THE
RIVETER

THE RIVETER

A Novel

JACK WANG

HarperVia

An Imprint of HarperCollins*Publishers*

THE RIVETER. Copyright © 2025 by Jack Wang. All rights reserved. Printed in the United States of America. No part of this book may be used or reproduced in any manner whatsoever without written permission except in the case of brief quotations embodied in critical articles and reviews. For information, address HarperCollins Publishers, 195 Broadway, New York, NY 10007.

HarperCollins books may be purchased for educational, business, or sales promotional use. For information, please email the Special Markets Department at SPsales@harpercollins.com.

First HarperVia hardcover published February 2025

The prologue of this novel appeared in slightly different form, as "The Jump" in *The Fiddlehead*.

Prologue Copyright © 2023 by Jack Wang.

Designed by Janet Evans-Scanlon
Title page and chapter opening texture behind numbers: © Unchalee/stock.adobe.com
Part numbers: © Hamza/stock.adobe.com

Library of Congress Cataloging-in-Publication Data has been applied for.

ISBN 978-0-06-308183-3

24 25 26 27 28 LBC 5 4 3 2 1

For Angelina and the Zeds

THE
RIVETER

Prologue

FOR THEIR FINAL MEAL, THE MEN HAD FEASTED ON MUTTON AND pork, and now they were sorry. All that food sat roiling inside them as their transport plane, an Albemarle, pitched and rolled in the dark. A night of buffeting winds, plus the wash of other Albemarles flying in formation. Every so often the plane would drop and their stomachs would lurch. During field exercises, the same man had always been first to retch, but in an unusual show of restraint, he had traded his dinner for cigarettes. Now they all waited to see who would do the honors instead.

The men had to squat on the floor of the cabin, under the weight of all their gear, the parachutes and the leg kit bags, every conceivable pocket crammed full of ammunition. With every dip and roll, they fought to stay upright. The whole plane roared with the gargling drone of the engines and stank of oil and gas and human tinctures—body odor, bad breath, and effluvium from all that mutton and pork—not to mention a miasma of cigarette smoke. Soon it would smell even worse.

Josiah Chang had an iron stomach, but even he had to close his eyes to settle the waves of nausea. In that more complete darkness, he pictured her face, or tried to, a face he knew so well yet somehow seemed to be forgetting. She had thin brows and heavy lids and dimples like wounds, yet each time he tried to train his mind's eye, her features eluded him, darting away like minnows.

He wasn't here for king and country but for her.

• • •

THE PLANE CONTINUED TO BUCK AND BOUNCE, A TIN CAN BATTED around by a bear. The men felt green, swirled like flasks. It was only a matter of time before someone lost it, and sure enough, someone did, though it wasn't clear who, and the spatter and the taint and the endless motion proved too much for the man beside him, and the one after that, and so came the chain reaction, men falling like dominoes, until the whole cabin was filled with a violent gastric stench. Only a few managed to find their airsickness bags in time. As the plane staggered, runnels of vomit slid across the floor. When the gruel lapped his boots, Josiah tasted bile but managed to choke it down.

The Albemarles flew in threes, arrowheads whistling through the dark. Arrow upon arrow, one after another. A magnificent storm. An armada. To avoid detection, they flew low, skimming the ocean. To achieve surprise, they had shied away from the target before wheeling around and taking an indirect approach, prolonging the flight. Men were cramping, their muscles on fire. They longed to stand, to stretch out the pain. To throw themselves out of that fuselage with all possible haste.

From somewhere came the distant sound of thunder. The floor door opened, letting in a bracing rush of air, the cleansing breath of God himself, which meant they were nearing the coast of France. Normandy.

THE PLANE BEGAN TO SHED ALTITUDE. EVERY MAN WAS ALONE NOW, in the silent vault of his skull, indulging whatever gave him succor: memory, prayer, incantation. Josiah thought of her. Wanted desperately to see her again. But even if he made it through this, would she still be his?

Outside, kettledrums sounded, a menacing overture, and the windows began to flash white. The fighter escort had engaged: the whining dive of engines, the prattle of machine-gun fire. And all the while, those drums: *boom . . . boom . . . boom . . .*

The red light came on, casting its oddly sensual glow. The jump-master ordered the men to hook up, and they clipped their static lines to the cable that ran the length of the cabin. Josiah was at the back of the plane, ten out of ten in the stick. He would be last man out.

The sky began to fill with bursting black clouds of antiaircraft fire. To the forces already battering them, the wind and the wash, was now added the spanking of flak. The plane jounced, and pieces of shrapnel tore through the cabin, through the tender membranes of the floor and the ceiling, leaving holes that emitted weird beams of light. But somehow no one was hit. In the carnival of chance that was war, their luck was holding.

But the crucible was getting hot, and pilots were already panicking, peeling off or climbing away from danger. This wasn't going to be the orderly drop of exercises, with the maximum number of men in the smallest possible space. No, they were going to be scattered all over the fucking place. But their pilot was holding steady, obeying orders. His only concession to fear was speed: he wasn't slowing down, at least not yet. Still, Josiah felt himself sending the man a badge of respect.

At last the light turned green and the jumpmaster yelled "Go!" and the first man dropped down into the void, then the next and the next, from alternating sides of the hatch. Through the windows, Josiah saw the familiar bloom of jellyfish, a massive swarm in the strobing light. It was all he could do to keep cadence, not push and shove and bum-rush the door, just to be out there.

Halfway through the stick, the plane got rocked, the men good and tossed. Josiah's helmet struck something, hard. Men fell over each other, tangled like marionettes, their static lines crossed. After yelling and screaming, unhooking and rehooking, they made for the hatch and threw themselves out, the exit cadence shot to hell. The three men before him, Gordon, Peavy, and Arceneaux, left the plane in quick succession, not so much jumping as being sucked out, the plane still going full tilt. They were nineteen and twenty years old. Never saw a camera that wasn't worth mugging for. Josiah would never see them again.

He lumbered to the hatch with his leg kit bag, air gushing and howling all around him. Pushed his static line at the jumpmaster and waited for the slap on the shoulder. Instead, the engines revved, the plane rose, and the jumpmaster shoved him back.

"We passed the DZ!" the jumpmaster shouted. "We have to go back!"

Josiah stared, bewildered. "To England?"

"No! Back to the DZ!"

His mind reeled. They were going to circle *back*? Do all that again?

At that moment, the plane was rocked a second time. Josiah was slammed to one side and fell on his back, head snapping against the floor. After blinking at the ceiling, those holes winking with light, he managed to get to his knees, but the jumpmaster was nowhere to be found.

He had fallen through the hatch.

The windows flickered orange and the cabin filled with thick black smoke. Only now did Josiah understand why their training instructor had made them practice blindfolded. With eyes closed, he groped for the floor door on his hands and knees, choking on burning oil and metal. The plane was banking, and he struggled for purchase, slipping on gruel.

When he felt a blast of air, he stretched out his arms, caught the lip of the hatch, and flung himself out.

HE WAS CARRIED AWAY ON THE SLIPSTREAM, THE TAIL OF THE ALBE-marle passing overhead, heading to some unknown fate. He had fallen out the wrong way, headfirst. Nonetheless, he felt the tug of the static line, followed by a more voluminous jerk, which slowed him considerably. With his hands on the risers, he gazed up and inspected the chute, its edges scalloped, its ribs perfectly formed. Everything checked out.

For a moment as he drifted, all that drumming, the whole mad symphony, seemed to fall away, leaving only a whistling silence. It was almost beautiful, the orange blossoms, the orange tracers, a light show just for him. Then, in the faraway bloom of jellyfish, he saw two tangled parachutes whirling like a dervish as they plummeted. He snapped to.

He reached for his quick-release straps and felt his right leg joyously freed of weight. When the leg kit bag reached the end of its twenty-foot rope, he felt a hard yank, followed by an unexpected lightening. Unlike most, Josiah hadn't crammed his bag full of extra gear, extra ammo, extra rations. Nonetheless, his kit had torn clear through the bag and was gone.

He had only a moment to rue the loss—ground was fast approaching. He checked his drift, scanned for hazards, but the world below was one dark mass. With a hundred feet to go, he thought he saw the boscage they'd been told to avoid, the trees and shrubs that edged the open fields, but he looked to be in the clear.

He was coming in hard and fast. He clamped his feet, pointed his toes. Hit the ground with a somersault and popped right up on one knee, all his senses alive.

He was down.

"COME BACK TO BED."

There were any number of ways she could have said this. Drowsily. Sulkily. Wantonly. But she said it mournfully, from a canyon deep inside her.

Morning light sieved in, powdering the room. He'd been sitting on the edge of her bed for what seemed like hours, staring at his uniform, his woolen green battledress and maroon beret, staving off the moment he would have to put it on and catch three planes and two trains for Camp Shilo. A trip of days, and he had no more to spare.

"I have to go," he said, his back still turned.

A draft entered the room, and a space opened between them. They stayed like that, taking each other's measure, until she said, "You should never have left."

Here they were at last, her real feelings. Feelings she had managed to fend off for a few days of concord. Happiness. Last night she had put on the evening dress she had worn the first time he saw her sing, just to stay in, the two of them dancing to records in her living room, sometimes fast, sometimes slow, and he couldn't believe how the music—the clap of a hi-hat, the swoon of strings—could rouse her, possess her, and rivet him with feeling. Now that was over. The space between them yawned.

"I had to."

"No, you didn't. I would have married you."

Her words, their particular construction, lanced him. "And then what?" he asked. "I have to make things right."

"You know I don't care about 'right,'" she said with the candor by which she lived her whole life.

"Well, I do." The words came out hot, a retort. He hadn't meant to sound so curt.

Her voice rose to meet his: "I'm not going to sit around and wait forever. That's not what I agreed to."

"I know," he said, though he hadn't known.

His back was still turned, and they stayed like that for a long time, in brooding silence, the seconds ticking down on what precious little time remained, and he thought something between them had hardened. Not like ice but like fire—a burning, a cautery. Then the bedcovers rustled, and the mattress sprang. Next thing he knew, her arms were around him, her face against the back of his neck, all of her clutching him tighter and tighter, until he could hardly breathe. My god. He didn't know he could be held like that. Enfolded so completely by fathoms of deep-sea pressure. Her whole body shaking.

HE WASN'T SURE WHERE HE WAS.

There was no moonlight, the sky plastered with clouds. He was on a dark plain, with darker uncertainties fringing it. If they missed the DZ they were supposed to face the line of the flight path and go left, but the planes he saw were small and moving every which way, like koi in a pond. He tried to remember the aerial photographs—surprisingly detailed, down to the cows—and the lectures at the sand table, the brigadier scratching and scrawling with his pointer. Nothing rang a bell. He was lost.

He had unstrapped his parachute but didn't have anything to take its place—he had lost his entire kit. His haversack and belt, his water bottle and respirator, his shovel, toggle rope, bayonet, and dagger. All his rations, all his rounds, except for a few in his pockets. His saving grace: he still had his No. 4 rifle, which he had kept slung around him and now carried at the ready. If not for that, he would have been naked as a lamb.

He headed for what looked like a copse, slipping like liquid through the darkness. It was some time after midnight. Hours to go before light, which worked both for and against him. When he reached what turned out to be woods, he entered cautiously, imagining unseen dangers: trip wire, an ambush. All his life, he had walked through forests at night. Knew their mysteries, their tells, but this was something else altogether. He stepped gingerly, ears perked. Treetops swished in the wind, muffling the distant sound of war-thunder. The air smacked of needles and bark and the unmistakable tang of vomit, deep in the fibers of his smock.

He had to piss but wouldn't stop. Didn't want to go out like that, with his pants down. But he wouldn't make it through a whole mission, much less a whole war, without taking a leak. If not here, deep in the woods at night, then where?

When the need became urgent, he parked himself next to a tree. By this point, he had decided he was thoroughly alone, but he still imagined sight lines before settling on a spot. With a hand on his rifle, he reached under his front flap, then released his bladder with a swollen ache, as if urine were flowing in, not out. At first, the sizzle of dirt seemed to resound, treacherously, but soon he relaxed. He was just taking a piss at night, something he had done a thousand times before, high in the Cariboo Mountains. For an instant, time and space collapsed and he was back there, a kid again. Had to remind himself that he was in Europe. France. A land of high-wheeler bicycles and curly mustaches, in his imagination. If nothing else, he had made it here in this one life.

When he was done, he buttoned up awkwardly, one-handed. Through the trees, he sensed the direction of the fight. Nothing for him but to go to it.

HE CAME TO THE EDGE OF THE WOODS. CAUGHT THE SOFT AROMA OF manure. This part of the world had been transformed into a mix of woodland and pasture. Faster to move out in the open, under the cover of dark, but the Germans were crazy for land mines. Better, then, to follow the boscage that fringed the fields, even if it meant zigging and zagging.

As he moved from tree to tree, shrub to shrub, his eyes large, feline— astonishing how much he could see in the dark—he wondered how the fight was going. If *he* was out here alone, then how many others were out here alone, and how many men were left to carry out the mission?

And if *his* leg kit bag had failed, then how many others' had failed, and what would the men be left to fight with? Were they finally gaining a toehold on Fortress Europa or was this Dieppe all over again?

He had to be miles from the DZ. His aim was to find not just the drop zone but also other men along the way, British or American, if not his own.

After an hour of winding along the boscage, stealing through countryside, something made him stop, turn. He looked again to be sure, and then he was running. At first he ran with rifle in hand, but when the situation became clear he slung his rifle around him and ran with both arms pumping—the kind of all-out running that makes you feel concussed.

What he had seen was a parachute, high in a tree. The brightest thing he had seen all night, a gray phosphorescence. Could tell by the way it hung that there was still weight at the other end. He thought at first that the man was tangled, unable to cut himself down. Then he saw the faint sheen of water and the man's legs pointing straight up, a diver frozen halfway through his entry. That's when he had slung his rifle around him.

He entered the water at a sprint but was instantly slowed by sucking mud. He began to wade, to thrash, as if dragging a monstrous weight behind him. Kept waiting for the moment to dive, but the water remained shallow. Shallow, yet deep enough to cover the man's head and shoulders. Josiah pushed on, harder.

At last he reached the man. Cradled him out of the water, as if he had just been baptized. The man's body was limp, sodden, impossibly heavy. Couldn't tell who he was, not in the dark, but whoever he was, he was gone.

Josiah felt a bolt of desolation. Yes, he'd been compelled by impulse and duty and brotherhood but also a terrible yowl of loneliness. With a struggle, he freed the man's legs from the lines and released his harness and dragged him out of the water, every form of resistance—weight, viscosity, suction, bloat—working against him. As soon as they were out, he paused to catch his breath. Then he took the man in search of a decent patch of earth.

It was only as he hauled the man farther that he saw, crawling out of the primordial sludge, the lucent balloon of his leg kit bag.

THE DEAD MAN HAD MADE A FATEFUL DECISION. HE HAD CHOSEN TO wear his shoulder-strap belt under his parachute—no easy feat—to make sure he arrived with gear and to save time upon landing. But all that weight had sunk like ballast, making it harder to keep his head above water. Yet by wearing his belt, he had lightened his leg kit bag, enough to ensure that it worked.

Josiah retrieved a shovel from the bag and dug a shallow grave. The ground was soft and crumbly, and the blade went in each time with a satisfying snick. As he worked, he thought of her. She had become a refracting presence, the eye in the sky through which he saw, admired, and pitied himself. And what he saw now was a man who had no need for gods but still believed in the unseen. Who couldn't lay claim to another man's things without squaring the debt to the man who had yielded them.

When the grave was dug, Josiah pulled off the man's helmet, slid the identification discs from around his neck, and put one back in the man's pocket and the rest in his own. Then, with difficulty, he peeled off the shoulder-strap belt, rigor mortis already setting in.

Once the belt was freed, Josiah took the man by the shoulders one last time. Hated the way the man's head lolled as he walked him backward. All that training, all those route marches, not to mention the jumps themselves, only to be snared by a tree. He imagined the man struggling, strung up like Houdini, only without the secret key.

THE LEG KIT BAG WAS A CORNUCOPIA. AMONG OTHER THINGS, IT yielded a haversack, a kerosene lamp and Sterno folding stove, a survey map and binoculars, a Bren gun wallet with an oilcan and a clearing plug—which meant the man had been the No. 1 in a Bren gun group—and best of all the Bren gun itself, its curved magazine already mounted on top like an angry horn. Josiah packed as much as he could into the haversack and clipped the haversack to the belt and strapped the belt over his shoulders. Everything else he slung around him or hung off the webbing until he felt like a packhorse. Right again.

The Germans had flooded mile upon mile of low-lying fields. He had come to one of them, which meant he was near a river, probably the Dives. If memory served, there was a bridge he could cross, if it hadn't already been destroyed. He tried to consult the map by squeezing the hand crank on a small dynamo-powered lamp, but the gears just whirred without producing light. He would have to go on instinct.

It was still the small hours of night, and he stole through a shadow play, dark upon dark. Continued to follow the boscage, always seeking dry ground. Eventually he came to a road lined with prickly walls of blackthorn, their tiny white flowers spectral in the dark. The only way across was to find a break in the hedgerow. When he came to one at last, he listened for the padding of footsteps, the rumble of engines. Once he was sure the road was empty, he pushed through the opening, crossed the road, and searched for a break on the other side. He slunk along the hedgerow, half crouched, poking around with his rifle, but the hedgerow refused to yield. He was just about to pull out his dagger when he sensed an opening. It seemed a little small but would have to do. He got on his hands and knees and crawled and felt himself snagging on all that bramble. Imagined his feet sticking out as headlights came bounding down the road. He thought about backing out and cutting off a few branches. Instead, he gave one final push and was through.

He kept moving. By this point, the skies were strangely quiet, but signs of the fight were everywhere: an empty wicker pannier with a parachute, the embers of a crash in the distance. By the time he reached the river the world was faintly dusted with light. He could see the straight line of the bridge a few hundred yards away, a simple farm bridge with iron guardrails, but the banks of the river were flooded, which forced him around to the road. Once he was close to the mouth of the bridge, he stationed himself behind a tree and waited for the moment to cross.

Just as he was about to dash, he heard the crunch of footsteps on the other side of the bridge. He shrank back, waited. Sure enough, someone was coming. A girl in a farm dress, her hair in a kerchief, carrying a basket like someone out of a fairy tale. Josiah watched her every step, until she spied him peeking out from behind the tree. Her dark eyes widened. The sight he must have made, his face blackened with camouflage paint. But he saw the effort not to flinch, not to break stride. Instead, she just stiffened a little and shook her head, ever so slightly. He shrank back.

Suddenly, crackling tires and shouts in German. A moment later, two soldiers came pedaling past. Feckless as they might have been on bicycles, the sight of jackboots and flared helmets still filled Josiah with awe. He kept watch to make sure they weren't after the girl, but they only yelled at her gratuitously as they passed.

When the soldiers were gone, he snuck across the bridge. By the time he looked back, the girl had disappeared into a house on the other side of the river. For the rest of his life, he would wonder about the girl, if she had outlived the war. He would never know.

• • •

AFTER CROSSING THE FARM BRIDGE, JOSIAH FOUND HIMSELF IN A village of a few scattered houses. The odd window flickered with life, and part of him longed to knock and be let in.

For the next hour, he followed the flooded banks of the river to the village of Varaville, next to the DZ, where he heard the chatter of machine guns and frantic shouting in English and German, as if war were a manic comedy. When he caught sight of muzzle flash, he scoured the scene with binoculars and spied, in a ditch by a gatehouse, webbed helmets with scrim camouflage, made to resemble leaves and twigs, the habitus of strange woodland creatures. At last he had found his own: Canadians.

1

AS SOON AS HE STEPPED OFF THE TRAIN, JOSIAH CHANG KNEW HE was somewhere else. The clamor, the bustle, the angle of women's hats—everything here was different. As he strode through the marble booking hall, he took in the coffered ceiling, the wheeled chandeliers, the clocks at either end keeping eternal time, and the frieze that ringed the hall with melancholy landscapes, depicting the kind of wilderness from which he had just decamped.

That morning, he had gotten up early, after a night of heavy drinking, the men in the bush camp sending him off with their usual batches of rotgut. He had hitched a ride with Ed Buckley in an old Moreland truck with solid tires, and they came down off the mountain in one long declension, Ed Buckley talking the whole way, through wads of snuff, until they arrived at the railway station in Kamloops. From there, Josiah sat on the hard wooden slats of coach class, mired in thoughts of all he was leaving behind: the Cariboo, the logging camps, his father in the hard earth. But as the train pushed on through the little towns of Savona, Ashcroft, and Lytton toward the great metropolis,

Josiah found himself tilting toward the future and its prospects, the unbridled sense of all that could be.

Directly across from the station were three hotels: the Grandview, the Almer, and the St. Francis, all of which offered European plan rooms for two dollars and up. Josiah stopped a passerby and asked where he might find a rooming house. The man took in Josiah's aspect, the rolled denim pants and caulk boots, the mangy work shirt and bulging duffel, and said, "What you're after, son, is Chinatown." The man pointed in one direction, then started off in the other.

Josiah felt a shard of irritation, but what did he know? He was the stranger. So he set off as directed, trying to maintain his expansive mood, that feeling of wildness and possibility that only comes from being in a city. It was late afternoon, the sidewalks still crowded, and faces kept coming at him in an endless phantasmagoria—more new faces in a single block than he'd been liable to see in a year.

Eventually he happened upon a little rooming house, an idyll in a sea of commerce. When he stepped onto the porch and knocked, curtains rustled, and the chain to the door fell, or so he thought. Instead, the door cracked open and a glinting pair of spectacles peered over a few brass links.

"How can I help you?" the woman asked, voice stingy.

Six months ago, on the same day as Pearl Harbor, Japan had attacked Hong Kong, where the Winnipeg Grenadiers and the Royal Rifles of Canada had put up a doomed fight. Maybe she took him for Japanese.

"I need a room, ma'am," he said in his deep, gravelly voice.

"We're full up."

He looked at the sign on the lawn, which suggested otherwise.

"I'm about to take that down directly," the woman said.

Her lips took on a hard set, but her eyes were damp and imploring, and he almost felt sorry for her, trembling at the sight of him.

"Have a good evening, ma'am."

Back on the sidewalk, he looked up Cordova Street, at its cafés and saloons, its furriers and haberdasheries, stretching all the way to the vanishing point. Somewhere in that direction lay Vancouver's Chinatown. A far cry, no doubt, from the dying cluster of storefronts that passed for Chinatown in places like Quesnel and Barkerville, but Josiah had never been one to glom to his own. His grandfather had already moved out of Chinatown, back when the Changs still lived in the great metropolis. So Josiah decided that wasn't the way for him.

It was late May, the air beautifully temperate, which gave him an idea, and he started back the way he had come. After a block, he looked over his shoulder. The sign on the lawn remained unchanged.

HE STOPPED AT A GROCERY STORE TO PICK UP SUNDRIES. THEN HE carried on, back to the station and beyond, past streetcars, yet more hotels, and one magnificent skyscraper that looked like a snowcapped mountain, the tallest thing for miles around. To the west, where the sun was setting, lay an improbable mass of trees, jagging the sky like a long black saw. Up north, he had heard talk of squatting in Stanley Park during the Great Depression. Men finding ways to live, as ever. That's what he would do.

He walked along Coal Harbor, past rail yards, storehouses, and tightly packed marinas. At the entrance to the park on Georgia Street, he came to a promenade lined with benches, its median a series of dots and dashes, like Morse code, all brightly planted. People were out and about, but no one paid him any mind. After crossing a footbridge, he followed the road around a lagoon before veering off into the woods. Suddenly light fell away, and sounds of the city thinned to a murmur. He found himself in a grove of Douglas fir, tall and skinny, just like the ones he used to cut. Most were old, their gray bark furrowed, like parched earth, but some were saplings, still bubbling with resin blisters. Deeper in the woods, he was met by western red cedar, their trunks absurdly wide, including one that would have taken a good seven hours to bring down. Here among them, he found what he was looking for: a clearing, free of roots.

He opened his duffel and pulled out a roll of heavy waxed canvas. With a kick, it unfurled, and he worked the poles and pegs until the pup tent was up. He threw in his bedroll and crawled in behind it. Then he lay down, surveyed his kingdom, and declared it good.

IT HAD ALWAYS BEEN THE TWO OF THEM, JOSIAH AND HIS FATHER, under the open sky. A few months each year when winter turned nasty, dropping to forty below, they would take to a bunkhouse and the amity and stink of other men, but otherwise, it was just them, cooking over an open fire, bathing in rivers and lakes, and sleeping under a great big diamond-encrusted sky.

Josiah's great-grandfather had been a forty-niner, but a poor one. When he caught rumor of gold on the Cariboo Plateau, he made the long trek north, from San Francisco to Yale by steamer, from Yale to Quesnel by mule train, and from Quesnel onward on foot, on rough trails. But the winters in Barkerville, where gold-bearing ground was frozen solid well into spring—the winters there killed him. So his son, Josiah's grandfather, took a different tack. Became an axeman and surveyor for the Grand Trunk Pacific Railway and eventually moved to the great metropolis. As a young man, Josiah's father had worked for a barrel-making company, bending staves of wood into iron hoops, before taking a job at Hastings Mill, where he manned a giant circular saw that made butter of wood. But after the Great War, men like Franklin Chang were replaced. That's when he went north.

From a young age, Josiah had wanted to fall and buck timber with his father, but for many years he was made to attend whichever one-room schoolhouse was at hand as they traveled up and down the Cariboo, from Lac la Hache to Dunkley. His father had gotten proper schooling in the city, all the way through junior matriculation, so he understood the value of book learning, and over the years, much of what he knew was slowly conveyed to Josiah, like water through a rope.

At twelve, Josiah could no longer be denied, so father and son became a team, either end of a two-man saw. Josiah came up in a particular world: he was too late to remember ox logging, almost too late to remember skid roads and horses, but too early for power saws, which were still in their infancy. He and his father had done things honestly, by hand. They would start with axes for the undercut, then draw the felling saw. Josiah had always loved the first rip, the bark sparking away and the saw biting into flesh. When the back cut was deep enough, they would hammer wedges into the breach until the tree finally keeled with a ground-shaking clatter. If the tree was big enough, they did everything on springboards high off the ground. That was their life for ten years.

Over time, Josiah got stronger as his father got weaker. Such is the way with fathers and sons. His father had always seemed vaguely surprised that a man so strapping could be his issue, but he wasn't one of those men who stubbornly refused to acknowledge the passage of time. No, Franklin Chang was that rare thing: a father happy to yield to his son. By degrees, he let Josiah do more of the heavier work, the hammering especially. He ceded as a tree cedes: slowly, then inexorably.

As his father got older, Josiah worried that a falling tree would vault and twist unpredictably and his father would be too slow to react. That something was bound to get him. In the end, it was a widow-maker, one of those branches that snaps in the wind and plunges hundreds of feet, like a bolt of black lightning. He and his father had been deep in the bush, working the felling saw. One moment his father was there, and the next he was not. Josiah had been looking up, keeping an eye out for falling branches, and would never know if he had failed to notice something he should have noticed sooner. But he did see something in time to cry out, and this he would forever regret, for his father had had time to look up, his Adam's apple bobbing, which meant he knew what was coming. The branch drove so hard into the ground that two men couldn't pull it out, except with a steam donkey. For the first and only time in his life, Josiah passed out. But he had seen, and would never unsee.

2

IN THE MORNING, JOSIAH CROSSED THE CITY AGAIN, THIS TIME
following a crude map on a rumpled piece of paper. Last winter, when
he and his father had gone to Quesnel for supplies, they had chanced
upon a man, a recruiter, who promised good wages and better hours at
a new shipyard in the great metropolis. "A tidy eight-hour shift or less,"
the man had said, handing them a flyer. "Not the ten or twelve hours
you work now, am I right?" The war was picking up steam, and the city
was a vortex, sucking in men from everywhere. Josiah and his father
listened politely before going about their business.

After his father was killed, Josiah found the flyer for the shipyard
among his father's things, and the way it reared up seemed full of por-
tent. He knew he would never cut again, not for a living, so he went in
search of a new one.

He walked east on Powell Street, past streetcars and storefronts,
dowsing his way to the star on the map. When he neared the chain-link
fence that enclosed the yard, he saw steel, row upon row of long, narrow
slabs. Beyond lay a cluster of low-slung buildings, and farther beyond,

at the end of the pier, the hulking shapes to which the yard was devoted, the air above them blackened by smoke and the smoke astonished by flashes of light, like clouds in a thunderstorm.

At length he came to McLean Drive and crossed four sets of railway tracks, under a billboard for MCGAVIN'S GOOD BREAD AND FINE CAKES. Just inside the main gate was a trailer marked PERSONNEL. When he entered, two women looked up, one at a long counter, the other at a desk behind, and the air changed, his reception somehow warm and cool at once.

"How can we help you?" asked the older woman at the desk. She had long, arched nostrils and a big blond pompadour that made her look leonine.

"I'm looking for work, ma'am," he said, holding up the flyer like a promissory note.

"Yes, of course," the woman said, suddenly crisp with action. She approached the counter with a form. When she asked for his address, he said, "Still getting settled, ma'am."

"Where are you for now?"

"At . . . the St. Francis Hotel."

"Very good," she said, scribbling. "And what about bonds, Mr. Chang? Will you take the standard ten percent deduction for Victory Bonds so we can win this godforsaken war?"

His father's dream had been to buy a block of woods they could cut themselves, but all that was left of that dream was a canister full of banknotes. Especially with no rent to pay, money was of no concern.

"Yes, ma'am."

She gathered his work history, then handed him a small brass badge and work slip. "You need to see Mr. Lewis, the foreman. He'll set you up, whatever's needed. But first, you need to see Ellie."

At this, the younger woman perked up. In fact, her whole body livened, now that she had his attention. This was something he had seen before, the effect his broad shoulders, sharp cheekbones, and slicked-back hair could have on women. Ellie filled out his union registration, then collected his fingerprints, rolling his fingers and thumbs. Her hands were cool and confident, yet she managed to slip and spoil not one but two cards and had to start again each time.

"What's the matter with me?" she simpered, a tube of sandy hair on each side of her head.

"Yes, what's gotten into you, Elizabeth?" the older woman asked. Only then did Ellie finish up expertly, with a sly smile.

As he turned to go, the older woman said, "There's a welder in the yard by the name of Louie Wong. A very fine young man. Very clean and very well-spoken. You should meet him."

Josiah smiled, and she smiled back, as if they'd reached an understanding.

"Yes, ma'am."

HE FOLLOWED THE MAIN ROAD, PAST A ROW OF OPEN ROLLER DOORS and the whir and whine of machinery. In one of the shops, he found Mr. Lewis, an old hand in a flat cap and coveralls. "A faller, eh?" the foreman said, taking his work slip. "I don't need an axeman but—" He looked Josiah up and down, all six feet of him, the broad expanse of his chest and the thick trunks of his thighs, sculpted by years of roughing it in the bush until he seemed physically capable of anything. "You look like a riveter to me. Training will take a few days. Paid, of course."

What Josiah knew about shipbuilding was next to nothing, but he liked the sound of "riveter."

They crossed the street to a large hangar where men were training at stations, welders mostly, joining steel through a torrent of sparks, in slotted masks that looked medieval. Strangely, one man appeared to be cooking: with a gloved hand, he prodded an iron pot with sword-length tongs. Every crevice of the old man's face was lined with soot, and sweat ran down his cheeks in dirty rivulets. When he pumped a lever, a pleated lung heaved in and out, sending up gusts of smoke and ash.

"How's it coming, Fergus? Getting the hang of it?" Mr. Lewis asked. He took the man's tongs, reached into the burning coke, and pulled out a red-hot rivet. "Not bad, not bad," the foreman said. "Ever seen one of these, Josiah? This here's the head and this here's the tail. Takes about three million of these to hold a Victory ship together."

Next to the pot, two perforated steel plates had been bolted together and mounted upright. Mr. Lewis pushed the tail of the rivet through one of the holes and asked Charlie, a large lumberjack of a man, to hold the rivet head in place with a bucking bar. "Now, your job," Mr. Lewis said, "is to take this rivet gun"—he picked up a sleek silver barrel, like something out of Buck Rogers, save for the hose of compressed air that snaked out of one end—"and jammer the hell out of the tail until you've formed a second head. Here, let me show you."

Mr. Lewis planted his feet, pressed the gun against the glowing tail of the rivet, and unleashed a volley of gunfire that bounded around the room, jangling the sheet metal walls. After ten seconds, he pulled away, leaving behind a perfect buttonhead, already cooled to black.

"Now you try it."

Josiah took the gun, a long cylinder that tapered at one end and widened to a ringed handle at the other. The gun had heft but still played lightly in his hands. He pressed the tip of the gun against the tail of a new rivet and squeezed the trigger. The tip of the gun jackhammered, and his whole body convulsed. After a few seconds, he let go.

Mr. Lewis inspected his handiwork, then leaned in closer, hands on his knees, as if his eyes were bad. Then he straightened, tipping back his cap and scratching his head, somehow unconvinced.

"Let's try it again," he said.

So they did. This time, after inspecting his work, Mr. Lewis said, "Let's try three-quarters." So they tried three-quarters, seven-eighths, and one inch, then steeplehead, conehead, and countersunk rivets, and each time, Mr. Lewis stooped to examine his work, only to propose something else. Josiah grew impatient with the man's cryptic judgments, but he did as he was told. Soon the board was filled.

"Good. Very good," Mr. Lewis finally said. "You done this before?"

"No, sir."

"Well, I'll be."

THE FOREMAN LED HIM DOWN TO THE WATER. THERE, THEY CAME to four berths, each one a giant nest of scaffolds. After a tunnel of posts and beams, the floor slithering with hoses, they came to a ship, the ribs of its hull still largely exposed, like the carcass of some leviathan. The air grew acrid and smoky and the clamor of the yard intense, Josiah's teeth resonating like tines.

"Cargo ships are what we do here," Mr. Lewis yelled over the din. "Ten-thousand tonners. Not as glamorous as battleships, but without cargo ships, we're done for. Last month, the Germans sank sixty-six cargo ships. Count 'em, *sixty-six*. They're sinking them faster than we can build them, which is why we've got to build more."

They took a set of plank stairs up to the first catwalk. There, Josiah was introduced to a riveter named Hank, a heavyset man in a hard hat who moved with wincing slowness. He took one look at Josiah and said, "That's what we need. Some young muscle."

For the rest of the day, Hank watched as Josiah fastened steel plates to the ribs. Each time Josiah fired the gun, the rivet would spark white, then anneal through shades of lava before turning a matte black. Sometimes Hank would offer a pointer or some small correction, but mostly he just nodded and murmured his approval. "Rivet gangs make twenty-three dollars a day, split three ways," he explained at one point. "Forty percent for the riveter and thirty each for the heater and the holder." Josiah was glad to know he had the hardest job and made the most, which matched his sense of himself. The only thing he didn't like was the noise, the blistering sound of gunfire, which echoed through the yard. So different than the quiet he was used to, out in the bush with his father, all of creation lulled by the swish of a two-man saw.

At the end of the shift, when Mr. Lewis reappeared, Hank said, "This man don't need no more training. He's a natural."

The next morning, Mr. Lewis put Josiah on a crew with Fergus and Charlie, the heater and the holder from yesterday. Both men had stubby cigarettes in their mouths, which made them look even more cockeyed, and neither extended a hand, just dipped their heads coolly. There were any number of reasons why they might have resented Josiah, including the fact he was new, his fingertips still stained with ink. Newer than them yet already done with his training—and a riveter to boot. But Josiah was unfazed. All his life, he had known hard men. Men so chafed by the elements that no part of them seemed uncalloused. Next to them, these men were baby soft.

In the end, it simply didn't matter whom he worked with, the best or the worst of men. None would ever be his father.

3

A FEW DAYS LATER, JOSIAH WAS SITTING OVER A NEW CAST-IRON skillet, tending to breakfast, when he looked up to see a creature eyeing him from the edge of the clearing. With its long neck, small head, and dark, shining eyes, it had the alien look of a greyhound, only this one was brindled, tan with black marbling and a shock of white on its chest. Josiah had seen his share of hounds in the bush, all mange and misery. This dog was different, but it looked gaunt, even for a greyhound. Possibly a racing dog put out to pasture. In any case, hungry.

As soon as he held out a strip of bacon, the dog came trotting up and promptly relieved him of it. Then it sat down, ears perked, waiting for more. That's when he saw the dog was a bitch, her ears covered in burrs. Gently, he picked them out.

He set out some water in a bowl and cooked up what was left of his bacon and fed himself and the dog, who waited patiently between offerings. By the time he was ready to leave, the dog had fallen asleep by the embers of the fire, her long legs crossed, as if hog-tied. Josiah studied her, dozing peacefully, and saw no reason not to let her be.

HE SET OFF FOR THE SHIPYARD. TOOK THE PEBBLED SHOULDER OF the railway line that ran along the inlet, past shabby little houses on stilts that jagged the water's edge. As usual, he was joined by a steadily growing procession of men in gabardine jackets and Cowichan sweaters, lunch buckets swinging. Still more came by car, bus, and trolley, rumbling and clacking down Powell Street. This was the thrice-daily change of shift, when the population of a small city traded itself out: between 4:30 and 5:00 in the afternoon, when the day shift gave way to the swing shift; between 12:30 and 1:00 in the morning, when the swing shift gave way to the night shift; and now, between 7:30 and 8:00, when the day shift came back on.

Josiah entered the yard by the railway crossing on McLean Drive, then followed the influx of men down to the berths. A year ago, this stretch of Burrard Inlet had been little more than garbage dumps and squatters' shacks. Now it was a thousand-foot-long pier.

Halfway to the berths, something caught his eye. He veered sharply, bumping against the flow of traffic, until he found himself before a poster on the side of a building. In the center of the poster was a young man not unlike himself in a flat cap, work shirt, and work pants, face steeled in concentration as he cradled a rivet gun. Below him were the words SPEED THE SHIPS and above him EVERY RIVET A BULLET.

Josiah swelled at the image. For the first time, he saw how others might have seen him, as young and rugged and able. Not just a workhorse but a stud—the very spirit of the yard. The very spirit, too, of a country at war. At the start of the war, Chinese had been allowed to enlist, but when Victoria and Ottawa realized that the Chinese might expect something in return, namely citizenship and the franchise, they were barred. When his father was alive, Josiah had had no thoughts of joining up; now the choice was no longer his. But in wielding a rivet gun, he, too, was fighting the good fight.

Every rivet a bullet.

AT THE ENTRANCE TO BERTH NO. 1 HE FOUND FERGUS AND CHARLIE hunched over cigarettes, like two rogues plotting, both of them scruffy with stubble, as if they had been there all night. As usual, they gave him cockeyed looks, but Josiah remained unfazed. Fergus and Charlie were stationed inside the hull while Josiah was stationed outside, up on the scaffolds, where he could afford to ignore them.

He started up the plank stairs. After a couple of flights, he stepped out onto the catwalk. Catwalks were only two planks wide and had no guardrails, only the occasional post, and the gap between the catwalk and the hull was wide enough to fall through. Compared to topping trees, this was nothing. Still, he had to be careful.

He found his equipment where the night shift had left it but didn't pick up his glove or his gun, not even when the whistle sounded. It would be a while yet before rivets were hot. Not only that, Fergus and Charlie were slow. Slower, it seemed, than any other crew.

Eventually, a rivet gun juddered somewhere in the distance. Soon it was answered by another, then another and another still, until the whole yard was bedlam, but Josiah had yet to pick up his gun. He wondered if Fergus and Charlie were down on the cargo deck, playing cards or pitching pennies, as men were wont to do, sometimes long after the whistle. He would have thought those with connections to the British Isles would be eager to win the Battle of the Atlantic, but rivet gangs were paid by the hour, not the piece, so they had no extra incentive.

As the minutes passed, Josiah grew impatient. This was hardly speeding the ships, so he put his mouth to a rivet hole and said, "What's going on?"

For a long moment, there was no answer, and he wondered if Charlie had even climbed the ladder to the catwalk opposite. Then, through a muffle of steel, he heard Charlie say, "Hold your horses."

Josiah felt his blood rise. If there was one thing he hated, it was being talked down to. Would rather have been called a slant or a Chinaman. That kind of crudeness could be sloughed off. But the subtle yet unmistakable condescension of "Hold your horses" was maddening.

When a rivet finally appeared, Josiah threw on his one glove, still clammy from the last man's sweat, and picked up his gun and channeled his feelings into the rivet. Here on the outside of the hull, rivets were countersunk, and he watched as molten metal sparked against his glove and mashed into the hole until the rivet head was flush.

He looked on, satisfied. Whatever was worth doing was worth doing well. That's what his father had taught him. Josiah had been there less than a week and already he prided himself on his work. That's what he couldn't understand about the likes of Fergus and Charlie, why they didn't take more pride.

He kept channeling his feelings into the rivets until his anger dissipated. When the whistle blew for lunch, he sat alone on the edge of the catwalk, two stories up, and opened his lunch pail. On his first day, he had gone down to the canteen and bought a sandwich against his wages, but now he brought his own. As sunlight spangled the inlet, he looked out over the water at the dark-green mass of Stanley Park and the bright-red cables of the Lions Gate Bridge, festooning the First Narrows, and realized with a quiet start that this was now home.

He worked through the long afternoon until the final whistle sounded. Then he followed the exodus to the time clock building, where he turned a lever on a large numbered wheel. When he punched in the same number as the one on his brass badge, a bell rang.

The sweet sound of freedom.

When he got back to camp, the dog—he'd forgotten—was where he had left her, only now she was lying on her back, weirdly splayed, and whimpering from some excited dream. It surprised him, how glad he was to see her.

"You staying, girl?" he asked.

That evening, the dog went bounding into the woods after squirrels. After a while, she came back with a creepy smile, tongue lolling. When he went to bed, she followed him into the tent and circled the floor next to the bedroll before dropping like a bag of bones. She stank, but he smoothed her ears as she snored. He couldn't really keep a dog. He was gone all day and had no way to make this or any dog stay. But as long as she hung around, he would let her.

4

ONE MORNING, ON HIS WAY TO THE BERTHS, JOSIAH CAME TO A sudden stop outside Plate Shop No. 2. A crowd had gathered, blocking half the road, and he was caught in the impasse. From the back of the crowd, he craned for a better look. Tall as he was, he couldn't see anything at first. An accident, he figured, or a fight, the kind that sometimes broke out in the yard, to the rabid interest of onlookers.

Eventually, through a sea of hats, he saw yet more hats filing out of the plate shop. So, new recruits. No big deal. Why, then, was the crowd transfixed, laughing and smiling—or glowering?

"You got to be kidding me," someone muttered.

Josiah's first thought: more Chinese. Or Blacks. Or Jews. For all the Scandinavians and Slavs, the yard was mostly British, and they liked it that way. He craned for another look. That's when he saw not just flat caps and hard hats but bandannas and headscarves.

So not just new recruits but women.

Which made sense. More and more men were going off to fight.

Even after sopping up all the men who had lain around during the Great Depression and all the men who kept pouring out of the mountains and the prairies, the yard was still short. Workers had to come from somewhere.

Still, he was a little surprised. He'd only ever seen women in the canteen and the front office, never in workshops or on berths, where these women appeared to be headed. Up north, most of the women he had known were weather-beaten and resourceful, as capable as any man of skinning deer or catching wild horses. Next to them, these women looked soft. This wasn't an airplane factory, where everything, including rivet guns, was light. This was a shipyard.

Women kept filing out of the plate shop, twenty or thirty in all. Most wore looks of grim determination, but one girl beamed, happy for attention. When she raised an arm to her ear and waved like someone in a pageant, the girl behind her gave her a shove. *What?* the first girl mouthed before turning back to the crowd.

From somewhere came a lewd whistle, which set off a wave of laughter. Emboldened, another man puckered his lips and said, "Give me a buzz, babycakes!" At this, one of the women, possibly the tallest, stepped forward and raised a fist, to more laughter. Josiah felt for her. For all of them. Knew something of what they must have been feeling. Yet he was glad not to be on the receiving end for once.

The door to the plate shop was being held by a matronly woman in a suit-dress. "Nothing to see here," she said, clapping twice as if shooing pigeons. But it wasn't until Mr. Thompson, the shipyard manager, emerged from the plate shop himself and said, "Move along, fellas," with an irritable swipe of the hand, that the crowd began to disperse.

THE NEXT DAY, JOSIAH CAME DOWN OFF THE SCAFFOLDS FOR LUNCH. As he sat with a large gathering in something resembling a square, a man appeared with a long coil of rope. After stretching it out on the ground, he marked the ground with chalk. That's when Josiah knew what the rope was for. The yard was fond of hosting picnics, bingo nights, softball games, and variety shows, anything to build esprit de corps. It even ran the largest bowling league in the world. Now it was staging a lunchtime tug-of-war.

Sure enough, eight sizeable men in work clothes lined up to one side, and a voice over the loudspeakers introduced them as members of the North Yard. Before the war, the North Yard had built ships start to finish; now the South Yard built the hulls while the North Yard did the outfitting. A little friendly competition seemed like a good idea, but there was a catch: everyone from the North Yard was a cable puller.

Laughter bounded through the crowd, and for a while this was the entertainment, the fact that no one was willing to step forward, not even when the North Yard began to flex and goad. Josiah looked around, confused. Was the yard just going to take it lying down? Again, where was the pride?

Josiah rose, dusting his hands, and walked toward the rope. He was wearing a white T-shirt and overalls, and the veins of his biceps bulged as he took up the *end* of the rope. A hush fell over the yard, including the eight men standing opposite. If the yard had been reluctant to step up before, it was even more so now.

At last, in a surfeit of shame, a second man stepped forward, then a third and a fourth, an ever-quickening stream that brought a rising cheer from the crowd. Soon there were seven other men on his side, who all looked more than capable.

Both sides took up the rope, and the rope grew taut, and the man who had brought the rope struggled to keep it from shifting. When he finally threw up his hands, the crowd sent up a lusty roar. For a long moment, neither side seemed to move, as if they were posing, figures in a frieze. Then feet began to scuffle and paw and the painted spot on the rope to slide, back and forth in a liquid way.

When it dawned on the crowd that it wasn't going to be a rout, another roar went up. Riled, the North Yard attacked and the South Yard skittered, but Josiah found his feet and sat down low, nearly on the ground, and started taking small, determined steps back, like a strongman pulling a train with his teeth, until the painted spot on the rope was nearly where it started. The pressure in his knees was incredible, as it was in his toes, mashing into the steel caps of his boots. High noon prickled his skin, and beads of sweat ran down his face, stinging him half-blind.

As the battle wore on, the crowd surged forward—faces screwed, spittle flying—urged on by the man over the loudspeakers, who kept calling for more noise. By this point, Josiah was starting to suffer, his thighs burning and his arms fraying and the fat knot at the end of the rope digging into his wrists and hands. Yet he kept going, determined to win. To send the yard into delirium.

But it wasn't to be. The North Yard found a rhythm, like a galley pulling in unison, and all at once the South Yard stumbled, all tension lost, like someone releasing a long-held breath. The whole yard groaned.

As the men shook hands, the yard rose up again in appreciation. Then a scrum descended on Josiah. Some of the very men who had looked at him askance now held out their hands and clapped his back. Part of him felt sheepish; after all, they hadn't won. Nonetheless, he felt himself growing in the eyes of the yard. Becoming someone.

5

THE FIRST TIME HE SAW HER, SHE WAS DRIVING A JITNEY. A SHORT flatbed on a Willys jeep chassis, custom-built to make tight turns in the narrow confines of the yard. She came barreling down the main road to the berths, faster than was altogether necessary. Josiah watched from the plank stairs, one story up.

The jitney came to a stop directly below and she hopped out in driving gloves and rough denim coveralls. A buoyant tentacle of hair had escaped her bandanna, and she paused to tuck it in. If there was one inviolable edict in the yard, it was that women cover their hair. For safety, yes, the real dangers of getting it caught in a drill or a lathe, but one suspected another no less important reason. In this case, though, modesty was useless. Anyone could see she was beautiful. Milky skin, high arched brows, and eyes so blue they seemed to smoke. When she smiled at old Sammy Taylor, the dockhand waiting to take her delivery, two long dimples bloomed on her cheeks.

What struck him more, though, was her verve. The way she tossed things off the flatbed with abandon, like a cowhand flinging bales of hay, and the way she tore out of there with a tight little turn, billowing smoke and dust, her whole body leaning.

THE NEXT TIME HE SAW HER, SHE WAS STEPPING OUT OF A STORAGE shed, looking exactly the same: gloves, bandanna, coveralls. A few seconds after the door closed behind her, it opened again and a man appeared, young and decent-looking, combing his hair with both hands. From the way he looked around guilelessly, it was clear what had happened.

Actually, if there was one inviolable edict in the yard, it was that women not do *that*.

But what she had done, what *they* had done, seemed to Josiah the most natural thing in the world. If anything was unnatural it was the architecture, the whole edifice of civilization, designed to keep the natural thing from happening. Suddenly he had a window into her, and the window was also a mirror.

He watched as she and the man walked in different directions, without acknowledging each other, the man more artful now. Maybe he was her beau or her husband, but somehow it didn't matter; he seemed of no consequence. Whenever Josiah imagined the mote-filled light of the storage shed, he saw her and only her.

AT THE END OF THE WEEK, JOSIAH WENT HOME AND FED HIMSELF and the dog, who had indeed stuck around. Queenie, he had taken to calling her, for the regal way she sat, like a sphinx. Then he went out to Second Beach, but instead of jumping into the bay, he used the public showers, careful to scrub the grime from under his nails. Back at camp, he put on his best work shirt and work pants and ran pomade through his hair and left without mussing the dog, afraid for once of her musk on his hands.

Earlier that day, at the end of shift, Josiah had been walking toward the time clock building when he saw a boy in the middle of the road, handing out flyers. Josiah tried to avoid him, but the boy was persistent. The yard was hosting a talent show that night at the Navy League Seamen's Club, and Josiah almost said no thanks. Talent shows were not the kind of thing he went in for. Then it occurred to him that *she* might be there.

The Navy League Seamen's Club was a squat building with a false front at the corner of Beatty and Dunsmuir, across from the Cambie Street Grounds. The building had once been home to the Vancouver Athletic Club, and all those facilities—showers, swimming pool, steam room, gymnasium—made it ideal for seamen ashore. Josiah made his way to the gym and took a seat in the back. As the benches filled, he quietly scanned the room. He recognized men and women from the yard, including old Sammy Taylor, looking rumpled in his suit, but there was no sign of her. If Josiah suffered from anything that might one day be his undoing, it was an unreasonable sense of self-belief, completely at odds with everything the world had ever told him. It was born of strength but also capability, which gave him a deep well of confidence from which to draw. In this case, he believed that if he could only meet this woman, this total stranger, who already seemed to have a lover, then he would have a chance, despite everything.

He watched and waited. By the time the lights dimmed, he still hadn't seen her. His only hope now was the show itself.

The curtains opened onto a band and a sign that read BURRARD DRY DOCK TALENT SHOW! For the most part, the show bored him, just song and dance routines and warmed-over radio bits. He only sat up between acts but was let down each time. With each passing act, the chances of seeing her dwindled, and he burned with shame and disappointment.

Then it happened: she swept onstage in a strapless blue gown, as if he had finally willed her into being. Her hair was long and dark as peat and moved with a soft jog. When the room began to whoop, she smiled, gouging her cheeks with those dimples of hers, but when the slavering continued, she looked at her accompanist with happy embarrassment, then broke into laughter, her pale shoulders quaking. Her name was Poppy Miller.

The song began with pretty little splashes of piano. As she waited for her cue, there in the incandescent moon of the spotlight, he found himself holding his breath, afraid she would founder. Then she began. The song, a slow ballad, was about two people meeting with a sense of déjà vu, as if they had talked and looked at each other in precisely this way before, only the speaker of the song couldn't recall where or when that might have happened.

Her voice was smoky and low. Each time she held a note, a wave, a physical force, passed through him, and everything fell away until there was only her in that burning tunnel of light. And in that transcendent myopia, she sang for him and him alone. But he knew this was just an illusion. Every other man in the room felt the same, and he resented their feelings, and their existence. Though the song was short, just three verses and a bridge, he would hear it for a very long time, but he didn't know that yet. That night, as she left the stage with a kiss, to rapturous applause, all he knew was that spark had leapt into flame.

AFTER THE SHOW, HE FOLLOWED THE CROWD TO THE CANTEEN. AT the far end of the room was a counter lined with stools, like a diner, where members of the Women's Auxiliary were handing out soda in small paper cups. Josiah stood in line and surveyed the room, unsure if she would appear or what he would do if she did.

Then, for the second time that evening, he willed her into being. She walked into the room and perched herself on a stool and promptly vanished into a huddle of men, and Josiah felt himself losing out already. Without thinking, he strode toward the counter. As he approached, her eyes met his and held their gaze, a summons that drew him right in, and the circle around her parted unhappily. For a long moment, she took him in with eyes of acetylene blue, waiting for him to speak, to fawn, as these other men were fawning, but he wouldn't, he refused, just stood at full height, letting her take him in with darting eyes.

Then the circle, the whole room, which seemed to have stilled, rose up again. The men, including a couple in seamen's caps and flap collars, went back to their banter, their wisecracks, their showy attempts at one-upmanship, until his silence seemed strange, even to himself, a boring kind of rectitude. More men joined the circle, boisterously, and Poppy laughed right along, her mouth a red ring, and he thought he had gotten her wrong, she wasn't daring but conventional, and the laughter became a drowning, sweeping him out to sea.

He'd been foolish to come. What did he think would happen? Someone like him and someone like her—

But just when all seemed lost, she tipped back her cup like a shot and clapped it against the counter, then slipped off her stool and came directly toward him.

"I need some air," she said. "Care to join me?"

6

THEY CROSSED THE STREET TO THE CAMBIE STREET GROUNDS.

"Did you see their faces?" Poppy asked, laughing.

For a moment, he feared she had chosen him simply for effect. Then she said, "God, what a bunch of boors," and he felt relieved to be outside her circle of scorn.

They made their way to the grandstand, its benches littered with soldiers and drunks. But the grandstand was long, almost a whole city block, so they had no trouble finding a section to themselves. As soon as they sat down, she reached into her purse and pulled out a pack of cigarettes. Sweet Caporal. Their advertisements featured a blond majorette in a shako.

"Smoke?" she asked, shaking one from the pack.

His father had smoked a pipe, and Josiah had always loved its rich, woody scent. But he also remembered the cough, the shortness of breath, the green-black oysters of phlegm.

"No thanks."

She pulled out a cigarette with her mouth. Through rolled lips, she said, "Let me guess. Your body is a temple," then let out a husky laugh.

She struck a match, but it blew out with a curl of smoke. She struck another, and he cupped his hands just as she leaned in, and the glow of the match redoubled against their skin.

"Let's see if I won." She slipped her fingers into the pack and pulled out what looked like a trading card. "A straight!" she said, flashing a picture of a poker hand. "My lucky night. What do I get?" She turned the card over and read aloud: "'Westinghouse Electric Iron. This standard type of iron is very suitable for general household use and carries the usual Westinghouse guarantee.' Hmm. Not sure I have much use for that."

He hardly knew what she was saying, but he liked watching her smoke and muse and the strong, dark smell of tobacco. They sat with their backs to the armory and looked across the parade grounds to a pretty row of two-story houses on Cambie Street. Now that blackouts had been lifted, windows burned through the dark.

"Did you ever come here for the carnivals?" she asked, gesturing at the grounds.

Once, when he was a kid, a traveling circus had come through the Cariboo: strongman, fat lady, fortune teller. That was the only carnival he had ever been to. He shook his head.

"I used to come here every year," she said. "They had everything. A merry-go-round, a Ferris wheel, a midway, you name it. The biggest thing was always a raffle for a new house. Not like the ones over there." She looked across the way at porches, columns, bay windows. "These were very modern, like something out of the future. My parents said they were ugly, but I always bought a ticket."

She took a drag of her cigarette and stared at some ghost of herself.

Then she smiled, alighting upon a memory. "One year, there was a hot-air balloon. I wanted to go for a ride, but my parents wouldn't let me. I begged and begged, but they still said no. So I slipped away and paid for a ride myself. Got a thrashing afterward, but it was worth it."

"How old were you?"

"Must have been eleven or twelve."

"Were you scared?"

"Oh god, no. I loved it. Never felt so free. When you're that high up, you realize everything down here, the whole world—it's just nonsense."

For a while they were silent, Poppy thinking to the slow pulse of her cigarette. Then she said, "I remember they used to have these . . . I don't even know what you call them. Sideshows, I guess. These pseudo-anthropological exhibits. I remember one called 'Igorot Dog Feast' and another called 'Savage Kawaba and Foster Baby.' You know what that was? A woman suckling a chimpanzee. Even as a child, I was horrified. By the whole idea of these shows, I mean. And I hated the carnival barker. Always some ruddy-faced man in a stupid pith helmet. I don't know how I knew all of this was terribly wrong. Sometimes children just have a natural sense of justice."

At that moment, a voice shot out of the darkness: "Why dontcha come over here, darling? You belong with us."

Men cackled, the sound strangely stereophonic, as if the whole grandstand were laughing. Neither Poppy nor Josiah flinched. But they didn't want trouble.

"Let's go back," he said.

Poppy stubbed out her cigarette, flicked it away, and stood.

"I've got a better idea."

WALKING AWAY, THEY RECEIVED A BARRAGE OF INVECTIVE. THE usual unimaginative things that slid off their backs like water. But when a bottle shattered nearby with an angry crash, she had to take his arm to keep him from turning around.

"Forget them. They're idiots."

She kept his arm as they walked, and he liked the feeling. He didn't know where they were going but was happy to be led. Since coming to the great metropolis, he had spent his nights in the park, avoiding drink, nightlife, and women altogether, especially after he took on the dog, so this was his first night out, and walking through the neon drench of downtown, he saw what a strutting young city it was.

She led him to the corner of Dunsmuir and Hornby, where they came to the Elks Lodge, or rather the alley behind, where a man in a suit and tie was standing at the top of a stairwell that led underground.

"Hi, Birdie."

"Hiya, Poppy," the man said, tipping his hat. "This a friend of yours?" Without waiting for an answer, the man stepped aside, and Poppy led Josiah down an unlit flight of stairs. At the bottom, they pushed through a door, then through heavy curtains, to a spray of light, and entered a low-ceilinged room of dark wood, brown leather, and red velvet, in the manner of a boudoir, all of it dimly lit by candles. Faces turned, took them in, paid them little mind.

They sat down on a pair of tufted leather armchairs around a small table with a votive. When two glasses of dark-amber liquid arrived, Poppy asked, "Are you scandalized?"

"No."

"Good," she said. "Cabarets are fun, but you can't get a drink. All the nightclubs are dry. You can get a drink in a beer parlor, but men and women can't sit together. Especially now, everyone afraid that soldiers will catch VD. Yes, that's what women are, a fifth column spreading our nasty diseases. God forbid that men and women should drink alcohol and—"

A bolt of black lightning flashed through his mind.

"There is no God," he blurted.

She stilled, brows raised, and he thought he had said too much.

"No," she said, "there most certainly is not."

WHEN A TRIO—DRUMS, PIANO, DOUBLE BASS—SET UP IN ONE COR-
ner and started in on an easygoing number, Poppy stood up and led
Josiah to where the trio was playing, even though there wasn't really
anywhere to dance, just a bit of Persian carpet that the trio hadn't taken
up. All the more reason just to hold each other and sway. The liquor
they had been putting down was doing its work; everything now had a
gauze to it. Yet he couldn't quite believe he was here with that girl from
the burning tunnel of light.

"Where did you learn to sing?"

He felt the heat of her breath as she laughed. "In church, actually.
Under the gaze of Saint Paul in Athens." She described the parish
church in the West End she had attended as a child, in walking distance
of the Queen Anne house on Seaton Street where her parents still lived.
"I used to love singing in church. St. Paul's has a pipe organ, and it's
just . . . magnificent. But at some point I realized my parents went to
church to be seen. That piety was just another way of keeping up with
the Joneses. Somehow I saw through that at an early age, too. That's
when I started to have my doubts. Sometimes I'm still shattered that
God's no longer there."

With that, she began to sing along with the band, her voice tremulous
in his ear. A crooning number about a guy who hoped to marry his girl
before someone else stole her heart away—

She stopped abruptly and said, "I saw you in that tug-of-war."

Now he understood the sense of recognition, the seemingly instant
attraction, each of them already aware of the other, but he wasn't sure

how she had managed to catch the tug-of-war. "Aren't women supposed to eat in the women's lunchroom?"

She laughed again. "One thing you should know about me. I'm not much of a rule follower."

Once again, he imagined her pale form in the dusty light of the storage shed.

"I've seen you, too."

"Really?"

"You're a jitney driver."

She leaned back and looked at him, her blue eyes aflame. "And you, my dear, are a riveter."

HE WASN'T SURPRISED WHEN SHE ASKED HIM BACK TO HER PLACE. He *was* surprised that she lived in North Vancouver.

It was late, the ferry done for the night, so they walked to the nearest taxi stand and took a cab to the North Shore. Poppy had worked in the main office at the North Yard, which was how she had managed to rent wartime housing in one of the new subdivisions that had sprung up all over North Vancouver. But as soon as there was a chance to do *real* war work at the South Yard, she had abandoned secretarial.

"Do you know Vancouver has a woman taxi driver now?" she said, her voice low in his ear so as not to rile the man up front. "It's a whole new world."

They came to a tract of new housing near Heywood Park, row upon row of little Cape Cods on streets with names like Churchill, Roosevelt, McNaughton, and MacArthur. She lived on Fell Avenue at the edge of Project No. 5, where she, a single woman, had managed to wrest a place for herself. Her house was tiny, just twenty by twenty-four, yet she had a living room, a bedroom, a bathroom, and a kitchen. Everything she needed.

He sat down on a velvety love seat with stylish metal arms, surprised he wasn't more surprised to be in the sanctum of a woman who just a few hours earlier had been a distant object of longing. As she kicked off her shoes and toed them against the wall, he had the pleasant feeling of being let in on her life. For the next half hour, as a record played, first one side, then the other—the same kinds of easygoing numbers they had danced to earlier, only fronted by a clarinet—they sat on the love seat sipping more whisky, Poppy with an arm propped up and a leg tucked under, those blue eyes fixed intently, even when she turned to exhale. When the record came to an end, she rose with sudden punctiliousness, took his not yet empty glass, and set both glasses on the table. Then she leaned over him, a hand on each thigh, exposing the deep, straight line of her décolletage.

"I showed you my talent," she said. "Show me yours."

7

SHE SAT ASTRIDE HIM, MOUTH TASTING OF SMOKE. HE REACHED
behind and unhooked her, once, twice, and caught the spill of her in his
hands, his mouth, her body taut and quivering. Soon she rose and led
him to the inner sanctum of her room, where they freed each other
completely, save for one thing she asked him to wear. Then they moved
together, her hands on his back, his head swimming with drink, both
of them urgent with need. He hadn't been drunk since his last night in
the Cariboo, and the glassed-in sense of delirium only added to the
dreamlike feeling.

Afterward, saronged in sheets, Poppy lit up, igniting the dark.

"You've done this before," she said.

He thought of the women he had been with, sometimes in the filth-
iest of rooms. They always seemed a little glad to see him, these women
whose lives were otherwise given to men who smelled like barnyards.
But this was something else altogether.

"*You've* done this before," he said.

She let out a gritty laugh. "I'll take that as a compliment."

"Even in the yard," he said brazenly.

She went quiet, her mood suddenly elusive. "Jimmy's a good kid. I've known him for a long time. He left to join up. I was just . . . sending him off."

This Jimmy didn't sound like much of a rival. Still, Josiah was glad he was gone—and suddenly glad he wasn't allowed to serve.

Poppy threw off the sheets, got out of bed, and put on a robe.

"Come on, I'm hungry."

THE KITCHEN WAS A MARVEL: BRIGHT, CLEAN, AND MODERN. RIGHT inside the swinging door was a white enamel stove with a silver stove-pipe that hooked into the wall. Next to it was a wall-mounted sink, also white, and across the room, a table and two chairs, their legs mirrored in chrome.

Poppy asked him to fetch some fuel for the stove, so he went into the small utility room at the back of the house and scooped sawdust from the hopper. His father had described how sawdust from a circular saw would get into everything—your hair, your eyes, your lungs—but how the dust was still of use, and how the mills would sell it. When the bucket was full, he looked out into the yard enclosed by a wooden fence and wondered if it wasn't time to come in from the past. To take his father's money, just lying there in that canister, and get a little place like this and wait out the war in comfort.

He came back with the bucket and she fired up the stove. When she pulled out bacon and eggs—camp food—he offered to cook.

She arched a brow. "Be my guest."

As she smoked at the table in her pink satin robe, its collar corrugated like a fan, he tended the cast-iron skillet to the popping of fat until the bacon was brown and the eggs ringed with a dark, lacy crust. This was his first time playing house, and he liked it.

When they sat down to eat, Poppy said, "Tell me who you are, Josiah Chang."

They both laughed, that she should be asking only now. He told her things he hadn't told her already about growing up in the Cariboo and falling trees. When he got to the part about his father, her eyes filmed over.

"What about your mother?"

Over the years, his father had told different versions of the story. In some, his mother died, either giving birth or shortly thereafter; in others, she ran off, with or without another man, sometimes crazed and sometimes not from the loneliness and wendigos of the North, until it seemed he wasn't born of a mother at all. That he had sprung full blown from the earth itself, from sea and sky and mountains.

Poppy, on the other hand, had a difficult relationship with her mother. "She was the one who set the rules, at first because my father was gone. Off in the Great War. Fought at the Battle of Ypres—the third, I think. But even after he came back, she was the one in charge. Her own parents were the worst sort of Victorians. The kind who refused to eat garlic and pronounced Spadina Avenue 'Spa-dee-na,' unlike those dirty Italians. My mother always says, 'As my father used to say . . .' as if her father's wisdom came from the hand of God. I've never understood why she never questions anything."

Something else he learned about Poppy as they sat there talking: she was older, twenty-five. This, too, he found alluring for the way it stretched the bounds of propriety, and she must have felt the same, for when her plate was empty, she set down her fork and strode to the swinging door.

"Come on. Night's still young."

THE NEXT DAY WAS SATURDAY, HIS ONE DAY OFF, AND THEY DIDN'T leave the house. Just stayed in, relishing everything that was theirs:

youth, freedom, each other. In the morning, as Poppy slept, Josiah took stock of her room. The sheer curtains and the blinds. The clock, hatbox, and framed photographs on her dresser, including one of a surprisingly handsome couple that could only have been her parents. The sizeable dressing table and bench angled into a corner, its counter an arsenal of jars, vials, and bottles. In the afternoon, he took a bath in her echoey, aqua-tiled bathroom, then plunged into the valley of a long, luxurious nap. In the evening, they raided the well-stocked refrigerator for dinner. That summer, the country had started rationing sugar, then coffee and tea, but not yet butter or meat, so they pan-fried steaks and whipped up a sauce and ate as if there would soon be no more meals of its kind. After dinner, they put on records and danced. There was no time of day when they weren't quietly orbiting, and by the time he left on Sunday, no season in which he hadn't known her: the spring of morning, the summer of afternoon, the fall of evening, and the deep winter of night.

On Sunday morning, as they lounged in bed, Poppy rolled over and laid a hand on his chest, her hair tousled, abounding. "Do you really have to go?"

The yard worked around the clock, seven days a week, but most didn't care to labor on Sunday, so Josiah had picked up a shift at double the pay. Now he resolved to change his schedule.

"Play hooky," she said.

He was sorely tempted. If he had been scheduled to work with Fergus and Charlie, he would have stayed, but he had a different crew on Sundays and didn't want to let them down.

"Okay, then, mister," she said, pinning his arms. "One more for the road."

As he left the house, a middle-aged woman next door pulled back the curtains. When he met her eye, the curtains fell, but not before he saw her unhappy look. All these houses were tightly packed and their walls thin. He could only imagine what the woman had heard, even over breakfast on the Lord's Day.

BEFORE WORK, HE WENT TO CHECK ON QUEENIE. WHEN HE GOT back to camp, she wasn't there, so he called out her name. For a long minute the forest was silent, and he had a stabbing premonition that one day she wouldn't be here. Then, with a leafy rustle, she came springing out of the brush. Usually, she could muster only a tired sort of affection, but today she came running, breath smelling of kill.

He felt guilty. For the past few weeks, the old girl had kept him from feeling lonely. He loved how she would nuzzle his armpit, clamoring for attention. How she would lie down beside him and sigh with resignation, as if she understood life and all its vicissitudes. He loved all that, but now he had found someone else.

He got changed and opened a can of dog food. Then he pulled her ears and said, "I need you to hold down the fort, girl."

He was running behind, so he hopped a streetcar. By the time he got to the berth, he was late and had to apologize. When he'd left Poppy's that morning, she had told him to call, and all day he worried her four-digit number like a diamond in his pocket, afraid he would lose it. But when the final whistle blew, he decided against calling. Instead, he took the ferry to Lonsdale Quay and walked up double-wide Lonsdale Avenue to Third Street, then Fell Avenue. When she opened the door, her blue eyes widened, and he thought he had made a mistake. Then she was upon him.

IN THE MORNING, HE WOKE TO POPPY SHAKING HIM IN A PANIC.

"We're going to be late for the ferry!"

He rolled over and looked at his watch, then sprang out of bed and threw on his musty clothes from yesterday. Poppy tore off her night-gown and threw on her coveralls.

"Come on, let's go!" she cried.

They ran down Third Street, past block upon block of the same Cape Cods. The farther they ran, the more the neighborhood devolved, from grass to dirt, from siding to framing, until there was nothing but empty lots. Even though they were late, they laughed with an air of high jinks. On Lonsdale Avenue, they ran downhill, and the perilous grade made them laugh even more. At the end of the street was the quay, and at the end of the quay the ferry, still docked. They relaxed, thinking they had made it, until the ferry began to pull away. They looked at each other. Caught the glint of mischief in each other's eyes. Then they started running, sprinting, all the way down to the end of the dock, where they leapt off. Josiah caught air, then the boat's railing, already a few feet out on the water. An instant later, Poppy did the same, if less gracefully, landing with the railing under one arm. Josiah caught her, as did a couple of men on board, and the back of the ferry broke out in applause. Still hanging off the railing, the couple grinned at each other and kissed—wildly, forgetfully. This time, applause was more tepid, but it only made them feel forged in the crucible of the world.

8

THE FOLLOWING WEEKEND, AS THEY SAT AT HER KITCHEN TABLE over cups of rationed coffee, Poppy in her satin robe, shimmery in the morning light, Josiah said, "There's something I should tell you."

"Uh-oh," she replied, setting down her cup uncertainly.

The night they had first met, when Poppy had asked, Josiah had said he lived with a roommate in the West End, which was, in a manner of speaking, true. It had seemed a small white lie, but now he feared the truth would catch up to him. So he told her about his first night in the city, how he had been turned away from a boarding house and how he had felt the need to be out of doors, to feel close to his father. And he told her about Queenie, how she had wandered into his life and how he was going back to the park every other night to check on her.

Poppy listened, smiling yet concerned. When he was done, she said, "Show me."

IT WAS A LOVELY DAY. IF THEY WERE GOING TO GO TO STANLEY Park, why not have a picnic?

After putting on a day dress, the fabric alert to her every movement, she pulled out a wicker basket with a gingham liner and handles that met in the middle. As they walked along Marine Drive toward the park, they stopped in at the butcher's, the baker's, the grocer's, and the cheesemonger's, until the basket was laden with provisions. Poppy owned a liquor permit, so they also bought a bottle of wine, and Josiah was glad to see her making an occasion of things.

The sun was high and beating down, especially on the bridge, but as soon as they entered the park, they were salved by shade. They followed the main road, to the whoosh of traffic, before veering into the woods. She wasn't exactly dressed for a hike, not in a day dress and heeled walking shoes, but she was intrepid, stepping over fallen trees and tramping through dirt and detritus.

At length they came to the clearing and the pup tent and all the things he had added in the weeks since, like a chopping block, clothesline, firepit, and stump stool. Poppy surveyed the scene as she might have a child's elaborate hideout: impressed, amused, and vaguely alarmed. When he pulled back the flaps of the tent, revealing a space that was now quite lived in, she hunkered down for a better look, the hem of her day dress riding up her thighs.

"My lover is a vagabond," she said dryly. "Where's this dog of yours?"

He whistled with his fingers. Before long, Queenie came scampering out of the brush, drawn less by his call, it seemed, than the promise of the basket, which she sniffed fervidly. Then she did the same to Poppy, who crouched again, scratching Queenie behind the ears.

"So you're the other woman."

They took Queenie out to the grassy knoll by Prospect Point and let her run, her broad chest and slender waist motoring. Then, as she snuffled beside them, they filled up on bread and wine and things Josiah had never tried before—a cheese with a soft center and a powdery rind, a salty ham with a delicate halo of fat—and Poppy took pleasure in watching him. Afterward, as a light wind ruffled the grass, she cradled his head in her lap and ran an idle hand through his hair. Her face eclipsed the sun, and each time she tossed her head back, he was blinded, her laughter filling the world with light.

THEY WERE BACK IN CAMP BY SUPPERTIME. HE HAD OFFERED TO walk her home, thinking she'd had enough, but Poppy had said, "No, we're here. Let's stay."

When he asked if she had ever split wood, she said no. When he asked if she wanted to try, she said yes.

He set a round of bigleaf maple on the chopping block, then looked for cracks in the end grain. "The grain has a natural tension you want to follow," he said, feeling in his element. "Remember, you're not cutting wood, you're splitting it. The wood is already in pieces. You're just taking them apart." He picked up his maul and stood with his feet shoulder-width apart. Then he raised the maul over his head and brought it down swiftly, bending his knees for power, and the round of wood split in two and fell off the block with a musical clatter.

Poppy set down a new round before taking her measure and swinging the maul. Her first swing was errant, sending the round lurching toward Queenie, who startled, but the next swing cracked the wood beautifully, and she punched the air with a laugh. She kept going, and he was mesmerized by the sight of her in those shoes and that dress, splitting round after round, her whole body liquid with motion. What a powerful attractant it was when a woman was good at something you loved.

At last she set down the maul and swiped an arm across her forehead.

"Okay, what's for dinner?"

• • •

JOSIAH WHIPPED UP A HASH OF CARROTS, ONIONS, POTATOES, AND bully beef. Then he sat on the stump stool as Poppy sat on the chopping block, and they ate by the fire, which crackled with deadwood that he had already split and stacked.

"Do things just taste better when you work up an appetite," Poppy asked, "or is this actually delicious?"

After they were done, Poppy lit a cigarette, and the ashy smoke of the fire was joined by something darker, sweeter.

"So nobody knows you're here?"

Once, he had come back to find the site disturbed, but nothing had been taken, so maybe just kids or someone who had wandered off the trail. He kept his father's canister of banknotes buried behind the pup tent, and it had still been there, unmolested. For the next few days, he kept waiting for a ranger or a constable to appear, but no one did, and then he relaxed again.

"How long do you plan to stay out here?"

He shrugged. "Maybe through the summer. As long as the weather's good."

She squinted at the sun, falling through the trees in tattered ribbons of light. "This is nice. I can see why you like being out here."

He was glad she approved. It *was* nice, sitting by the fire on a cool summer night and feeling the hum of the other's presence, Queenie balled up at their feet, her hind legs all the way up by her head, like a diver in the pike position. But he sensed Poppy intimating more. That she didn't mind him living this way, at least for now. That she wasn't above the things that gave him pleasure. That her station in life was in no way irreconcilable with his.

They stayed out all evening, until stars poked out through the break in the canopy. Then, after flicking one last cigarette into the fire, Poppy slapped her knees and got to her feet with that sudden punctiliousness of hers.

"All right, Joe. Time to show me your tent."

ALL THOSE NIGHTS HE HAD LAIN HERE THINKING OF HER, AND NOW here she was in the greasy darkness of the pup tent, moving above him, hands on his chest, in the flesh and yet somehow unreal, as if she weren't really here. As if he were dreaming again.

Afterward, he held her on the narrow bedroll.

"Do you always carry . . . safes?"

She laughed huskily. "Yes. If you must know."

Women had asked him to use them before, but he had no idea how to get one. "Where do you find them?"

"Drugstores keep them in the back, but you have to ask. Most places require a marriage certificate. I remember one druggist: 'Don't you know you can go to jail?' But you can go to jail even if you're married. And just for selling. But that wasn't stopping him."

"Really?"

"It's not likely to happen, but it's in the Criminal Code. You know, a crime against God and nature. The sad thing is, it's not just the liberal-minded who want birth control. Some want to keep the working classes from 'breeding.' It goes without saying that most of these people feel the same about Indians, Japanese, Chinese—" She squeezed his thigh. "Honestly, these people are no better than Hitler." For a moment, the thought hung in the air. "Anyway, it took forever to find someone who would sell to me. Three for fifty cents. Not cheap, but money well spent."

It was too dark to see the tin she kept in her purse, but he could picture the little blue boxes in her room. SOLD FOR PROTECTION AGAINST DISEASE. GET NEXT TO NUTEX. Each rolled circle was flattened into an oblong and wrapped with paper, like shoelaces. Three to a box.

"You know what's funny? Watching men trying to buy condoms. My god! The way they hem and haw. You would think sex would be important to them, but some walk out, too ashamed to buy anything! Me, I go right up and say, 'Rubber safes, please,' and watch whoever's behind the counter go red."

Suddenly they heard Queenie whimpering outside. She had fallen asleep by the fire, but the fire must have gone out.

"Aw, poor thing," Poppy said. "Should we let her in?"

"No, not yet," Josiah said. "There's another safe in the box."

9

BY THE TIME JOSIAH MADE IT THROUGH THE TIME CLOCK BUILDING, Poppy was already waiting on the other side, standing with hip slung, one hand over her eyes, like someone looking out on a vista, and the sight of her through the parting crowd made his heart rise.

The night before, Poppy had said, "We should go out to dinner. Oh, wait. You probably need a suit, don't you? Then let's go shopping tomorrow after work." So that's what they did. Took the streetcar to the Hudson's Bay Company at the busy intersection of Granville and Georgia. Josiah had been to the Bay before, but only to the War Worker Shop in the basement. Today, they took the elevator to the men's section, where Poppy helped him pick out a light-brown three-piece, made of botany wool and lined with Celanese for "graceful drape" as the tag said. In the dressing room, with a little help from the salesman, Josiah managed a Windsor knot. When he stepped out, Poppy's blue eyes went soft.

"My goodness, you clean up nice."

They went back to Fell Avenue. By the time she was done with all her little rituals, the powders and the lotions, the makeup and the hair, she, too, was remade in a striped summer dress with a plunging back, her dark hair falling in waves.

"Let's go to Mandarin Garden," she said as she checked herself in the mirror by the door.

His brows furrowed. "Where's that?"

"Chinatown."

"No."

"Why not?" she asked blithely. "It'll be fun."

"No," he repeated.

She turned from the mirror, finally catching on. "It's not what you think, Joe. It's a regular cabaret. There's an orchestra at ten. They have a Canadian menu and everything—"

"I said no."

She rolled her lips, resisting the urge to say more. Then she brightened with effort. "Okay, let's go somewhere else."

They went to the Cave downtown instead, which did indeed look like a cave inside, the ceiling dripping with papier-mâché stalactites. For dinner, Poppy had the crab Louie, Josiah the steak special. Like every other cabaret, the Cave was dry, so they drank Old Colony soda. When Poppy ran out of cigarettes, she turned to a cigarette girl whose legs were clad in fishnet. On the surface, everything was fine. The food was good and Poppy cheerful and the venue lighthearted, but Josiah felt a small tear in the fabric of the evening. He wished he hadn't acted the way he had. Peevishly, almost irrationally. He wanted to explain but didn't know how. It had simply been a feeling.

When the orchestra came on, Poppy said, "Come on, let's dance," in a way that seemed designed to change the mood. She showed him the rudiments of swing, the rock step and the triple steps and the underarm turn, and they laughed to find themselves suddenly dancing. But Josiah could still feel the strain and felt relieved when the music slowed and he could just hold her, and even more relieved when she finally said, "I'm tired. Let's go home."

On the ride back, she sat at arm's length in the lighthouse sweep of oncoming traffic. Once home, they lay in bed, listening to the sound of the other's thoughts crackling in the dark.

At length she said, "Want to tell me what that was about?"

He didn't know how to answer. He still wasn't sure where his feelings had come from. Maybe it had to do with the Bay. Before going in, they had passed a few storefront windows, all of which had been given over to the war effort. One had been dedicated to the Chinese War Relief Fund and featured a stiff-looking mannequin in a peasant suit and a bamboo hat, his eyes strangely drawn, and it bothered Josiah to think that that was how others saw him.

Then there was the time two men had approached him in the yard, so excitedly that he thought they must have seen him in the tug-of-war. But they started speaking to him in Chinese, and he couldn't understand, much less answer, and the light drained from their faces, and he was left feeling embarrassed. Somehow, the world never saw him the way he saw himself.

But it seemed too hard to explain, so he told her about the man he had met outside the train station on his first night in the city, who had taken one look at him and directed him to Chinatown, as if he belonged nowhere else.

After a moment, she said, "You think I'm like the man at the train station?"

The question was rhetorical, meant to point out the patent absurdity. If anyone saw him the way he saw himself, it was Poppy. And yet.

"How long has your family been in Canada?" he asked.

All her grandparents, she said, had been born in England.

"My family has been here twice as long," he said. "I guess I just didn't like that the first place you thought to take me—"

He didn't finish the thought, and they lapsed into silence, until she said, "Look at me."

For a petulant moment, he refused. Then he turned and looked her in the eye. Even in darkness, face half-sunken, she had a fierce and resolute beauty.

"I can't say I never notice. That you're Chinese. That you're different. That wouldn't be true. But I like that you're Chinese. I like that you're different."

He thought he knew why. Because being with him affirmed the way she saw herself and wanted others to see her: as open and unafraid. Which, he supposed, was the way he saw himself.

"I'm sorry I upset you," she said. "I thought that . . . well, never mind what I thought. All of this is new for me, but I'm learning."

At this, he softened, enough for her to put a hand on his chest. "Just think, very few people have ever done what we're doing. We'll figure it out, I promise."

That was it. They were doing something so untried. Of course it wouldn't always be easy. The knot in his chest loosened. If Poppy said they would figure it out, then he believed her.

10

ON A BEAUTIFUL DAY IN AUGUST, AS SHE TOOK THE FERRY TO WORK, on one of those increasingly rare mornings when she crossed the water alone, Poppy stood on deck in the whip of a cross breeze and scanned the south shore, from the Second Narrows to the First. As always, the primeval swath of Stanley Park made her think of Josiah. Today, what came to mind was Queenie, who had smelled of something dead the first time they met. Nonetheless, Poppy had scratched her behind the ears, knowing Josiah was watching. In the weeks since, they had gone back to the park a few times to split wood, build a fire, cook a meal, and spend the night, which she enjoyed, well and truly, especially with the run of weather they were having, but she knew it was largely for Queenie's sake. Same when he didn't stay over, which was fine, not just because they needed something to slow their headlong falling, but because she knew from the way Queenie lay at his feet and looked at him with those dark, rheumy, possibly clouding eyes that the old girl loved Josiah. Which made two of them.

The first time she saw him was in that tug-of-war. She had been on her way to the women's lunchroom, where she planned to have lunch with Betty and Edith, when she heard a booming voice over the loudspeakers. When she worked her way into the crowd, she was greeted by what looked like a farce: a single man lined up against eight others—and a man of Asian extraction, no less. Never mind that he was young and powerfully built; he looked utterly forsaken, standing there alone. She imagined stepping forward, and the shock of the yard as she strode out to meet him, and if she thought her doing so would hasten anything other than his demise, she would have. As it was, she could only look on with pity and admiration until seven other men finally joined him. Watching him in that tug-of-war was incredible. The way he pulled, his legs straight out, his biceps stretched like zeppelins. There were seven other men on his side, but somehow *he* was the oak that had to be uprooted.

The next time she saw him, he was up on the scaffolds wielding a rivet gun, arms rippling in the heat. Since then, she had only confirmed what she knew from the first: the man was beautiful. But it wasn't just his beauty she loved. She had known beautiful men. Plenty, in fact, but what they wanted from her was the very thing that left her wanting. She could still remember the man whom she had thought self-respecting who actually said, "It's been fun, darling, but I need a girl I can bring home to Mother." But Josiah didn't think that way. To him, she had no past, as he had none to her, and that made everything possible.

After disembarking, Poppy made her way past the gate guard at the women's entrance to the dingy locker room above Plate Shop No. 2, where Betty and Edith, a bolt threader and a plate marker, were tucking their hair into snoods. As Poppy joined them, tying on a red bandanna, one of the office girls appeared.

"Poppy, Miss McGhee would like a word with you."

Betty and Edith tittered, as if she had been called in to see the Mother Superior.

"Really? What for?"

"I'm not sure."

Poppy was shown through a door with a frosted window that read MISS MARY MCGHEE, SUPERVISOR OF WOMEN. The office was dated, the windows draped in heavy brocade, and Miss McGhee was ensconced at her desk in a woolen suit-dress, her hair a sexless cloud of gray. At the sound of the door, she looked up. "Ah, Poppy. There you are. Have a seat."

As soon as Poppy had settled in, Miss McGhee clasped her hands and smiled. "How much do you know about me, Poppy?"

A strange way to begin. "Not much, I'm afraid," Poppy said, though she sensed a good deal. Everything about the woman reeked of fustiness, like the doilies and antimacassars her mother insisted on using. On their first day, Miss McGhee had lectured all the women on decorum and forbearance. Poppy knew what this was about.

"Do you know I used to supervise women at the aviation plant on Sea Island? For many years. And quite successfully, I might add. That's why Mr. Thompson, the shipyard manager, recruited me to work here. You see, the president of the shipyard didn't want to hire women. Was quite opposed, in fact. Not to women per se, but the problem of women and *men*." She let the word hover for a moment. "But I gave the president my personal assurance that women in my charge would comport themselves. That's the only reason he relented—and the only reason you're employed here."

Poppy supposed she owed this woman a debt. If not for her, she might never have escaped the cloister of the typewriter. But Poppy didn't care for her methods, the way they catered to men and their fears about women.

"So I expect women in the yard to be on their best behavior."

"Yes, ma'am."

Poppy's voice was tart, and a veil of cordiality slipped from Miss

McGhee's face. "Do you know someone in the yard by the name of Josiah Chang?"

"Yes."

"And how would you describe your relationship?"

Poppy bristled. What right did she have to ask? "We're friendly."

"I see." Miss McGhee jotted something down in a folder before clasping her hands again. "I'll be frank. I've received reports that the two of you have been . . . consorting in the yard."

"Consorting?"

"Yes."

One of the keys on Poppy's key ring sprung the padlock to one of the storage sheds, but the door couldn't be locked from the inside. The first time, Josiah had stood with his back to the door; the second time, she had pressed her hands against it. Both times, she was the one who had said, "Meet me for lunch."

"I don't know what you mean."

"You don't?"

"No."

Miss McGhee frowned but pressed no further. "It's important to remember that what you do in the yard reflects on me. I gave my word, and I intend to keep it. In fact, what you do reflects on all of us. There are those who don't want women in the yard. We can't let them be right."

Poppy hated the double bind: be what people expect or confirm their worst fears. And she hated giving the skeptics ammunition. Being the exception that somehow proved the rule.

"What if they're wrong? About everything?"

"I confess, the evidence is circumstantial," Miss McGhee said, misunderstanding. "But it's important to be above reproach. Sometimes, appearance and reality are one and the same. Especially when it comes to a woman's reputation."

Poppy wanted to laugh. What about the men in the yard and their pinups, their girlie magazines, their endlessly vulgar talk? What about *their* reputations? And what about Josiah's, for that matter? Was *he* getting a talking-to?

"My reputation is sterling."

To her credit, Miss McGhee remained unruffled. She simply squared her papers and closed her folder. "I think our interview is over. Just remember, there are rules in this yard I expect my girls to follow. If you can't, you'll be let go. We have plenty of girls to choose from."

Only now did Poppy feel the first real quaver of fear. She remembered what it was like during the Great Depression when there had hardly been any jobs for girls like her, much less good ones. Now she had not only a job but a place of her own. Freedom and a life. She couldn't risk all that.

"Yes, ma'am."

Poppy was shown out by Miss McGhee, but not before the woman held the door to keep her a moment longer.

"I know your parents. They're good people. And you're a bright girl. Pretty, too."

Poppy braced herself. All this obsequiousness was leading somewhere.

"Do you think a girl like you should be . . . friendly with the likes of Josiah Chang?"

And there it was. Poppy's eyes brimmed with anger, but not just at Miss McGhee. She loved Josiah, but she knew her love was shot through with other feelings. Novelty, for one. Daring, for another, especially in public, a flouting that matched her sense of herself. And, if she were honest, a feeling of self-abasement that was feral, reckless, and thrilling. All of which made her burn with shame.

"A very good question," Poppy said. "I'll be sure to consider it."

11

JOSIAH WOKE UP AT FIRST LIGHT AND FED HIMSELF AND THE DOG.
Then he followed the endless scroll of railway ties to the yard, alone at
first, then joined by others. At one point he overheard a man say, "Did
you hear?" and another man reply, "Just now." That was the first inkling
that something was up. The yard had finally gone from an hourly wage
to piecework. Mr. Thompson, the shipyard manager, had called a meeting and said, "Rivet gangs in Quebec are pushing seven hundred rivets
a shift. We're averaging three hundred. That's not good enough." The
news had put Charlie and Fergus in a permanently sour mood. But that
was weeks ago. It had to be something else.

When he entered the yard, the feeling that something was off only
deepened. The whole place seemed both unusually quiet and strangely
abuzz, the chatter low and indistinct. Before the whistle sounded, a
radio report came over the loudspeakers, which finally explained what
was going on. The same reports had already appeared at breakfast
tables all over the city, but Josiah had caught none of it.

After training in England for nearly two years, Canada had pressed the British for action, and it finally came in the form of a raid. Supported by over a thousand Allied planes, the Canadians, along with British, American, and Free French forces, had landed on the beaches of Dieppe in France. It was not an invasion, the report took pains to point out, but a "great commando raid" and a "daring, dynamic attack"—the most significant fighting in Europe since Dunkirk. The Canadians had shown well and met their objectives, destroying a gun battery and an ammunition dump.

The yard broke out in a thunderous cheer, and to his own surprise, Josiah felt a pang of envy. He remembered another storefront window at the Bay, full of cardboard cutouts of soldiers carrying Bren guns. One cutout was blank, except for the words YOUR PLACE IS VACANT. YOUR GUN IS READY . . . CANADA CALLS YOU! At the time, he couldn't imagine heeding the call, leaving Poppy. Now he felt the first stirrings of something else.

THAT WEEK, SHIPWRIGHTS BEGAN TO BUILD THE LAUNCHWAYS, which meant the ship he'd been working on was almost done. The sliding and standing ways—that is, the skis on which the ship would rest and the ramp down which the skis would slide—were built out of thick wooden beams and coated with two kinds of grease, one hard, one soft. Then came the difficult part: transferring a three-thousand-ton cargo ship onto the launchways. This meant driving wedges between the hull and the sliding ways, first by hand, then by pneumatic hammer— ramming up, it was called—until the entire ship lifted off the keel blocks.

When the South Yard had launched its very first ship back in the spring, there had been bunting, dignitaries, a military band, and a beribboned bottle of champagne, not to mention a live broadcast on the CBC, but this time there wouldn't be fanfare, especially after Dieppe.

In the days since those first flattering reports, more sobering details had emerged. On the channel crossing, the Canadians had been intercepted. By the time they came ashore, those beaches were bright with flares, as if all the lights had been thrown on in a house being burgled. From high above, the Germans opened fire. The Canadians were hit so badly that the yawning maws of landing craft jammed with bodies. Those that made it out were raked by cross fire. Within hours, surrender. There had been acts of valor, but in the end fewer than half of the five thousand Canadians who set out made it back to England.

"I'm glad you don't have to fight in this war," Poppy said one night, shutting off her upright radio and putting on a record instead.

They were sitting in her living room by the dim light of her lamp. Josiah knew what she meant, but still.

"You don't think I could?"

"Joe. I know you *could*. I just don't want to wake up to your picture in the papers."

Full-page spreads had begun appearing in the *Sun*, the *Province*, and the *News-Herald*. What looked like high school annuals of the missing, killed, or captured. Josiah had no interest in dying, but now that dying had begun in earnest, he felt he had a right to lay his life on the line if he wanted.

"This is my country, too."

"It is, Joe. But I'd take my mercies where I can get them."

He said nothing else. If this was what a raid on Europe looked like, then the war was far from over. Things could change. Only time would tell.

On launch day, the mood was somber. Men and women looked on silently from the scaffolds as the last of the safety shores were knocked out. A man in black vestments blessed the ship and its crew. Then Mr. Lewis started pacing with stopwatch and whistle in hand, the yard so quiet that one could almost hear the stopwatch ticking down. At last the whistle blew, and triggermen swung their heavy hammers, and the ship began to slide. Eerie, watching something so colossal move so impassively. More eerie still, no one cheered. Instead, grown men, roughnecks and old sea dogs, looked on, glassy-eyed.

The inlet was deep enough to launch stern first, so the giant rudder and propeller were first to vanish underwater. After months in the berth, it took only thirty seconds for the ship to slide into the saltchuck with a foamy surge, the wooden beams of the sliding ways bobbing in pieces and tethered by ropes, to be saved for another day.

And that was it. Launch over. The only nod to ceremony was a tugboat in the harbor blasting a few discernible notes of its horn: dot-dot-dot-dash.

V for Victory.

12

BY THE END OF AUGUST, THEY HAD BEEN TO THE CAVE, THE ALEX-
andra Ballroom, and the White Rose Ballroom, but they had yet to go
to the Commodore, the premier cabaret in the city, so Poppy put on a
pleated sea-green dress that came down to her knees and they went
down to Theatre Row, the rakish heart of the city. It was Friday night
and Granville Street was a sleek black river of Lincolns and Buicks and
Cadillacs, everything bathed in the sensuous glow of neon signs and
flashing marquees, now that night was falling.

The Commodore Ballroom was nestled between the soaring neon of
the Capitol and the Orpheum theaters. After paying the cover, they
found themselves at the bottom of a grand staircase, one side lined with
patrons waiting to check their coats. Walking up arm in arm, they ran
a gauntlet of looks, but Josiah felt undaunted. He knew he looked good,
and that he and Poppy looked good together. Then he noticed some
women wearing corsages and felt remiss, but when he said as much, she
squeezed his arm and said, "I'm not worried about that, darling."

At the top of the stairs, they were met by the manager, who shook their hands effusively. Then they were led to the ballroom by a silver-haired maître d'. After being seated at a table draped in floor-length linen, they looked out onto the ballroom, at the six-sided columns and the Art Deco chandeliers and the lit trays in the ceiling. In the center of the room was the dance floor, a whole tennis court of polished blond wood. It was empty for the moment, but it was the reason everyone had come.

"If you think this is nice, you should see back there," Poppy said, nodding at doors marked SILVER ROOM, PLANET ROOM, and EGYPTIAN ROOM.

Aside from Jimmy, they had never really talked about their pasts. Each knew the other had one, but that was about all. If Poppy had had a great love, she hadn't thought to mention it, and he hadn't thought to ask. But now he found himself wondering when she might have had occasion to go behind those doors, and with whom.

There was only one thing on the menu, chicken à la King with a buttered roll and greens, so that's what they ordered. Then Poppy curled a finger at the waiter and whispered in his ear. Moments later, he came back with a tea set, and Poppy greased his palm discreetly. With a flourish, she lifted the lid of the teapot, which turned out to be full of ice, and plinked a cube in each cup before slipping a small silver flask from her handbag. Josiah smiled, impressed.

Over dinner, Poppy explained that the Commodore had been built with bootlegging money. "The owners ran beer to the States during Prohibition and used the money to build this place. They wanted to rival the Crystal Ballroom in the old Hotel Vancouver, which used to be the best ballroom in the city. I used to go there all the time—and argue with my mother when I got home late."

She described Peacock Alley, the entrance hall that ran the length of the ballroom, with its brass railings, Persian rugs, and chaises longues.

The old Hotel Vancouver and its seven hundred rooms now served as a barracks, so all of this must have been before the war. She would have been young, in the first bloom of youth, even lovelier than she was now, if such a thing were possible, and Josiah could only imagine the men, the attention, on all those late nights.

It was no different now. Men kept walking past and smiling. When they saw Josiah, their faces fell. That or they kept smiling, as if he weren't there. As if he were no one. If he wasn't more galled, it was only because Poppy didn't seem to notice—or looked unhappy when she did.

At eight thirty sharp, Ole Olsen and His Commodores appeared in the orchestra shell in white tuxedos, to wild applause. Almost instantly, the dance floor flooded with people. Poppy took Josiah by the hand and together they waded into the crowd. Over a number of evenings, Josiah had learned how to dance. Not well, but well enough to give her the pleasure of dancing. He couldn't do much beyond the basic step, just turn her and swing her out, but she knew all the embellishments, all the little kicks and swivels, hips twisting in a waddling way, and it made him laugh, how good she was.

When the orchestra started in on a waltz, another couple pulled up alongside them. "Mind if we cut in?" the woman asked. This was what the Commodore was known for, everyone dancing with everyone else. Poppy looked at Josiah, who raised a brow and shrugged. The other man was tall and dark and foppish. As soon as Josiah stepped back, he took Poppy in his arms and whisked her off. Soon they had whirled to the other side of the room. Josiah didn't know how to travel the floor like that, so he and the woman just stayed where they were. She was young and blond and patient, and willing to dance with him in the first place, which was no small thing, but Josiah's attention kept turning to Poppy and the man she was dancing with. Clearly, he was good and knew how to show her off to effect, each of them leaning away from the other, as if in disgust, but every time she came into view, she was beaming. Suddenly, he saw all the ways that Poppy might be better off with someone else. The world was full of suitors, waiting to cut in.

At the end of the song, Poppy came back smiling, with a show of dimples, but Josiah still felt thrown. He was glad when the orchestra started in on the radio hit of the summer, Jimmy Dorsey's "Tangerine," so he could just hold her. Poppy laid her head on his shoulder, smelling of whisky and smoke. At that moment, he had a strange vision, that the two of them were clinging to each other on a lashing sea, and he quietly vowed never to let go. Then he realized with a start that he had the means to forestall the pain of ever losing her, and the knowledge gave him a feeling of such elation, such tenderness and peace. As his vision blurred and his nose fizzed painfully, he pressed his mouth to the whorl of her ear and said, "Marry me."

13

AFTER THEY WENT HOME AND MADE LOVE SWEETLY, JOSIAH LAY IN the dark, remembering how Poppy had turned to him, eyes shining, and said, "Yes, Joe. Yes," and how they had kissed then and there, for all the world to see, and how for the rest of the night she had clung to him, refusing to dance with anyone else, shaking her head adamantly whenever she was asked, with a touch of the frightened child, and how he had felt assured, his effort to keep her already working.

But now that he was lying here, with her, he felt ashamed of the unexpected jealousy that had gripped him at the Commodore. He was used to feeling self-possessed, not so helplessly otherwise. But maybe that was love.

"So," she said, looking at him, "how long are you going to stay in the park?"

Unlike the time she had asked in camp, the question now carried a whiff of judgment. Clearly, she saw things now in a new light. But he gave her the answer he had given before: "As long as the weather's good."

"Why don't you just move in?"

"With Queenie?"

"Of course."

Part of him wanted to. He spent so much time here already. But Queenie liked it out in the wild, and so did he. Living out of doors still made him feel close to his father. To the life they had shared. Once he moved in, that life would be gone forever.

"As soon as summer's over. Won't be long now."

She said nothing, and he thought he had upset her, on this of all nights. Then she said, "I suppose we have the luxury of time."

Since Dieppe, another wave of men had enlisted, and many had scrambled to marry before shipping out. But Josiah couldn't go to war, which meant they had all the time in the world.

SUMMER CONTINUED. NIGHTS BY THE FIRE, NIGHTS ON THE TOWN, and nights when they just stayed in, putting on records and dancing. Things they had always done, yet everything felt touched with a new poignancy. Sometimes he would watch her sleeping, in the still of night or the first flush of morning, and his throat would catch, to think this would be his life till the end.

Then came the day Josiah exited the yard and saw a man he recognized standing on the other side of the tracks. A week earlier, Josiah had answered the door at Poppy's house, thinking it was her, arms full of groceries. Instead, it was the man from the photograph on her dresser, looking sheepish but not altogether surprised to see Josiah. When Josiah said that Poppy was out, the man said, "Will you let her know her father came by?" Then, with an uneven gait, he hurried back to the car, black and shiny as a beetle. Later, when Josiah told Poppy, she didn't seem troubled in the least. "You were going to meet soon enough anyway," she said before going back to the groceries.

Now, outside the yard, her father said, "Josiah, am I right?"

The man was dressed in a suit and tie and trench coat, and he had about him an air of softness, like uncooked dough, his brows so pale he seemed to have none. He didn't bear much resemblance to Poppy, save for the same unsettlingly blue eyes.

"I'm sorry, Mr. Miller. Poppy doesn't come this way. There's a women's entrance."

The man smiled uneasily. "Yes, I know. I was hoping you and I could talk. Can I interest you in a cup of coffee?"

After the two men met the first time at Poppy's house, she had been invited to dinner at her parents' bay-windowed house on Seaton Street. According to Poppy, when she broke the news of their engagement, her parents had been "remarkably well behaved." If her father wanted to talk, then this could only be one thing: the interview.

They crossed the railway tracks to Powell Street and stopped at a coffee shop with a neon star above the door. At that hour, the coffee shop was clearing of those fueling up for the swing shift and filling with those coming off the day shift. With a small hitch in his step, Mr. Miller led Josiah to a booth next to the window, where he took off his hat and smoothed what was left of his hair, a laurel at most. His manner seemed reluctant, as if he had been prevailed upon to be here. He looked at Josiah doubtfully, unsure how to begin.

"Do you know that Poppy was a war baby?" he asked finally.

Josiah remembered Poppy saying her father had served in the Great War, but Josiah had never thought of her in precisely those terms.

"She was born while I was gone. Didn't see her for the first two years of her life."

"Is that why you named her Poppy?"

"Actually, she was named after my mother. But yes, I was in Flanders. Took a bullet in the knee at Passchendaele. That's why I walk funny." He laughed, then looked out the window, searchingly. "Nothing I ever wanted the world to see again. Yet here we are."

Josiah tried to imagine it, the abattoir of heavy rain and sucking mud at Passchendaele, and could hardly fathom such misery. Yet Poppy's father, newly married and admitted to the bar, had gone of his own volition. Josiah had to admire the man for that.

When the waitress came by, Mr. Miller ordered two cups of coffee, with the air of someone used to deciding for others. But before the waitress could leave, he caught himself and said, "Is coffee all right?"

"Yes, thank you, sir."

As soon as the waitress disappeared, they were left to fumble again in silence, until Mr. Miller said, "I hear you're staying at the St. Francis Hotel."

Josiah had told Poppy about his small white lie in the personnel office on his first day in the yard. Repeating the lie made perfect sense. One could hardly tell one's parents that one's betrothed was vagrant. Yet he felt a little surprised, and it made him wonder what else she might have kept from her parents.

"Yes, sir. For now. But I wouldn't mind some shipyard housing, like Poppy has." Remembering that the Millers lived in what was by all accounts a fine house, he added, "Not that it's anything special."

"Nothing to be ashamed of," Mr. Miller said, eyes glazing again with that faraway look. "You learn the value of a roof, any roof, when you don't have one."

Once again, Josiah pictured Mr. Miller in the drowning mud of Passchendaele. Clearly, the experience had given him perspective. According to Poppy, her mother was always beseeching her husband to leave downtown for Shaughnessy. The West End, her mother felt, was not what it used to be, but her husband refused to indulge her. The war, it seemed, had taught him how much in life to covet.

The waitress returned with two cups of coffee, and Mr. Miller took this as his signal to begin in earnest. "I understand you want to marry my daughter."

Josiah straightened. "Yes, sir. I'm sorry, I should have asked you first."

Mr. Miller laughed appreciatively. "We both know Poppy does what she wants. She's always been like that, ever since she was a child." Josiah imagined Poppy at eleven or twelve, stealing away from her parents in a hot-air balloon. "I remember meeting Poppy for the first time after the war," Mr. Miller continued, retreating into memory. "She didn't seem like she was mine. What I mean is, at two, she already seemed her own person. Fully formed. Already beyond my influence as a father. Her mother called her 'willful.' I preferred to call her 'spirited.' Perhaps it's my fault. Perhaps I encouraged her a little too much. To be whoever she wanted to be. At least, that's what Gladys says." He looked down, contrite. "I appreciate that you want to marry her, I really do. Frankly, not everyone would. I'd like to see her settle down," he said, with a father's earnest hope.

Josiah wasn't sure where this speech was going.

"If Poppy wants to get married, I can't stop her. She's a grown woman. And you're a grown man," Mr. Miller said, and for a moment, Josiah felt buoyed. "But Gladys and I—well, we're still her parents. We still want what's best for her. We don't want her life to be hard. And I don't just mean the slings and arrows the two of you will face, though there's that to consider, too."

Josiah felt his brows knit. He wasn't sure what hardship he meant, beyond the obvious. "Sir, with all due respect, my family has been in this country longer than yours."

"I know, son," Mr. Miller said, suddenly firm. "It's not what you might think. When I was in Europe, I served with Japanese Canadians in the 52nd Battalion. Some of the finest men I've ever met. And I doubt we would have won the war without the Chinese Labor Corps. Trust me, a bomb will teach you that God favors no one."

Josiah was now even less sure of what the man was driving at. "I'm a riveter, sir. I make good money."

"The war won't last forever. Afterward, your prospects won't be the same. But that's not the issue." Mr. Miller looked down and worried his cup with the edge of his thumb. Then, to his credit, he managed to look Josiah in the eye. "You're not a British subject, son. You're a resident alien. If Poppy marries you, she'll lose her citizenship."

Outside, a klaxon blared, and a cloud bank cast a sudden penumbra. Josiah knew what his status was, but he hadn't known his status—or lack thereof—could doom someone else. Even if Mr. Miller weren't a barrister, Josiah had no reason to doubt his understanding of the law.

"I'm not saying it's right, of course. Quite the opposite. But that's the way it is. And Gladys and I are loath to think of what will happen to Poppy—and the children."

How strange, the invocation of children. It should have been bright with promise. Instead, Josiah felt bereft. He couldn't speak, his lips fat with self-consciousness, and Mr. Miller could see that his unpleasant work was done. He pulled out his billfold and laid a dollar on the table.

"I'm sorry we had to meet under these circumstances, I really am. But I hope you'll do what's best for Poppy."

With that, Mr. Miller put on his hat, hobbled to the door, and left with a jangle. Josiah stayed where he was, there in the booth, the world around him clinking with confusion, and there he remained, staring at his cup, long after his coffee went cold.

14

THE NEXT MORNING, JOSIAH WENT TO WORK IN A BLACK MOOD. HE had lain awake all night, unable to sleep. Rain had pelted the tent with a bassy crackle, as loud and tempestuous as his thoughts. He had never been naive. Had never thought being with Poppy would be easy. He knew he was asking her to live a more difficult life, and wouldn't have asked if he didn't think her strong enough. But he didn't know he carried a kind of contagion that could render a person nobody. He loved Poppy, but he couldn't do that to her.

What he had wanted, sitting there in the coffee shop, was to hate Mr. Miller. To make him the face of every ugliness he had ever endured in his life, but he couldn't. He was filial, and believed in the rights of fathers. Plus, the man had a sense of proportion. What he had said was not unreasonable. It wasn't wrong to point out the law. If Josiah had been a father, he might have done the same.

And yet.

On McLean Drive he crossed the tracks and entered the gates. As he walked along the main road, he had the strange feeling that people were eyeing him, as if his abject state were clear for all to see. Halfway to the berths, he came to a crowd near one of the hangars. People were piling up, three, four, five deep. The feeling that others were eyeing him intensified.

Suddenly, Edith, one of Poppy's friends, appeared before him, stricken. "Don't look."

"What's the matter?"

"Believe me," she said, tugging his elbow, "you don't want to know."

He shrugged her off and shouldered his way through the crowd. Kept pushing and shoving, frantically, imagining the worst, a crash, Poppy broken and bleeding, until he reached the front of the crowd. What he found was not the scene of an accident but a crude painting on the side of a building. Two stick figures lying horizontally, one on top of the other. What stunned him most was not the malice but how such simple iconography—dotted circles for breasts, slanted lines for eyes, two squares for bucked teeth—could convey so completely what was happening, and to whom.

The crowd had left a cautious space between itself and the graffiti, and without quite realizing, Josiah had wandered into it, his vision wavy with disbelief. At the sight of him, the crowd laughed with recognition.

When someone appeared beside him, he thought it was Edith, maybe even Poppy. All the more galling, then, to see Fergus and his withered face.

"Spitting image, wouldn't you say? The work of a real *artiste*."

Synaptic lightning bounced from Josiah's spine to his fist, which landed in the middle of the old man's face. His nose cracked like ice, his cap flew off, and he stumbled backward, drunkenly, before toppling, his head striking pavement with a wet smack. The crowd gasped.

Then someone struck Josiah on the chin, hard, snapping his head to one side and setting his neck ablaze. As the world tipped and sloshed, a large lumberjack of a man appeared, complete with plaid shirt. Charlie. Up north, Josiah had gotten into his share of scraps. His father had never liked the welts, the deep cuts yellow with fat, but even his father knew that sometimes you had no choice.

The two men circled each other, fists raised, like a couple of bare-knuckled boxers. Clearly, Charlie could throw a punch. Josiah had already taken one and wasn't sure he could take another. So he kept his distance, biding his time, waiting for Charlie to make the first move. Eventually, Charlie came in with a jab, more startling than painful. In fact, it was bracing. Clarifying. He wasn't going to outbox this man. To have any chance, he would have to brawl.

Josiah lowered his shoulder and charged. Charlie caught Josiah and staggered but managed to stay upright. With a quick move, he put Josiah in a headlock. Josiah felt his head crushed, chafed by coarse flannel, but this was where he wanted to be: in close, free from blows. He hooked a leg around Charlie's and pushed, and they both fell, Charlie still holding on. A mistake. With nothing to brace himself, he landed with all of Josiah's weight on top of him. Charlie's head snapped back, and he let go, dazed. *Hold your horses*, Josiah heard Charlie say, but he didn't. He raised a fist and brought it down, once, twice, three times, unleashing all his anger since yesterday, a wetness spritzing his face.

When he raised his fist again, someone caught his arm. He whipped around, ready to turn his blows on whomever, only to see Poppy, her blue eyes wide and trembling.

"Run, Joe."

He gave her a wretched look. It was one thing to fight in the yard, another for someone like him to assault the likes of Fergus and Charlie. He knew he'd upended his life, and he took in the sight of Poppy and her trembling blue eyes as if for the last time. Then he bolted. Bulled his way through the crowd until he was running past the gate guards, who looked on, confused. He wanted to go to Poppy's, to hide out at her place and stay forever, but the powers that be would know to look there, right after they checked the St. Francis Hotel.

He ran all the way back to Stanley Park, slowing only as he entered the woods. When he reached camp, he threw all his clothes in his duffel, then clawed at wet earth for his father's canister of banknotes. When Queenie and her small, alien face came trotting out of the bush, he buried his face in her neck and breathed in the wild, piquant smell of her. Only then did he truly understand he was leaving.

He abandoned almost everything, just left it as it was, but Queenie, sensing some ripple in the air, followed him as he left. She did this sometimes, but never for long, so he let her trail behind him. As they took the path he had worn through the woods, he said, "I'm sorry, girl, you can't come." He didn't know how long he would be gone and didn't want her wandering around in the city. She would be safer in the park.

But when they reached the edge of the woods, she followed him out onto the road. He told her to get, but she wouldn't go, so he told her to stay, and she would stay for a while, but every time he looked back, she was slinking after him. "I told you to get!" he said, picking up a stone and throwing it. It landed wide. He picked up another. This one caromed and struck her in the side, in those strangely articulated ribs, and she skittered and yelped and lowered her head, mournfully. "Get out of here!" he yelled, throat raw. At last he threw a handful of pebbles, which pattered like rain, and only then did she turn with sudden decisiveness and bound back into the woods.

Within the hour, he was on the train out of town.

THE GATEHOUSE WAS A WIDE TWO-STORY BUILDING MADE OF YELLOW brick. A road ran through its arched gateway, from the village to the château. C Company had been tasked with taking out the German garrison in the village, a bridge over the river Divette, and the château's gun emplacement.

Josiah slipped toward the gatehouse. Save for birdsong, the world was eerily quiet, on its knees for matins. When the dusky silhouette of the gatehouse reared up, its roofline serrated by gables and dormers, he noticed one sawtooth was missing. Blown away.

At one end of the building was a door, guarded by one of his own, the orange tip of a cigarette pulsing through the gloom, foolishly. Smitty was a nervous kid, the youngest in the battalion. Josiah wasn't going to risk a shadowy approach. Instead, he whisper-shouted the password: "Moose Jaw." Smitty raised his rifle, scoped around, traces of orange sparking at his feet, until Josiah stepped out from behind a tree, hands in the air for good measure.

They locked eyes, and the rifle deflated. Only then did Josiah scamper the few open yards to the gatehouse.

"Jesus, Chang, you made me shit my pants."

Josiah now stood with his back to the building, keeping an eye on the copse from which he had just emerged. "How long have you been here?"

"Since we hit the DZ."

"How's it going?"

Smitty lit up again with a few sharp clicks.

"Major's dead."

Josiah snapped his head. "What?"

"Did you see that hole?" Smitty asked, raising his cigarette over his head. "Krauts got a heavy gun back there." He lowered his hand and pointed at the château. "Seventy-five millimeter, at least. Holloway tried to take it out. But he missed."

Josiah imagined Holloway shoulder-firing his PIAT and giving away his position, and the Germans, unscathed, sending back a deadly rejoinder.

"They got Holloway and the major—and four others."

Josiah felt a little ill. He hadn't even fired a shot and already—

"Where *is* everybody?"

"You tell me. Only fifteen of us at the rendezvous. Picked up guys along the way, but the major sent half of us to blow up the bridge."

"Who's in charge?"

"That's the other thing. Half our officers are missing. But the lieutenant's inside."

"Okay," Josiah said and walked through the door.

HE ENTERED A NARROW HALLWAY WITH ROOMS ON EITHER SIDE. This wing of the building hadn't been hit, but the walls were still

spidered with cracks and everything was dusted with plaster. The first
room was home to six double bunks, all unmade. A makeshift barracks,
abandoned in haste. The jump had been preceded by heavy bombing,
which had sent the German garrison scrambling.

In the second room, also full of bunks, Josiah found the lieutenant
and a man with three chevrons—a sergeant. The light in the room was
watery, and all of their faces were blackened with paint. It took a moment for the lieutenant to realize who had walked in.

"Where'd you get the Bren?" the lieutenant asked. Lieutenant Morrison was a world-weary man who regarded even the most pressing of
matters as little more than personal irritants. Josiah respected him.

Josiah explained how he had gotten the Bren, then pulled out the
dead man's identification discs and handed them to the sergeant.

"Let's put that gun to use," the lieutenant said. "It's the best we got."

"Sir?"

The lieutenant sniffed. "You heard me, Chang. We already lost the
PIAT. Now we're down to three Sten guns, a dozen rifles, and this"—he
held up his pistol—"plus some grenades and Gammon bombs. I sent a
runner to Le Mesnil for the seventeen-pounder, but who knows if we'll
get it." The lieutenant gave him a trusting look. "I need you to harry
that German gun."

Josiah felt himself straighten. "Yes, sir."

HE LEFT THROUGH A DOOR THAT OPENED ONTO THE GATEWAY. THE
heavy wrought-iron gates were open and the road was lined with plane
trees, and he scurried from one to the next. When he reached the ditch
that ran perpendicular, he dove in.

"Nice of you to join us, Chang."

It was Walker, scrunched down uncomfortably, like a man in a
child's cot. He already looked unshaven, as if he had been out here for

days, but his eyes were crinkled to say he was only joking. Walker was a wily and louche sort of character. Could get whatever contraband you wanted. Not the kind of guy to play cards or make bets with, but precisely the kind to bring to a gunfight.

Josiah crawled in his direction, then curled up in a fetal ball of his own.

"Who we got?"

Walker rattled off some names from C Company, plus a few stragglers from B Company, and Josiah felt a twinge. Antoine, Heikkinen, Van den Berg—no one from his stick had made it. At least not yet.

The ditch overlooked a field that stretched all the way down to the château. In the rising light, they could see the German line: a long trench of mounded earth with machine-gun nests at intervals and a concrete bunker at each end, all of it barbed with wire. Normally, German defenses were trained on the main intersection by the château, but now all of it, including the heavy gun, was pointed at the gatehouse. Since the small hours of night, Walker and maybe a dozen others had lain in the ditch, sniping at Germans—and trying not to get sniped themselves. But the fighting had ground to a halt.

"Where's the gun?"

Walker described where he had seen the flash, somewhere beyond the trench. Josiah pulled out his binoculars and sidled up to the edge of the ditch. Through the twitchy gaze of the viewfinder, he scoured the German line until, with a double take, he spotted the gun, its black hole poking out through drapes of camouflage netting.

He nodded at Walker, who called out to the next man, and the order carried on down the line, like signal fires. Then Walker got up on one knee, fearlessly, and fired his Lee-Enfield—the No. 4. At the first crisp report, the fusillade began, including the cracking of Sten guns, the morning suddenly dimensional with sound. For a moment, Josiah was mesmerized by the sonic storm, and by Walker himself, his total calm, working the bolt so fluidly and firing with his middle finger, with nary a hitch, round after round, the gun spitting shells. Then Josiah sprang into action.

Swiftly, while the Germans were down, he lifted the Bren out of the ditch and onto its bipod, his vision collapsing into the peephole of his scope. He wasn't sure the gun would work after lying in water, but when he squeezed the pistol grip, the gun let out a smooth barrage. In the distance, spouts of dirt. He aimed higher. Through the tempest, he thought he heard pings and cries of pain.

The Bren held twenty rounds and emptied quickly. He dove back down, just as the ditch was raked by gunfire. Dirt rained, prickling his lashes. Walker looked up from the bottom of the ditch, smugly.

"Having fun yet?"

The pattern repeated itself: one side shot, the other returned fire. Every time Josiah rose from the ditch, he felt himself tempting fate. How many seconds, half seconds, quarter seconds before a bullet came the other way? Could he afford to empty the chamber, or was that a bridge too far?

But the Bren was making a difference. The Germans pulled their heavy gun back, deeper into the boscage. Josiah moved along the ditch, collecting magazines and letting his gun cool. The Bren was getting hot, but he didn't have an extra barrel.

Just when he thought the gun might seize up, he caught sight of something astonishing, rising from the German trench: a white flag.

2

A LONE GERMAN CROSSED THE FIELD. HE WORE A GRAY FIELD CAP and tunic and walked in fits and starts, sometimes breaking into a jog, cognizant that others were waiting, which suggested low rank, no great dignity to maintain. Indeed, he was young, wide-eyed, and sweating profusely. Lieutenant Morrison, who had ordered the men to stand down, walked out to meet him. They talked briefly, the young man upright, the lieutenant at ease, their voices carrying indistinctly. Then they turned and walked in opposite directions.

After the young man made the long walk back to the German line, a cart emerged from one of the bunkers, pushed by two soldiers. As the cart trundled along the road to the château, three walking wounded emerged from the trench and followed. The Germans had asked for permission to bring their casualties to the aid station at the château. Josiah was surprised. In the midst of battle, you could call . . . a time-out. War had rules, refereed by honor.

Josiah wondered how badly the men in the cart were wounded and if he had done the wounding. Had he already killed, or could he make it through a whole war without killing? Quietly, he hoped the men would live. Despite all the talk of Krauts and Huns and Jerries and Boche, he felt no great animus toward the Germans. In some ways, his fight was not against them but against his own country.

"Giddy up, fellas," the lieutenant said.

For a moment, the fields, the French countryside, were verdant and lovely. Then the wounded disappeared, the white flag came down, and the fight resumed.

SHORTLY AFTER THE FLAG CAME DOWN, THE WORLD WAS SHAKEN BY sound. An explosion flowered in the air, in petaled layers, and sent a tremor through the earth, one that Josiah could feel in the muscular hinge of his jaw. It sounded like some almighty being come to chastise man for mindless goings-on.

But it wasn't the voice of God; it was the bridge. The other half of C Company had managed to blow it up. As the knowledge descended, a throaty cheer rose from the ditch. For the Germans, the cry was malevolent, for the Canadians, cathartic. It bucked them up.

WHEN THE EXPLOSION WENT OFF, JOSIAH WAS LYING IN THE BOT-tom of the ditch, in a slurry of mud, thinking of Poppy. Of the day he had lain with his head in her lap at Prospect Point, staring up at the same wispy sky . . .

The barrel of the Bren had cooled, but no one had yet fired the first resumptive shot. No sense wasting more rounds; they didn't have enough firepower to take out the German gun. Their only hope was to wait for more—maybe the seventeen-pounder. With the bridge gone, the Germans were stranded. Only one side was poised to get stronger.

Josiah had made his way to the other end of the ditch, until he was near the copse from which he had emerged. In time, from those same trees, another man appeared. Instead of the gatehouse, he headed straight for the line, but his manner was blithe, unguarded. It wasn't until someone yelled "Get down!" that the man started, sniffed the air, and began running, half crouched. Excruciating, watching him out in the open. German snipers were expert, and Josiah kept waiting for the moment of impact.

At the edge of the ditch, the man dove and landed in a heap, just as the trough was swept by machine-gun fire. When the barrage subsided, the man looked up and pushed his helmet back into place.

"Well, fuck me," he said, sheepishly.

It was Corporal Larson, a member of the mortar platoon. He, too, had been dropped in the bumfuck middle of nowhere and had felt his way through the dark, until he was drawn by the sound of a firefight. But the fighting had stopped for so long that he'd thought it was over.

Josiah filled the corporal in, then saw the khaki tube—the two-inch mortar—strapped to the corporal's back.

"Think you can hit the gun from here?"

The corporal considered. "I saw a little drainage ditch that runs from here to the German line. If I can get a little closer . . ."

With that, the corporal crawled down the main ditch until he came to a smaller one, so shallow that Josiah could see the scrim of the corporal's helmet flouncing down the edge of the field. After the corporal had advanced a hundred yards, Josiah was amazed to see him rise from the ditch and lean the base plate of the mortar against a tree and hold the mortar on his shoulder like a bazooka. Without thinking, Josiah popped up to cover him. Twenty rounds in no time flat. Before he dove back down, he heard four hollow whumps and saw the German line explode four times.

Josiah expected a counterattack, but none came. Instead, feverish shouting on both sides. The German line was billowing smoke. Within minutes, the white flag reappeared.

THE GERMANS MARCHED DOWN THE ROAD THAT RAN THROUGH THE gatehouse. Even in defeat, the gray mass of them looked imposing, even picturesque, the way they were flanked by plane trees, as if marching down the Champs-Élysées. There were nearly eighty of them, including the walking wounded and those left behind at the aid station.

At the gatehouse, they were disarmed. Some were confused by the sight of Josiah—"Didn't expect *you*, now did they, mate?" someone said jovially, clapping Josiah's shoulder—but most were more perturbed by the size of the enemy force. The Germans had surrendered to a small band of lightly armed paratroopers, and they weren't happy about it.

The sun shone and a breeze tousled the air. For the first time since emplaning, the men were at ease, out of harm's way, and it felt tremendous. What a strange schizophrenia: life and death, life and death, right on the heels of each other.

The radioman radioed headquarters. Mission accomplished.

It was ten o'clock in the morning.

3

AFTER THE GERMANS SURRENDERED, THE CANADIANS WENT DOWN to the château. There, among gardens and steeply pitched gables, they found not only Germans dead or dying but a few POWs, including Simmonds, the man from Josiah's stick who was prone to throwing up, looking more wan than ever. "Leave it to me to land right on a German bunker," he said, laughing skittishly. Josiah had never been happier to see him.

They took up the German position to guard the main intersection. With their newfound stockpile of weapons, they were poised for a counterattack—almost wanted one, fatuously—but it never came. Instead, they were met in the afternoon by British Commandos, who had come up from the beachhead to a chorus of whooping. Fortress Europa had been breached. The great invasion was underway.

The company was relieved of duty at the château, but their day wasn't over. Their job was to help hold the eastern flank. So after some rest, some rations, maybe a catnap, they roused their weary bodies and set off for Le Mesnil.

• • •

LIEUTENANT MORRISON LED THE WAY, ON A QUIET STRETCH OF ROAD that skirted the hamlet of Petiville. Houses with shutters and moss-eaten roofs lined the edge of the road, their hedges low and neatly trimmed. Outside of one, an old woman was hanging billowing sails of laundry. When the men passed, she hardly noticed. The sun was high and the fields around them green with oats.

At one point, the men encountered fire and dove for either side of the road, in two great waves, like a puddle splashed by a tire. If the day had lulled them into a trance, they were entranced no longer. The lieutenant sent a dozen men to deal with the nuisance. Josiah watched as they slithered up the ditch on either side of the road, then vanished into the boscage. He waited for the sound of a firefight, but none came, and the longer the silence continued, the more menacing it became. The wildwood ahead betrayed no signs of life, as if the men had been swallowed whole.

Eventually, a lone figure appeared on the crest of the road. One of their own, moving at a light jog. The man went up to the lieutenant, who nodded and ordered the men to move out. When they caught up to the others, they were sharing a smoke with two knobby-faced men in gray field uniforms. Not Germans but reluctant Poles, who had surrendered without a fight.

The men carried on. Along the way, they rounded up half a dozen more deserters.

THEY KEPT MOVING WEST, ON ALTERNATING SIDES OF THE ROAD. AT times the road was open, at others closed, the boscage pressed right up, ominously. One of the fields they passed was filled with "Rommel's asparagus," wooden poles strung with razor wire to guard against airborne landings. Another was filled with poppies, a tremoring sea of red. Josiah couldn't stop staring.

The last part of the trek was uphill. That's what gave the crossroads at Le Mesnil its value: high ground. As Josiah dug in his toes with each step, creasing the vamp of his boots, his feet positively throbbed from all the miles he'd already clocked.

They reached the crossroads by evening, the day still light. The roads didn't form a perfect cross but rather a pinched X. In one of the larger quadrants was an apple orchard, still white with bloom. Across the way was an ivy-covered cheese farm that served as brigade head-quarters. In one of the smaller quadrants was a brickworks with a too-visible chimney, where some of the men were being fed. There were fervent halloos as men reunited, including men from Josiah's stick. Josiah was relieved to see Syd Antoine, whom he had known since he was a boy, high in the Cariboo. Syd Antoine was Carrier and the best tree climber Josiah had ever known. He flashed Josiah a shit-eating grin, cheeks plumping.

"Can't get rid of me that easy," he said.

AS THEY STOOD IN THE CHOW LINE, SYD ANTOINE DESCRIBED HIS long night, beginning with the opening shock of his parachute, which ripped off the knee strap on his leg kit bag. With his bag hanging loose by the ankle, he couldn't reach the other quick-release strap and landed with the bag still attached. "Came down hard. Thought I broke my ankles," he said. For a long time, he lay in the dark, lost and in pain. When he heard the coughing of engines, he forced himself to move. By turns, he found others, and together they felt their way to the crossroads.

"Seen Heikkinen?" Josiah asked. "Van den Berg?"

Together they pictured the bookworm and the big fella. "No," Syd Antoine said, solemnly.

When a group of them sat down to some slop, Simmonds said, "I'm right famished," and the men laughed, remembering how he had skipped his mutton and pork, a lifetime ago.

It felt good to sit and get some food in their bodies, to kill that scrunching pang in their stomachs, but the respite was short-lived: they had to dig in. All roads led through Le Mesnil, and it was only a matter of time before the Germans collected themselves and tried to drive the invaders back into the sea. The Allies had pushed through massive double doors to Fortress Europa, and it was their job to keep one of those doors propped open.

THEY FORMED A CONTINUOUS PERIMETER AROUND THE CROSSROADS. Josiah was ordered to man the road that stretched west to Caen, where the Germans were still firmly ensconced. Under velvety evening light, he dug in, there by the side of the road, but unlike before, when he'd dug a grave, the ground here was willful, sending up a jangling shiver each time the spade struck, forcing him to paw out rocks with his bare hands, dirt swelling under his nails. It was late and the men were tired, working on little to no sleep, and they left their trenches shallow. Then they hunkered down and waited.

As night fell, the chirr of crickets gave way to the weird mating calls of frogs, which sounded like ducks cackling. Josiah was glad to be out here with Syd Antoine, who apprehended night, unlike some of the city boys, who were practically scared of the dark.

"Hear that?" Syd asked at one point. Josiah heard a plaintive wail, like a child crying. "Peacocks," Syd said, which seemed right. They had seen a few strutting around the farm.

Above it all, the unholy sounds of man. A soft booming in the distance, attended by a flashing sky that limned the trees and strobed the clouds, like a thunderstorm on the horizon. The fight had not yet reached the crossroads, but it raged elsewhere, and Josiah was grateful that war was the burden of other men. For now.

As night wore on, his vision began to waver. He hadn't slept for more than a day and felt a nauseating hollowness in his chest. At times, he flirted with sleep, and it was in that shadowland that he keened for her most, her pale form rising out of the darkness, like a drowned thing out of black waters. But he had to stay awake, stay focused. Stay alive for her.

4

THE FIRST ASSAULT CAME AT DAWN. THE WORLD WAS JUST STARTING to reappear in staticky grays when they heard the whistling of mortars. Men who were standing hit the dirt. They had been taught that shrapnel shot upward, but these shells spewed their jagged fragments right along the ground. Men cried out. Some scrambled for cover, but the trenches were only half-dug. Of little solace when shells exploded midair and rained hot metal. Josiah lay with his face in the dirt, utterly pinned down.

Those who weren't there can never truly know the chaos and the terror of moments like that, dirt blown into your eyes, your mouth, your nose, the earth itself shaking you. And you, little you, hoping against hope that your luck will hold.

When the pummeling slowed, Josiah looked up to see Syd Antoine dragging a man into the trench. Josiah followed suit, leaping out, grabbing another fallen man by the webbing, and pulling him off the road. The man's right knee was unnaturally kinked, his trousers blooming darkly where shrapnel had torn clear through. The man gritted his teeth and snarled.

As they waited for a medic, Josiah did his best to dress the man's wounds, to stanch the gouts of blood that flooded the holes in his knee like groundwater. All the while, they listened out for more whistling. They were on a ridge, surrounded by rugged terrain, as well as flooded fields on one side, a half moat, yet the enemy seemed to have all the advantage. As a child, imagining medieval sieges, Josiah had always thought it better to be in the castle, arrowing from towers and parapets. Now he wasn't so sure.

When the pounding resumed, the whistling of mortars was joined by a new sound: the thunderous reports of tanks. At the end of the sloping road, two Panzers materialized, two mechanized beasts, trundling at a clip, and the sight was awesome. Awesome yet irrational. They were flanked by infantry, a whole company, it seemed, all in close formation on either side of the road. A full-frontal assault, with little room to maneuver. The Germans were sitting ducks.

With no radioman nearby, a runner dashed back to headquarters. The Canadians had their own mortars by the brickworks, plus the seventeen-pounder. Syd and Josiah laid low, waiting for the salvo of their own artillery. The Germans were fast approaching—five hundred yards, four hundred yards—and lobbing deeper, aiming for the chimney, but there was no response. Had the runner been hit? Had their own guns been taken out? Were a few bedraggled paratroopers supposed to take on a whole German company?

"Come on, boys, come on," Syd muttered under his breath.

Josiah mounted his Bren. The tanks were now so close he could see the iron cross. Feel his heart swelling.

At last, the deluge: a whomping cannonade, followed by counter-whistling. Then the spectacular landings. Earth thrown into the air. Men. The first tank erupted into inferno. A direct hit from the seventeen-pounder, which must have had a clear view.

The barrage continued. Germans slumped to the ground. Others seemed to vaporize in a cloud of blood. Once, when he was young, Josiah had swiped at a long thread of spider's silk. He had expected the thread to swing down, like a rope dropped at one end. Instead, the whole thread had vanished with a puff.

It was like that.

Josiah opened up, into the screaming and shouting, the Germans walled in by hedgerows on either side. The second turret began to swivel, the black cyclopic eye at the end of the barrel turning slowly in his direction, like a giant noticing an irritant behind him, before it, too, exploded out of existence. The world became a maelstrom of sound, of human misery. Then, almost as quickly, all that noise reverted to silence, save for the roaring of flames.

THE GERMANS HAD BEEN ROUTED. NONETHELESS, THE CANADIANS had been hit hard. The dead were buried and the wounded carried back to the main dressing station in the brickworks. Those left standing spent the day digging deeper trenches with half roofs. Correcting fatal mistakes.

Their ranks were even thinner now. Too thin for anyone to stand down. By nightfall, none of them had slept in two days. Lieutenant Morrison walked the perimeter, kicking men awake.

"Get some rest," Syd said. "I'll let you know if I see Fritz—or the lieutenant."

Josiah felt scooped out. Every shitty bed he had slept in from the Horse Palace to Camp Bulford now taunted him with their kingliness. But he couldn't leave it all to Syd.

Deep in the night, Josiah spied a figure on the road, walking directly toward him. A silhouette that slowly luminesced in the moonlight, until it seemed lit from within. A woman, pale, ethereal, naked, her arms crossed, as if she were cold. Then her arms unfurled and her hands reached out, beseechingly. He blinked and blinked, but she kept walking, until she was standing above him. When he tried to touch her, craven with longing, she vanished.

"Syd, I better close my eyes."

BUT SHE STALKED HIS DREAMS, TOO, HER BODY KEEN, SCANDALOUS with need. Visions suffused with ache and desire—

"Joe," Syd said, shaking him awake. "I hear something."

Josiah had the bends, coming up from dream. It took a long moment to grasp where he was and why. When he finally did, he mourned. The dream had seemed so real.

From somewhere ahead came the sound of rustling. Mass movement. A ghost army floating through the dark. When a branch snapped, Syd and Josiah looked at each other. Were the Germans back already?

Through the trees, they saw helmets. Not smooth and flared but scrimmed and leafy.

"Moose Jaw," Syd called out.

"Swift Current" came the reply.

It was Major Decker and members of B Company, along with British paratroopers they had picked up along the way. They had waited for Airborne engineers to blow up the bridge at Robehomme—the very one Josiah had crossed. Afterward, they had only traveled under the cover of dark, since their numbers were large. So many shadows emerged from the trees that Josiah thought he was still suffering from mirage. There had to be a hundred men, maybe a hundred and fifty. It did tremendous things for the spirit.

The following night, Josiah was finally able to stand down for the first time in three days. Just curled up and closed his eyes, right there in the slit trench. An instant and mercifully dreamless sleep that ranked with any in his life.

5

THE BATTLE FOR THE CROSSROADS QUICKLY REACHED AN IMPASSE. The Canadians could not be driven from the castle, but nor could they drive the enemy away. Sometimes they were shelled for hours on end—the worst was twelve hours straight—with little recourse but to curl up in their trenches, like animals in their hovels, waiting for the storm to pass.

Then the Germans began to snipe. To pick off Canadians one by one, from lurking vantage points all around the crossroads. One moment a man would be standing and the next he would be down, the air ringing with the crack of a Mauser. It got to the point where nowhere within the perimeter was safe. So many officers were wounded or killed that Lieutenant Morrison finally tore off his insignia. Their nerves were frayed.

The best way to deal with sniping was counter-sniping. Patrols were sent out day and night. Just like all the practice patrols they had gone on, only now there was no rising from the dead. The first time Josiah went out, he stumbled across someone from the battalion who had gone out before him, a third eye gaping from the middle of his forehead.

One night, Josiah was sent out on night patrol with Walker and Syd Antoine. These were the guys he preferred to patrol with, especially after dark. Not the guys who were jumpy or trigger happy, who lacked sense. The three of them set off down the road before veering into woods. In time they came to a high-walled house with a sloping roof, where they spotted sentries and the low luster of a candle in one of the windows. Syd Antoine scribbled in his writing wallet. Then, through glances, they agreed to head back. They had gotten what they had come for.

As they retraced their steps, Syd Antoine came to a stop and held up his hand. Josiah and Walker froze, ears perked. Sure enough, a crackling, somewhere in the darkness in front of them. After another exchange of looks, Josiah took cover behind a fallen tree with his No. 4 rifle while the others slipped off to flush out the enemy. The fallen tree smelled of decay, of earth returning to earth, and he thought of the men already dead, returned to the slick from which they were born.

A smooth helmet appeared through the trees, the thinnest of crescent moons not twenty or thirty yards away. Popgun range, as the men liked to say. The man looked lost, turning his head from side to side, and Josiah felt something like pity. Just a boy alone in the dark, full of fear and eager to live.

A rifle cracked, rending the night. The German boy snapped his head and stalked in a new direction. Josiah was almost inclined to let him go, but when the boy raised his own rifle, Josiah fired a single shot, and the boy fell. Or rather, flailed so theatrically that it seemed he had time to think. To mourn the coming of the end.

The others found Josiah standing over the dead boy: young, handsome, astonished. If Josiah hadn't killed before, he had now.

THE GERMANS HAD NOT YET GIVEN UP HOPE OF BREAKING THROUGH the Allied front and driving all the way to the beaches of Normandy.

They kept probing the eastern flank, looking for a soft spot, and they found it at Bréville, a mile north of the crossroads. They sent in unit after elite unit of grenadiers and Panzers, determined to smash the line. After six days, they were almost through.

That's when Brigadier Hill, their British commander, appeared at company headquarters, asking for men. He wasn't an unfamiliar sight; he came to the crossroads every other day to check on the Canadians, his cheeks gaunt, his face mostly skull. During the drop, he'd been wounded by friendly fire—Allied *bombs*—that killed a number of men and tore out a chunk of his backside. Now he moved with an awkward gait, aided by a longstaff. The men, who had always admired him, only admired him more.

The Black Watch was having a tough go in Bréville, the brigadier said, and needed help. C Company's ranks were thin, but Major Decker agreed to spare all the men he could, including Josiah.

"Come along, chaps," the brigadier said. "Nothing to worry about."

He led forty men off the ridge and down the road to Bréville. Josiah carried both his Bren and his rifle, all the firepower he could muster. In the distance, plumes of smoke filled the air.

After half a mile, they entered the woods near Château Saint-Côme, to the sound of artillery. The château itself was already ruined, just a dark abscess in the ground. In the woods, they came to a trench full of dead Germans. There had been so many attacks and counterattacks that both sides wound up using the same trenches. As he crossed, Walker stepped on the chest of a fallen man, who grunted in protest. They all turned, some with rifles raised. But the man was dead. Just one last pocket of air forced from his lungs.

At the edge of the woods, they saw where the Scots had gone wrong: they had tried to cross an open field between the woods and Bréville, only to be mown down. The field was pocked with craters and strewn with bodies, many charred, the stench of seared flesh already rising in the heat. In one lonely corner of the field, a Bren gun carrier smoldered.

The Canadians dug in, taking up where the Highlanders had left off. When the brigadier asked who could handle a heavy machine gun, Josiah stepped forward and gave up his Bren. There were three abandoned Vickers guns near the tree line, complete with tripods. He took a seat behind one, his legs straight out, but a round was jammed in the breach, the lock seized, so he and O'Connor, the boy assigned as his No. 2, took up one of the other guns.

No sooner had Josiah sat down than enemy shells began to whistle. They burst overhead, shearing the treetops like buzz saws and showering metal and wood. O'Connor got clocked by a branch, but the boy carried on, eyes wet and gleaming. Josiah peered into the sight, down the length of the thick, corrugated barrel. With two hands on the grips, he pressed the triggers with his thumbs, unleashing a torrent into the boscage, and O'Connor fed him the whole belt, all two hundred and fifty rounds, before he let up.

Simmonds and another man were cowering in a trench nearby. Suddenly, the brigadier came hobbling past, fearlessly. "Are you chaps in the picture?" he asked, pointing at the men with his longstaff. Sheepishly, both men rose and began to fire.

"Attaboy, Canada!" the brigadier said.

The battle continued for hours. There was plenty of ammunition, and Josiah kept his thumbs depressed, and the Vickers, the "old reliable," kept sending out its smooth ejaculate. Meanwhile, bullets and shells kept whizzing by like corpulent mosquitoes. At one point, the Vickers they had abandoned took a direct hit. Went up in a cloud of dirt and vanished from the earth. Josiah and O'Connor looked at each other, the boy still watery-eyed, but neither said a word.

C Company had bolstered what was left of the Black Watch, but in the end, the only way to break the stalemate was to call in naval artillery.

And with that, the Germans were beaten back. The line had held.

But the costs were high. Half the men who had set out from C Company did not return to the crossroads, including the boy O'Connor, who finally took a bullet in the shoulder with a startlingly modest yelp. He was carried off in a jeep and ferried back to England and tended to in a hospital by stout young nurses. In fact, he would go on to marry one and live a long and decent life.

THEY CONTINUED TO GUARD THE CROSSROADS. MORE PATROLS, MORE skirmishes, more shelling, plus days that were astonishingly calm, just wind tousling the trees and the sun pouring down. Then, eleven days after falling through the inky void and touching down in France, the 1st Canadian Parachute Battalion was relieved. Sent back to Ranville, a mile or two behind the line, where they dug in next to a field and jumped into the cleansing embrace of the Orne River. At the nadir of his plunge, Josiah opened his eyes and saw green-brown waters streaked with light and the pale forms of other men rising and falling in a slow ballet all around him, and he wondered, how? How could life be beautiful in the midst of so much hell?

The men were issued clean underwear. Thus purified, they went back to doing what they did best: drink. In this case, bottles of Pernod and demijohns of Calvados, one tasting of licorice, the other of apple, and both of fire. Again, that strange schizophrenia: life and death, life and death, one after the other. But this wasn't something he tried to explain as he holed up in his slit trench with pencil and paper. He just wanted Poppy to know he was alive.

6

AFTER EIGHT DAYS OF REST ON THE ORNE RIVER, THE CANADIANS returned to the crossroads at Le Mesnil. It was strange, going back to the front, picking up where they had left off, as if the war had held itself in abeyance, waiting for them to return. They found themselves on the same perimeter, in the very same trenches, which gave them a cruel sense of déjà vu.

Enemy shelling and sniping continued, if less frequently. Despite leaflets urging surrender, it was clear the Germans were now on their heels. Unlike the first frantic days, when the battalion had sent every available man forward, it could now afford to keep one company back and rotate in and out, which gave everyone more time to eat, clean, rest, and sleep.

One overcast day, when Josiah and his company were behind the line and eating near the brickworks, the air began to thrum. The sound wasn't unusual. The Allies now controlled the skies over France, but the day was muddled by low-hanging cloud and there hadn't been any sorties. As the thrumming grew louder, a single propeller dropped from a cloud bank. For a moment, it looked like a Spitfire or a Hurricane, but instead of roundels, they saw black crosses. Mess tins clattered as men ran for cover. Some, like Josiah, only had time to drop. Lying prone, face in the crook of his elbow, he heard the juddering pulse of machine guns, the zinging and thudding of bullets, and the Doppler of the plane whooshing overhead.

When the noise receded, Josiah looked up and saw that he and everyone else were all right. For a spell, men laughed, with a mordant sense of relief. Then the plane tipped its wings and circled back. Walker, already stubbled from a day of not shaving, grabbed a Bren and lay on the ground and shot from the hip, just as they had been taught in basic. Josiah followed suit. Lay on his back with one knee up and tried to concentrate fire. The Messerschmitt swooped down with the same uproar, only this time Josiah saw the plane's yellow nose and two rows of bullets streaming down from the wings, ploughing the earth on either side of Walker, who vanished in a dirty fog.

When the cloud dissipated, Walker rose like Lazarus as the Messerschmitt puttered off.

"Was that fun or what?" Walker said, with a roguish grin.

Their second tour of the crossroads also lasted eleven days. Then they went back to the Orne River and its ablutions—and to drinking indiscriminately.

AT THE END OF JULY, IN THE MIDST OF A DOWNPOUR, THE MEN returned to the line. Not to the crossroads, mercifully, but the Bois de Bavent, a forest to the southeast—a sign that the Allies were starting to push the Germans back to the Seine. They dug in along the edge of the forest, two to a trench, as rain came down in slashing sheets. Trenches kept crumbling and flooding, even when they moved to higher ground. When they were done with theirs, Josiah and Walker found themselves sitting in brown broth.

"This is bullshit," Walker said.

"What, the rain?"

"No, the fact that we're still here. This is a ground war. We should be using infantry."

"We are."

"We shouldn't have been reinforced, we should have been *replaced*. We're fucking Airborne, man. Think of what it took to train us. They should be saving us for the next jump. We're too valuable to use as regular tommies."

Josiah could see his point. All that training, all those jumps—no one else could do what they could do. Their mission was supposed to last a few weeks, a month tops. They were the tip of the spear. Get in, get out. Yet here they still were, nearly two months in.

War did different things to every man. Walker, it seemed, was already starting to sour. Before the war, he had been a rumrunner on Prince Edward Island, the only province that still had Prohibition. When he was arrested for the third time, the judge told him he could go to jail or join the army. If he had volunteered for Airborne, it was only for the extra seventy-five cents a day in jump pay. Josiah liked to think of himself as made of sterner stuff. That his own reasons for being there were unassailable.

Rain came down for three days, without letting up. Their groundsheets doubled as ponchos, but they still got soaked to the bone. When it came time to eat, they took turns leaving the trench to fetch food behind the line, but by the time they got back, their mess tins would be soaked. A few weeks ago, the division had set up a field bakery, and the first taste of hot bread had almost made Josiah weep. Now their bread turned to mush. It tested a man's resolve.

What had Poppy's father said about the value of a roof?

When he had to take a leak, Josiah would get to his knees and piss in a can. They were supposed to use a pissing station, a piece of black stovepipe jammed into the ground, but that seemed like a perfect place for snipers to lie in wait. Every time Josiah whipped himself out, he was startled by how much detritus could lodge in the folds of his skin. Hard to believe, looking at himself like that, that his body had ever been a means of pleasure for him or anyone else.

Eventually it occurred to Josiah that Walker used neither can nor station. "When do you go? When you get food?"

Out came that roguish grin. "I just piss in the pool."

"For fuck's sake, Walker!"

"I do what it takes to survive, brother. Feel free to do the same."

Josiah glowered. "Just don't shit in here."

Walker made a horribly constipated face. "Whoops, too late."

They slept, or tried to, in two-hour shifts. Then came the witching hour, that time each night when they had to leave the relative safety of the trench to check their trip flares or go out on patrol, all the worse for the deafening rain, the darkness full of primeval fears and every bit the enemy as the enemy out there.

By this point, Josiah had received a letter from Poppy, which he kept in a waxy pouch in his breast pocket. As much as he wanted to pull it out and smooth its soft pages, he didn't, for fear that it would turn to pulp. But he didn't really have to, since he practically had it memorized. He was glad that Poppy hadn't feigned cool or bravado. Instead, she had gushed with relief—and fear. *I can't believe you're in France. In a trench somewhere, facing real bullets. I can't think about it too much or else I'll go crazy. I know it hasn't been easy, these years apart, putting up with me, but now that you're there—well, there's nothing for me to do but pray for you in my own way. It's taken me all this time, but I've learned to keep vigil. I've learned devotion. In a strange way, it's brought me back to the feeling of God. I love you, Josiah Chang. That's all you need to know. Don't spend a second worrying about me. About us. Not a second that might distract you from what you have to do. Just fight and live and come back to me.*

AFTER THREE DAYS, THE RAIN FINALLY STOPPED. OUT CAME THE sun, along with steaming humidity and a whole new problem altogether: mosquitoes. Dense black clouds of them, filling the air with a drone, a sinister warble. So many that men couldn't open their mouths without swallowing one. Repellent was standard issue, but no matter how much they used or how much they slapped at themselves with bloodstained fingers, they got bitten. Little red pustules that turned into misshapen welts, then hard mounds. Some men scratched themselves so raw they had to go to the makeshift infirmary. With gallows humor, they laughed at themselves, at their lumpy faces and swollen eyelids. "Krauts are gonna run when they see us!" they joked. But they felt besieged. Life, all of life, was against them.

7

IN THE MIDDLE OF AUGUST, AFTER MORE THAN TWO MONTHS IN Normandy, the battalion went in pursuit of the Germans, now retreating to the Seine. Their task was to hound and harry the German rearguard, to keep them from easy escape and from blowing up too many useful things. After so many weeks of languishing in trenches, it was thrilling to finally be on the move.

But after all those weeks of inactivity, the men were out of shape. Just a few miles of hard pursuit and their muscles and lungs were burning. All that effort to get into fighting form, only to see it deteriorate. "I told you," Walker said. "Should have sent us back to England."

They were also slowed in other, more devastating ways. One morning, Josiah and his platoon were walking down a road, men flanking in the woods on either side, when they heard a muffled boom that was neither grenade nor artillery. Then came screaming and shouting, followed by a second explosion.

"Fuck," Lieutenant Morrison said, wearily, as if he had just remembered something important he had to do. He ordered the men to follow him into the woods, now haunted by sounds of agony. As he stepped cautiously through large prehistoric ferns, clearing a path, men walked behind and marked the path with tape.

Eventually they reached a dozen men lying on the ground, some more badly hurt than others. Someone had tripped a shrapnel mine, which had leapt out of the ground and into the air, spraying ball bearings in every direction. Those who hadn't been hit began to run, until someone tripped another S-mine, at which point, anyone still standing crumpled to the ground in fear.

Some men stopped to help the fallen, but Josiah moved deeper into the woods, scouring the ground for the three deadly prongs of the S-mine. The next man he came to was lying on his back. He had been hit in the stomach, and through the man's bloodied hands, Josiah could see the dark gleam of entrails. It was Smitty, who had guarded the gatehouse on D-Day, looking pallid and scrawny and every bit the boy he was.

"Shoot me, Chang," he said, trembling.

Josiah was quietly horrified, above and beyond the overwhelming smell of shit. He kneeled and took off his haversack, remembering things he had learned in basic: *Never clean a wound with water. Never replace a protruding gut.* When Smitty sensed what Josiah was about to do, he clenched his teeth and said, "Save the fucking morphine and shoot me! For god's sake, just shoot me!"

Smitty began to convulse. By the time Josiah got out the morphine, the boy was dead.

There was a lighter and an unlit cigarette on the ground. Josiah remembered Smitty at the gatehouse, the orange tracer of his cigarette burning foolishly in the dark. Smitty was a dedicated smoker of Craven

A's and would countenance no others. Every man is a universe of his own delights, and in the end it all goes with him.

THEY LEFT THE SERIOUSLY WOUNDED FOR THE MEDICS. THE DEAD they left behind. Those who were lucky, wounded but not badly, got sent back to England. Everyone else pressed on.

Four miles east of Le Mesnil, they crossed the Dives on a portable Bailey bridge. In Goustranville, they marched past whitewashed houses with enormous thatched roofs and a church whose yellow brick had been licked by flame. Then they came to a canal where the Germans were still dug in. Under the cover of dark, Lieutenant Morrison led a platoon to a cobbled cow bridge on the canal. They scurried through trees, where night was especially dark, each with little to go by except the man in front of him. When they came to within fifty yards of the bridge, they could just make out a German gun nest, the gun mounted on sandbags. It didn't seem a tall order.

They crept as close as they could within the tree line. Josiah lay on his belly, the Bren propped up on its bipod. When the lieutenant gave the signal, they opened fire. Josiah unleashed the Bren in bursts while Walker stood on one knee, firing with his middle finger.

Just as they were about to launch grenades, the air hissed with bullets, slashing leaves and snapping branches. A man staggered and fell. Walker hit the deck, cursing a blue streak. They were being met by cross fire from somewhere off to the right. Everything was confusion.

The lieutenant scrambled up from behind. "Walker, Chang, Antoine. Follow me."

Together they slipped through the dark, toward the winking of muzzle flash, Josiah lugging his Bren by its wooden handle on top, like a heavy suitcase. When a second gun nest came into view, he set the Bren down and lay directly behind, his cheek pressed to the smooth grain of the gunstock. Through the circle of his scope, he spied flashing orange light. His trigger finger itched, but he had to wait for Syd and Walker to get into position.

When the lieutenant nodded, Josiah squeezed the trigger in bursts of four or five rounds, and the orange light vanished. Then two grenades glinted through darkness, and the gun nest went up like a geyser.

THEY CAPTURED THE BRIDGE AND KEPT MOVING EAST, FROM DO-zulé to Annebault before veering north to Tourgéville. These were all little communes, each one a perfect pastoral save for the bullet holes and the craters, the dead cattle and the rotting horses, their once magnificent flanks now wizened and deflated. When bombs were falling, even chickens knew to flatten themselves on the ground. War spared nothing and no one.

From Tourgéville, they followed the coast toward the Seine. They were moving steadily, two or three miles a day. For the most part, resistance was light. Once, however, they found Germans dug in on the far side of a railway. Artillery softened up the German line first. Then the battalion advanced under a creeping barrage, the world before them going up in clods of earth and the men using that earth for cover. When they got to within throwing distance, they pulled out their Mills bombs. For the first time since landing in Normandy, Josiah pulled a pin and lobbed a grenade, with a vicious sense of excitement.

When the smoke cleared, every German was dead or gone.

As they moved east, they lost men, good men. Too many to name. There seemed no rhyme or reason why some men lived and some men died. Why some were spared and others cut down. But they didn't have time to mourn. Facts simply shifted and became the new reality. Nothing could assail the redoubt of being alive. If you lived, you were glad and carried on.

They ended up in the town of Beuzeville, a few miles south of the Seine. Here as elsewhere, they were greeted joyfully, as the liberators they were, but the mood in Beuzeville was unusually ecstatic. Everyone seemed to be clutching a dusty bottle of wine, and even Josiah got caught up in the mood, clasping shoulders with men in a tavern and swaying to rowdy accordion.

Eventually, he stepped outside, into the town square dominated by yet another sandstone church, and sat before the doors. What gave him a reverent feeling, sitting there, was not the church but the stars, adamantine with light, and arrayed as he had always known them.

Suddenly, the stars were drowned out by a burst of fireworks. Sequins of light that dazzled and died, as if it were New Year's Eve, and it made him bitter to think he had already missed two with Poppy, first in Longueuil, then in England, and was bound to miss a third and possibly more, what with the way the war was going.

From Beuzeville, they slouched to the coast. Then, exactly three months to the day that they first descended into chaos, they boarded a ship and made the short but momentous journey back to England. As he stood on deck, watching the coast of France recede, he felt tremendously glad to be alive. But he also felt guilty, leaving the dead and the dying to others.

1

WARM AUTUMNAL LIGHT POURED THROUGH THE WINDOWS OF THE great hall. Small cathedral windows high above the concourse, plus a four-story arched window at each end. Encircling the hall was a frieze, etched with the names of every place where the Grand Trunk and Canadian Pacific railways made stops, including the city from which Josiah Chang had just absconded. But everything about the hall—its cavernousness, its grandeur—told him he was somewhere else.

The Queen City. The Big Smoke. Hogtown.

At Waterfront Station in Vancouver, Josiah had paid the fare for his own sleeper, a tiny cabin with a windowless door and marvelous little space-saving features, like drop-down shelves, a sink-cum-vanity, and a built-in hanger above the bed, where he hung his three-piece suit. On the first leg of the journey, he retraced his steps to Kamloops. If his purpose had been simply to run away, to disappear, he would have kept going north and vanished into the bush. Instead, he had humped it over the Rockies, through avalanche sheds and spiral tunnels, then chugged past endless grassland from Calgary to Winnipeg, endless woodland from Sioux Lookout to Sudbury Junction, and with every passing mile, every passing railway tie, he felt Poppy receding from view. Each time the train stopped, he thought about finding a pay phone, but each time, he stayed in his cabin, his DO NOT DISTURB sign dangling outside, afraid that authorities might be on the lookout. Maybe it would have been wiser to get off the train sooner, but the more distance he put between himself and the incident at the yard, the better he felt. And the farther east he went, the more likely he would be able to do what now had to be done.

For five days and four nights, he had holed up in his cabin, venturing out only for food or the toilet, and only in his suit and tie, hair pomaded, looking as unsuspicious as possible. And during those many days and nights, staring out the window or into the mirrored wall across from his bed, he kept thinking through his plan, turning it over in his mind. He could see no other way to be with Poppy, to make things right, except to do his duty, earn the things that would then be his due, and come back whole. There was a chance, of course, that he wouldn't come back at all, but better to die with honor than to live in shame.

Since Dieppe, he had felt guilty that others were doing the fighting for him—and angry that others could fight when he couldn't. He didn't want to leave Poppy, but he couldn't see that he had a choice. If he married her, she would lose her birthright. If he didn't marry her, they would lose a life together. And if he didn't fight, it would surely come back to bite him, for when the war was over, the very people who had denied him the right in the first place would ask, *Where were you in our darkest hour?* and use that as grounds to deny him further. He couldn't let that happen. He would have to do what he had always done: prove himself.

There was only one small problem: Chinese still couldn't join. Not the army, not the navy, not the air force, especially in British Columbia, where most Chinese lived. The province had opposed conscription for fear that Chinese would earn the franchise. But rumor had it that some had managed to join up east of the Rockies. Sometimes, enlistment depended on the whims of the recruiting station, even the officer on duty. That was his only hope, so he kept going. The farther he got from the coast, the better his chances would be.

HE WEAVED HIS WAY THROUGH THE CROWD, CARRYING THE SUIT-case he had bought at Waterfront Station. In the center of the great hall was a clock tower with a banner that read NAVY / ARMY / AIR FORCE, which spurred him to his purpose. However, before he reached the stairs to street level, he saw a bank of telephone booths under a grand arch and knew he couldn't put off calling any longer.

He entered one of the booths and closed the bifold door behind him. Poppy's exchange and number were now seared into memory, but he wasn't sure how to call long distance. When he dialed the operator, she put him through to another operator, who took his information and told him to hang up. As he stood in a cone of light, waiting for the operator to call back, he pictured Poppy at home, in the house he had come to think of as theirs, sitting down to breakfast in her pink satin robe, the peal of her black Bakelite phone breaking the spell of Saturday morning.

When the phone finally rang, he picked up right away. "Miss Poppy Miller on the line," the operator said before asking for the toll. Only after he had parted with an absurd number of coins did the operator say, "Please go ahead."

"Poppy."

"Joe."

For a long moment, they were both silent, each breathing in the presence of the other. What a strange, disconcerting experience, hearing her voice across the miles. She was right there with him in the booth, yet not.

"Where are you?"

"Toronto."

Another swell of silence. "Why?"

He didn't want to say, not yet. If he couldn't enlist, he didn't want the shame of her knowing. "You told me to run."

She let out a short, stilted laugh, one that didn't ease the tension. He hated the telephone, he realized. It made him feel like he didn't know her at all.

"When are you coming back?"

"As soon as I can."

Another unsatisfactory answer. "Come back, Joe. Everyone is fine. Everything's going to be okay. Nothing's going to happen."

He knew why she was speaking cryptically: the operator was still there. But he understood her perfectly. The worst hadn't happened. It had simply been a fight, and he'd won. Nothing that called for the law.

"I'm coming back, Poppy. I promise. Just . . . wait. Wait for me."

Only the slightest hitch before she said, "I'll be here, Joe."

"Can you do me a favor, Poppy?"

"Of course."

"I hate to ask—"

"Joe."

"Can you try to find Queenie?"

He was fearful of the answer, but it came as a relief. "I have her, Joe. I went to find you, but I found Queenie instead. Couldn't leave her out there by herself, now could I?" Suddenly, everything seemed as it should be. She was still the person he knew. Nothing could have proven it more.

Despite all the coins, time evaporated, and the operator came back on, asking if he wanted more.

"I better go," he said.

"Okay."

"I'll write as soon as I can."

"I'd like that."

"Goodbye, Poppy." And then, because that seemed no way to part: "I adore you."

"Oh, Joe. I adore you, too."

2

JOSIAH STEPPED THROUGH THE PORTICO ON FRONT STREET AND found himself across from the Royal York Hotel, a château-style building not unlike the new Hotel Vancouver, only larger, much larger. This, he gathered, was going to be the theme: if Vancouver was big, Toronto was bigger. Part of him wanted to splurge on a room, to take a long, luxurious bath and savor a few last hours of freedom, but mostly he just wanted to get on with it.

He hopped a red-and-white streetcar on Front Street, then got off at Bathurst and took another out to the exhibition grounds. This was what the officer on the train had told him to do: take the Bathurst Tripper, then Fort Lansdowne. The train had been full of raucous young men in uniform, their spirits high, and their vaunted air of camaraderie had impressed him. When he asked where he might enlist in Toronto, the officer directed him to No. 1 Manning Depot on the grounds of the Canadian National Exhibition. "They might not take you," the officer warned, apologetically, "but keep trying."

At the end of Fleet Street, Josiah stepped out of the trapped, sun-baked air of the streetcar into the clemency of October and walked through the exhibition grounds, past the shuttered stalls of the midway, until he came to a sprawling complex of buildings punctuated by four towers, each with an oxidized green dome. Normally, the complex was used for agricultural fairs, but now a sign outside read GO ACTIVE NOW!

Josiah straightened his tie, his mouth a little parched, and walked into the main building through one of three sets of double doors. Sure enough, right inside the entrance hall was a table manned by two men in peaked caps.

"What can we do for you?" one of the men asked.

When Josiah made his intentions known, the two men glanced at each other.

"Identification, please," the same man said.

Josiah caught the stench of livestock. He reached into his breast pocket and produced his certificate of registration, which he was required to carry at all times. The first man examined it, then passed it on to the second. Josiah pictured the fine print: *This certificate does not establish legal status in Canada.*

The second man rose, still holding the certificate. "I'll be back," he said to the first man. "Why don't you get started?"

The first man took Josiah to a cool, dusky cinder-block room that served as a makeshift medical station: hospital curtain, cotton balls, eye test. An older man in a lab coat handed him a form on a clipboard, and he answered no to syphilis, gonorrhea, and every other possible affliction. Then he was told to undress.

"How long will this take?"

The man in the lab coat adjusted his glasses. "Physical, urine test, blood test, chest X-ray. Might be a while."

As soon as Josiah felt the cold bite of the stethoscope on the thick slab of his chest, the door to the room opened, and the man who had left with his certificate reappeared with yet another man, similarly dressed but gray-haired and mustached, with more swatches of red on his uniform, who took one look at Josiah, standing there completely naked, and said, "Oh yes. He'll do."

JOSIAH WAS GIVEN SHOTS FOR EVERYTHING FROM DIPHTHERIA TO typhus fever and told he might feel sick in the next few days, though he never did. Then he was issued identification discs, service record and pay books, and most importantly a uniform. Under the watchful gaze of the quartermaster, Josiah took off his suit and tie and put on his army-issued underwear and socks, his army-issued shirt, trousers, and tunic, the word CANADA emblazoned on each shoulder. Then he laced up his boots and strapped on his anklets and put on his field cap, which the quartermaster tipped sideways to a perilous angle, and just like that, he was a soldier.

Standing before the mirror, feeling the itch and scratch of the wool and breathing its wintry, animal scent, he felt the way he had the night he met Poppy: that he had willed something into being. Through sheer impressiveness, he had forged his own reality, and would go on forging it, until it bent to his will.

He was shown next door to the Horse Palace, a horse ring surrounded by two floors of stables. There were over a thousand wooden stalls, all of which were being used for billeting soldiers. Each stall came with a wooden bunk bed, a small writing desk, and the sweet, warm smell of manure. The Royal York it was not.

Josiah claimed the top bunk. Before long, another man, tall, pale, and gingery, appeared in the stall. When he saw Josiah, his eyes grew.

Then, remembering himself, he thrust out a meaty hand and introduced himself as William Flanagan from Douro, Ontario. "Call me
Bill," he said. A farm boy, wet behind the ears, with a thumbprint of a
cleft in his chin. Josiah could tell they would get along just fine.

FOR THE FIRST FEW DAYS, ALL THEY DID WAS DRILL. SOMETIMES ON
the cakey dirt of the horse ring, other times on the hard, dusty pavement of the exhibition grounds. Quick time, double time, mark time.
It was all easy enough, yet some men didn't seem to know their left foot
from their right. If they couldn't march, Josiah had no idea how they
were going to fight. It dissolved any feeling he might have had that he
didn't belong. If this was the caliber of men they were admitting, then
he had every right to be here.

When they weren't drilling, they were showering and shaving, eating in the mess, and writing letters home. Josiah had promised to write,
but every time he sat down at the small writing desk in his stall, he
couldn't find a way to tell Poppy he had joined the army. That it would
be some time before he saw her again. Basic training took eight weeks,
but the Horse Palace wasn't even basic, just a literal holding pen until
he was shipped off to basic, after which there would be advanced training, and then . . . Every time he tried to explain all that, he would catch
the weirdly bitter smell of the fountain pen and put off the task for
another day.

On their first weekend, half the men at the Horse Palace, including
Bill, went down to the Palais Royale, a dance hall on the lakeshore,
where the walking-out uniform worked like magic, but Josiah didn't
go. Instead, he lay in his bunk, staring at the ceiling. The roof directly
above the horse ring was made of glass, and through it, Josiah could see
stars, as if he were back in Stanley Park. Some of the men here were

young, away from home for the first time, and as he lay in the dark, he could hear the ghostly sound of sobbing. Maybe some of them were racked by the same question he was: How had he come to be here, in a manning depot redolent of horseshit, when he could have been home, with her?

3

A WEEK LATER, THE MEN WERE FINALLY PUT ON A TRAIN. AS USUAL, Josiah found himself sitting with Bill, and as they jogged around the rocky shores of Lake Simcoe, Bill looked out admiringly. Like most of the men, he was seeing the world for the first time and took it all in with wonder. There was something slow, almost bovine, about the man, but he also had a quick and easy loyalty, as if he and Josiah, having shared a bunk, were now bonded for life. He always sought Josiah out, always sat with him in the mess, and had a boyish way of saying each night, "Good night, Joe. Sleep tight."

The train stopped in Orillia, eighty miles north of Toronto. As they marched from the tiny railway depot on the lakefront through the center of town, they were greeted by dewy-eyed smiles from men, women, and children. Some looked surprised to see Josiah, but he was happy to let them stare. He was proud to be in uniform and to sear that image into their minds.

They trekked out to what had once been a farm, now a sprawling complex of forty-some-odd buildings, including a hospital, each one covered in a red roof and green tar paper. Officially, this was No. 26 Canadian Army Basic Training Center, but everyone called it Champlain Barracks. Each barrack had two long rows of bunks with a potbelly stove in the middle. Unlike the Horse Palace, the bunks here had headboards and footboards. "We're moving up in the world," Bill said. Once again, they shared a bunk.

No sooner had they settled in than a man with the beady eyes of a ferret came up to them. Josiah didn't recognize him from the train, so he must have come from somewhere else.

"The name's Wilkerson. What's yours, mate?" the man asked in a cracking, high-pitched voice. When Josiah told him, the man said, "Chang, eh? What's that, Chinese or Japanese?"

Josiah wouldn't deign to answer, but Bill was quick to jump in: "What do you think?"

Despite this, Wilkerson squinted, even though he seemed a little cowed by Josiah. "Good. Wouldn't want any Japs in this unit, now would we, boys?"

In different company, this might have gone over well. Men in the army did not suffer from too much delicacy. There had been plenty of talk of Japs and Nips and slopes. But some of the men already knew Josiah, and it made for uneasy laughter. Not what Wilkerson had expected, and it knocked him down a peg, and he shuffled off, confused.

Josiah had almost begun to think he might make it through the army without meeting the likes of Wilkerson. Wishful thinking.

THE NEXT DAY, THE BUGLE SOUNDED AT 0600 HOURS. JOSIAH LEAPT out of bed, ready to fire a gun, to hump a pack for miles on end. Anything to get on with the business of battle. Instead, his unit was led out to a grassy field, where they stood in open formation and wheeled their arms, twisted their trunks, and touched their toes in unison. Part of the "daily dozen" meant to keep them limber. It was almost effeminate, their synchronized stretching, less army than dance troupe. Not exactly what he had hoped for.

More disappointing still, most of the first day—in fact, most of the first week—was devoted to more drilling, starting at the very beginning, with standing at attention and standing at ease. So endless were the squad drills and the arms drills that Bill, usually uncomplaining, said, "Apparently we're going to parade the Germans to death." Despite their instructor's exhortations—"You're learning discipline, you're learning coordination, of mind and muscle. You're learning to think and act as one, and someday that may save your life"—Josiah felt terribly impatient. The sooner he learned how to fight, the sooner he would get to the war, and the sooner he got to the war, the sooner he would get home to Poppy.

THEY ALSO SPENT TIME ON FUNDAMENTAL TRAINING. THINGS LIKE personal cleanliness, military law, and recognizing rank, all delivered by lecture in front of a dusty chalkboard. A few lectures were also devoted to what their syllabus described as "a basic knowledge of democratic government and the responsibilities of a British citizen under such form of government." This rankled.

What he *did* enjoy in those first early days was hand-to-hand combat. The handholds and the legholds, the knee lifts and the headlocks. They practiced in pairs in a gym that smelled of leather, horsehair, and feet, and one day, as they worked on breaking a rear bodylock with a hiplock, Josiah found himself paired with Wilkerson. As Josiah stood with his back turned, Wilkerson came up from behind and grabbed him around the waist with what felt like a punch to the gut. Nonetheless, after throwing Wilkerson over his hip and onto the mat, Josiah was careful not to land on the man too heavily. Then they switched places.

Josiah clutched Wilkerson from behind, face pressed to the shockingly sour smell of his shirt. Suddenly, Wilkerson flipped Josiah through the air and came down on top of him, hard, knocking the air from his lungs. As he pinned Josiah, he leaned in and said, "You're nothing special. You're not even British." On cue, the session came to an end, and Josiah was left to fume. He hadn't thought he could have any more reason to want to be British. He was wrong.

4

EVERY SPRING FOR AS LONG AS JOSIAH COULD REMEMBER, HIS father had burned joss paper on the anniversary of his own father's death so his father would be rich in the afterlife. Sometime after dark, he would call Josiah over, and together they would stoop over a brazier, a small gold dish with three stubby legs. The joss paper was so fly-wing thin that the instant it was touched by flame it would blacken and curl and lift off in pieces, but for a brief and tender moment, the fire would light up all the somber features of his father's face.

A year to the day his father was struck down, Josiah decided to do the same. The thought occurred to him as soon as he awoke, but he didn't have a moment alone until that evening, after supper, when he finally managed to slip away from the others. He didn't believe money was of any use where his father now was. Didn't believe they would ever again fall trees, sit by the fire, or sleep under the stars. Not for a day, much less eternity. But he did believe in love and honor and duty and even mysticism, so he sought out the dark serenity of the woods behind the barracks and dug a hole in the ground. He didn't have any joss paper, but he did have plenty of money in his father's canister, so he pulled out a two-dollar banknote from the Bank of Canada, which held the face of the King. As the banknote burned reluctantly, a pitiable flame in all that darkness, Josiah envisioned a bolt of black lightning and once again felt the raw scrape of guilt. But if not for the accident, he would never have left the Cariboo, never have met Poppy, and never have wound up here, in basic, on his way to war, and he marveled to think of how a gust of wind could set so much fate in motion.

As the King's face blackened and crumpled, Josiah thought of not only his father but also his grandfather, Reginald Chang, whom he'd hardly known, except through this very ritual, and his great-grandfather, Chang Lee Chien, whom he hadn't known at all. These men had once walked the earth, every bit as alive as he was, yet somehow nothing of them remained, except through him.

5

IN THE SECOND WEEK, THEY WERE INTRODUCED TO THE OBSTACLE course, which wound its way through woods. The first time, they weren't allowed to try. Had to walk the course slowly, watching the instructor demonstrate, which made Josiah wild with impatience. When they finally got the chance, Josiah made it through in no time. "Normal pace! Normal!" the instructor kept barking, trying to get him to slow down. "Easy, tough guy," Wilkerson said, but Josiah ignored him. Eventually they went at normal pace in battle order, packs and pouches bouncing. By the end, they were doing everything at the double in full kit. Some men sprained ankles or broke arms, jumping down from the high wall or falling off the hundred-foot rope slide. They were some of the first to wash out.

In the second week, they also went on their first march, a four-mile trek through open country with a rifle and belted dagger. As they tromped on unpaved roads, their instructors pointed out tactical features in the rolling fields and low scrub all around them and explained how to use them against attack from the ground or the air, and only then did Josiah feel the first real premonition of war. Over the next two months, as the days cooled, they marched for longer, six, eight, ten miles in full kit.

It took a while, but they were finally taught how to fire small arms, starting with the No. 4 rifle in the indoor range, lying on their bellies and shooting over sandbags. Josiah had fired rifles in the bush, but nothing like this. With its short bolt throw and lightning-fast action, the No. 4 was a beautiful friend. He could get off five rounds in five seconds, the gunstock kicking with each cracking report.

Every rivet a bullet no longer.

They graduated to the open range, then to the open range with a Bren gun. The first time, Josiah was paired with Bill, and they took turns switching out the curved magazine on top while the other fired, with a steady *tuk-tuk-tuk*, the hillsides billowing smoke and dust. If the No. 4 was a beautiful friend, then the Bren was something even more intimate and responsive.

The final phase of weapons training was the antiaircraft course. Their instructors would send up large balloons, gibbous as the moon, and men would either stand and fire rifles or lie on the ground and fire Brens. They learned to work together to keep the imagined plane high. It was fun to shoot balloons and watch them burst, but it was going to be something else altogether when a real Messerschmitt or Stuka bore down, pumping hot lead the other way.

EVERY NIGHT AFTER SUPPER, MEN LINED UP IN THE BARRACKS FOR mail. For the longest time, Josiah got none, until he was quite possibly the only one without. As soon as he had learned he was headed to Orillia, he had written Poppy. Told her he had joined the army, and why, though he made no mention of her father. He knew it took time for mail to travel across the country. Still, he started to feel a needling resentment that a letter had yet to arrive. Her silence felt like judgment. For leaving. For not consulting her. For taking so long to tell her.

Then one night, Josiah heard his name called, and an NCO handed him an envelope with one eyebrow raised. Usually, a spirit of horseplay pervaded the barracks. Men running around, snapping towels, kicking top bunks from below. The exception was mail time, when a hush fell over everything. Josiah sat up in bed and opened the letter, to a roaring in his ears.

Dearest Joe,

I'm sitting at the kitchen table in my wool robe, looking out the window and thinking of you. The weather has taken a turn. Not as cold as Ontario, mind you, but I've got the oil burner going. It's only in winter you realize how poorly insulated these little houses are.

I can hardly believe you've joined the army. I understand the reasons why, but I hate to think of you in harm's way. And I hate the thought of you being away for so long. I wish you didn't have to do this. I wish the world were otherwise.

But I'm proud of you, Joe. There are only two kinds of people in the world: those who believe in everyone's freedom, and those who do not. You know what side I'm on. The side of freedom, always.

And don't worry, Queenie is fine. It's made a difference, having her around. She misses you, too, I can tell.

Am I terrible for hoping the army will find a reason to send you home? What can I say, I love you, and I'm selfish.

All my love,

Poppy

The letter seemed contradictory, both reticent and effusive at once. Part of her was holding back, not saying what she really wanted to say, that she wished he'd never left. Which was understandable. Her ambivalence was natural, akin to his own, and simply a sign that she loved him. In any case, the hard part was over. He'd told her what he'd done, and now they could go on.

IN THE FINAL WEEKS OF BASIC, THE FOCUS WAS ON FIELDCRAFT, which they practiced through elaborate games of hide-and-seek. Sometimes they worked in teams, other times alone. In one such game, Josiah found himself up against Wilkerson. They started on opposite sides of a copse, and each had to track down the other. Josiah would have felt eager to win regardless. In this case, it was imperative.

But it was hard to move through the woods with stealth. Winter had set in, and his breath smoked, and the trees were naked, which made it easier to see but harder to hide, and he couldn't move without the sound of crunching underfoot. Yet the copse seemed not just eerily quiet but devoid of life, as if every creature save for him had been swept up in some kind of rapture. They had been taught to use all their senses to survive, so he sniffed the air, trying to catch a whiff of Wilkerson's sour smell. From the first, Josiah had made every effort to avoid the man, but Wilkerson kept turning up and giving him pointers on whatever it was they were doing—tying a rifle splint, putting on a light service respirator—eager, somehow, for Josiah's attention, his approval, even. It was strange.

In time Josiah saw a black toe cap peeking out from the base of a tree and felt a rush of excitement. He raised his rifle—just for pretend, no bullets, not even blanks—and stepped sideways. The instant he realized, to his horror, that the boots were just sitting there, attached to no one, he caught the sour tang of sweat behind him.

"Bang. You're dead."

6

"CAN YOU BELIEVE WE'RE ALMOST DONE?"

Josiah and Bill were sitting in the mess, amid the clamor and clink of suppertime. Yes, it was in fact hard to believe they were almost done. At first, basic couldn't come fast enough. Then, in the grueling middle, it seemed like it would never end, and now, just like that, it was almost over.

"Where do you want to go for advanced training?" Bill asked.

Josiah had proven to be a good shot and might have made a good sniper, but he wanted to carry a machine gun. A light machine gun at the very least, but maybe a heavy one, like a Vickers. Those were the guns he liked best. Reminded him most of being a riveter.

"There's a machine gun training center in Three Rivers, Quebec. Wouldn't mind that."

Bill looked down at his plate, shyly. "Wouldn't mind that, either."

ON THEIR LAST DAY AT CHAMPLAIN BARRACKS, ALL THE MEN STOOD in formation in the parade square as a light snow dusted their lashes. After being lauded by their commanding officer, they were addressed by an adjutant. When the Germans had blitzed Poland, Denmark, Norway, the Low Countries, and France, they had made use of an entirely new military force, the Fallschirmjäger, the adjutant explained. That's when the British and the Americans saw the need for airborne troops of their own. Now Canada, too, was forming an airborne unit, and the adjutant was there to recruit volunteers. "We want men who are motivated and confident and capable of becoming extraordinary fighters," he said. Volunteers could not exceed thirty-two years in age, six feet in height, or a hundred and ninety pounds in weight, and could not be nearsighted, flat-footed, or dyspeptic. "This new outfit will be the tip of the spear and will only take the best of the best."

Josiah was instantly drawn to the idea of an elite corps. So far, he hadn't been much impressed by the quality of the men around him and was eager to be among better, for the more such men there were, the more likely he was to live.

"Jumping out of a plane? No thanks," a voice behind him said. "That's suicide."

Josiah could understand the sentiment. Most men, himself included, had never even been on an airplane, much less jumped out of one. But the voice behind him belonged to Wilkerson, and the fact that he didn't want to join made Josiah want to all the more.

But he was mostly spurred by Poppy. Somehow, he felt the need to prove he had done the right thing by joining. That it wasn't just an impulse but a special calling. And what better way to prove that than by joining a special force. Surely she would feel better knowing that he was among the few, the chosen.

After the men fell out, Josiah said, "I'm going to volunteer."

Bill looked crestfallen. "Gee, it's going to be lonesome without you."

"Then come with me."

Bill brightened in his slow, bovine way. "You know, I could."

Together they went to see the adjutant. Unwilling to be bested, Wilkerson tagged along, tail between his legs. Half a dozen men stepped forward, none of whom, to Josiah's mind, was the best of the best. Except himself.

Before any man could go on, he had to pass a battery of tests, starting with another physical. Once again, Josiah found himself probed as he stood stark naked. The physical eliminated one man who couldn't hear a forced whisper ten feet away. Next was the physical fitness test: push-ups and sit-ups in the same dank gym and a two-mile run around the camp through jagged December air. This eliminated a second man. Then they were given a general intelligence test. They all passed.

Finally, each man met with an army psychiatrist. Before the meeting, the adjutant stressed that they needed to be completely forthright. Anything short of total honesty would get them disqualified. The psychiatrist was a relatively young man who looked older for his hairline, receded to an island in front. He began by asking about Josiah's family, schooling, and work history. Josiah told the truth: he had grown up with his father, gone to school through sixth grade, and worked as a faller, then a riveter.

"When you were a boy, were you afraid of the dark?"

"No."

"Did you wet the bed?"

"No."

"Did you have nightmares?"

"No."

"Were you afraid of small, enclosed spaces?"

"No."

The man jotted on a clipboard. When asked about sports, Josiah cited athletics as well as pole climbing, which he used to do in logging camps, with gaffs and a rope.

"So you're not afraid of heights."

"No."

"Have you ever fainted?"

A bolt of black lightning flashed through his mind. "No," he lied.

The psychiatrist studied him, then asked him to hold out his hands. The man examined his palms, then ran a finger down each one before rubbing his finger and thumb together, testingly. Then he asked Josiah to stand with his arms straight out on either side and placed a small piece of paper on the back of each hand.

"Are you sure you've never fainted?"

"Yes."

The man studied the pieces of paper carefully. When they didn't fall, he told Josiah to sit down.

Next they played word association. Josiah didn't overthink it, just said whatever came to mind. "Swim" for "water," "killer" for "lion." Then the psychiatrist asked if he was married. When Josiah said no, the man said, "Good. Married men tend to be . . . preoccupied. Any thoughts of marriage?"

"No," he lied again.

"Have you ever been with a woman?"

"Yes."

"Have you ever masturbated?"

"Yes."

"What do you think about when you masturbate?"

The question confused him. "Sex."

"Do you ever think about men?"

"What?"

The psychiatrist waved the question away. "I'll be honest. Your service record, your qualification data, the things the colonel says about you—it's all good. But your people—Chinese, am I right? Your people are rather . . . meek."

Josiah bristled. "I don't see *you* in uniform."

The man's lips curled faintly. "Touché," he said. "Have you ever hurt a man?"

"Yes."

"How?"

"With my fists."

"Could you kill a man with a bayonet?"

"Yes."

"Could you jump out of an airplane from a thousand feet?"

"Yes."

"Tell me, Private Chang. Why do you want to be a paratrooper?"

"Because I'm the best of the best."

"HOW DID IT GO?" BILL ASKED AFTERWARD.

"Fine, I think," Josiah said, though he wasn't sure. "How 'bout you?"

Bill looked contrite. "I know we weren't supposed to lie, but I might have fibbed a little."

That night, they both slept fitfully, waiting for the verdict. The truth was, Josiah didn't know if he could do it. Jump. Didn't know if he had it in him, though he liked to think so. And he didn't know how Poppy would feel about him going such a dangerous route. But now that he had come this far, he dreaded the thought of not making it.

At dawn, Josiah was called in to see the colonel—white-haired, eminent—who looked uneasy, the bearer of bad news, it seemed, which made Josiah lose heart. The thought that he hadn't gotten in—and Wilkerson had—filled his mouth with bile.

But the colonel handed Josiah an envelope and said, "Hate to lose you, son. The infantry needs more men like you. But I know you'll make a fine paratrooper."

7

THE LETTER INSTRUCTED JOSIAH CHANG TO REPORT TO NO. 4 Military District Depot in Longueuil, Quebec, so he took the train back to Union Station in Toronto before taking another to Bonaventure Station in Montreal, accompanied by Bill, who'd been given the same assignment. As they swept around Lake Ontario, fringed with ice and dark with waves in the distance, they talked amiably, glad to be done with basic and on their way to jump school, though neither knew what to expect.

"Did you see Wilkerson's face?" Bill asked, eyes crinkling with satisfaction.

Indeed, Josiah had. When Wilkerson learned he hadn't been selected, he took the news with ugly disappointment, and that more than anything made Josiah glad he had volunteered. But he was surprised that Bill had gotten in. Bill was a perfectly fine tommy, but average in every way. Josiah still believed that none who stepped forward were the best of the best, save for himself, and the fact that Bill was still here left him to wonder just what kind of outfit Airborne would be.

By the time they arrived in Montreal, night had fallen. From the station, they walked on rue Notre-Dame in greatcoats and woolen caps, dry snow scudding along the sidewalk and a sharp wind coming off the river. As they passed the basilica and the courthouse, it occurred to Josiah that he had now seen the three largest cities in the country in ascending order. At one point, in quick succession, he spied a sign above a grocery store and an ad on the back of a streetcar for Sweet Caporal cigarettes, complete with blond majorette, and it made him lonelier than ever for Poppy.

They took the Jacques Cartier Bridge over the lightless expanse of the St. Lawrence River to the depot in Longueuil, known as Cartier Barracks. They were let in the gate by a guard and shown to their barrack by a staff sergeant. That night and in the days to come, they shook hands with other Airborne volunteers who arrived from across the country, their regiments still emblazoned on their shoulder titles: the 12th Manitoba Dragoons, the Cape Breton Highlanders, the Sherbrooke Fusiliers. All young and hale and proud as hell to be there.

They stayed at Cartier Barracks through the end of the year. On Christmas Day, in the spirit of Saturnalia, when Roman slaves were freed for a day, officers switched places with the enlisted men. At dinnertime, everyone above the rank of master corporal put on a chef's jacket and a chef's hat and served the junior ranks. The menu consisted of club salad and cream of celery soup, followed by roast turkey, fried oysters, and baked ham, plus sage dressing, snowflake and candied potatoes, fresh corn, cream peas, diced carrots, and hot rolls with butter. For dessert, fruitcake, mince pie, plum pudding with brandy sauce, and all the cigarettes and cigars they could smoke. It was quite possibly the most lavish meal of Josiah's life.

Yet everything was tinged with melancholy. It was hard not to think about how he could have been celebrating. How bacon and eggs on Fell

Avenue would have surpassed any meal the army could have dreamed up. As soon as he had arrived at Cartier Barracks, he had written Poppy. Told her he was off to jump school. Now he was waiting to hear back, and this, too, made him a little morose. Her letters had warmed; now he feared another chill. But there was nothing to be done. He had made the call, and the right one. This was where he belonged.

LIKE THE HORSE PALACE, CARTIER BARRACKS WAS SIMPLY A HOLDING pen until fifty men—the weekly number the army was now sending to parachute school—could assemble. But Canada was new to airborne training and didn't yet have a jump school anywhere in the country.

It was Matti Heikkinen, a bookish and towheaded fellow from New Finland, Saskatchewan, who broke the news: "Haven't you heard? The only Airborne school this side of the Atlantic is in Fort Benning, Georgia."

Bill turned to Josiah. "Jiminy Christmas. We're going to America."

AS SOON AS FIFTY MEN HAD ASSEMBLED, THEY LEFT FOR FORT
Benning, their departure more momentous for the dawning of a new
year. At Bonaventure Station, Josiah spied a bank of telephone booths
and felt a pang of conscience. When he wrote to say he was going to
jump school, he didn't know he would be venturing to a far-flung end
of the continent, and he felt Poppy had a right to know before he left.

"Happy New Year," he said when she came on the line.

"Happy New Year, darling! Is it really 1943? Where are you? Longueuil? Am I saying that right?"

She sounded blithe and upbeat, which made him feel guilty. "I'm at
the station in Montreal."

"Are you shipping out?"

"Yes."

"Where?"

"Fort Benning."

"Where's that?"

"Georgia."

The line crackled with silence, and suddenly he remembered how much he disliked the telephone. Save for the night she had proposed going to Mandarin Garden, it had never felt like this in person. The strangeness. The distance.

"Why didn't you tell me?"

"I didn't know."

"Why there?"

Fort Benning was the only parachute school in North America, he explained, at least until they finished Camp Shilo in Manitoba. "Which should be soon, I think."

"But not soon enough for you."

He heard the regret in her voice and felt irritated that she wasn't being more relenting.

"How long will you be there?"

"Not that long. Only four weeks."

"And then?"

He paused. "Then Shilo will be ready."

The line went still, and he could picture her standing by the little alcove between the living room and the bedroom, where the telephone sat, clutching at her wool robe. Perhaps because she was looking onto the living room, she said, "I still have the Christmas tree up."

"You do?" he asked, feeling an ache at the thought of tinsel, garlands, ornaments.

"And I got you a Christmas present, but I sent it to Orillia. Maybe it's on its way to Longueuil. Hopefully, they send it on to Fort Benning."

That was the strange thing about mail, the lag, their lives forever out of sync. "I'm sure they will. What did you get me?"

"I can't tell you!" She laughed. "It's a surprise."

For a while, they talked of other things, Montreal, mostly. The Palace and Cinema Paris on rue Sainte-Catherine, the movies he and the men had gone to see, but it all felt a little strained, a little false, as if they were performing. Then, before the operator could come back on, she blurted, "Why, Joe? Why did you do it?"

The question vexed him. He didn't know how to explain what seemed so clear in his mind. That it wasn't enough to be good; he had to be the best. Only then might the world see him for who he really was.

"It's an elite unit. It's where I belong."

"Won't it be dangerous?"

"All war is dangerous."

Another oceanic silence. The eternal tide, roaring.

"Okay, Joe," she said, with a crack of what might have been anger or sorrow. "But please, please, please, take care of yourself."

After setting down the receiver, Josiah stood in the cloistered light of the booth, feeling no better than he had before calling. He had hoped that by joining Airborne, he would make Poppy proud, and in so doing, make her understand. But it seemed he had only succeeded in slipping farther and farther away.

9

THEY TRAVELED DOWN THROUGH ALBANY AND THE BLANKETED stillness of the Hudson Valley to the sooty clamor of New York City, Philadelphia, and Washington, in train cars specially fitted with bunks, as if barracks had been set on wheels. Whenever they came to a city, men craned to look out the windows, then hurried onto the platform to stretch their legs and hunt for souvenirs. At Grand Central Terminal, a few men slipped through the catacombs to the main concourse, where signs of the war were everywhere: women in uniform, a servicemen's lounge, a huge mural for war bonds. Josiah bought a postcard and dashed something off to Poppy.

Much like in Champlain Barracks, Bill stayed close to Josiah, sitting across from him in the passenger car and next to him in the dining car. If he had been wide-eyed seeing more of Ontario, then he was all the more so now.

"Never thought I'd leave Douro, never mind the country," Bill said.

In that respect, the two of them weren't all that different. Josiah had never imagined leaving the Cariboo, yet here they both were, out in the great wide world.

After the Northeast Corridor, most of the men slept. By the time they awoke, they were somewhere in the lushly carpeted hills of Appalachia, bound for Atlanta. Astonishing, going from winter to summer in a day. Escaping to warmer climes was the reason some men had joined. Others had languished in training for years and were looking for the fastest way to see action. Still others were hoping to avoid the horrors of trench warfare by joining a quick strike force that could get in and get out. They all wanted to prove themselves.

The men bantered, played cards, sang, and got on, and no one seemed to regard Josiah as anything other than one of them. Canada's regimental system was designed to build esprit de corps based on place of origin, but it was only here, among men from all nine provinces, that Josiah felt the first stirrings of brotherhood.

EVERYWHERE THEY WENT, THEY WERE GREETED WARMLY. PEOPLE nodded and smiled, waved and saluted, even ran up with hugs and kisses. It wasn't just the uniform but its different stripe. They were cousins, brothers, guests of the nation. When the train slowed to a crawl outside of Columbus, Georgia, a fruit truck pulled up alongside them and a scrawny boy with the makings of a big-league pitcher threw oranges from the cargo box, and the men leaned out the windows to catch them, raucously.

When they finally reached the humble little railway station in Fort Benning, they were greeted by a master sergeant. Even without his uniform, he would have looked American: beefy, ruddy, swaggering. "Welcome to the finest goddamn parachute training school in the world," he said. "Your training starts right now. We're marching to the barracks. If any of you dog it, you'll be right back on that train." He looked down his finger with one eye shut. "Now pick up your kit and follow me—on the double."

It was a beautiful evening, the sky awash in gold and bigger for the flatness of the landscape. Instantly, the eye was drawn to the latticework of three jump towers, hundreds of feet high, looming in the distance like crosses on the mount. "Jesus H. Christ," one man said, fittingly, knowing that was where they were bound.

Fort Benning was massive, a city unto itself, so sprawling it had its own light railway. Champlain Barracks was twenty acres; Fort Benning, a hundred and fifty thousand. They weren't in Orillia anymore.

It was five miles from the railway station to the barracks on Sand Hill, one of three new cantonments that had sprung up during the war. The barracks were two-story clapboard buildings, yellow with green trim, and they did in fact sit on a sandy hill.

"That sand is full of chiggers, so keep your boots on," the master sergeant said. "This ain't no beach."

Men were already filing into a barrack when the master sergeant raised his hand and said, "Hold up." Everyone stopped in their tracks.

The master sergeant approached Josiah. "What's your name, private?"

"Josiah Chang, sir."

"Where you from, Private Chang?"

"Canada, sir."

The master sergeant's face contorted. "You take me for a goddamn idiot, private? Where you really from?"

Josiah knew he was playing with fire. "The Cariboo. In British Columbia. Sir."

The master sergeant took another step forward, until Josiah was staring directly at the leathery crease across his nose. "You can't be here, boy. You need to be down on Wold Avenue. With all them other darkies."

After waking up somewhere in Appalachia, Josiah had begun to see signs at every stop: WHITE, COLORED, and sometimes NEGRO, once in playful neon, as if it were all quite harmless. That's when he realized the South was a different world, or the same world made plain. But he was neither Black nor white, and it was confusing, never really knowing where you stood.

Josiah kept his eyes straight ahead, on that leathery crease above the ball of the master sergeant's nose, but he sensed the men around him tensing. No matter how they might have felt about someone like Josiah before—and there was no telling—soldiering had taught them not to abandon one of their own.

Before he could turn to leave, their commanding officer, Major Evans, an impressively compact man, came trudging up the hill to welcome the new recruits. He sized up the scene, trying to mask his own surprise, then spoke in hushed tones to the master sergeant. The two men shared a small laugh. Then Major Evans ordered his men—all his men—to carry on.

EXCEPT FOR THE FLOORS, OILED TO A DARK SHEEN, THEIR QUARTERS were raw and unfinished. Instead of one floor of double wooden bunks, they got two floors of single metal beds. "Now we're *really* moving up," Bill said. But the barrack still suffered the usual lack of privacy. One communal shower stall. A row of toilets without partitions.

As soon as they were out of earshot, men came over and slapped Josiah on the back. "'Where are you from?' 'Canada! The Cariboo!'" they repeated uproariously, as if Josiah had just been taking the piss, and maybe he had been. Bill was the only one who said, "If he'd made you go, I would have gone, too."

At first the barrack was soupy with heat. By lights-out, the air had cooled considerably, and would cool further still. That was Fort Benning in winter: hot by day, cold by night. After Bill said, "Good night, Joe. Sleep tight," Josiah lay in bed, taking in all the night sounds, the squeaky call of mockingbirds and the raunchy blathering of frogs. This was the country where it all began for his family. The Beautiful Country, as the Chinese called America, only this time someone had to make good.

10

IN THE MORNING, AFTER JOSIAH SAT DOWN TO BREAKFAST AT A
long picnic table in the mess with Bill and others, two more Canadians
came up to their table, carrying metal trays. Josiah didn't recognize
either, so they must have been in a different cohort.

"Looks like we got some new recruits," one of them said, without
taking a seat.

"Ready to get your asses kicked?" the other asked.

The table glanced at each other. "I hear the Americans are tough,"
said Heikkinen, who always seemed in the know.

"Tough?" the first man said. "The Americans aren't tough. They're
fucking sadistic."

"It's not just them. It's our own brass," the second man said, nodding
across the room at Major Evans, chortling away at the officers' table.
"They don't want any chaff in this unit."

"What did we lose our first week? A quarter of the guys?"

"Baloney," said a boy named Crocker, who slept in a bed next to
Josiah's.

"Maybe not a quarter," the second man said, "but plenty. Some of you boys won't be here next week."

The table went quiet.

"But we're Canadians," the first man said, bucking them up now.

"That's right," the second man said. "Show those bloody Yanks what we're made of."

IT STARTED WITH RUNNING ON THE DOUBLE, WHAT THE AMERICANS called "speed marching." Men in two columns, running in sync, their instructors calling cadence. They ran up and down the roads of the main post and all three cantonments, Sand Hill, Kelley Hill, and Harmony Church. They ran past the baseball stadium, the football stadium, the golf course, and the polo grounds, past the officers' club and the infantry school, past men in open cars on the light railway who jeered them. They ran all over Fort Benning. All over kingdom come. Airborne was simply infantry dropped into war without any means of transport. Anywhere you had to go you went on foot, which required men of exceptional endurance. The goal of the first week was to weed out anyone who wasn't supremely fit. No sense training you to jump if you didn't have the stamina.

In addition to running, they went on long route marches. The first was fifteen miles, and they only got longer. They hoofed it through the countryside, over dusty red clay roads, sometimes near the banks of the Chattahoochee River, in the inconstant shade of slash pine. It was one thing in the morning, when the world was cool, another as temperatures rose, air thickening in the mouth. In full kit, they slowly burned up. Josiah felt in his element, living the life of the body, but even he was not immune to the heat, or that blasted red dust, which rose in the air and got in your eyes and your lungs and mixed with your sweat and turned back to clay in every crevice of your skin.

At the end of each day, before the men were allowed to crawl back to the barrack and shower, there were dog shows—foot inspections—just like in basic, only now those same feet were bloodied and blistered and sometimes pimpled with little red dots.

"What did I tell you about those goddamn chiggers?" the master sergeant said, disgusted.

IN A STAGE, THEY ALSO SPENT TIME IN THE SAWDUST PITS, WORKING on hand-to-hand combat. Their instructors, in hallmark white T-shirts and khakis, took savage delight in demonstrating on the Canadians. There was one instructor in particular who seemed out to get them. The man was easily six foot five, two twenty. With his golden coif and perfect musculature, he looked like Flash Gordon. That's what Crocker called him once, to laughter, and the name stuck.

At the end of each session, Flash Gordon challenged any man to take him down. The first to have a go was a big fella from Calgary named Machiel Van den Berg, who liked to go all out. He had a hound dog face with sad, drooping eyes and surprisingly small teeth for a big man—taller, clearly, than the supposed six-foot maximum. His mother had abandoned him at an early age, which drove his father to drink, and young Machiel was sent to live with an aunt in Calgary whose view of life was mean. Maybe that's why he always had fire in the belly. On this occasion, he charged headfirst, with a full frontal attack, but Flash Gordon brushed him off with a straight-arm and chancery before finishing with a knee to the solar plexus. Van den Berg grunted loudly before rolling around in sawdust, gasping for air. The men looked away.

Afterward, still struggling for breath, Van den Berg said, "I'm gonna get that bastard."

AT THE END OF THE WEEK, THE MEN WERE ROUSED IN THE MIDDLE of the night and ordered to march fifty miles before supper. Anyone who didn't make it back in time would be sent home.

As the men geared up, blinking away sleep and the glare of electric lights, their bodies already heavy with exhaustion, the master sergeant barked at them: "Think you're going to get a bed in Europe or the goddamn Pacific? Eight hours of sleep every night? If you think this is bad, wait till you see combat."

They set off into blackness north of Upatoi Creek, marching on either side of the road, behind the master sergeant, who rode in the sidecar of a Harley-Davidson. By the time the sun rose, a creeping orange bleeding into pink, they had already marched for hours and would go on marching all day, in the rising heat, stopping only once for rations and sometimes to piss and shit, right by the side of the road. At one point, deep into the march, Josiah saw a red-tailed hawk circling overhead, its wings outstretched, and imagined it was Poppy. This was how he liked to think of her, as an ever-watchful presence high above. The feeling of being watched ennobled his pain and gave him the strength to go on, to conquer the miles and the hours.

On these marches, there was nothing in the way of tactics or maneuvers, just dumb, plodding animal movement. The closest thing to strategy was making their water last all day. Each man carried only one bottle, dangling from his belt, and by midafternoon they were starting to cramp and stagger. Late in the day, one man fell to his knees and retched. Others tried to get him up, but he stayed down. It was Crocker, a boy of eighteen going on twelve. Josiah put a hand on his shoulder, and the boy looked up, eyes raw.

"I'm not gonna make it."

"Get up. We're almost there."

"I can't," he said and began to cry.

When Sand Hill finally came into view, Josiah passed Major Evans and the master sergeant, inspecting the men as they came in, and he made a point to look them in the eye, saying nothing and everything at once.

That night, as he lay in pain, the bed next to his was empty, but he felt no pity. He had made it. He was still here. That was all that mattered.

11

MERCIFULLY, THERE WAS NO TRAINING ON WEEKENDS. INSTEAD, they were all given forty-eight-hour passes, which some men used to go as far as Atlanta. Josiah used his to sleep in. By the time he stirred on Saturday morning, Bill was already up, writing to his mother, and Heikkinen was reading magazines, as he was wont to do, everything from *Maclean's* to *Look* and *Argosy*. Even Van den Berg, who'd had the wherewithal to go drinking the night before, was awake. "'Bout time, Chang," he said, scratching his belly. "Let's go get some fucking food." After five days in the mess, where every other meal consisted of eggplant, they were ready to eat. So they joined a group of Canadians at a café near the post, where they drank Coca-Cola and Dr Pepper and munched on boiled peanuts and ordered local delicacies like fried chicken, fried catfish, and something called a scrambled dog, a chopped-up hot dog and bun topped with chili, onions, pickles, and oyster crackers. At last, they were having fun.

When talk turned to jumping out of a plane, Heikkinen said, in that knowing way of his, "Didn't someone die during jump training?"

"That was before our time," said a man who had been there longer, "but yes. A major, no less. That's why we have Evans."

Airborne was so new that even commanding officers had to learn how to jump.

"Plane behind him sheared his parachute," someone else said. With two fingers, he snipped the air.

"Lovely," Bill said, blanching.

There were any number of things to do on post, any number of libraries, bowling alleys, and movie theaters to go to, but after lunch, Josiah took the "Dinky Line"—the light railway—out to King's Pond, where he whiled away the afternoon writing to Poppy. Besides the rigors of the first week, he told her about two curious incidents on post. The first was speed marching through the main post and coming across a marble arch on Morrison Road inscribed in both English and Chinese. Later, when he went back for a closer look, he discovered the monument was dedicated to the 15th Infantry Regiment for keeping the peace around Tientsin in 1924—but only by reading the English. His father had tried to teach him Chinese, but Josiah had been a poor, reluctant student. Now he wished he had done better.

The second curious thing happened on the Dinky Line. He was sitting on an open-air bench, enjoying a warm, rustling breeze, when a man in khakis, including a khaki tie and side cap, appeared and introduced himself as Bobby Yang, his drawl as thick and viscid as any Josiah had heard, and Josiah was surprised by his own surprise. Bobby's family had picked cotton in the Mississippi Delta before opening a general store, surviving on those whom whites wouldn't serve. He had gone to college and enlisted in the National Guard before being called to active duty, then selected for Officer Candidate School. The school produced more than a thousand second lieutenants a week. "'Ninety-day wonders,' they call us," Bobby said.

"How much longer do you have?" Josiah asked.

"Just a couple more weeks."

"Then where are you off to?"

"Not sure," Bobby said, shrugging. "Philippines, maybe."

His casual tone belied the prospects of that distant and daunting place. "How 'bout you?" Bobby asked. "Where you jumping?"

This was a subject of endless speculation, where they might wind up, Asia or Europe or elsewhere. "Don't know, either. Maybe I'll see you in the Philippines."

They laughed. "Couple of Orientals in Asia," Bobby mused. Then he asked, "Just you in the jump school?"

Josiah knew what he meant and nodded. "And you?"

"Not many of us in OCS," Bobby said, "but plenty of us in the army."

As the Dinky Line trundled along, Josiah thought he saw some of their own wielding bayonets in the distance.

"Nah, those are Mexicans," Bobby said, languidly. "Gonna take all kinds to win this war."

12

IN B STAGE, THEY FINALLY GOT TO THE BUSINESS OF JUMPING.

They started by jumping from a low wooden platform, with a shoulder roll or a back roll. Then, after learning how to strap on a parachute and check equipment and how to stand in the exit door, they jumped a few feet from a mock fuselage, a perfect replica of a C-47 made of wood and thick with heat, like a shed in summer. The first time, Josiah's stick made it out in seventeen seconds. They had to do it in eight.

Then came the mock tower. Another exit door, this time thirty-five feet in the air. Not nearly as tall as the jump towers they'd seen on the first day, but a step in that direction. To simulate exits and landings, they jumped out in a harness and slid down a long cable. On the first day, Josiah stood in the pounding heat and watched as other men went up and came down first. It was hard to come down smoothly, to keep from bouncing and swinging, but some men flopped egregiously, like fish on a line. One man spun with his arms out, like a maple key. It was embarrassing.

When Josiah's group was finally called, they climbed the plank stairs that zigged and zagged inside the tower's legs and entered the top of the tower through the floor. From there, they could see the green-brown waters of the Chattahoochee, which hairpinned around Fort Benning. Bill was in the same group and he strapped into the harness first. He had gone a little pale just climbing the plank stairs; now he looked positively ashen. Apparently the interview question to which he had lied was *Are you afraid of heights?*

Bill felt his way to the exit door like a rickety old man. "When I slap your shoulder, I want you to jump," their instructor said, but when the signal came, Bill just stood there. "It's perfectly safe," the instructor said, but trying to reason seemed pointless. Every man ahead of them had come down safely, yet Bill was still paralyzed.

They heard Heikkinen shouting up from below: "Come on, Billy Boy! You can do it!"

"Let's go, Bill," Josiah said sharply, feeling responsible. He was the one who'd encouraged Bill to come, which meant that Bill reflected on him.

But it was no use; the man wouldn't move. Any man could be forgiven for bad technique, but no man could be forgiven for not jumping at all. That would get him sent home. Maybe that's why the instructor finally pushed Bill out. He fell with a strangled cry, twisting and flailing as he went, then landed in a heap, to laughter. Another instructor ran up and berated him.

Josiah was next, and determined to do better. When the harness came back up, he strapped in and readied himself at the door, knees bent, arms wide. Then he saw something that made his heart start. His father was standing below, dressed as he was on the day he died, in work shirt and work pants. Josiah shook his head and blinked, trying to dispel the vision, but his father was still there, looking up, Adam's apple bobbing.

"Don't look down," the instructor said. "Eyes on the horizon."

Josiah did as he was told but still sensed his father below, radiating like heat. Josiah's heart was surging, his breath short. Why was his father here? Was it some kind of warning?

When he felt a slap on his shoulder, he wavered for only a moment before jumping out with a quarter turn. For an instant, he was weightless. Then he was falling. He feared something bad was about to happen. That his tether would break, and he with it. But he reached the end of the tether with a bounce, just as he was supposed to. All the while, he counted out loud: "One thousand! Two thousand! Three thousand!" In a real jump, if you didn't feel the shock of the canopy after three seconds, you were supposed to pull the ripcord on your backup chute.

He did his best to tame all those wild, unruly forces as he zipped down the cable. When he came to the end, he hit the sand with a somersault and popped right up on his feet. The instructor who had screamed at Bill clapped once, loudly.

"Helluva jump, private."

Josiah looked back. His father was gone.

AT THE END OF THE WEEK, A LETTER ARRIVED, AND JOSIAH WENT out to King's Pond to read it. There was almost no one else around, save for turtles and eagles and herons and a father fishing with his son in the distance, and he relished the chance to read the letter alone. *I'm glad we talked, Joe. It was good to hear your voice. I'm trying my best to understand. It's just that you're getting farther and farther away, this before you've really gone anywhere at all. I hope you can understand why that's hard for me . . .* She went on to say, *When I look at that postcard from New York, it just fills me with feeling. I've only been to Whidbey Island, which hardly counts. I suppose I'm a little jealous that you get to see America without me. Tell me all about Georgia. Are there really a lot of peaches?*

Tucked inside the letter was an article from the *Vancouver Sun*, which read in part, "Picture men with muscles of iron dropping in parachutes, hanging precariously from slender ropes, braced for any kind of action. These are the toughest men who ever wore khaki, the sharp, hardened tip of the dagger pointed at the heart of Berlin." It was a puff piece, designed to help with recruiting, but it had a salutary effect on Poppy. *I'm coming around, Joe. I'm proud of you, I really am.*

Encouraged, he wrote to her about B Stage, except for the part about his father. Every time Josiah had jumped, he had seen him, clear as day, standing there with a look both wounded and wounding. Josiah didn't know what he was seeing, something imaginary or otherworldly. In the end, he wasn't sure there was a difference, or if the difference mattered. But it seemed too hard to explain, so he kept that part to himself. Maybe he would tell her when he knew what it all meant.

THAT WEEKEND, JOSIAH DREW KITCHEN DUTY. THE NIGHT BEFORE, he draped a towel over the foot of his bed so the charge of quarters would know to wake him. Despite having to get up early, Sunday was not a bad day for kitchen police. The mess was always quieter on Sundays, after a night of heavy drinking.

Like the barracks, the mess hall was a yellow clapboard building with a green roof, except only one story. The kitchen sat in the back, behind the three-windowed wall where men were served. The heart of the kitchen was four large cast-iron stoves, pushed together to form one large appliance in the middle. Josiah was assigned to work alongside a man named Lloyd in a white chef's beanie and apron, who gave him a long, curious look before showing him how he wanted his vegetables chopped. Then he left Josiah to it. Lloyd was a barrel-chested man with a finely pitted face, and he belonged to that class of persons who did all the lowly work in Fort Benning—in all of America, it seemed—and he didn't appear much interested in conversation.

They stood side by side at a long wooden table, facing the wall, knives rapping politely. As they worked, Josiah sensed the man glancing in his direction. Eventually, he turned to Josiah and said, "You Chinese or something?"

Josiah couldn't tell if Lloyd was perceptive or using "Chinese" as a catch-all. When he nodded, Lloyd said, "Whatcha doing in this war?"

Earlier in the week, Josiah had finally caught a glimpse of Wold Avenue, between Anderson Avenue and Edwards Street. As they ran past a little redbrick post exchange and a little redbrick theater, they received a host of looks. These were the men of the 24th Infantry Regiment, and this was the heart of the segregated area, which, for some reason, the Canadians were traipsing through. Like Lloyd, some of the men on Wold Avenue had given him long, bemused looks. It reminded him of himself as a boy, seeing a Black person for the first time and wondering if he was seeing a particularly dark sort of Indian. Looks, he supposed, went in all directions.

"Is that what you ask the men of the 24th?" Josiah replied.

"You damn right," Lloyd said. "You seen where the commandant live?"

Josiah had also run past the commandant's house, an all-white mansion with two stories of columns and wraparound porches. Riverside, it was called.

"That used to be the big house. *Still* the big house," Lloyd said, laughing.

At that moment, a staff sergeant happened through the kitchen, and Lloyd went back to his chopping, but once the staff sergeant was gone, he leaned in again. Clearly, the man had things to say; he just hadn't had anyone to say them to. "Last year, a man from Deuce Four with good conduct was shot by military police for cutting up on a bus. Man who shot him said he had a knife, but there weren't no knife. Got off scot-free. That's America for you. I'm telling you, she ain't worth dying for—and not no Canada, neither."

"It's the only way things will change," Josiah said.

Lloyd looked at him askance. "Oh, you one of them Double V folk. Victory abroad, victory at home." He smiled, tutted. "Ain't nothing going to change. You know when Deuce Four was raised? 1869, my friend. 1869."

Josiah felt the ground shift beneath him. It hadn't occurred to him that all of this might be for naught. He had counted on being made whole, for when this war was over, he wasn't going to be able to wait a year to marry Poppy, much less seventy-four.

13

AT THE START OF THE THIRD WEEK, THEY WERE ISSUED AMERICAN jump boots. Unlike their Canadian boots, which were black with six pairs of eyelets, their American boots were muddy brown with hard rubber soles and a dozen pairs of eyelets. These boots were instantly prized—loved, even. They announced to the world that they were Airborne.

In C Stage, they finally reached the place they were bound for: the *real* jump towers. The towers stood in Eubanks Field, right in the center of the main post, each an airy lattice of steel, two hundred and fifty feet high. At the top of each were four arms in the shape of a cross, and it was from those arms that the men would be dropped.

"Nothing to it," Heikkinen said. "They have one of these at Coney Island."

They started on the controlled tower, where descents were guided by cables. The first piece of equipment was the chair rig, which looked like a porch swing attached to a parachute. Men were strapped in two at a time, winched to the top, and released, to get them used to the feeling of falling.

On his first attempt, Josiah was paired with Bill. After mounting a set of portable stairs, they belted themselves into the chair. There was no trace of his father, but he felt Bill tensing beside him.

"Relax. It'll be fun."

"I don't know," Bill said wanly.

With a sudden jerk, they began to rise. At first, it felt like a Ferris wheel, their view of the world climbing. Then they rose beyond any tree, any height Josiah had ever known. With another jerk, they came to a stop, all of creation spread out before them. The sky was baby blue and stippled with bolls of cotton, and a light wind set them swaying. When a fussy hinge began to creak, even Josiah felt a mewl in his guts.

Bill closed his eyes and clutched the cable next to him. "Hail, Mary, full of grace—"

Suddenly, something gave way, and they were falling. Bill let out an audible groan from the hard yank on their innards. The parachute was already open, so there was no shock, just a straight descent, maybe eight or nine seconds, the world below rushing up, returning to size.

With a jolt, the chair hit bottom and began to bounce. To steady them, an instructor ran up and grabbed a rope dangling underneath.

"See?" Josiah said. "Fun."

Bill looked at him with drowning eyes, then leaned over the chair and threw up.

THE NEXT DAY, THEY WERE BACK ON THE CONTROLLED TOWER, only this time they came down one by one in a parachute harness. Bill was one of the first to go and strapped on the harness like a man condemned. As he rose straight up in the air, he kept mumbling with his eyes closed. If he managed to come down, it was only because he had no choice in the matter, but he did little more than fall like a rock. The instructor called for a quarter turn, but Bill just kept his hands on the risers. When he hit the mat, he crumpled. Yesterday, after heaving, Bill had seemed morose. A kind word would have gone a long way, but somehow Josiah couldn't bring himself to offer one, just as he couldn't now. Bill's apprehension was starting to grate, and Josiah found himself growing impatient.

Next came the free tower. They were winched up four at a time, one at the end of each arm, and set loose one by one. The first time Josiah strapped into the harness, he drew position number four, which meant he would go last. An unlucky number, four, since it sounded like "death" in Chinese. As he rose through the air, he saw his father again, standing in the middle of Eubanks Field and looking up with sad eyes. The first sight of his father had spooked him, yes, but it had also seemed a kind of gift. Maybe that's why Josiah had failed to see the obvious, that his father, too, was a bad omen.

When he reached the top, his father was still there, two hundred and fifty feet below, his face little more than a smudge. As Josiah dangled with his back to the tower, waiting for the others to come down first, he kept his eyes straight ahead, on the far and dusty horizon, ignoring whatever his father was trying to say.

At last, a voice came over the loudspeakers: "Number four, drop your paper."

To gauge wind drift, Josiah released the slip of paper in his hand, and it fluttered north, like a lonely piece of ticker tape, toward the white bulb of a water tower in the distance.

"Release number four."

Rather than falling, he found himself rising. When he reached the very top, some mechanism let go, and his parachute detached from its metal frame, and for the first time he was completely unleashed and free to fall, and he felt a surge of the most unexpected joy. As he came down in a lazy corkscrew, the magnitude above him crackled like fire and steered him gently but firmly, like a father's hand.

"Make a body turn, number four."

Josiah crossed his arms overhead and pulled on the risers and turned to face the direction of drift. But his body was swinging slowly, like a pendulum, and he couldn't tell which way he would be swinging, forward or backward, when he touched down.

"You're okay, number four."

He could feel the quivering tension of the lines and the world coming at him with pace. He bent his knees, pointed his toes, and kept his feet together.

"Now let's have a good tumble."

Josiah braced himself for impact, but the pendulum kept swinging back. When his feet touched down, he was pitching forward, and as he tried to roll, he smacked the top of his head, or rather, the modified football helmet he was wearing. More painful than the jolt to his neck was the shock of an ugly landing. The parachute dragged him along the ground, so he pulled on the lines, hand over hand, just as they had practiced with wind machines, until the canopy collapsed. Then he rolled onto his back and threw off the harness. By the time he got to his feet, his father was no longer there. Instead, a white T-shirt was coming toward him, and he knew he was in for some pointers, maybe even some push-ups, but he didn't care. He was alive.

THERE WERE SEVERAL MORE JUMPS FROM THE FREE TOWER, BUT that wasn't the end of it. There was still one more diabolical contraption to get through, the shock harness, designed to mimic the shock of a canopy opening—something they had yet to experience.

As always, Van den Berg was gung ho. When his name was called, he ran into position at the base of the tower and dropped face down on a mat. Something resembling a trapeze was then fastened to the back of his parachute harness, and he was hoisted fifty feet in the air, his whole body spread like a starfish.

"Pull your ripcord!" the voice on the loudspeakers ordered.

Van den Berg did as he was told and promptly fell fifteen feet. Then he came to a sudden stop, limbs curling. After bouncing a few times, he was lowered to the ground.

"Piece of cake," he declared, flashing those babyish teeth of his.

When Bill was called, that doomed look came over him, a look that Josiah had come to resent, despite himself. He disliked the air of frailty and the way it attached to him by association, but he said nothing, just left Bill alone, superstitiously.

Bill was hooked up and raised fifty feet and ordered to pull his ripcord, but to no one's surprise, he refused. Just dangled there, like a spider from a thread.

"I repeat, pull your ripcord, private!"

They all waited. Now that the choice was his, he was paralyzed.

"Fifty more!" the voice barked.

Bill was raised another fifty feet. Counterintuitive, making a frightened man go higher. But he needed incentive to pull.

They waited again. Still nothing. He was raised another fifty feet, and Josiah felt his impatience curdling into anger. The only time you needed to pull your ripcord was to open your backup chute, which meant if you didn't, you were as good as dead.

That night, at one of the long picnic tables in the mess, Heikkinen regaled those who hadn't been there with the rest of the story: "So they haul him up *another* fifty feet. Now he's two hundred feet in the air. The instructor says, 'Pull the goddamn ripcord or we're sending you straight back to goddamn Canada,' but he still won't do it. So they haul him up to the very top. And they leave him there, spinning like a piñata. Finally, they start to lower him—or so I thought. But after fifteen feet, he comes to a stop. I couldn't believe it. He pulled the ripcord!"

"Won't pull the damn thing at fifty," Van den Berg said, "but he pulls it at *two hundred* and fifty!"

The table roared as Bill smiled sheepishly.

"But here's the best part," Heikkinen said. "When he's finally back on the ground, the instructor starts tearing into him—"

"And we all hear a splat," Van den Berg said, jumping in irresistibly, "right on the man's boots!"

14

AT THE END OF THE THIRD WEEK, THE MEN WERE IN HIGH SPIRITS. They were done with the jump towers, done with the shock harness, and they were the holders of fresh forty-eight-hour passes, which meant they were free to go wherever. The others—Bill, Heikkinen, Van den Berg—had already been to Columbus, Georgia, and its twin city, Phenix City, Alabama, which sat across from each other on the Chattahoochee, and they were ready for something new.

"You should come," Bill said, meaning, *I'm still here. Let's celebrate.* "We won't be down here much longer."

This was true. In a week, they would be on their way back north. After a couple of weekends of sitting out by King's Pond, Josiah was finally keen to see a bit of America. So the four of them took the train to Birmingham, Alabama. On the ride up, they sat at a table playing a fervidly studious game of five-card stud. At one point, as they rolled through fields of cotton stubble, Van den Berg turned to Josiah and said, "You're keeping a secret from us, Chang."

"What are you talking about?"

"You're hiding something in your footlocker."

A few days earlier, Josiah had received a package. It wasn't until he saw the original address in Orillia that he remembered his Christmas present, which turned out to be an LP, *Moanin' Low* by Lena Horne. *I couldn't find it at Western Music or Kelly's*, Poppy wrote, *so I ordered it by mail*. He wasn't sure why she had gone to such lengths until he looked at the track list and saw it included "Where or When," the song she had sung at the Navy League Seamen's Club. There was a record player in one of the recreation rooms, but the room was always full of men, and he didn't want others to know, to pry or josh or sully her name in any way. He preferred to keep her to himself, as he'd managed to do so far, so he stashed the record in his footlocker.

"Just a Christmas present," he said.

"From who?" Van den Berg snapped, looking up from his cards.

"My . . . girl," he confessed.

At this, Bill's eyes went a little flat. "What's her name?"

Before he could answer, Van den Berg grinned wolfishly. "Is she a dish?"

Exactly why Josiah had kept Poppy to himself. "What about you?" he asked in reply. "You got a girl?"

"Hell yes," Van den Berg said. "I got a girl in Columbus, I got a girl in Phenix City, and I'm gonna get me a girl in Birmingham!"

By the time they pulled into Terminal Station, a wide brownstone building with a dome and two towers, the sky was streaked in dying shades of violet. In the station, they passed a sign that read COLORED WAITING ROOM, and Josiah was troubled again by the feeling of never quite knowing where he belonged. Beyond the station, on 5th Avenue North, they were greeted by a soaring wrought-iron sign:

BIRMINGHAM

THE

MAGIC

CITY

"That's what I need," Van den Berg said, "some fucking magic!"

They wandered through the stout civic air of downtown, feeling their way through the pulse of a clamorous Saturday night. When they turned onto 3rd Avenue North, Josiah was startled by the flashing marquees and the gaudy neon colors. If he hadn't known better, he would have thought he was back on Granville Street. There was even a Lyric Theatre, just like in Vancouver, and for a beautiful and bewildering instant, he was walking arm in arm with Poppy to the Plaza, the Paradise, the Vogue.

They hopped from bar to bar, and everywhere they went, drinks were free, either on the house or paid for by strangers. This was the Southern hospitality—the magic—that men were always going on about. But sometimes a barkeep would look at Josiah sideways, then serve him with a little too much magnanimity. And all night, people kept asking where he was from. When he pointed at his shoulder title, they laughed.

Everywhere they went, there were women, all the more alluring for being American, everyone taken by everyone else's way of talking. At the end of the night, they found themselves in a smoky, softly burnished nightclub, all of them swaying with a girl, but each in their own way. Heikkinen clung to his with quiet desperation. As soon as he had enlisted, his girl in New Finland had left him, unwilling to be a war widow, and he was still reeling. Bill, a good Irish Catholic, danced politely, in formal dance position, as if a nun were taking a ruler to the pocket of space between him and the girl. Van den Berg, meanwhile, was all hands. After clutching and grabbing and kissing openly on the dance floor, he and his girl absconded to a dark corner.

Josiah, for his part, danced with a pretty little blond in a skirt and sweater set. Her name was Daphne, and she was studying school library service at the state university in Tuscaloosa and visiting Birmingham for the weekend. She had warm skin, kissed by the sun, and a spray of freckles across the bridge of her nose. She wasn't the least bit daunted by dancing with the likes of Josiah. Seemed, in fact, oddly excited. Part of a larger desire, he sensed, for a bit of weekend daring, and through the aquarium of his dulled senses, he indulged the possibility. She had honey-brown eyes, and lashes like Venus flytraps. More than once, their cheeks brushed, hers so shockingly soft that it sent a pulse right through him. Now he remembered why he hadn't gone to the Nite Spot in Columbus or Beechie's in Phenix City, whiling away his weekends out by King's Pond instead. Because once the body was roused, it was easy to lose your head.

Over three months. That's how long it had been since he had seen Poppy. Long enough to make a man feel tempted. He held Daphne close, and she felt good in his arms, this sweet little bundle of love and heat . . .

But in the end, nothing came of it. They just danced. Three months was a long time, but not long enough to make him forget. At the end of the night, when the lights came on, Josiah stepped back with a look of apology, and the girl smiled, eyes misty with understanding, and said, "Take care of yourself, soldier," and disappeared from his life forever.

15

ONLY ONE THING STOOD BETWEEN THE MEN AND THEIR JUMP wings: actually jumping out of a plane. Five jumps, to be exact, one for every day of jump week.

Before their first jump, there was one last dress rehearsal in the mock fuselage. Then they were off to the checkered hangars at Lawson Field. In the supply area, each man grabbed a pack at random. Earlier in the war, men had learned how to pack their own parachutes, but now all the packing was done by riggers.

"Hope I didn't get a dud!" Van den Berg said.

This was how men dealt with their fear.

As they sat on long benches, waiting for jumpmasters to inspect their chutes before emplaning, a French Canadian chap named Oberg, one of the few men who had ever been in the air, kept going on about his trip from Montreal to Vancouver and back in a Lockheed Super Electra, how utterly charming the flights had been, the single seats and the in-cabin service, until someone finally said, "Did you jump out of the fucking plane, Oberg? Then shut up already."

Then they were walking across hot tarmac in their gear and Riddell helmets, toward stout-looking C-47s sitting up on their large front wheels. As they entered from the back, through a doorway with the door removed, Josiah noticed the rivets that quilted the entire plane. He was now on the other side, counting on those rivets to hold.

The inside of the plane looked just like the replica, only made of metal: a metal bench on either side and metal ribs all along the fuselage, like the belly of a whale. In all their gear, they fit snugly. They weren't allowed to smoke in the hangars, but as soon as they were aboard, men lit up.

The right engine started up with a chop. Propeller blades sputtered and whirred, and puffs of blue smoke drifted past the windows. Then the left engine churned, until the whole cabin was filled with the deafening sound of mechanical coughing—the longest, loudest, most labored throat clearing they had ever heard.

"It was nice knowing you fellas," Van den Berg said.

The plane taxied from the apron to the runway, where it sat for a long minute. Then the engines changed key, and the plane began to hurtle, jogging the men as it went. Through the window opposite, Josiah caught a passing glimpse of his father, standing next to the runway and staring straight at him. Then, to his astonishment, his father appeared again and again, until he was flickering in the window like an image in a zoetrope, and Josiah felt that now-familiar mix of joy, pain, terror, and confusion, wondering what his father was trying to tell him.

Then the tail rose and someone shouted, "Let's go, baby!" and the plane achieved a sudden lilting weightlessness, and to the many things Josiah had experienced for the first time in recent months was added the sensation of flight.

Soon he was looking down at a sharp relief map of Fort Benning and the winding S-turns of the Chattahoochee River. At first, their distance from the ground was unsettling, but soon they were so high up that height became an abstraction. Like the engines themselves, which went from hacking to purring, most men went from disquiet to a kind of distillated calm. But some of the men looked anxious. Then there was Bill, mumbling with his eyes closed. If Josiah didn't feel his usual impatience, it was only because he was gripped by his own doubts. After the free tower, he had decided his father had come to guide him, to watch over him, but now that he was up here, it seemed obvious what his father was trying to say: that the sky was no place for a man to be. But what choice did he have? He couldn't be like Bill. He had to face death head-on.

The jumpmaster was a strapping fellow in the usual white T-shirt and khakis, except he wore a parachute, as well as a soft helmet and aviator goggles, like a pilot from the last war. As they neared the drop zone, he lowered his goggles, braced himself against the doorway, and stuck his head out fearlessly before turning back to the men.

"Remember, on this first go-round, we're jumping in groups of four."

When the red light came on, he ordered the first group to stand and hook up, and Van den Berg leapt to his feet. When the moment came, he threw himself out with abandon and took three others with him, as if they were all chained by the ankle. The plane let out a cheer.

They circled the drop zone and came in for another pass. This time, Bill and Josiah's group was up.

"Get ready!" the jumpmaster shouted.

Each man grabbed the snap hook at the end of his static line.

"Stand up!"

Four men got to their feet.

"Hook up!"

They clipped their static lines to the cable that ran along the ceiling and tugged a few times to be sure.

"Check equipment!"

Every man checked his own gear, then the parachute of the man in front of him. As last man, Josiah turned around so that Bill could do the same for him.

"Sound off for equipment check!"

"Four okay!"

"Three okay!"

"Two okay!"

"One okay!"

"Is everybody happy?"

The four of them cheered obsequiously. Something was definitely coursing through Josiah, jangling his nerves and scraping his veins, but he wouldn't have called it happiness.

"Stand in the door!"

The first man stepped into the doorway with his arms to either side, sleeves rippling in the slipstream.

"Go!"

The man jumped, followed quickly by another, both of them slipping from view. Then Bill stepped forward, pivoting smartly into the doorway, one foot over the lip, with what seemed like newfound confidence. But when the jumpmaster slapped his shoulder, he just stood there.

"Go, private!"

But he wouldn't move, and Josiah felt his impatience return. Up here, a second felt like forever, and too many had already elapsed.

"Come on, Bill!" Josiah shouted, over the roar of the engines.

Bill stooped a little, like a child trying to shorten the distance to the ground, but he still wouldn't jump. By this point, Josiah's impatience had turned molten. It was one thing to imperil yourself, another to imperil others. Freezing up like this in war could cost men their lives.

In a fit of pique, he grabbed Bill by his chute and yanked him out of the doorway before they missed the drop zone entirely. But when he got to the door and saw the strange patchwork of fields below, he, too, froze. For only half a second, maybe less, but in jump-time, it felt like a small eternity. Time enough to wonder if he had failed to heed his father. If he was making a terrible mistake.

As soon as he was out the door, he was met by the unfamiliar smack of the prop blast, which shot him under the tail. For a moment, he was in free fall, his eyes, his entire head, swollen with pressure. *One thousand* . . . He felt the tug of the static line and the top of his bag tearing off. *Two thousand* . . . Then he heard a loud unfurling snap and instantly started to slow, to still greater forces on his body, all of his blood now pooled in his feet.

He was hundreds of feet in the air, where no man was supposed to be, but now that his chute had deployed, he was certain, almost certain, he would live, and in that certainty, he took it all in, the sky above and the earth below and his infinitesimal place in between.

He was swinging again as he neared the ground, but this time the pendulum swung perfectly, and he landed upright, rolled forward, and sprang back up on his feet. As he ran around the chute, spilling air, silk collapsed in the field all around him, like so many brush fires being snuffed out. Men were whooping and shouting and already recounting their exploits. Every man's story was the same, except it had happened to him. Josiah felt the same exhilaration, but also a tinge of sadness. Somehow he knew, now that he had crossed the Rubicon, that he would never see his father again.

16

JOSIAH MADE HIS WAY TO THE CANOPY TRUCKS LINED UP TO TAKE them back to the hangars. Van den Berg was waiting to pump his hand and say, "Welcome to the club, pal!" as if he hadn't beaten Josiah by mere minutes. Then Van den Berg glanced around and said, "Where's Bill?"

"Didn't jump."

Van den Berg threw up his hands. "You got to be kidding me."

More men came in from the field, to more handshakes, including Heikkinen, grinning like a fool, and together they waited for every last man to come in. Anyone who didn't jump the first time got a second pass. If not for that, Josiah wouldn't have pushed Bill aside, or so he told himself.

But no one would get a second chance until every other man had gone. They were jumping today with Americans from the 507th Airborne Infantry Regiment, so a good many men had to come down first.

"Is he going to do it?" Van den Berg asked grimly.

"Don't know," Josiah said. More to the point, he didn't know if he *wanted* Bill to jump. From the first, he'd had his doubts about Bill, and those doubts had only grown, and he didn't want to be in a unit with men about whom there could be any doubt. But he kept these thoughts to himself.

Half an hour later, after every other plane had dropped its human payload, a lone C-47 finally circled back toward the drop zone, a dark, banking shadow that slowly grew larger and louder.

"Come on, Billy Boy," Heikkinen muttered.

As the C-47 approached, Josiah thought he could see a speck of a man in the doorway and kept hoping he would fall out, someway, somehow, if only to keep him from feeling guilty. But the plane thundered overhead, and kept on thundering, without dropping a thing.

"Fuck," Van den Berg spat.

On the ride to the hangars, as other men continued to celebrate, Josiah sat in a muted world of his own, wondering if he had been too callous. Yet each time he pictured Bill in the doorway, dithering before their one essential duty, his anger returned. No one could falter at the moment of truth.

By the time they reached the hangars, Bill was already there, looking even more distraught than they might have imagined. He was standing in socks. They had already taken his jump boots.

BILL WAS DRIVEN BACK TO THE BARRACKS TO FETCH HIS THINGS, then taken directly to the train station for the long, lonely journey back to Montreal, but not before he shook hands with the men and found a moment alone with Josiah. His eyes were raw, and the cleft in his chin unsteady. What had happened on the plane crowded the air between them.

"Guess the adjutant was right," Bill said. "Shouldn't have lied."

Josiah recalled that curious interview with the army psychiatrist and wondered how many other questions Bill had lied in response to. For Josiah now understood that what a man truly feared, standing there above the void, was not the long fall down but whatever pain was deepest within him. But he didn't know what it was that Bill had yet to stare down.

"Remember the Horse Palace?" Bill asked, and suddenly Josiah was back there, lying under a spray of stars, listening to homesick boys crying themselves to sleep at night. It felt like a lifetime ago. The army did strange things to time.

"Smelled like shit," Josiah said, and they managed to smile.

When a nearby jeep rumbled to life, Bill grimaced, then looked at Josiah earnestly and said, "Thank you, Joe."

Josiah arched a brow. "What for?"

"For taking this boy on the greatest adventure of his life," he said happily. "I won't forget you, Joe. You're a very fine man."

The words made Josiah feel like a bastard. Part of him still felt guilty, as if his own lack of faith had sabotaged Bill, but part of him felt relieved, that some chaff had been shucked and was no longer under his care. It scared him a little, that he put himself above fraternity—the opposite of what they were supposed to be learning. It spoke to a smallness, a meanness, in him that he'd always known was there. No, he was hardly a fine man.

Eager to take his leave, Josiah thrust out his hand. "See you in Tokyo. Or Berlin."

Bill's eyes shone, but he smiled bravely at the prospect. "See you then."

That night, the beds on either side of Josiah's were empty, but he tried not to feel remorse. War was not for the faint of heart. His goal was to live, and that required the best of men. Still, he wasn't insensible to the fact that his oldest friend in the army was gone.

17

THERE WERE FOUR MORE JUMPS, MOST INVOLVING PLANELOADS OF men at once, the whole sky blooming. It made Josiah think of the cherry blossoms in Stanley Park, the way they fell in dense flurries. With men that close, they could talk on the way down. "Bring me a cuppa!" they would say, joking about their little tea parties. They had learned to jump so fast that they were right on top of each other. Sometimes, a man could even walk on another man's chute, until the man below told him to fuck off.

It was strange and surreal, humans falling through space.

ON THE LAST DAY, THEY HAD ONE MORE ROUND IN THE SAWDUST pits. One last chance to take down Flash Gordon. By this point, men had wearied of the exercise, but Van den Berg was determined to give it one last go. Once again, he was first in the pit, where he and Flash Gordon circled each other like a pair of Gargantuas. Flash Gordon had always let his opponent make the first move, but today, he seized the element of surprise, lunging and grabbing Van den Berg by the collar.

Then he put a foot to his stomach and rolled backward, sending the big fella sailing through the air and onto his back, in spectacular fashion. The men groaned.

"Who's next?" Flash Gordon asked, dusting his hands theatrically.

A mutter went through the crowd. So this was how they were going to leave Fort Benning. With their asses handed to them.

"No one?"

"Come on, Josiah," Van den Berg said, bristling with indignation. "Someone's got to take the bastard down."

So far, Josiah had avoided getting into the pit with Flash Gordon. No sense getting hurt for the sake of a foolish challenge. But now that he had earned his wings, the calculus seemed different. He stepped forward, to wild approval.

"About time, Chang," Flash Gordon said, smiling. "About time."

Josiah entered the pit, his opponent looming before him, a thick vein running down the side of each bicep. Josiah had no plan, no strategy, other than lasting as long as he could. For a while, they stalked each other, pawing the air testingly. Then, obeying an impulse that wasn't entirely conscious, Josiah charged. When Flash Gordon raised a hand for a straight-arm, Josiah juked, hooked the man's waist, and put him in a rear bodylock, and the men roared. Fed by the crowd, Josiah squeezed harder, his cheek flush against the hard slab of Flash Gordon's back. The American reached for his ankle, but Josiah stepped back. Then the American grabbed Josiah's wrist and tried to hook his leg with his own, but Josiah kept turning away, still clinging fiercely.

Finally, with a swift and inexplicable move, Flash Gordon broke Josiah's hold and put him in a headlock. At that point, he could have easily finished Josiah off. Instead, he toyed with him, like a predator taunting its prey. "What have you got, Chang? Show me what you got."

Josiah tried a body slam, but the man could not be moved.

"That's it? That's all you got, Chang?"

Suddenly, Josiah was back in the shipyard, his head being crushed by Charlie, and all the anger and anguish of the last time he saw Poppy came rushing back at once. He hooked a leg around Flash Gordon's, then reached up and shoved his face, gouging the man's eyes as he did, with a savage cry, and the man began to falter. Slowly, then inexorably.

One moment, Josiah was on the ground, breathing a cloud of sawdust, the next, in the air, riding on shoulders. He was carried around the sawdust pits, in full view of the vanquished American, who seemed oddly pleased, a jouncing and jubilant victory lap in the glare of a bright and beating sun. If he wasn't one of the men before, he was now.

18

LATER THAT DAY, THEY LINED UP ON THE TARMAC AT LAWSON FIELD
to receive their wings, both American and Canadian, the former a small
silver pin, the latter a badge with a golden maple leaf. They also received the coveted maroon beret—and got to keep their jump boots.
After Major Evans gave a speech, the brigadier general who lived at
Riverside, the "big house," read the Airborne Creed in its entirety and
ended by saying, "It's thrilling to know that so fine a body of men is an
ally of ours in the struggle against tyranny."

Then it was on to their last night in Fort Benning, which meant one
last chance to get shit-faced. They started on post in the enlisted men's
club, where every new graduate was served a drink called "The Opening Shock," a glass of corn whisky and vodka that went down like sol-
vent. Everyone wanted to buy Josiah a drink for taking down Flash
Gordon, so he was already good and soused by the time he got on the
bus for Columbus. An ad on the bus promised THE UNIFORM ALWAYS
GETS THE GLAD HAND AT THE GOO GOO! so that's where Josiah,
Heikkinen, and Van den Berg went for dinner. The place served chicken,

steaks, chops, and seafood, and Josiah splurged on the Special Goo Goo T-bone for $3.50. Halfway through dinner, Van den Berg raised his glass to the empty seat at the table and said, "Here's to Bill. May he find his balls," which bothered Heikkinen, and the rest of the meal passed in silence. Josiah didn't care. He had his own plans.

After dinner, he found the waitress. "Do you know how to get to the 5th Avenue USO?"

The waitress crinkled her nose. "You sure 'bout that, honey?"

"Yes, ma'am."

"Fifth Avenue ain't but two blocks thataway." She pointed. "Just keep walking south from there."

Josiah told the guys he would see them in the morning.

"Where are you going?" Heikkinen asked, surprised.

"Something I got to do."

"Don't we all, brother," Van den Berg said. "Hope you brought some prophylactics!"

Josiah walked to 5th Avenue, then turned south, to the squeaking and clattering of a nearby rail yard. Large houses with stables and coops gave way to densely packed shotgun houses, oil lamps burning in the windows. The farther he went, the darker the streets became. At one point, an older man in a hat stopped him and said, "You know where you at, son?" Josiah said yes and carried on.

Eventually he came to an intersection with a drugstore, millinery, and funeral home. Nestled among them was a new two-story building with a large USO shield hanging outside. As he made his way to the door, through a host of sidelong glances, he felt a hand on his arm.

"Hey, soldier. Looking for a good time?"

Through dim streetlight, he saw red-painted lips and dark, liquid eyes, and his blood thunked with an old impulse, but he took his arm back and walked on.

He stepped through the front door of the USO, where a handsome woman looked at him uncertainly. "What can I do you for, mister?"

"I'm here to see the show, ma'am," he said, pointing at the poster behind her.

"Of course," she said, warming. "Right this way."

He was shown to an auditorium with red stage curtains, and he took a seat in the back, trying to remain inconspicuous. The 5th Avenue USO was also known as the Colored Army and Navy YMCA, and he wasn't sure he had a right to be here.

As the auditorium filled, a man with freckles and a pencil mustache slid in next to him. He was chewing a toothpick, and it flipped like a switch as he studied Josiah.

"Canada, huh?" the man said, eyeing Josiah's shoulder title. "What are you doing down here?"

"Jump school."

"Well, dang," the man said, rearing back. "They won't let *us* do that."

"You Deuce Four?"

"Aren't we all," the man said, laughing. "You must like music."

"I like *her*," Josiah said, nodding at the still-empty stage.

Shortly after getting his Christmas present, Josiah experienced a moment of serendipity: he was speed marching again on Wold Avenue when he saw a poster for a show starring none other than Lena Horne.

"Ma Rainey used to live a few doors down from here," the man said. When Josiah looked blank, the man said, "Oh, you should hear yourself some Ma Rainey. Where are you from?"

"Vancouver," he said, for simplicity's sake. "You?"

"Pittsburgh. Different world down here, isn't it?"

Josiah couldn't tell if he meant America or the South. "How do you stand it?"

The man's toothpick flicked up and down. "I trust in the Lord."

Josiah found the answer unsatisfying. "You believe in Double Victory?"

The toothpick kept flicking, then stilled. "It's no victory to get to the starting line. I prefer to call it liberation."

At that moment, a man in a double-breasted suit and wingtips strode onstage to kick off the evening. Then the lights dimmed and the curtains opened, and there she was in the flesh, in a shimmering shoulder-strap dress, her hair done up with a flower. The applause was deafening. "Good evening, boys!" she began, and all the men fell over themselves. She was absolutely gorgeous, a genuine star, and held the men in the palm of her hand. Josiah had managed to find some time alone to listen to *Moanin' Low*, enough to recognize most of that night's set list, but he didn't need any help recognizing the one song that mattered most. As soon as she started in, Josiah was no longer there, he was gone, hurtling through time and space, back to the Navy League Seamen's Club and that girl in the burning tunnel of light.

19

OF THE FIFTY MEN WHO HAD SET OFF FROM MONTREAL, ONLY thirty-eight made the long journey back at the end. For the most part, they slept, torpid from drink and exhaustion. As ersatz summer gave way to real winter, the trip took on a blue feeling, which made them even more listless.

They had to report to Camp Shilo in Manitoba, now up and running, but not before they all got a week's leave. This late-breaking news lifted spirits considerably. Josiah, however, was bitterly disappointed. A week was not enough time to take the train to Vancouver and back. Then he remembered Oberg.

"Where do you catch a plane to Vancouver?" Josiah asked.

"Dorval," Oberg replied. "It's a pretty penny, though. You got that kind of money?"

After shaking hands with Heikkinen and Van den Berg and the other men at Bonaventure Station, Josiah took a cab to Dorval, on the outskirts of the city. As the cab approached the airport, he saw fat dolphin-headed planes that looked like C-47s, only they were silver and dusted with snow. He paid the driver from his canister, still spiraled with banknotes.

At the ticket counter for Trans-Canada Air Lines, a woman in a blue suit swelled at the sight of his uniform. When he asked about Vancouver, she beamed.

"There's a flight leaving tonight. And there's one seat left."

HE FOUND A PAY PHONE AND CALLED POPPY.

"You're back in Montreal?"

"Poppy, I'm coming home."

"What? When?"

"Today. Tonight. I'm flying. I'll be there in the morning."

"Don't tease me—"

"I only have a week's leave. It's the only way."

"Oh my god, Joe."

He left Montreal at eight thirty that night. By eleven in the morning, he was back in Vancouver. It was teleportation, sheer sorcery, and it still wasn't fast enough.

From Montreal, the plane had made stops in Toronto, North Bay, Kapuskasing, Winnipeg, Regina, and Lethbridge, through blustery veils of darkness. On the first leg, a young woman in a blue suit and side cap served him food and drink—every bit as pleasant as Oberg had said it was. After Toronto, Josiah tried to sleep but slept fitfully, partly from sitting upright and all the takeoffs and landings, which made him long for the comforts of rail, but mostly from restless anticipation, the scenes of reunion that kept playing out in his mind. On the last leg, dawn broke over the Rockies like a supernova, and Josiah thought he could see the Cariboo somewhere along the bending horizon.

On Sea Island, two runways formed an X, as if to mark the spot. As the plane descended through drizzle, over swales of brown grass,

Josiah sensed her presence below, just minutes away, drawing him in like a vortex.

IN THE BACK OF THE CAB, POPPY SAT WITH HER HEAD AGAINST HIS shoulder, her hair dewy with rain and smelling sweetly of smoke. At the airport, she had taken mincing steps that sprang into strides until she was in his arms. He had stooped to set down his duffel, and the act of rising and the force with which they met lifted her off her feet. They hadn't let go of each other since.

On the Second Narrows Bridge, he was struck by the North Shore Mountains, how close they seemed. So close he could see individual trees powdered with snow. On Third Street, they entered the same war-time subdivisions, only grown, the empty lots now framed and the framed houses now finished and bleeding smoke. Strange, the way the world both stayed the same and went on faithlessly without you.

"Look at you," Poppy said, drinking in his uniform with those eyes of acetylene blue, and he kept thinking the same.

Poppy's house resembled every other in the neighborhood, yet he had no trouble picking it out. As they started up the walkway, the curtains next door ruffled, and Josiah felt triumphant in his uniform, maroon beret, and jump boots. At the door, he heard whimpering and frantic scrabbling. As soon as the door opened, a sleek face appeared, and the threshold pattered damply as the old girl lost control.

He was home.

POPPY AND JOSIAH PROCEEDED DIRECTLY TO THE BEDROOM AND DID not come out until the whole room was briny with sex. After more than three months, they were both monstrous with need. They would make love, lounge through an interregnum of smoke, then start all over again.

For months now, his body had known only pain. Pain was the price of being with her, and he was willing to pay. But now, at last, the prize.

"'PICTURE MEN WITH MUSCLES OF IRON,'" POPPY SAID, RAKING A hand over the cobblestones of his stomach.

All those runs and marches had etched his body further, his buried form brushed into sharp relief. He and the other men had often gone shirtless in the broiling heat, and a clear line between light and dark now bisected him at the waist. He was pleased that she was pleased. He wanted her to think him beautiful.

"DO YOU HAVE TO GO TO WORK?"

"No, I'm taking the week off."

"They let you?"

"I don't care if they let me or not."

They didn't have to leave the house. As soon as he had called, she had gone to the grocery store, the liquor store, the druggist.

HE GOT UP TO LOOK AT HER DRESSING TABLE. STUCK IN THE FRAME of the mirror was the finely waffled linen postcard he had sent from Grand Central Terminal, captioned MIDTOWN SKYLINE SHOWING CHRYSLER BUILDING AND RADIO CITY, NEW YORK, and it had the slightly cartoonish quality of color reproduction. And there, around the postcard, on both sides of the mirror, were all the other postcards he had sent from Toronto, Orillia, and Montreal. From Columbus, Fort Benning, and Birmingham.

He pulled out the card from Fort Benning, which showed scenes of infantry and parachute training inside curving 3D letters, and flipped it over to confirm that the card had really been sent by him. Strange to think he had just been there, that he had been to all these places, and in so short a time. For better or worse, the war was opening up the world.

"Did you really do that?" Poppy asked from bed. "Jump out of airplanes?"

He looked at the C-47 flying across the top of the card and the little men tumbling out, their chutes in various stages of distension.

"Got my wings, didn't I?"

As he put the card back, he realized she was staring at him and his reflection, taking him in all at once, front and back. She stubbed out her cigarette.

"Bring that beautiful body back to bed."

SHE WAS WILLING TO DO ANYTHING. HER WILLINGNESS WAS ASTON-ishing. But her willingness with *him*—that was the miracle. And yet, for all their desire, a space, a strangeness, hovered between them, maybe from being apart for so long or maybe from being any two people, and no matter how hard he tried, how fiercely he shut his eyes and blinded himself with effort, he couldn't obliterate that final distance between them.

WHEN THEY FINALLY CAME OUT, QUEENIE WAS ASLEEP ON THE love seat, torqued and splayed in that weird way of hers. In the time he'd been gone, she had aged. The white on her chest had spread, and those eyes of hers looked cloudier, and her stomach was lumpy with fatty tumors.

"Not much we can do," Poppy said, sitting down and rubbing Queenie's chest. "Doctor says she's just getting old."

"Let me pay you for the vet," Josiah said.

"Joe," Poppy said, looking up admonishingly.

• • •

JOSIAH TOOK A BATH, EVERY DRIP AND PLASH RESOUNDING AGAINST
the aqua-blue tiles. It wasn't just his first bath but the first time he
had bathed alone in months. After a punishing day of training, a
shower was the best feeling in the world. Sometimes the water in Fort
Benning had that special quality of heat that only comes from being
warmed all day in the sun. But that shower stall had always been full
of men, shouting and laughing and soaping each other's backs. What
a relief to finally have some privacy. This was just a temporary war-
time house—no basement, easy to tear down—but it might as well
have been the Royal York.

LIFE AS THEY KNEW IT RESUMED. DINNER, RECORDS, AND DRINKS,
only now with Queenie snuffling nearby.

"I have something for you," Josiah said. "A belated Christmas
present." As he rummaged through his duffel, Poppy set down her
drink in anticipation.

"Aw," she said when he handed her a signed photograph of Lena
Horne. "Where did you get it?"

"I met her."

Poppy's eyes grew. "You *what?*"

He told her about the USO in Columbus, how he had gone there on
his last night and met a man from Pittsburgh named Ormes, and how
they had gone up to the singer afterward, with Ormes as a kind of
emissary—"My friend here is Canadian"—and asked for an autograph,
and how Lena Horne had smiled her dazzling smile and said, "Pleased
to meet you, soldier!" before they were crowded out by all the other men
in line.

"Was she every bit as beautiful in real life?"

"Second most beautiful woman in the world."

"Stop it," Poppy said. But her cheeks dimpled as she grinned from ear to ear.

LIKE A BOOMERANG, THE RECORD SHE HAD SENT HIM HAD COME ALL the way back in his duffel. After she put it on, they held each other in the living room. When Lena Horne sang the title track, "Moanin' Low," about the sweet man she loved who was mean as could be, Josiah asked, "Am I mean?" He was being facetious, sure of the answer, but instead of laughing, Poppy slivered her eyes and said, "Depends on what you mean by 'mean.'" For a moment, he didn't know what to think. Then he realized she hadn't come around, or hadn't come around completely. She was still nursing some anger or hurt. That he had left her, joined the army, joined *Airborne*, all without telling her.

A few songs later, when Lena Horne started in on "Where or When," Poppy pulled him closer and buried her face with tender despondency, and he felt like the speaker in the song, lost in time and bewildered, unsure whether this was past, present, or future.

20

THE DAYS PASSED. SOMETIMES JOSIAH WOULD SIT ON THE LOVE SEAT with Queenie, rubbing that shock of white on her chest, while Poppy sat at a small secretary, writing letters or paying bills, which gave him a pleasant sense of the everyday. Mornings and afternoons, they took Queenie on walks, sometimes along Mosquito Creek, which ran right behind the house, for as long as the old girl would go, and on those walks, the most frequent subject of conversation was all the things he had seen and done in the time he'd been gone—almost four months now. One day, he told her about a film he had watched in basic on sex hygiene. At first, the men couldn't help but snicker and crack wise. Then came footage of pus and hard and soft chancres and antibiotics syringed directly into the urethra, which sobered them right up. At this, Poppy smiled and asked, half teasing and half testing, "Did you meet any nice girls?"

They were walking along a shallow creek in MacKay Park, through a stand of naked alders, the old girl puttering in and out of the water. The pretty little blond in the sweater set reared up in his mind, and some look of contrition must have crossed his face, because Poppy started a little and said, "Oh. You did."

He had danced with a girl in Birmingham, he muttered. Otherwise, he had stayed in.

"Do what you want, Joe. It's okay to have a little fun."

"That's the thing. It's *not* fun. Not without you."

She looked at him doubtfully. "That's sweet of you, Joe. But really, I don't mind if . . . if you have a little fun." She had paused to consider her words but had settled on the same phrase. "As long as you're safe— and come back to me."

At that moment, Queenie bolted after something in the underbrush. She was good at leaving and returning, but Josiah felt strangely pan- icked. "Queenie, come back!" he shouted, and in very short order she did, trotting nonchalantly. But his heart was racing, and his breath ragged, and he felt confused. By all of it.

"What?"

Again, she seemed to tread carefully. "The war is going to be hard. And we're going to be apart for so long."

Was she saying what he thought she was saying? Did she really think him that faithless? That weak?

"And you think I'm going to mess around."

"That's not what I mean."

"What do you mean, then?"

At the sound of his voice, unexpectedly sharp, her eyes dimmed. "Never mind, Joe. Forget I said anything."

ON THEIR SECOND TO LAST NIGHT, THEY WENT TO SEE A MOVIE. Poppy wore gloves and a dark mohair coat with three big wooden buttons, Josiah his walking-out uniform, his shirt and tie peeking out from under the collar of his tunic, and they walked arm in arm down luminous, rain-slicked Granville Street—to looks, as ever. But the looks were changing, softening, which reminded him why he had put on the uniform in the first place.

They went to see *You Were Never Lovelier* at the Dominion, starring Fred Astaire and Rita Hayworth. The movie was about an American dancer in Buenos Aires who falls for a nightclub owner's daughter. When she falls for him as well, the nightclub owner tells the American to leave Buenos Aires, and Josiah couldn't help hearing a distant echo of his own life. He hadn't said anything to Poppy about her father. Hadn't wanted to cause friction in ways that might work against him. But after the movie, as they waited at the taxi stand, he felt compelled to tell her.

He watched as Poppy struggled with the sudden new view of her father—and of him.

"Is that why you joined the army? To prove something to my father?"

He supposed there was a grain of truth to this. If he didn't serve, other men, including her father, whom he admired for serving, would always have something over him. But after all the pain and hardship he had been through, her simple logic vexed him. He wanted to say he was doing this for them, for *her*, as he so clearly was. Instead, he put it in terms he was sure she would understand: "It's not about your father. It's about liberation."

She pursed her lips and said nothing.

AND JUST LIKE THAT, IT WAS THE LAST NIGHT. "WAIT HERE," POPPY said before coming back to the living room in the strapless blue gown she had worn the night they had met, her shoulders and back and décolletage as smooth and pale as marble. He put on his uniform again, but they didn't go anywhere, just stayed in listening to records and dancing. Sometimes Poppy would dance with a glass in one hand

and a cigarette in the other, rolling her hips and shoulders in ways that roused him. But mostly they just held each other fast, Poppy clinging with the same despondency he had felt since he got back. He was going off to war for who knew how long, and to what end.

So far, they had managed to keep all those feelings at bay, but they were running out of time to say whatever needed to be said. "What's the matter?" he asked.

He felt the muscles of her back clenching and unclenching. "Nothing, darling. Nothing's the matter."

21

SHORTLY AFTER JOSIAH HAD JOINED THE ARMY, POPPY HAD SUNDAY dinner with her parents at their turreted Queen Anne Revival on Seaton Street, on the lower slopes of the West End, overlooking the inlet. As always, a profusion of doilies and antimacassars made the house seem fusty—a fustiness she had spent her youth trying to escape. At some point during dinner, as they sat at a long table similarly smothered in lace, her mother at one end in a dinner dress and pearls, her father at the other in a suit and tie, Poppy noticed that her slice of roast beef was strangely iridescent, like the wings of a fly, and wondered why her parents continued to believe this meal the very height of cuisine.

Toward the end of dinner, Poppy was surprised when her mother asked about Josiah. A few weeks earlier, Poppy had told her parents that Josiah had proposed, to a quiet consternation she was happy to see, especially in her mother. Now she wished she hadn't mentioned it. If her parents hadn't known, she wouldn't have had to say anything. Now she had to tell them that Josiah had joined the army. When her father asked how, she said he had gone east. When he asked why, she did her best to explain, and her parents exchanged a look that struck her at the time as opaque.

But that look came back to her with sudden clarity at the taxi stand on Granville Street, when Josiah confessed that her father had spoken to him. She had already been feeling miserable about the end of his visit, and the revelation only unsettled her more. She was angry at her father, but also her mother, whom she strongly suspected of influence. Angry at the way they had used Josiah's honor against him, and angry at Josiah, too, for letting himself be used. For volunteering to go away, which was for her parents the best of all circumstances.

She supposed she'd been angry with Josiah ever since that awful day in the yard. Yes, the graffiti was upsetting, humiliating even, but she wished he hadn't indulged that all too masculine impulse to resolve problems with one's fists. It had shocked her, his capacity for violence. She had thought him gentle, as he always had been, at least with her, but clearly that was a misapprehension. If not for the punches thrown, he wouldn't have had to run, and if not for the running, who knows if he would have gotten it into his head to join the army. Not just the army but *Airborne*, his momentum taking him farther and farther afield. She would have thought her gravitational pull strong enough to keep him close. Now she was being punished for hubris. For presuming she had that kind of sway on anyone.

On the morning of his departure, she woke to find him sitting on the edge of the bed staring at his uniform, draped across the bench of her dressing table. She could see every ripple of muscle in his broad back, there in the shadowy dark, and had a sickening feeling she couldn't name. She could tell he didn't want to go, and she didn't want him to, either.

At the thought of his leaving, her throat caught painfully. "Come back to bed," she rasped.

For a long moment, he sat there as if he hadn't heard. Then he said, "I have to go."

She knew as well as he did that he had a long journey ahead. Flights through Lethbridge and Regina to Winnipeg before a train to Brandon and a spur line to Camp Shilo. They had tried to find a way for him to stay a day, even an hour, later, without success. But she just wanted to hold him for a moment. Denying her this one small request brought all her pain into sharp relief. She pushed up on her elbow.

"You should never have left."

His back tensed. "I had to."

Frankly, she couldn't see why. No, he wasn't a British subject, yet he lived in this country, worked in this country, loved in this country. That's what they could have done. Just lived and worked and loved. They would have found a way.

"No, you didn't. I would have married you."

He flinched. True or not—and she wasn't entirely sure—she meant she would have done anything, the world be damned, but she heard how the words must have sounded.

"And then what?" he asked. "I have to make things right."

"You know I don't care about 'right.'"

"Well, I do."

His words were sharp, just like that day in MacKay Park, only this time she didn't back down. "I'm not going to sit around and wait forever. That's not what I agreed to."

Finally, she was saying what she hadn't been able to say the whole visit, and all these many months. That she had agreed to one life and been left with another, and she felt betrayed. She knew herself, knew what she wanted, and the one thing she did *not* want was to sit around helplessly for months or even years waiting for a man to come back from war. She thought she had been spared all that. Now she found herself facing the very thing she had tried to avoid. That day in MacKay Park had surprised even her, but it wasn't that she didn't trust *him*. She didn't trust herself. To be steadfast, unwavering. She simply didn't know if she had it in her. Better, then, to be weak and honest than weak and dishonest. But he hadn't understood, and she didn't know how to make him understand.

For a while they were quiet, and again she had that sickening feeling. It tasted like metal and soured her stomach and made her heart pound, and she realized the feeling was fear. She was scared, just so scared. That a time would come when the world set out each day to destroy him. Stifling a cry, she threw off the covers and clambered across the bed and launched herself upon him, with all the love and terror in the world.

22

THOSE MONTHS AT CAMP SHILO WERE SOME OF THE LONELIEST OF Josiah's life, especially with snow well into spring, the world a flat and frozen whiteness. The only thing visible for miles around was a single jump tower, and the way it stood there, silent and alone, seemed for all the world like the figure of his own desolation.

Those who had already earned their wings had it better than the new recruits, who slept in unheated barracks and shaved with ice-cold water and ran two miles every morning before breakfast and washed out of jump school in droves. But life was hardly easy for the qualified men. They kept up with physical training, long route marches in sub-zero temperatures, the oil of their weapons gumming in the cold, and naturally, they continued to jump. At least one jump a month from Lockheed Lodestars that took off from Rivers, Manitoba, fifty miles away. Now that they had their wings, they couldn't balk, had to jump. Otherwise, they got a hundred and twenty days in the clink.

On his first night drop, Josiah landed in snow, so deep and so soft that he couldn't help but laugh. But sometimes on those windswept plains, men were blown about wildly and would land on their backs and get knocked out. Increasingly, jumps were combined with ever larger maneuvers at the section, platoon, and company levels. Once, they were dropped in sticks of ten within a fifty-mile radius of Camp Shilo and ordered to get back to camp without asking for directions. Upon landing, Josiah was heartened to see the lights of the jump tower pricking the darkness, but on the boundlessness of the prairies, things were farther away than they appeared, and they spent hours trudging toward a beacon that never seemed to draw closer.

Yet it was all welcome distraction. He was glad to be back with the men, with Heikkinen and Van den Berg and the others. For months, he had yearned to go home; now he fought to keep all those memories at bay. What had she meant the night she said, "Depends on what you mean by 'mean'"? Or that day in MacKay Park as they walked along the creek? Poppy was a modern woman, with modern ideas, but that seemed a bridge too far. And what, above all, had she meant when she said, "I'm not going to sit around and wait forever." Despite the return of her tender despair in the cab, at the airport, their parting a final clutching goodbye, she didn't take back the things she'd said and offered no assurances. Were they done? Was it over? He didn't know.

When Poppy's next letter arrived, he didn't open it for a day, afraid of what it might say. *I'm sorry, Joe. It wasn't how I wanted our last morning to go. I just hate being without you. Hate the thought of you in harm's way. It scares me, now more than ever, and I know I'll feel this way for some time. If I'm angry, I'm angry at the world for giving you such a terrible bargain: prove yourself and we'll let you be human. I know who you are, Josiah Chang. You have nothing to prove to me.*

He was heartened. And yet, for all her conviction, there was still no clarity, no assurance. Now he understood, as he hadn't quite understood before, that so long as he was away, her letters would always have, to a greater or lesser degree, form. She would never hurt him expressly; there would always be kindness, politeness, decorum. No matter what any letter said, there was simply no proof, no promise of anything, until he came back whole.

SHORTLY AFTER ARRIVING AT CAMP SHILO, JOSIAH SAW A NEW RE-cruit who brought him back to childhood. Specifically, the day he arrived at yet another isolated logging camp, this one somewhere north of Williams Lake, where he came across a pair of old spar poles that people now climbed for fun, and he decided to get some exercise. But no sooner had he sat down to strap on some gaffs than a voice said, "You can't be here."

Josiah didn't look up, but from the corners of his eyes he saw a face-less gray mass of boys. Usually, the only way to settle these kinds of scores, especially in a new place, was to fight, but before he knew what to do, another voice interceded: "Who says?"

The second voice belonged to a Carrier boy in a straight-brim hat, his hair center-parted. Without a word, he strapped on the rusty heel spikes Josiah had meant to put on himself, then buckled into a safety belt.

"Race ya," he said to the other boy, and the other boy sneered gleefully.

The Carrier boy took off his hat and set it down gingerly. Then he threw a length of rope around one of the poles before tying the loose end to a D ring on his belt. Soon both he and the other boy were stand-ing at the ready, one leg raised. By this point, all the boys, including Josiah, had gathered around, buzzing with excitement.

When someone yelled "Go!" both boys pulled on their ropes and began to climb. With a lashing rhythm, they kept tossing their ropes and stabbing their gaffs and spidering upward. Soon they were twenty, thirty, forty feet in the air. The Carrier boy rose smoothly, on a ladder of his own making, but the other boy had a hitch in his step, and a small space opened between them. Some of the boys yelled encouragement, profanely—"Come on, Tom, for fuck's sake!"—but Josiah watched in awed silence. At some point he realized what he was feeling was envy. Josiah was a good climber, but the Carrier boy was born to be a high rigger.

At the top of each eighty-foot pole was a cowbell. The Carrier boy didn't even lunge, just clanged the bell with a casual flip of his rope. Then he leaned back on his gaffs, crowned by the sun, and flashed Josiah a shit-eating grin—the very same grin he was flashing now on the flatlands of Manitoba. Josiah hadn't seen Syd Antoine in over a decade, but they recognized each other instantly.

"Damn, you already got your wings," Syd Antoine said, after a long embrace.

"Beat you," Josiah said. "For once."

Now that Syd was here, Josiah finally believed that Airborne was the best of the best.

AS WINTER GAVE WAY TO SPRING, RUMORS ABOUNDED. THAT THOSE trained at Fort Benning would be the first to embark. That they were going to jump into China or Burma, Denmark or Norway. "I don't care if it's the Japs or the Krauts," Van den Berg said. "Let's get this fucking show on the road." Then word finally came down in July that six hundred members of the 1st Canadian Parachute Battalion were headed for England.

"So this is it," Poppy said when he called.

The connection was bad, her voice tinny and hollow, as if she were speaking from the other end of a very long funnel. They hadn't talked in some time, and it had been a relief to avoid the awkwardness of the telephone. But here they were again.

"Yes," he replied.

"When are you leaving?"

They had been granted embarkation leave, but only for a few days. Hard as he tried, he couldn't find a way to Vancouver and back in time. Only those who happened to live nearby would get to go home, briefly. Everyone else was going to Winnipeg for one last hurrah. But he had no interest in Winnipeg.

"Day after tomorrow," he lied.

"Oh god, Joe."

The line went still, and they listened to the sound of the other's breathing.

"Wait for me, Poppy."

For a moment, there was no answer. Then, defiantly, she said, "I'll be here. Send me a postcard from Berlin."

THEY LEFT CAMP SHILO A FEW DAYS LATER AT MIDNIGHT. ONCE THEY were past Montreal, Josiah was farther east than he had ever been, in places like Sherbrooke, Mégantic, St. John, and Moncton. Somewhere in Nova Scotia, crates full of boiled lobsters were brought on board, courtesy of local lobstermen, and the men had a riotously good time wagging those claws and sucking out that sweet, succulent meat and flinging the shells right out the train windows.

When they arrived in Halifax, they proceeded directly from the station to the harbor, where the RMS *Queen Elizabeth*, an ocean liner turned troopship, awaited them at Pier 21. The whole place was teeming with soldiers, as far as the eye could see, yet the air was subdued, almost hushed, and every man walked the gangplank with a feeling of solemnity, for the odds were that a great many were seeing their country for the last time.

23

AFTER CROSSING THE GANGPLANK, THEY FOLLOWED A MEMBER OF the Army Service Corps down a series of dank corridors and stairwells into the bowels of the *Queen Elizabeth*, until they arrived at a strange-looking room with a giant white-tiled depression in the middle.

"It's the fucking pool," Van den Berg said.

So it was, only now the whole room, including the pool itself, was filled with metal-framed canvas bunks, stacked three high.

Syd Antoine climbed down into the pool and made himself at home, claiming a bunk, closing his eyes, and lacing his fingers over his chest, but Van den Berg was having none of it. When an officer happened past, Van den Berg said, "Sir, it's too crowded down here. We need a proper cabin."

The officer took him in with quiet loathing. "The top three decks are taking turns sleeping outside. I can arrange for you to be up there."

Van den Berg shut up right quick.

• • •

THE *QUEEN ELIZABETH* WAS COLOSSAL, ITS MOTIONS ALMOST PLANE-
tary, but so many men had been crammed on board that movement
had to be restricted and everything done in shifts, including eating
and sleeping. In a twist, enlisted men took their meals in the first class
dining room, since it was largest. The *Queen Elizabeth* hadn't even been
outfitted before it was commandeered for war, but in the stately columns of the dining room and the volume of space overhead, one still
got a nascent sense of luxury.

"So this is how the other half lives," Syd Antoine said.

"Which half?" Van den Berg asked, grim-faced. "Have you seen the
latrines?"

This was a central problem of the voyage: how to dispose of so
much waste. Hygiene in general was suspect. They had water for only
two hours a day.

"Food's decent, though," Syd Antoine said, looking at his plate of
beefsteak with boiled onions and potatoes.

"Problem's on the other end, mate," Van den Berg said.

At that moment, the ship tremored with a muffled boom. The whole
room looked up.

"Gun drill," Heikkinen said, in that knowing way of his. "Nothing
to worry about."

Van den Berg scoffed. He had gone up on deck and seen their one
and only escort, a destroyer, peeling away in a lonely arc and heading
back to Halifax.

"No escort?" Josiah asked, surprised. He knew what kind of
gauntlet the Atlantic was for cargo ships. One in four didn't make it
through.

"Ol' Lizzie here is too fast for a convoy," Heikkinen said. "She can
outrun anything in the ocean."

"Doesn't mean we're not a big fat target," Van den Berg said. Apparently Hitler himself had offered a bounty to any U-boat captain who could sink either of the Cunard Queens, the *Queen Elizabeth* or the *Queen Mary*. "Divide a quarter million by fifteen thousand. Then you'll know how much your life is worth."

But for all the talk of danger, the crossing was uneventful. The weather was a lamb, and save for the ship's occasional zigging and zagging, there was no sign of submarines. When it came time for air, Josiah would go up on deck, which thronged with men. The ocean made him feel tiny, like nothing, and he wondered if with every passing mile he was becoming similarly insignificant to Poppy. But no sooner did he have the thought than he checked himself and resolved not to wallow in cynicism or self-pity. Whatever else could be said of her, she hadn't abandoned him, not like Heikkinen's girl had. Poppy still wrote and professed love, and so long as she did, he had every reason to soldier on.

For four days, he saw nothing but the steel-blue waters of the North Atlantic, touching sky in every direction. Then, on the fifth, he looked out and saw land.

THE *QUEEN ELIZABETH* SAILED THROUGH THE FIRTH OF CLYDE TO Greenock, Scotland, which rose straight out of the sea, up into lush green hills. For fear of attack, the ship didn't dock; instead, she kept her engines running as men were lowered into boats and brought ashore. It took two days for fifteen thousand men to disembark.

When Josiah finally came up on deck, he saw battleships, so many battleships, there on the deep-blue waters of the Clyde, the entire Home Fleet, it seemed, which gave him a fearsome premonition of all that was to come. Then he heard a clamor, an endless salvo, that gave him déjà vu. He listened harder. Sure enough, from up and down the Clyde came the unmistakable din of riveting, and for a beautiful instant, he was home.

FROM GREENOCK, THEY TOOK THE TRAIN TO RAF RINGWAY NEAR Manchester for conversion training. The British didn't have C-47s, just old converted bombers like the Albemarle and the Whitley, so the Canadians had to learn how to jump the British way, through a hatch in the floor where the belly turret had been. "What the hell?" Van den Berg asked, indignantly. They had their wings, their maroon berets, their American jump boots. Why did they have to start all over? Then they learned the British didn't jump with a backup chute, which knocked them down a peg. "No room for a backup when you're going through the hatch," one of their British instructors explained. "Besides, we drop much lower than the Yanks. No time for a backup."

They started by jumping through a hole in a wooden platform a few feet off the ground. Sat with their legs dangling and pushed off with both hands, like a child slipping into a pool. The key was to make sure your parachute cleared the edge. Otherwise, you would flip forward and smash your face on the other side. More than one man got bloodied. A few broke their noses.

Then they were taken a few miles west to Tatton Park for practice jumps, only the British didn't use jump towers. Instead, they used rickety wooden gondolas suspended from barrage balloons. The men rolled up in lorries to a field full of pudgy zeppelins tethered by steel cables.

"Look, it's the bloody Macy's Day Parade," one man said.

"Jesus, haven't these guys heard of the *Hindenburg?*" asked another.

They went up in groups of eight. Josiah was in the same group as Simmonds, a sallow-looking man with a twitchy little mustache who was always first to get airsick. As the cables let out, the gondola swayed, and Simmonds slowly turned pale until he threw up right through the hatch. The men took the piss out of him, but their British instructor was patient. "You'll be fine. Happens to the best of us," he said. America had millions of men to spare, but England had none and treated them accordingly.

Unlike Simmonds, Josiah was enjoying the ride, the strange sense of levitation, so smooth compared to a plane. From here, he could see the whole estate: the mansion, the beautifully manicured gardens, and the green fields dotted with lakes, and he thought of young Poppy in that hot-air balloon, having the time of her life.

Each man jumped from the gondola twice, then five times from a plane, just like at Fort Benning, only a Whitley was nothing like a C-47. There was only room for ten, and they had to sit on the floor, as if curled in a sewer pipe. And when they fell through the hatch, there was no prop blast to blow their chutes out, which gave them another endless second to wonder if their chutes would open. Those who couldn't bring themselves to jump got sent back to regular infantry, and Josiah was glad. A chain was only as strong as its weakest link.

IN AUGUST, AFTER EARNING THEIR BRITISH WINGS, THEY SETTLED into Carter Barracks at Camp Bulford in Wiltshire, some eighty miles west of London. Carter Barracks had sprung up during the war, row upon row of Nissen huts north of the Droveway—Tin Town, the men called it. This would be home for a long time.

Every day except Sunday began with a five-mile reveille run across the beautiful desolation of Salisbury Plain, sometimes out to the ruins of Stonehenge, followed by a longer run in the afternoon. In between, they continued to ready themselves for war, training in everything from wireless to demolitions. They were now attached to the 3rd Parachute Brigade of the 6th Airborne Division of the British Army, under the command of Brigadier James Hill, a dashing and elegant warrior eager to get the men up to standard. The brigadier had jumped in North Africa with the famed Red Devils and brooked no nonsense. The men admired the hell out of him.

A letter from Poppy arrived in September, after his own had made the long voyage back and disclosed his new whereabouts. She told him that work in the yard had slowed, now that the Allies were winning the Battle of the Atlantic and losing fewer cargo ships. She also told him that Jimmy, her friend from the yard, had been shot down over the Netherlands, his fate unknown, and Josiah tried not to see this as a dark omen. *I want the war to end*, she wrote, *but I hope the invasion never comes.* Josiah knew this was her way of saying she loved him, but he couldn't have felt more differently. He was tired of waiting. He had already been away too long. He was desperate for the great invasion to begin. To fight this war and get back to her.

24

TIME BEGAN TO REPEAT ITSELF.

In October, after three months in England, the battalion was given ten days leave, and Josiah made his first trip to London, with Heikki- nen, Van den Berg, and Syd Antoine. There was a time when the larg- est city in the world would have baffled him, but he had worked his way up from Vancouver, Toronto, and Montreal. At one point as they wandered the city, from one famous sight to the next, places that had always existed vaguely yet talismanically in his mind—Buckingham Palace, Piccadilly Circus—Josiah slipped off to Limehouse in East London, where the Chinese had set root. The area was badly damaged, but some shops remained in all that rubble, persistent as weeds, and lo and behold, he found what he was looking for. Back at Carter Barracks, he stole a moment alone behind the Nissen hut and set the delicate paper aflame, and it burned the way he remembered such paper burn- ing, so diaphanously as to take wing. How had it already been a year since he did the same at Champlain Barracks? Two since his father had died?

And then, just like that, it was Christmas again, turkey and all the trimmings, plus fat cigars, and once more, the officers served the enlisted men, only this time it was a gawky beanpole named Smitty who got to be lieutenant colonel for a day. How had it already been a year since Christmas at Longueuil? How did time move so quickly and so slowly at once, and how much more time would it take?

THE LONG-AWAITED OFFENSIVE DID NOT COME BEFORE THE weather turned, which meant another season of waiting. In the meantime, they continued to train. A battle drill course at Hardwick Hall in the Midlands. A street fighting course in the bombed-out lanes of Southampton. In his letters, Josiah was candid about the dangers—the tear gas, the thunderflash grenades, the live bullets zipping overhead as they crawled under barbed wire—but there was one thing he didn't tell her. The one time a man's departure left him shaken.

On one of their jumps, Josiah had come out smoothly in his British X-type parachute, much better all around than the American T-5, when he saw a man plummeting through the air, his parachute streaming above him like a flame. His lines were tangled, and his chute wouldn't open. For a few eternal seconds, the man struggled, trying to turn his body and untwist the lines. Then, with a couple hundred feet to go, he gave up. Just stilled himself. That was the most harrowing part, the resignation. An instant later, the ground exploded.

By the time they got back to camp, members of the Women's Auxiliary Air Force, who packed the chutes, were already inconsolable. Afterward, Brigadier Hill came to address the men, his sharp cheeks more drawn than usual. "I know this comes as a terrible shock," he said in his nasally, aristocratic voice. "We are a brotherhood, and today we lost a brother. But you mustn't lose courage. You must be stout of heart. For today is but a shadow of all that is to come."

• • •

LIVING IN A NISSEN HUT WAS LIKE LIVING IN A SUBWAY TUNNEL. Josiah shared his with twenty-three others, who slept in beds on either side of the hut, Josiah next to the skinny coke-burning stove, which kept the hut surprisingly warm. Whenever rain fell, as it often did that winter, the whole hut rumbled with a somber music that Josiah would hear for the rest of his life.

When they weren't training from dawn till dusk and sometimes even at night, in pure darkness, they were whiling away the hours in that Nissen hut. Each man had his own way of killing time—Heikkinen by reading, Van den Berg by yammering, Syd Antoine by closing his eyes—but every man pored over letters, there in the quiet sanctum of his bed. A letter was a tether to the world, a reminder that they had once been men, and before that, boys, held in the bosom of life before they became mere fighting animals.

The frequency of his letters—and Poppy's—had slowed. He wanted to blame it on the long transatlantic voyage, but of course it wasn't that. They had simply reached that stage of a journey when one is less talkative, less inquisitive, than one is at the outset. Nonetheless, they continued to write, and one quiet Sunday, when most of the men were scattered on leave, Josiah received a letter from Poppy. *Hard to believe, but I haven't seen you for a year now*, the letter began, and only then did Josiah realize how much he had lost track of time. From the distance of a year, it was hard to recall the pain and confusion of the last time they saw each other. It wasn't just that time had passed and sanded the edges; rather, time itself was a kind of achievement. Simply by writing, continuing to write, however dully and laggingly over a year, devotion had become a habit, or maybe habit a devotion. On this occasion, Poppy described an unexpected snowstorm in January, this after a relatively mild winter. She also gave him an update on

Queenie, how she was now licking her joints and limping with what seemed like arthritis, and he fell asleep that night dreaming of the old girl, for the first time in a long time.

THEY ALSO KILLED TIME BY PLAYING CARDS. ONE NIGHT, JOSIAH was playing five-card stud with some of the men, including Walker, a man with blue cheeks and a loose, shifty grin. As the company's resident smuggler, Walker could get you whatever couldn't be had at the Army & Navy Stores in Bulford. Booze, smokes, smut. Anything for a price. That night, as usual, Walker was winning, in a way that always made Van den Berg bristle. More than once, after losing his shirt, Van den Berg had said, "That guy's fucking cheating, I swear."

On this night, Josiah was nursing a pretty hand and anxiously waiting to throw down his card when Van den Berg leapt up from the edge of the bed, lunged across the footlocker that served as their table, and closed a fist around Walker's collar. "I saw that, you bastard!"

"Whoa! Whoa! Whoa!" Heikkinen said, leaping in to separate the two men and knocking over a lamp in the process. Heikkinen held back Van den Berg as Syd Antoine held back Walker, grinning impishly. In the spilled light, they made for a tense tableau.

"Check his sleeves! I saw him!" Van den Berg said, but Syd Antoine refused. Instead, Walker held up his hands in the way of the innocent. Then, very showily, in the manner of a magician, he pulled down one sleeve and then the other to prove there was nothing.

"I saw you," Van den Berg snarled, unconvinced. "You can't fool me."

The game ended, and the lights went out, and Josiah found himself staring again at an arc of corrugated tin and knew that what had caused tempers to flare was not poker so much as the endless waiting. It was starting to wear, to make them surly. They'd been cooped up too long. They needed spring to come, and fast.

• • •

UNDER BRIGADIER HILL, THE MEN CONTINUED TO MARCH. AT LEAST three marches of fifteen miles or more each month, up to a hundred miles in full kit.

On one such march, a relatively modest fifty-mile road march, the men set off at dusk, in the gloaming, a fault of lava running along the horizon.

"Just like Fort Benning," Van den Berg grumbled, and Josiah recalled being roused in the night and marching behind the master sergeant in the sidecar of his Harley-Davidson. In Georgia, they had felt the need to prove themselves to the Yanks; here, they felt the need to prove themselves to the Brits. The Canadians were outsiders in the 3rd Brigade and couldn't let the British 8th and 9th Battalions get the best of them.

So they marched on into the night. At first, they marched in formation, talking a little. In time, each man found his own pace, and suffered alone. For hours, Josiah trudged in solitude, accompanied only by the crunching of his own steps and the silver glint of his breath. That and thoughts of Poppy, ever his compass, his polestar.

As day broke, so, too, did the weather. It started as a few tinny drops on his helmet. Then, with a crack, the sky burst open and rain came down in torrents, sluicing down his back and all the way into his boots, until he was soaked to the bone, the wind so strong he staggered. Compared to the Cariboo, winter in England was balmy. Rain and fog, but very little snow, just the occasional ornamental dusting. But this was different. All that wet wool was like being wrapped in a compress. There was no escaping the cold; it stuck to you.

For the last twenty miles, all he could really see was the beaded curtain dripping from the brim of his helmet. When his mind began to lose touch, he saw Poppy on the other side of that curtain, her blue eyes beckoning, and all he had to do was step through . . .

By the time he reached camp in hour seventeen, he was shaking uncontrollably. As soon as he saw the brigadier, who stood in the rain and marked his return with a nod, he stumbled to the Nissen hut and threw off all his wet clothes and put on blessedly dry ones, as much wool as he could muster. Still shaking, he fed the stove more coke before piling under the covers.

Over the next few hours, men who had not been sent to the infirmary returned to the hut and did the same, threw off their clothes and leapt under the covers, until the whole room was febrile with misery.

Truly, spring could not come fast enough.

25

WHEN THE WHOLE PLAIN BEGAN TO BLOSSOM WITH LITTLE YELLOW cups of cowslip, the entire 3rd Brigade began to rehearse mass drops. The goal was to put as many men in as little space as possible, in as little time as possible, then vanish like ghosts from the drop zone. Each plane blew out a trail of dandelion seeds, the whole sky seeded at once.

As time passed, Josiah had to admit that they were becoming better soldiers, better *fellow* soldiers, learning to think and act as one. That a spirit, a confidence, was growing. That all that time had counted for something.

Toward the end of May, the brigade was inspected by none other than the King himself, looking dashing in his Sam Browne belt, accompanied by the Queen, a long fur stole draped over one shoulder, and a shy-looking Princess Elizabeth in a lampshade hat and a Peter Pan collar. In honor of the royal family, there were demonstrations of every kind, including a parachute drop, but no one in Josiah's brigade was allowed to jump. That's when he knew the hour was finally at hand.

• • •

AT THE END OF MAY, THEY WERE ORDERED TO LEAVE IN TWO HOURS
with only their essentials. Josiah grabbed his gear and his rifle and left
everything else: Poppy's letters, the Lena Horne LP, his brown American jump boots. Then they set off into the night in the backs of
three-ton lorries.

"Traveling under the cover of dark," Heikkinen said. "This must
be it."

"'Bout fucking time," Van den Berg said.

"Which way are we headed?" Syd Antoine asked.

As usual, Simmonds had been made to sit next to the tailgate in
case he got sick. He lifted one of the canvas flaps, letting in a slash of
moonlight.

"North, I think."

They didn't go far, maybe fifty miles, before the fat tires of the lorry
crackled to a stop and they hopped out to find themselves in yet another
camp. After lugging their gear to a field of bell tents, blowing with an
alien wind, they were greeted by a regimental sergeant major with a
handlebar mustache from the last century.

"You are now in a security transit camp," the regimental sergeant
major said. "The things you will hear are vital to the fate of Europe and
must not be shared with anyone. Under no circumstances is anyone to
leave this camp. Anyone who steps beyond that barbed wire"—he
pointed to a single filament glinting in the distance—"will be summarily
shot. I advise you not to go anywhere near it."

OVER THE NEXT FEW DAYS, THEY SAT IN BRIEFING ROOMS AS OFFI-
cers of the highest rank detailed the great invasion of Europe. The
invasion force would take a longer route to the beaches of Normandy,
not Calais, for the element of surprise. The task of the 6th Airborne

Division was to hold the invasion's left flank so the British 3rd Infantry Division could move out from the beachhead. The Canadians would operate in the area between the Orne and the Dives rivers. C Company was tasked with blowing up a bridge and taking out a gun emplacement near the village of Varaville before meeting up at the Le Mesnil crossroads.

Josiah studied the maps, photographs, and dioramas, trying to commit every last detail to memory. It wasn't enough to know your own mission; everyone had to know everyone else's. For if the next man, the next section, the next platoon did not arrive, their mission became yours.

When they weren't being briefed or conducting final maneuvers, they were knocking around a football or lounging around the bell tents. Impossible not to feel the electric charge in the air, the brash hopefulness of June. Men were loose and in high spirits. They were young and hardy and spoiling for a fight.

WHEN THE ORDERS FINALLY CAME DOWN, THE MEN CHEERED lustily, suddenly keyed up. But every man also felt a quiet, a stillness, in the eye of all that excitement. With ritual purpose, they blackened their buttons, cleaned and oiled their weapons, and went to get their parachutes fitted one last time. They also wrote last letters. Writing his, Josiah counted the months: ten since leaving Halifax, sixteen since he last saw Poppy, twenty since he first left Vancouver.

Dear Poppy,

This is my last night in England. By the time you get this, I'll be somewhere in France. This is the day I've been waiting for, and I'm ready. I know you'll worry, but try not to. We all know our jobs, and I'm not afraid.

Today we had to fill out forms for contacting next of kin. I didn't have to, since I have no family. It reminded me why I'm here, why I'm fighting. To make you my flesh and blood.

For almost two years, the road has only led away from you. Today, the road begins to turn back, and every day hereafter is one step closer to seeing you again.

> *Love,*
>
> *Joe*

That evening in the bell tent, the air still syrupy with light, Josiah turned to Syd Antoine, sitting on the edge of his folding cot, and held out a piece of paper. "Here's Poppy's address. She isn't next of kin, so they won't—"

"You're gonna make it, Joe," Syd said, laying a hand on his shoulder.

"Still. Better take it."

Syd took the piece of paper and gave it a long look. "You know why the French called us 'Porteur'? Carrier? Because our widows used to carry the ashes of their husbands on their backs while they mourned."

Josiah knew Syd was thinking of his own girl. "You're gonna make it, too, Syd."

Syd Antoine considered, then pulled out his writing wallet. "Better give you an address, too. Just in case."

THAT NIGHT, JOSIAH FELL ASLEEP QUICKLY AND WOKE UP ONLY once, briefly, to the sound of the tent rippling. By the time the bugle sounded, though, the tent was snapping wildly. Outside, storm clouds filled the sky, dark and unforgiving, like an angry god ready to mete out punishment.

"Not looking good," Syd Antoine said.

They waited anxiously all morning. Prepared for the fight as if nothing were different, which only succeeded in making time crawl. By noon, the invasion was called off.

For the rest of the day, the mood was downcast. At dinner, taken at long wooden tables in a much larger tent, men picked at their food and said little. It was hard to escape the feeling that fate had dealt them a blow.

"There's a reason there's no painting of the second-to-last supper," Simmonds remarked.

"Shut up and eat," Van den Berg said. "You won't be puking tonight."

That night, Josiah slept poorly. The letter he had written to Poppy was already untrue, and he wondered how else the universe might thwart him. Maybe all of fate had shifted by a day, and the bullet that was going to miss him was now coming his way.

THE NEXT DAY, THE INVASION WAS BACK ON. THEY WOULDN'T LEAVE until midnight, under the cover of dark, so they had plenty of time to get ready. Some men packed their weapons in their leg kit bags; others decided to carry their weapons on them. Then there were those who couldn't decide, who went back and forth. They had too much time to think.

That night at dinner, the men were again in high spirits, putting down greasy platefuls of mutton and pork, knowing it would be their last square meal for a while. Van den Berg ate like a man possessed, but Gordon, Peavy, and Arceneaux, three young Turks in their section, were in particularly fine form, helping themselves to thirds. The only one who didn't eat was Simmonds, who traded his dinner for cigarettes.

"Now you're thinking," Van den Berg said.

UNDER A BRUISED AND DARKENING SKY, THE MEN PARADED ONE last time. Then they were driven to Down Ampney, the back of each lorry full of silent contemplation. At the airfield, they strapped on their parachutes and gathered in the staging area, smoking and talking and laughing, or lying down and napping. At one point, a man in vestments pulled up in a jeep, and a good many men sought him out. The need to feel seen, to feel watched and loved—some men called that God. For Josiah, however, the watcher was someone else, and it was to that someone else he prayed.

The night was dark and sickly sweet with gasoline and glycol. Josiah shook hands with their RAF pilot, then led his stick across the tarmac to the stuttering chop of propellers. When he reached the plane, he ducked underneath and passed his leg kit bag to the jumpmaster before hoisting himself through the entrance hatch. Then he clambered to the back of the plane. First man in, last man out.

The Albemarle was soon crammed and the entrance hatch closed from below, and the already darkened fuselage went darker still. Lighters flared and the plane filled with smoke, and a voice full of bravado said, "Next stop, motherfucking France."

With a lurch, the Albemarle began to move and take its place in the queue, one that stretched across aerodromes all over England. As engines roared by the thousands, Josiah could feel the tempest gathering. C Company would be the first Canadian company in—the very tip of the spear—so it wasn't long before their plane began to hurtle. As they jostled in the dark, Josiah felt the thrumming presence of the men before him, including Simmonds, Heikkinen, Van den Berg, and Syd Antoine. They were all bound for mystery, for one great saga of the unknown. Some were down to their very last moments of love, joy, pain, sorrow, and memory, beyond which lay neither redemption nor reunion nor yet immortality, only cold, black nullity. Which was why he had to live. Live and get back to her.

Poppy. Penelope. Wait for me.

1

AFTER NORMANDY, THE MEN WERE GIVEN TEN DAYS LEAVE. SOME
went to stay with family, others with strangers through the country's
billeting system. The luckiest went to see a girl they had met before the
great invasion. Josiah went back to Camp Bulford, prepared to ride out
his ten days in quiet solitude. It was strange, returning to the barracks.
The same streets, the same huts, unchanged except for men who looked
at him with sneaking reverence. There were now only two kinds of men
in the world, those who had been to the fight and those who had not,
and walking through the camp, he felt like a specter of death in a garden of innocence. Of the five hundred and forty-one Canadians who had
set off for Normandy, fewer than two hundred had returned. When he
entered the corrugated tunnel of his Nissen hut, he was greeted by
empty beds and gave a long moment to those who were gone.

THEN A SHOCK. ON HIS WAY TO THE MESS, HE SAW WHAT COULD
only be a ghost: Van den Berg, standing right there in the middle of the
road with his hound dog face and babyish teeth. Josiah was vaguely

terrified as the figure approached, grinning like a madman, then astonished when Van den Berg picked him up, raucously.

"You're alive?" Josiah asked, still unsure.

"What does it look like?" Van den Berg laughed.

In the mess, over a meal of coffee, Spam, and bread fried in lard, the big fella recounted his Normandy campaign, such as it was: landing in a tree, trying to climb down, falling thirty feet, and breaking his leg. Nothing he could do but shoot himself full of morphine and wait. At one point, he had to drag himself behind a hedgerow to dodge a German patrol. Took two days for help to arrive, by which point there was nothing left to stanch the pain.

"Got sent to a hospital in Sheffield. I tell you, those nurses couldn't wait to undress me!"

"Was O'Connor there?"

"Who?"

Josiah told him about the battle in Bréville, how O'Connor had been his No. 2 on a Vickers and how they had lost twenty men that day. A mix of pain and envy played across Van den Berg's face.

"What happened to Heikkinen?" Van den Berg asked.

"I was going to ask you."

"You didn't see him at all?"

Josiah shook his head.

"Shit," Van den Berg muttered.

That night, there was no dessert with supper. It made Van den Berg wonder what Josiah was doing in Tin Town, eating army slop, when he was supposed to be on leave.

"I've got some letters to write."

Van den Berg rolled his eyes. "Let me guess, you miss your girl. Listen, you're not going to get through this war by moping around. Let's go to London. You can write bloody letters from London if you want."

Josiah had no great desire to see London again, but the sight of Van den Berg had lifted his spirits—and made him feel guilty. From the first, he had hardened himself to any man's leaving, so he hadn't mourned Van den Berg, not as much as he should have. And Van den Berg was right: his stomach was ready, positively howling, for something other than Spam.

THEY TOOK THE TRAIN FROM THE DEPOT IN BULFORD TO WATERLOO Station, then wandered around South Bank. At first, Josiah felt the chaotic excitement of London. Of all the cities he had seen, London was by far the most sprawling and magnificent, all the damage notwithstanding. But as they walked around, the normalcy and even gaiety of London began to seem sinister. At that very moment, the Allies were clearing the channel ports of France and Belgium, and somewhere, everywhere, men were deep in the fight. How could you live and be happy while others were out there killing and being killed?

Josiah's solution was to drink, or rather, to keep up with Van den Berg as he stopped in at every available pub. In London as elsewhere, people bought them drinks, especially since Van den Berg made no bones about jumping on D-Day. "I only made it to D plus two, but this guy was there for three months," Van den Berg kept repeating, with what sounded like growing bitterness. Josiah hated using the war as a gambit, a token for drinks. It was one thing to talk to Van den Berg or tell Poppy about what he'd seen and done, another to regale total strangers. Yet he recognized in the eyes of their listeners, these blitzed and battered Londoners, a fury and a need for solace, so he tried to indulge them a little, which required ever more drink.

They went all afternoon and into the evening, until the only pubs open were those with two sets of doors to keep light from spilling. By the time they found themselves standing across from two members of the Auxiliary Territorial Service, the room was already pitching wildly. Both women were dressed in olive-green service jackets and skirts, as well as matching cloth caps, puckered on top like a chef's hat. As Van den Berg went into his routine, delivered with almost comic facility, the woman across from Josiah stared at him with dark intensity. Her name was Phoebe, and she was tall, possibly taller than him, and handsome, almost mannish, with skin so tightly drawn that the apples of her cheeks shone. At first, Josiah didn't think much of her spidery length, her austere gaze, but then they began to talk, just the two of them, shouting over the din, and her hot breath against his ear was electric. When she said she had helped build Churchill tanks, he said he had helped build cargo ships. "So you were saving us long before Normandy," she said, putting a hand on his arm. By the time they looked up from their own little world, Van den Berg and the other woman were gone.

Josiah and Phoebe left, too. The blackout gave her a perfect reason to take him by the arm, and together they lurched through the dark. When they came to a park surrounded by wrought-iron bars, they took a seat on a bench, to the fecund smell of vegetation. There in the dark, they felt unseen, as if the blackout was meant to give refuge to lovers. Indeed, the park seemed ghostly with the sounds of rustling and soft moaning. Phoebe sat close, playing with the hair at the nape of his neck, her breathing shallow. "You're a pretty man," she said, which seemed an odd but indelible way of putting it.

When they started to kiss, Phoebe with a smile across her lips, Josiah felt strangely disembodied, as if he weren't really there. As if nothing were real. But this woman *was* real. Flesh and blood in the here and now. It was Poppy, an ocean away, who was now the abstraction. Now, at last, he finally understood what Poppy had meant that day in MacKay Park. The war was going to be long and hard, and it was okay to have a little fun. As long as he was safe. As long as he went back to her. It wasn't about being weak; it was about avoiding needless guilt and suffering. She wasn't being critical; she was being clear-eyed. She was giving him a gift.

He thought he and Phoebe were going to lie down in the cool grass until she said she had a key to a friend's flat. As they made their way there, Josiah had the pleasant sensation of falling, like the first seconds of a jump, when all you can do is surrender. After they entered a villa with columns flanking the entrance, Josiah watched her long, reedy calves climb a flight of stairs and pictured her bony sternum, her small, high breasts, so unlike Poppy and all the more alluring for the difference. And yet, the two women seemed to blur in his mind: Phoebe, Poppy, Phoebe, Poppy.

On the second floor, she produced a skeleton key and entered the flat but didn't turn on any lights. Instead, she took off her cap, undid her hair, and pushed him against the door. Her mouth was wet and greedy, and he felt himself rousing, coming back to life. He wanted this, needed this, *deserved* this. He had walked through the valley of the shadow of death.

But when she reached down, he felt scalded and he recoiled. She laughed, thinking this part of the game, but when he took her by the shoulders to separate them, she stared, incredulous.

"What the hell is wrong with you?"

"I'm—in love with someone."

"So?" she asked caustically.

When she understood the night was over, her dark intensity returned. "Do you know what I was willing to do? With *you*?"

Josiah stumbled back down the stairs. Outside, the world seemed unusually sharp, as on a cold winter's night, and he shook to think how close he had come to throwing it all away. To marring his own devotion, which was all he really had. He had been right, right all along. It mattered whether or not they were steadfast, and he resolved to be just that. True.

2

HE WROTE TO SAY HE HAD MADE IT BACK FROM FRANCE. IN HER next letter, Poppy seemed high, almost manic. *I knew you'd make it, Joe, I just knew it!* She wasn't just overjoyed but sanguine, as if having survived one campaign he would surely survive the rest. She had been following the battalion in the papers—strange to think their exploits on the ground were being reported a world away—and apparently they were earning quite the reputation. *They say your battalion has never failed to meet an objective.* He supposed this was true, but it didn't feel that way. The battalion was spent. Had to be refitted, reorganized, and brought up to strength. While he was in France, others had been training in England. Now the old and the new had to be molded into one, and this required more route marches, more mock assaults, and above all, more jumps. Now they were dropped over rivers, which meant their next jump would likely be over the Rhine.

TIME CONTINUED TO REPEAT ITSELF.

They were back to reveille runs across the plain as winter encroached.

Back to strict discipline, doing up top buttons and everything at the double. In October, Josiah found himself back behind the Nissen hut, staring into flames as joss paper blackened and crimpled, wondering how yet another year had passed.

Then, in December, as Christmas came hurtling back like a comet, word came down that Christmas leave was canceled. They had to be ready to ship out on six hours' notice, and the only one who was happy was Van den Berg. But a drop on the Rhine seemed premature, especially in winter. Where were they headed? No one knew. Confusion reigned.

They took Christmas dinner early. As always, the enlisted men were served by the officers, and the youngest man got to be commanding officer for a day, but the spirit of Saturnalia had lost its luster. This time last year, Josiah was sure he would be home by now, but the great invasion of Europe was seven months in, with no end in sight, and it scared him to think he might still be here next Christmas, and the one after that . . .

On Christmas Eve, they took the train from Bulford to Folkestone, a small town on the coast of Kent, across the Channel from Calais, where they entered another transit camp. Here, they expected to be fully briefed before sand tables, photographs, and table-size maps, as they had been before Normandy. Instead, they weren't briefed at all.

"How are we supposed to carry out a mission," Walker asked, "when we know sweet fuck all?"

On Christmas Day, orders came down to leave their parachutes and leg kit bags and to carry their gear in battle order, which set off waves of consternation. Not only was this not the Rhine, it wasn't even a jump. They were going in as regular infantry. "What the hell was all that training for, then?" Walker asked. Josiah wondered the same and felt a little spooked. If they were going in like this, then everyone was being thrown into the fight. Even Van den Berg was put off. He wanted to jump, to redeem himself. Only Syd Antoine seemed indifferent. Ready for anything.

Late that night, under the cover of dark, they were trucked from the transit camp to an embarkation point on the Channel. There, to the smell of brine and the lapping of waves against pilings, they shuffled down a wooden pier into a ferry turned troopship for an ordinary sea crossing. The iron hold reeked of vomit, which portended the long night to come: the pitching and rolling, the spattering stench, the susurrus of agony. Some men braved the floor and tried to sleep, but Josiah stayed awake, wrapped in a blanket, thinking a Channel crossing would be short. Instead, the voyage took all night, which only deepened the mystery of where it was they were going.

In the morning, as they came ashore, they couldn't see anything for the fog, an impenetrable miasma. Had to walk right up to read the signs for Ostend.

Belgium.

FROM THE DOCKS, THEY JUMPED RIGHT INTO AMERICAN TRUCKS and left in a long convoy, on roads packed with snow. Someone in Josiah's truck threw down a blanket for dice, and for a while the back of the truck was rollicking. Then the man got cold and took his blanket back. As Josiah sat to one side of the cargo box, trying to sleep, he could feel a whistle of air coming up from under the tarp and cutting right through him.

"Where do you think we're headed?" Simmonds asked, from his usual spot by the tailgate.

Just when the war had seemed poised for a Christmas hiatus, Hitler had launched a massive counteroffensive. His goal was to smash his way to Antwerp, in one last desperate attempt to push back the Western

Front. By all accounts, the Americans were taking it on the chin in the forests of Ardennes. The line had bent but not broken. If they were in Belgium, it could only mean one thing.

"We better be headed to the front," Van den Berg said.

"We're paratroopers. Lightly armed," one of the new men said. "How are we supposed to take on whole armored divisions?"

"By being the elite fucking soldiers we are," Van den Berg replied.

There was still a schism in the ranks between the old and the new, one that wouldn't go away until they were all battle born.

"That's right, we're elite," Walker said. "Should be saving us for the Rhine."

"Come on, we gotta help the Yanks," Van den Berg said.

"With what?" Walker asked. "Forget winter camouflage. We don't even have greatcoats. We're gonna freeze our balls off."

By the time the convoy came to a stop, the world was dark and the men chattering with cold. An unhappy prelude to all that was to come.

FOR THE NEXT FIVE DAYS, TO VAN DEN BERG'S DISMAY, THEY STAYED well behind the lines in the town of Rumes, billeting in an unheated school gymnasium. There was very little to eat but compo rations and very little to do but maintain weapons, clean new grenades, and wonder what the hell was going on.

Finally, on New Year's Eve, they were ordered to move out. A cheer went up, and they piled back into American trucks. By the time they were let out, the world was purple with dusk. They found themselves on the crest of a hill, looking down on the dark spill of Rochefort. The town had been overrun, then recaptured, but the Americans desperately needed to be spelled. The Canadians were ordered to man a perimeter in case the Germans tried to push through again.

They started down the hill, boots creaking on hard-packed snow.

The tips of their ears stung; their breaths came out in smoky plumes. As they entered the town, they passed haggard-looking American sentries, their eyes hollow. The town itself was dark and lifeless, under curfew, but signs of battle were everywhere: burned-out Shermans and Panzers, abandoned M-1s and Mausers, and bodies, so many bodies, just lying in the streets, shrouded by only a scrim of snow.

"Goddamn it," Van den Berg said. "We missed the fight."

WHEN THE BATTALION WAS REORGANIZED, JOSIAH WAS FINALLY made the No. 1 in a Bren gun group. His No. 2 was a new boot named Harrison, a small man with soft, round features and drowsy-looking eyes. His family had been United Empire Loyalists who had moved to Nova Scotia during the American Revolutionary War. At the turn of the century, his grandfather had played for the Halifax Eurekas, and in the twenties, his father for the Africville Sea-Sides. Josiah had never heard of the Colored Hockey League of the Maritimes.

The leader of the Bren gun group was Campbell, a lance corporal and another greenhorn. He had gone to university somewhere in Ontario, which was one reason why he and not Josiah was the officer, and this created a quiet tension over who was the natural leader.

They were ordered to man the road on the other side of Rochefort, so they walked through the lifeless town and beyond. A few hundred yards down the road, on a desolate stretch of ground, Harrison pulled out his shovel and cleared away a patch of snow. After bringing his shovel down a few times, he declared the ground frozen.

The lance corporal pulled out his machete and chopped at the ground ineffectually. Josiah and Harrison looked at each other, as if to say book learning only got you so far. Josiah took the shovel from Harrison, raised it above his head, and brought it down with a clang, sending a painful shiver through his arms. The ground was hard as rock, but some of it flinted away. Since Normandy, he had regained strength. Now he put it to use, slamming the shovel again and again and dreaming of D-Day, when his blade had sliced through earth with ease.

"Getting somewhere," Harrison said, impressed.

Campbell merely grunted his assent.

Josiah and Harrison took turns, until they were both sweating in the cold. At length the trench was dug, and they stayed there all night, watchfully, Josiah with his Bren gun mounted and pointed at the road. At midnight, the lance corporal glanced at his watch and said, "Happy New Year, gentlemen," and Josiah remembered the fireworks in Beuzeville, how they had presaged this night, and now this night was already here yet the war so very far from over.

3

FOR THE NEXT TEN DAYS, THEY SAT IN THAT TRENCH AND EYED THE
road, which stretched across a wide expanse of open ground to a narrow
defile between two hills. American trucks kept rumbling down the
road and disappearing into the gap, toward the frequent sound of artillery. Something was happening beyond those hills, but they couldn't
say what that something was. Every time there was movement in the
distance, Josiah readied the Bren, but it was only ever those same trucks
returning, minus men and munitions.

Those ten days were miserable. Those hours of sitting in the frozen
earth, their bodies slowly losing all sensation. Even on a good day,
their faces went numb. Then came the biting winds, the drifting
snow, the all-out blizzard conditions, the world a blinding tempest of
white. They didn't have rubber boots, so they took to wrapping
their boots in burlap to keep them from freezing. They also slit blankets for ponchos, socks for gloves, anything to stay warm, and still the
cold seeped in. Sometimes, Josiah would tense to keep himself from

shivering, which only made him shiver more, in violent spasms, as if he were possessed. At those moments, he dreamed of long route marches in the Georgian sun, of warm French rain and being eaten alive by mosquitoes.

Above all, he dreamed of his one and only summer with Poppy, including the times they had gone to Second Beach in Stanley Park and raced out to the wooden platform in the bay, Josiah in woolen trunks, Poppy in a skirted two-piece. When it came to swimming, Josiah had power but no form; Poppy had power *and* form, slicing through the waves like a blade, and they raced doggedly, never knowing who would win. Whenever she touched the platform first, she would beam, the sun beating down and spangling off the water . . .

Pain was the price of being with her, and he had always been willing to pay. But now, for the first time, he wasn't sure it was worth it. Even Poppy wasn't worth this. It was just the cold talking. The cold was crazy-making. Still, he felt a crack in his resolve, and it scared him.

HE LIVED FOR THE TIMES HE COULD GO INTO TOWN TO WARM UP. One time, he walked into company headquarters to find Van den Berg and Syd Antoine thawing out by the fire, a snapping blaze in a stone hearth that drew Josiah right in.

"What kind of army sends its troops out in winter without gear?" Van den Berg groused. The cold was getting to everyone, even Van den Berg.

"Gets a lot colder in the Cariboo, am I right?" Syd Antoine asked.

It was true, they had known worse, but never for so many hours on end while being so ill-equipped.

"If you think this is cold," Lieutenant Morrison said, eavesdropping from across the room, "try being a tail gunner in a bomber. At twenty thousand feet, it gets to fifty below. If you don't blink, your eyeballs will freeze."

Van den Berg was unmoved. "Look what we have to resort to," he said, raising his arms.

The khakis that had served them so well in Normandy made them easy targets out here. The gray of their blankets helped, but many like Van den Berg had covered themselves with white sheets they had scavenged.

As he sat by the fire, skin burning with a rush of blood, Josiah unwrapped and unlaced his boots, peeled off two pairs of socks, and inspected his feet. They powdered and rubbed their feet twice a day, but some men still lost toes to frostbite. Josiah's felt arthritic with cold, but at least none were black.

"What's there to eat?" Josiah asked.

"What do you think?" Van den Berg asked. "Root fucking vegetables."

"They're all right," Syd Antoine said.

With little to eat besides compo rations, men had taken to foraging in the cold earth, digging up turnips and potatoes, which the company cook had learned to whip up a dozen ways. Honestly, some warm turnips and potatoes sounded good.

"Might all be worth it if we were in the fight," Van den Berg muttered.

So that's what was eating him, the fact that they were being held back. More than most, Van den Berg was desperate to see action. The battle-hardened couldn't help but feel superior to the greenhorns, and Van den Berg wanted to feel the same. But he was somewhere in between, experienced yet not.

Josiah powdered his boots, rubbed his feet painfully, and ate some boiled tubers. Then, with a feeling of lassitude, he went back to the line. On his way through town, he saw a horse-drawn cart coming down the road. The driver looked forlorn, as did the horse, tramping with its head down. The cart appeared to be stacked with logs. Upon closer inspection, Josiah realized they were dead Americans. Their boots and socks had been removed—saved—and their blue feet stuck out the back, with the innocence of children who had lost their shoes. As the cart passed, an open eye, visible through the slats, raked Josiah, and he shuddered with something other than cold.

AFTER TEN DAYS, C COMPANY WAS ORDERED TO CLEAR AND HOLD the village of Roy, about ten miles to the east. They followed the river Lomme out of town, past snow-covered fields and the dark scrawl of trees, glad to finally be on the move. They looked ragtag in their blankets and sheets, their shower-capped helmets, like dress-up versions of winter soldiers.

En route, there was no sign of the enemy. Then, outside of Roy, which seemed little more than a cluster of houses, they heard the whomp of mortars and saw them wobbling through the air, lazy and aimless enough to dodge before they kicked up fountains of earth and snow. The Bren gun groups stayed back while the rifle groups scampered into the village, with Van den Berg out front. Back in England, when they had practiced street fighting in Southampton, men had been blown out of doorways with guncotton and thunderflash grenades, and that's what Josiah kept expecting: pandemonium. But the village was eerily still. Soon the Bren gun groups were ordered to move forward.

They made a sweep of the village, going from house to house. Mostly, they were met by grateful villagers, but one house was deserted and in a strange state of disarray, half the floorboards missing, cannibalized for firewood. There were signs the Germans had been there, including bowls of thin gruel, still warm to the touch.

JUST LIKE IN NORMANDY, THE GERMANS WERE ON THE RUN. IT WAS the same the next day when they marched into Bande, a steepled village to the south. Some half-hearted mortar and machine-gun fire, followed by a hasty retreat.

As they swept the village, Lieutenant Morrison came up to Josiah and said, "Chang, I need you to come with me." The lieutenant looked agitated—the first sign that something was off. Josiah was led to a cobblestone house with a slate roof, where Simmonds was retching by the front door, a long string of mucus dangling from his mouth. Taken alone, this wasn't surprising. Then he saw Walker rushing out for air and bracing himself against the door. That's when he knew something was wrong.

He entered the house through a set of French doors. At some point, the house had been set on fire, and what remained was charred and ruined. As he went down a flight of stairs, he was met by something noxious. A mix of blood, excreta, and death. He pulled his blanket turned poncho over his face, but the stench was overwhelming. He followed the lieutenant into a stone cellar, and there they came to the source: dozens of bodies laid out in rows on a thin bed of straw, some with arms in the air, levitating with rigor mortis. One boy, barely of age, lay with his head against a wall, his bruised eyes half-open, as if waking or falling asleep, his lips pulled back in a rictus, his teeth still enviably beautiful.

Josiah and those who could stomach the task were made to carry those bodies outside, where they were laid out again, this time in snow. They worked in pairs, those bodies stiff yet sagging. Thirty-seven males of fighting age, including boys, all of them shot in the back of the head.

From the heel prints and cigarette burns, it was clear they had suffered first.

For the rest of the day, villagers dressed in black came to identify the bodies. Many were old, in caps and headscarves, rheumy-eyed and grimly determined, as if knowing were the only solace. For the rest of his life, Josiah would hear their anguish. The wives and the children. The mothers.

4

AFTER THE MASSACRE AT BANDE, THE BATTALION WENT FOR A FEW days of rest in the village of Pondrôme, west of Rochefort. To help raise spirits, Brigadier Hill decided to organize a sports day. Men made toboggans out of anything they could find—doors, bathtubs—and raced down a hill to maniacal cheering. There were also lumberjack games, and Syd and Josiah put everyone to shame, especially on the two-man saw.

"Just like back in the day," Syd said, throwing an arm around him.

But Josiah had trouble enjoying himself. Bande continued to haunt him. The first thing he had learned in France was that war had rules, refereed by honor, so he was incensed by what the Germans had done, and though he tried not to give in, a hardness, a darkness, began to seep in.

THE AMERICANS AND THE BRITISH HAD SUCCEEDED IN REPELLING the Germans in the Ardennes, so after a few days in Pondrôme, they took a pulverizing thirteen-hour truck ride to a new front: Holland.

After all the letdowns of Belgium—the cold, the lack of action—Van den Berg was glad to be going to the country of his father's birth.

"I got relatives," Van den Berg said. "You can all stay with me."

For the first few days, they did in fact billet with locals in the town of Roggel. Josiah and Syd Antoine walked out to a farmhouse with a large thatched roof and half-timbered walls. A man with saggy eyes and a scraggly beard stepped out of the house, took one look, and walked back in without so much as a word. It fell to the child of the house, a girl of no more than eleven or twelve, to greet them. Her name was Isabelle, and she wore her hair in a bob, barrette to one side, and her large brown eyes seemed larger for the hollowness of her cheeks. "Don't worry about Papa," she said. "He's good at heart." When Syd praised her English, she said, "Most Hollanders speak English."

That night, Syd and Josiah slept in the hay barn attached to the farmhouse, across from a Jersey cow and a donkey that father and daughter used to draw a small cart. Much better than a slit trench, but still. Here they were, risking their lives to save Europe, yet some wouldn't deign to let them in.

"He's just trying to make us feel at home," Syd said, and they laughed.

Syd's grandparents had once moved freely about the Cariboo, until the Oblates of Mary Immaculate convinced them to stay put and grow corn and send their children to school at St. Joseph's Mission near Williams Lake. Syd's father, who had always thought the school not too bad a place, sent his son in turn to the newly built Lejac Residential School near Fraser Lake. Syd was there the year two boys ran away and nearly made it back to Nadleh Whut'en reserve before freezing to death on a lake.

Nonetheless, Syd, who missed his family, ran away himself and begged to go falling with his father, just as Josiah had.

"What are we doing here, Syd?" Josiah asked.

Syd Antoine went quiet. "I don't know," he said. "At Lejac, you had to be good for a year before you could be baptized. But I was too wild. Always breaking the rules. Father Jean-Louis said I would amount to nothing. I can still see him, jabbing his finger in my face." He paused, remembering. "Sometimes I think I'm here just to spite him."

After a moment, Syd said, "They look hungry," meaning Isabelle and her father. "We should bring them some food."

The battalion was now better provisioned, and they gave their hosts whatever they could spare: canned vegetables, canned beef, lemonade and chocolate powder, and, whenever possible, fresh bread and cigarettes. They even took to milking the cow, to the plangent sound of the pail, and leaving the pail on the doorstep, along with everything else.

"Papa says thank you," Isabelle said.

Nonetheless, they remained in the barn.

FROM ROGGEL, THEY MARCHED A FEW MILES SOUTHEAST TO THE town of Buggenum, where C Company took over a few abandoned houses on the river Maas. Mist came off the river like smoke, its waters burning. The Germans lay in wait on the other side, Düsseldorf and the Rhine just forty miles beyond.

Here in Buggenum, they were finally issued rubber boots, leather jerkins, and winter camouflage, which they greeted with cynicism. "Would have been nice to have these," Van den Berg said, "three fucking weeks ago." Josiah, Harrison, and Campbell found themselves back in a slit trench, only this one was already dug and sandbagged, and it was large, as far as trenches went, with room enough to move around. Still, they were back to the cold for hours on end, just staring across the river, into leafless trees, where German snipers lurked. Sometimes, out of boredom, the Canadians would raise a helmet at the end of a rifle, and the Germans would pick it off for fun.

One night, when the cold and the boredom seemed especially deep, Harrison turned to Josiah with those sleepy-looking eyes and asked, "What was it like in Normandy?"

Josiah considered all the things he could have said but said nothing.

"Wish I could have been there," Harrison said, moonily.

"Don't worry," Campbell sniffed, "there's plenty of war left."

Josiah's second tour of Europe had been underwhelming so far. To date, they had lost more men to frostbite than to the enemy. Part of him was glad; his aim was to live. But another part of him wanted to go charging across the Maas and bring the war to an end. So Campbell's prediction rankled.

"We'll be in Berlin by summer," Josiah declared boldly, then rued how far away summer still was.

IN THE SMALL HOURS OF THE NIGHT, HARRISON SAT UP.

"I see something."

They were still in the trench, only now Campbell was snoring, sleeping out of turn.

"Where?" Josiah whispered.

Harrison pointed, and Josiah turned his gaze upriver. There, he saw what appeared to be a ripple on the water, an undulating blackness, a hundred yards away. Both sides had taken to probing the other at night, crossing the river in small inflatable rafts. Entirely possible that this was German reconnaissance. But exhaustion could make you see things, and the lieutenant wanted fire control. They had to be sure.

"Not one of ours?"

"Not tonight," Harrison said.

Josiah looked again, this time through binoculars, until he caught sight of movement and the telltale flare of helmets. Three of them. He held his breath to clear the air and aimed his Bren, struggling to find the target through the pinhole of his scope. Once he was certain the first man was in his sights, he squeezed the trigger, to a blaze of orange, traversing one way, then the other, and the night was rent by the sound of screaming. He felt a little sick, the way he had the first time he slaughtered a chicken, by chopping off its head, the chicken's eyes still darting until its spinal fluid ran out. But he also felt a new darkness within him. After a few seconds, the screaming stopped and the world went silent, save for the sound of air leaking.

"We got 'em!" Harrison whisper-shouted.

Josiah wasn't inclined to celebrate. For him, the only pleasure was Campbell startling awake and asking, stupidly, "What happened?"

5

WHEN JOSIAH WENT INTO THE HOUSE THAT SERVED AS HEAD-quarters, where their own snipers were stationed upstairs, he was debriefed by Lieutenant Morrison. Then the lieutenant clapped his shoulder and said, "Get some sleep, Chang. You're on night patrol."

"Yes, sir."

"I want you and Campbell—"

"No, sir," Josiah blurted. "Not Campbell."

The lieutenant regarded him. "Who then?"

"Syd Antoine." There was no one he trusted more.

The lieutenant considered, then turned to a runner and said, "Tell Antoine to come in for some food and rest. He's going out tonight."

Holland was not just cold but dark, daylight gone by four in the afternoon. Nonetheless, they didn't set off on patrol until midnight, when the world was truly stygian. Before they left, there were handshakes all around.

"There's a shot of rum waiting for you when you get back," Lieutenant Morrison said.

They set off into the night, Josiah carrying a Sten, lighter and better suited to the cold than the Bren gun was. They had been ordered to find a way over the Buggenum railway bridge, which lay in a heap to the south. Crossing the bridge wouldn't be easy, but after gunning down the Germans, Josiah was glad not to have to cross by boat.

The bridge was a long series of trusses, and the three directly over the water had collapsed. Syd and Josiah slipped to the shore and took off their winter camouflage, which would give them away on the blackness of the Maas. They studied the trusses lying in the river. The top of each truss was still above water. That was the only way across.

They slung their weapons around them and started up the first beam, which went up at a steep angle. The beam was slick with snow and ice but thoroughly pimpled by rivets, which gave them purchase. At the top of the truss, they straddled the beam and belly-crawled. Once across, they slid down the far side, braking with their feet, until they reached a concrete pile cap, large enough for both of them to stand on.

The second truss had folded in on itself, like an M, which made the angles even steeper and required a short but difficult jump in the middle, from sloping beam to sloping beam, over gurgling black waters. Josiah could only assume the Germans were guarding the bridgehead, and he imagined snipers lining them up and picking them off clean.

When they reached the second pile cap, Syd said, "Let's wait. In case someone heard us." This was precisely why Josiah had wanted to come out with Syd, because his instincts were always good. They squatted with their backs to the pillar, relatively safe for the moment, and shared a wry look. As boys, neither could have imagined being here.

"If Father Jean-Louis could see you now," Josiah said.

When no German onslaught seemed forthcoming, they clambered the rest of the way. On the opposite shore, they camouflaged themselves again and skulked into the woods. For the next few hours, they trudged through a perfect fondant of snow, senses on high alert. The snow was knee-high and soft as soufflé, collapsing with every step. The whole scene might have been beautiful if not for the enemy who knew where.

At length, Syd Antoine raised his hand and they stopped. Sure enough, in a clearing some distance away was a mortar pit, neatly dug and sandbagged, the mortar itself sitting on its base and bipod, like a telescope tipped to the ground. There were four men in the mortar crew, dressed in all white, including white-painted helmets. They might have disappeared completely if not for their dark belts and bread bags. This must have been the crew that occasionally harassed the Canadians from the other side of the river.

Syd and Josiah were only there for reconnaissance, so they pulled out their writing wallets and took notes, their fingers stiff with cold. Then they retraced their steps, visible in the snow, and crossed the bridge again before sunup.

When they walked into headquarters, they were greeted like men who had returned from the underworld, and maybe they had. As it happened, Brigadier Hill was visiting the company. This was what the men admired about him: he showed his face, led from the front, not like some of the other brass. After debriefing Syd and Josiah himself, the brigadier said in his nasally voice, "Lieutenant, pick a dozen men and take out that mortar pit tonight." Then he handed Syd and Josiah each a shot of rum.

THE LIEUTENANT DID AS HE WAS TOLD: PICKED A DOZEN MEN, including Walker, Van den Berg, Harrison, and Campbell, and of course Syd and Josiah, who would lead the way. The men planned their mission, ate and slept, then set off for the railway bridge at midnight.

Syd and Josiah led them down to the bridgehead and pulled off their winter camouflage, and the others followed suit.

"What in the devil," Campbell said, staring at the sunken trusses.

"Just do what the man in front of you does," Syd said before leading off.

The crossing went largely as planned, but the wind was sharp and scalded their eyes. At one point, they heard a clang, then a plunk in the water—Campbell, dropping his machete—and everyone froze until the moment had passed. When it came time to make the short jump on the M-shaped truss, Campbell slipped. He managed to catch himself, but not before he had slid halfway into the drink. There was some hushed talk with the lieutenant about whether or not he should go back, but Campbell, to his credit, wanted to stay, even though he was already shivering.

The moon was brighter tonight and lit the way. Syd and Josiah had marked some trees with their daggers, but mostly they just followed their footprints, vague with new snow. This time, Josiah carried the Bren and felt the weight of it. At one point, they heard the haunting cry of an owl and another calling back.

In time they came to the mortar pit, which looked as it had the night before, except the Germans were hunkered down and hard to see, even by moonlight. The lieutenant signaled, and the Bren gun group slipped off, Campbell's teeth chattering so loudly that Josiah was sure the Germans could hear. The rifle group would attack from the front and the Bren gun group would flank. Josiah was nearly to the mark when something like fireworks went off behind him, lighting up Harrison's face and its look of pure astonishment. Shouts from the mortar pit, followed instantly by machine-gun fire. Campbell, standing next to the smoking light of a trip flare, stumbled backward. Josiah and

Harrison dove for cover, and the world erupted into chaos. The Germans were still shooting in their direction, pinning Josiah and Harrison, when the others opened fire. The mortar crew yelled and turned its attention, which gave Josiah the moment he needed to rise from the snow, mount the Bren, and open up. One magazine, then another, Harrison changing them seamlessly. Then came the heavy bass of one, two, three grenades, followed by a long patter of sand and earth.

When the smoke cleared, the mortar pit was silent. And Campbell was dead.

THE ENCOUNTER HAD BEEN SO QUICK THAT THE TRIP FLARE WAS still sputtering. When it finally went out, the world went darker than before. Cautiously, from different directions, they approached the mortar pit. When they found dead Germans and no sign of the mortar, they relaxed.

Then, through the darkness, they heard a soft groan and the icy scrape of movement. With a click, Walker raised his rifle and strode a few paces. A lone German soldier was crawling away, leaving a dark stain in his wake.

Walker stepped closer, until he was nearly over the man, and pointed his rifle.

"Don't," Josiah said.

"He's a dead man. I'm doing him a favor."

"Fight's over, Walker."

Walker looked in his direction. Josiah couldn't really see his face but could easily imagine the look of disdain. "Don't tell me you weren't shooting five seconds ago."

Josiah swallowed dryly. It did seem an absurdly fine line. But that's what honor was.

"He needs help."

"What are you going to do, Chang? Patch him up and carry him over the fucking bridge?" Walker asked.

Josiah turned to Lieutenant Morrison, but the lieutenant said nothing, his face inscrutable in the dark. Neither he nor anyone else seemed willing to intercede. Syd Antoine would probably have said something, but he was off guarding the perimeter. That darkness Josiah had felt was seeping into all of them.

"You saw what they did at Bande," Walker said.

"And this one's a coward," Van den Berg spat. "He was running away from the fight."

Josiah well understood the dark forces they were fighting. But there was darkness on every side, and light in every man.

"Just shoot him already," someone said. As if he understood, the German began to crawl more frantically, grunting and indignant. When the effort proved too much, he heaved himself onto his back and lay there, breathing raggedly. In a final effort to live—or maybe die—he reached into his coat and tried to draw a pistol. Walker shot him in the chest.

The crack of the rifle echoed through the woods. When the waves subsided, Walker came up to Josiah with a steely glint in his eye and said, "Don't go soft, Chang."

6

THERE WERE MORE PATROLS, MORE MIND-NUMBING HOURS OF STAR-
ing at the misty waters of the Maas, through bitter winds and fluttery
curtains of snow. Then, just as they had spelled the Americans in Belgium, the Americans came to spell them in Holland, and their tour of
the continent came to an end. After another miserable truck ride, they
found themselves back in Ostend, on the SS *Canterbury*, and headed
once more for England.

Upon returning, the men were given seven days leave. Despite Van
den Berg's exhortations, Josiah had no interest in London. What he
wanted was a few days to himself, away from army life, so he asked to
be billeted and was sent to a farm in Oxfordshire. The farmhouse had
a large black roof, white walls, two chimneys, and leaded windows
with black trim. The woman of the house, Mrs. Foster, was plain but
lively, with three little girls—Emily, Beatrice, and Margaret—in her
thrall, each one a version of the others, like nesting dolls, their hair the
color of dishwater. Mr. Foster was young but weather-beaten, with a
touch of elephant hide about the neck. When he found Josiah in his

kitchen, he nodded curtly, then left the room, ostensibly to wash up. Once again, Josiah had been put in the barn, only this one had a bed, neatly made. In fact, there were a number of handmade beds and straw palliasses. Maybe Mr. Foster had simply seen one too many billeters.

At supper the first night, Mrs. Foster said, "I'm sorry to say we've brought you here on false pretenses, Mr. Chang. I'm sure you were expecting some rest and relaxation, but we're going to put you to work." They needed to clear some acreage, she explained, her manner light and disarming. "We'll get some help from the Women's Timber Corps, but not for a few days yet."

"Fine by me," Josiah said. "I used to be a faller. Back in Canada."

At this, Mr. Foster looked down sheepishly, but Mrs. Foster clasped her hands and held them to her chin. "Why, Mr. Chang, you're heaven-sent!"

Every morning for the next five days, Mrs. Foster sent Josiah and her husband off with a bundle of bread and cheese, and they walked to the woods at the edge of the fields, the air fecund with the first hints of spring. Josiah didn't mind the work. Was glad for it, in fact. The weather was cool, ideal for cutting, and the trees, mostly pine, were soft and easy to get through. It felt good to handle a saw again, even if Mr. Foster labored to keep up. At first, they didn't say much, but by degrees Josiah learned the farm had once raised livestock, but after the war began, they'd had to stop growing feed and start growing flax and wheat. Mr. Foster still mourned the loss of the pigs and the sheep; all they had now were a few hens and Guernsey cows, whose eggs and milk were not theirs to do with as they pleased. The War Agricultural Executive Committee dictated everything, down to what to feed the chickens. After years of frantic production, his fields were spent, which was why he had been ordered to clear more land.

In the evenings, they took supper in the kitchen, a large room with a farm table to one side and a coal-burning stove in the fireplace. The wallpaper was dingy, and the windows were still blacked out, and the table was lit by the burning coil of a single dangling bulb, powered by a petrol generator. The whole room smelled of sour milk, from cheese that hung in dripping sacks of muslin. Mrs. Foster served parsnips, whole boiled onions, and a seemingly endless supply of baked beans, but she served meat only once. One night, sitting at the table, the girls on the bench across from his, Josiah realized this might be the first close-up of a proper family he had ever had in his life, and it gave him a sense of everything he might want for himself.

One evening, when conversation turned to the war, or rather, the action Josiah had seen, Mr. Foster listened intently before pushing up and leaving the table, and Mrs. Foster smiled and said, "Don't mind him. He's seen a lot of friends go off, but he can't, since he's been deemed 'essential.' Makes him feel guilty, I know. But I like him right where he is."

On Josiah's last day, he and Mr. Foster were joined by four members of the Women's Timber Corps, who had arrived a day early. They were young and spirited in their green berets, green jerseys, and khaki breeches, and they worked with aplomb. None was exceptionally beautiful, but taken together, they were as charming as naiads.

As the women felled trees, Josiah and Mr. Foster measured all the timber they had already cut, down to the last cubic foot, all of which had to be reported to the government. When Mr. Foster grew impatient with all the numbers in the Hoppus Tables, Josiah took over the calculations, scrawling on a piece of paper with a snub-nosed pencil. When word got back to Mrs. Foster, she said, "Why, Mr. Chang, I hear you're brilliant at maths!"

In the evening, all ten of them sat around the farm table, the Fosters on one side, Josiah and the Timber Corps on the other, at least until the

Foster girls went crawling onto the laps of the naiads, the whole room crackling with laughter and youthful energy. For dessert, Mrs. Foster served plum duff, a pudding made of flour, bread crumbs, suet, raisins, and powdered eggs, the last given to her by American soldiers. "It's a triumph!" one of the naiads declared.

Afterward, Mrs. Foster pulled Josiah aside and said, "The girls will need the barn."

He nodded. "I'll leave tonight."

"No, you mustn't, Mr. Chang. We have plenty of room in the house."

That night, lying by the dying embers of the fire in the living room, on a straw palliasse that Mrs. Foster had brought in from the barn, Josiah felt purged of some of the darkness that had started to seep in, and vowed to keep the darkness at bay. And lying there, he had the same feeling he'd had before, that this was a life he might like for himself. A family. A hearth. It made him want to fight for the Fosters. So they could live their lives in peace. Go back to raising pigs and sheep if they wanted.

In the morning, as he took his leave, Mrs. Foster seized his hand in both of hers. "I shall remember you, Mr. Chang. I shall."

"Come see us again," Mr. Foster said, "when this bloody war is through."

7

AS ALWAYS, THE FIRST THING SHE DID WAS CHECK THE MAILBOX. Look for proof that he was alive, or had been however many days ago when the letter was sent. Last she heard, he was somewhere on a river in Holland, playing weird shooting games with the Germans. He sounded safe, or as safe as one could be in war, but getting a letter was always better than not, and she felt a little fizz of deflation when she found the mailbox empty.

When she entered the house, Queenie roused herself from the floor and followed her through the kitchen and out the back door. As recently as six months ago, Queenie had clamored for a walk whenever she came home, but in the past half year, the old girl had slowed down considerably. Now she preferred to tramp about the yard and squat shakily, then come back in and go back to sleep. In her dotage, she seemed to dream of someone she used to know and still loved.

After taking a bath, Poppy picked through the fridge, then settled into her usual Friday night routine: records and drinks in the living room, then Ole Olsen and His Commodores on CKWX, until she fell asleep. At a small bar cart, she poured herself a finger of whisky. Then, with her head turned away so as not to drop ash on her record, she set down the needle with a crackle, and the silence of the room was lifted. There was a time when the prospect of such an evening had frightened her, when she had dreaded the thought of sitting at home by herself. But a funny thing happened: over repeated months and now years, she got used to it. When Josiah was in France and she was sick with worry, she had kept vigil by staying in. By that point, though, the habit had already taken hold. Of course, she still went out, still made plans with Betty and Edith, but now she wasn't afraid of being alone. Love, it seemed, wasn't just a feeling but a practice, and she had been practicing for years.

But tonight she felt oddly restless, maybe because she hadn't received a letter. It was a strange way to live, never knowing from moment to moment whether your beloved was alive or not, even when a letter *did* arrive. Or maybe she was restless because her life seemed clouded in other ways. That afternoon, another clutch of girls had been let go from the yard. She loved her job, loved driving a jitney, the smooth grip of the wheel at the end of its long steering column, but she knew her days were numbered and that she would have to turn to the future, only she didn't know what that future was. Vancouver may have had a woman taxi driver, but after the war, the world wouldn't have much use for drivers like her, and she wasn't sure she wanted to keep driving in any case. All she knew was she wanted to avoid the cloister of the typewriter—unless that typewriter was her own. She had been following the war in the papers, reading the likes of Ross Munro, who was one helluva writer. Maybe she could study literature and writing and become a reporter. That way she, too, could go off to war.

She sipped her whisky as the record crooned, first one side, then the other, but even after the record was through, there were still hours to go before Ole Olsen and His Commodores came on the radio, and she felt a throb of impatience, and that same restive energy. Despite the music, her walls seemed unusually mute. The mirror next to the front door had crooked a little, and she realized from the sliver of paint that was now exposed that her walls had yellowed with smoke. It was the kind of change that was imperceptible from one day to the next, but now she saw it all at once.

Obeying an instinct that wasn't entirely hers, she rose from the couch and put on a dress and did her makeup and hair, in a flurry of motion. Then she slipped on shoes and a winter coat. As she checked herself in the mirror by the door, a klaxon blared, right on cue.

"Where to, miss?" the driver asked, after she had sidled into the back.

All this time, there was only one place she hadn't gone back to. "The Commodore," she replied.

They crossed the Lions Gate Bridge, downtown sparkling in the distance. Once they had stopped directly in front of the Commodore, she paid the driver and strode through the doors. It was March, the dregs of winter, and the queue for the coat check was long, but she waited until she reached the top of the grand staircase, where she handed her coat to one of the coat check girls. She was wearing the same sea-green dress she had worn the night Josiah proposed, and like that night, the manager shook her hand, and the maître d' showed her to a table, and a waiter in a white mess jacket brought her a teapot full of ice.

She looked about the ballroom and saw Josiah everywhere and had the strange sensation that he would appear at any moment. This was why she had come, to remember that night and feel close to him. At the time, she didn't think he could join the army, and if she were honest, that was part of his appeal. She would get to marry without any pain or suffering, to the envy of so many around her. Maybe that's why she had been angry, because he had thwarted her so completely. But she couldn't be with Josiah, or be the person she imagined herself to be, without believing in the things he believed in. It had taken time, but she'd come around. It helped to read about the battalion in the papers. She had to admit, imagining Josiah a part of that now-famous battalion was thrilling. It certainly had a tonic effect on her parents, who now seemed weirdly admiring. But if anything had brought her around, it was Josiah himself, who had already seemed a different person by the time he came back from jump school. She remembered that night at the taxi stand on Granville Street, when he spoke of "liberation"—language he had never used before. Apparently, the army had taught him civics, what it meant, ironically, to be a British subject. Plus, he had just been to America, and concluded that Canada and America weren't all that different. By the time he was training in England, he had decided that Canada and Germany weren't all that different, either. The Chinese Immigration Act had barred Chinese for over twenty years, but Canada didn't just exclude; by making it next to impossible to marry, the country was also trying to *uproot*, which meant Canada had its own Nuremberg Laws. More recently, he had pointed out that the law didn't strip citizenship from men, only women, which meant he was fighting for her rights as much as his own. He wasn't an educated man, but the army—experience—was giving him an education. She felt it almost jealously every time she got a postcard from yet another new place in the world. It was hard not to admire the person he was becoming.

In the midst of her reverie, the orchestra struck up, and men began to approach, to smile and ask her to dance. She smiled back but shook her head each time, pleased by how easy it was to say no.

In time, a man approached and stood right next to her, so close she was forced to look straight up, but even from that odd angle, she recognized him right away, tall and dark and foppish. He had grown a pencil mustache, which somehow managed to look both dashing and ludi-crous. He didn't say anything, just stood with his hand out, so presump-tuously that she almost refused on principle. Then she remembered how well they had danced together, and how fun it had been. There was nothing wrong with a little fun. You had to live, go on. You couldn't get through a war by being an anchorite.

So she took his hand, dry and papery to the touch, and followed him onto the dance floor, that gleaming expanse of polished blond wood. There he took her in his arms, smelling of lavender and mint, bergamot and cloves, and whisked her off on what would be the first of many dances. He wasn't here with the blond he had come with last time—or anyone, for that matter—so they had each other to themselves. He was still an excellent dancer. If anything, he had only gotten better, more supremely confident, able to whirl them both so briskly that she felt lightheaded. Her skills, on the other hand, had atrophied. But it didn't matter. He had a strong lead. All she had to do was follow.

At the end of the set, he led her to a darkened corner of the room. As she stood against the wall, hands tucked behind the small of her back, he propped an arm beside her head and leaned in, and she felt a fillip of heat, her chest rising and falling. When he touched his face to hers, she didn't flinch, just felt the rasp of his skin, her whole body sighing with pleasure, and she wondered if this was what she had really come for, this feeling of desire she had gone so long without. But when he moved his lips to hers, she snapped her head away.

She could feel him scouring her, trying to parse her mood.

"Are you sure?" he asked.

Afterward, standing alone in the dark, she smiled a disembodied smile, realizing why she had come. It had been a test, to fathom her feelings, and she had passed.

SHORTLY AFTER JOSIAH RETURNED FROM THE FOSTERS' FARM IN Oxfordshire, the battalion was taken by lorry to a transit camp at Hill Hall in Essex, northeast of London. This was how quickly the war was now moving. But they hadn't had a chance to train for some time now. In fact, no one had jumped since November.

"What if we're rusty?" Harrison asked as they bounded along in a lorry.

"That's what I've been saying," Walker grunted. "Should have been training in England, not freezing our asses off in Belgium and Holland."

"If we weren't there," Syd Antoine said, "Hitler might be in Antwerp."

"I'm sick of exercises," Van den Berg said. "Just jump out of the plane and run like hell for the rendezvous. What's there to know?"

"Let's get this war over with," Josiah said. No one disagreed.

OVER THE NEXT THREE DAYS, THEY WERE FULLY BRIEFED ON THEIR mission. Gone was the murkiness and confusion of the Ardennes and the Maas. This was much more reminiscent of their first jump: sand

tables, oversize maps and photographs, and dioramas made of Plasti-
cine. The plan was to cut across Germany in three great swaths. The
Canadians were part of the northern swath led by Field Marshal
Montgomery, bound for Wismar on the Baltic Sea.

Then came the familiar rituals of fitting parachutes, cleaning weapons, and packing leg kit bags, which were now reinforced. Familiar, at
least, to some but not most. For the new men, it was baptism, and they
tried not to let their apprehension show. For Josiah, it was simply the
next mission, and he readied himself like the veteran he now was.

On D minus two, a singer came to entertain the troops. Men by the
thousands sat outside before a small wooden stage. The singer had wavy
blond hair and very white, very large, almost buck teeth. Her singing
seemed a little operatic and old-fashioned, but from the way the Brits
sang along, it was clear she was some kind of national treasure. When
she started in on the first soft strains of "Where or When," Josiah felt
stricken, but not in the way he might have imagined. As thousands of
men sang along, teary-eyed, he realized the giant feelings he'd been
hauling around for years, which had seemed uniquely his, were in fact
common, possibly even vulgar. It had always seemed his feelings might
afford him special protection, but every man was full of the same desperate longing, and his was no more likely to save him.

On D minus one, they racked out early, since they had to get up in
the small hours of night. Before lights-out, Josiah turned to Syd Antoine and asked, "Still got my girl's address?"

"Yeah," Syd said. "You?"

Josiah patted his breast pocket.

REVEILLE CAME AT 0200 HOURS. JOSIAH'S FIRST THOUGHT UPON
waking was that men were crossing the Rhine at that very moment in
assault boats, to a hail of bullets in the unfeeling dark, paving the

way for those to come. That the war never stopped, even when it stopped for him.

Their final meal was steak and eggs. The men were upbeat if a little tired, their bodies thrown off by the early hour, no matter how well they had slept. But the wait was over. For nearly ten months, they had clashed in the castle. Today, they finally attacked the keep.

Once again, Simmonds traded his meal for cigarettes, just as he had before Normandy. "If it ain't broke, don't fix it, am I right?" he asked, puffing away.

"You're a goddamn genius," Van den Berg said.

At quarter to five, they climbed into lorries and sat there breathing petrol for a long time before finally making the short half-hour trip to the aerodrome at Chipping Ongar, which looked like every other RAF base they had seen, except this one had been turned over to the Americans, which meant flying in C-47s. After gearing up, they walked out to their respective planes, parked on either side of the runway, nose to tail, one after the next, as if rolling off an assembly line, their silhouettes traced by the first light of dawn. The sight of their American pilots in baseball caps, smoking cigars, made some men long for the RAF. Others took heart.

As men sat on the grass, waiting to emplane, Josiah lay on his leg kit bag and closed his eyes. Neither Harrison nor Somerville, the new lance corporal who had taken Campbell's place in the Bren gun group, had jumped before, and both of them seemed on edge. Josiah felt calm, but he also felt himself performing calm, for their sake.

The battalion's four chaplains, strapped into parachutes and ready to jump themselves, prayed with those inclined to pray, and the brass came by with handshakes and bullish words of encouragement. Glory, et cetera. Then, in noisy preparation, every engine began to hack.

After all those jumps from C-47s, it was only fitting that Josiah would get to jump from one for real. Once again, he would jump last, so he led his stick of twenty up the folding stairs and through the port side door. Without having to stoop, he walked to the front, through the belly of the whale, and took a seat. Soon they were all packed in, leg kit bags between their knees.

They took off at 0730 hours. After bumping along for what seemed like a mile, engines roaring through the open side door, the plane lifted off with that sudden leavening feeling. They joined two other Dakotas in an arrowhead, then two other arrowheads in a still larger arrowhead, just like the night of Normandy, but already this flight was so different. There was room to stand, to take off their gear and use the toilet, and the ride was smooth and no one retched. Best of all, they were flying by day, which banished all their irrational fears, leaving only the rational ones.

They flew low enough over the North Sea to see whitecaps but high enough that the sea seemed motionless. The sky was a perfect blue, with a kind of corona along the horizon. Somewhere over Belgium, they joined up with thousands of other planes that had taken off from airfields all over England and blackened the sky like starlings. Josiah looked out in awe and realized their first weapon against the Germans was fear, the unholy terror of so many men and so much materiel come down to destroy them.

Harrison was sitting beside him and bouncing his leg like a restless child, and Josiah resisted the urge to reach out and still him. To each their own, in what could well be their very last moments.

They flew toward the Ruhr Valley and their drop zone north of Wesel. By the time they were over Germany, there was still no sign of the Luftwaffe, still no dent in the fighter shield, and for a while every man lived in the warm amnion of his deepest hope: that there would be no resistance at all.

Then they saw it, the Rhine, long, snaking, and dark. Before the crossing, the Allies had bombed relentlessly. Now everything east of the Rhine was on fire. Wesel was a conflagration, a single black tower of smoke. At just four hundred feet, they could see everything clear as day.

Then they heard the sound they had all been dreading.

"We got ack-ack," Syd Antoine said.

Sure enough, the booming of antiaircraft fire, which gave Josiah a terrible sense of déjà vu.

"Buckle up, boys," Van den Berg said. "Reception's hot."

Suddenly the sky filled with bursting clouds of black smoke, to say nothing of tracers, zipping past with alien speed. Already, one plane was falling from the sky with a desperate groan, one wing sheared, a few men dribbling out. The downside of overwhelming force: so much to shoot at. But so far, their plane was threading the needle.

At last the red light came on, and the jumpmaster ordered the men to their feet. "Remember, when you meet the Hun, treat him with extreme disfavor," the jumpmaster shouted over the roar. Then the light turned green, and the jumpmaster yelled, "Go! Go! Go!" In seconds, Josiah was at the door, pivoting into the gale. The moment he left the plane, he was cuffed by the prop blast and shot down the slipstream. His parachute opened with a bang.

He saw the drop zone, shaped like a boot atop the Diersfordter Forest, where C Company was supposed to rendezvous. In the middle of the drop zone were two coppices, one large, one small, and both heavily fortified. Everything looked like the diorama they had studied, except already littered with silk.

As he fell through the air, he heard the fizzing of bullets, an effervescence all around him. Here, truly, was the pure chance of war. The sky was a barrel and you were the fish, and only luck could save you. Some men were already slumped in their harnesses, others gamely shooting from the hip. One man who hung limply sprang back to life an instant before touching down, having feigned death to escape it.

Josiah was coming in near the toe of the boot, where men below were running for the forest en masse, like a herd of prey. He released his leg kit bag, which fell with a yank to the end of its now-shorter rope. The bag hit the ground first, Josiah an instant later, with a hard tumble. He dialed and punched the quick-release button on his chest, and his harness sloughed off. Then he hauled in his leg kit bag and pulled out his shoulder-strap belt and slung it on with theatrical urgency.

He ran, crouched, for the wood line, maybe fifty yards off. A few men lay on the ground, some crying out. Machine-gun and sniper fire were coming from the coppices, as well as some nearby farms. Josiah had the urge to stop and fight, but it was up to the Brits in the 8th Battalion to secure the DZ. His job was to get to the rendezvous.

After ten, maybe fifteen yards, he heard his name called. Despite himself, he dropped to the ground, in case it was an officer. He looked back. It was Simmonds.

"What?" Josiah hissed.

"I got hit in the leg!"

Josiah felt a spike of anger. "Then patch yourself up," he said, beginning to rise.

"Wait!" Simmonds cried. "Help me to the woods."

For all their fraternity, Josiah's goal was to live, and he wasn't going to get himself killed in the DZ, least of all for Simmonds. Their orders were clear: leave the fallen and get to the rendezvous. There was a reason the battalion had medics.

"Doc will be here soon enough. Then you'll be on your way back to England," he said, with a tinge of envy.

"Don't leave me here, Chang."

As men kept running past, Josiah spied a medic kneeling in the grass nearby, working on a man, and was just about to point him out when, despite the red cross on each arm, the medic fell over to a spray of blood from his chest.

"Just stay down," Josiah said.

"Come on, Chang!" Simmonds pleaded, more plaintive for lying prostrate, his mustache flecked with mud and his sallow face even more wan than usual. Josiah felt that smallness, that meanness, that hatred of frailty he'd felt toward Bill.

Just then, the whizzing around them seemed to abate, and men in the sky began to jerk. The guns in the large coppice were firing in a pattern: down, then up.

Seizing the moment, Josiah ran back to Simmonds, took his arm about the neck, and forced him to his feet, to a cry of pain. Then they shambled as fast as they could, three-legged. When they reached a post and wire fence, Josiah crawled through first, then took Simmonds by the wrists and dragged him underneath, perhaps more roughly than altogether necessary.

For a while, they lay low. The frothing of bullets had resumed, and they waited for the sound to fade. When they started running again, Harrison appeared out of nowhere, and together they practically carried Simmonds the rest of the way.

In the relative calm of the woods, they propped Simmonds up against a tree. Only now did they see the ragged hole in his trousers, spewing darkly. The man was pale with sweat, as if all the effort had been his. But he was fine. He would live.

"Dress your wound," Josiah said, "and take your wound tablets—morphine if you want."

With that, he and Harrison set off for the rendezvous.

9

THEY SLIPPED THROUGH THE WOODS, TO THE SMELL OF GUNPOWDER and high explosives, the battle still raging just beyond the tree line. By the time they reached the rendezvous, almost everyone else was there. Somerville, Walker, Syd Antoine. Nearly all of C Company.

"Took your sweet time," Van den Berg said.

No sign, however, of Lieutenant Morrison, so a sergeant organized the men. Their objective was to clear a farm called Hingendahls, on the western edge of the DZ. The Bren gun groups would flank; the rifle groups would charge.

They followed a stream that ran through a gully, protected by trees and the gully itself, until they were nearly upon the farm, which comprised a barn, a dairy, and a three-story farmhouse, its windows winking with muzzle flash. While the Germans kept their attention fixed on the drop zone, the Bren gun groups set up their guns at the edge of the trees, on a little slope of sun-warmed grass that rose from the stream. When the signal came, the Bren gun groups opened fire. Instantly, the farmhouse began to blister and fray to the sound of splintering wood and breaking glass. After twenty rounds, Harrison changed the magazine with his usual poise, then filled the empty magazine with charges from his bandolier while Josiah continued to rake.

While the enemy was down, the rifle groups charged. Went running toward the farm, fearlessly, Van den Berg leading the way, still determined, it seemed, to make up for Normandy. One man was felled but got up and hobbled until he could throw a grenade, at which point he was felled again. Walker was there, too, running with his rifle raised. Since the night of the mortar pit in Holland, the two of them had kept their distance, each wary of the other. But Walker was still the kind to bring to a gunfight.

As soon as they were in range, the rifle group tossed grenades, breaking windows before blowing them out entirely. Then they kicked down the front door. From inside came gunshots and panicked voices yelling in both English and German. It was a wonder that any German was still alive after all that carnage.

After a few long minutes, the first German emerged with his hands on his head. Thirty minutes into the Rhine drop and C Company was through.

WITHIN TWO HOURS, ALL RESISTANCE CEASED, AND THE 3RD BRIGADE was left with an unwieldy number of prisoners. But unlike those who'd surrendered at the gatehouse in Varaville, these prisoners weren't angry or disgruntled but afraid, and they seemed all too happy to ferry the wounded and dig trenches and graves, so long as they weren't shot on sight.

Just about everyone had made it out of Hingendahls farm, including Van den Berg, Walker, and Syd Antoine. The only man they lost was the one who had gone down twice. A far cry better than the Germans had fared.

Josiah's section was sent on patrol to make sure there were no more Germans lurking. They followed a road that ran north, along the edge of the DZ, to the audible crunch of their own boots. After the mayhem of the drop, the quiet was a little unnerving.

In time they reached a copse, which seemed quieter still, despite the shushing of leaves. Here they found a few snagged parachutes, lying shriveled on the trees, their harnesses empty. Then they came to one with the leaden weight of a man inside, his body riddled with stigmata.

"Holy fuck," Van den Berg said.

It was Lieutenant Morrison, dangling in the air with his head slumped and his eyes closed. Josiah saw again the lieutenant on D-Day, crossing the field to speak to the German envoy after the Germans had raised the white flag. The lieutenant was the one who had shown him that war had rules, refereed by honor. The one who had led him into battle from the first. Now he was gone.

Even without gaffs and a rope, Syd Antoine scaled the tree with ease and worked to free the lieutenant and lower him as gently as he could into the arms of the other men, waiting to receive him.

As someone ran back for a jeep, the others stood around solemnly, sucking on cigarettes. Van den Berg wore a distant look, perhaps recalling his own ill-fated jump in Normandy. From his wounds it was clear the lieutenant had been shot at close range. Not as he was coming down but as he hung from the tree. If anyone had seemed shrewd enough to outwit the war, it was the lieutenant. Yet he had not only died but ignobly.

"Lieutenant was first man out," Van den Berg said. "That's why he missed the DZ."

"The man had a wife," Syd Antoine said. "Kids."

When the jeep arrived, they laid the lieutenant out in the back and brought him to the makeshift cemetery next to the main dressing station, where German POWs were digging shallow graves. The lieutenant was shrouded in parachute silk and buried under a mound of earth, to be reinterred later.

Every mound was marked with a cross. Josiah couldn't help but notice that one belonged to a chaplain. Proof if there ever was that God absconded from battlefields.

10

C COMPANY DUG IN ALONG THE NORTHERN EDGE OF THE DIERS-
fordter Forest and waited for signs of a German counterattack. Sometime in the night, as he manned the trench, Josiah felt something brush
his leg. At first he was vaguely horrified, thinking it was something
wild, like a badger or a groundhog, but it turned out to be a mutt,
likely a stray from one of the farms. The dog smelled foul, but Josiah
gave him some food, and the dog lay curled up beside him all night,
and Josiah thought of the old girl and how she used to do the same. By
morning the dog was gone.

"Did you see where the dog went?" he asked Syd Antoine.

"What dog?" Syd replied.

AS DAWN APPROACHED, MEN ROSE FROM THE TRENCH AND SET OFF
in tactical formation, on alternating sides of the road. Once again, the
Germans were on the run, and the Canadians in pursuit. Josiah walked
five yards ahead of Harrison and five yards behind Somerville, the lance

corporal, but unlike Campbell, Somerville understood natural rank, and whose was higher.

The morning was shrouded in fog. Even when daylight broke, Josiah could hardly see his own rifle group, just thirty yards ahead, much less B Company, way out on point. But the fog seemed apropos. They were marching toward the unseeable, the unknowable. Toward who knew what.

For hours, they met no resistance. Then from somewhere in the pall came spasms of small-arms fire, plus the booming report of a tank, and everyone dropped. Word came down the line that it was a Tiger I, a tank so heavily armored that anti-tank guns were next to useless. For a long time the tank seemed to rage with impunity, and Josiah imagined B Company getting cut to ribbons. Then, at last, the whump of a PIAT. Josiah could picture the heavy trigger, the long delay, the bomb's feeble range, which meant the PIAT crew had had to crawl right up to the tank. But it seemed to work. The booming of the tank receded.

At that moment, two jeeps mounted with Browning machine guns—British reconnaissance, most likely—came bounding down the road like a godsend, to a rolling wave of hurrahs, vanished into the fog, and opened fire.

After half an hour, all sound ceased, and the men rose. In the woods ahead was a small village, just a few farms and houses, half of them on fire. There was no sign of the tank or the jeeps, but dead Germans littered the ground, and half a dozen had been taken prisoner. To Josiah's surprise, B Company looked remarkably intact.

In the village, they found men and women of French, Polish, Italian, and Russian extraction, forced to do farmwork for the Nazis. From the bruises and scars and emaciation, it was clear they had all been ill-used. Freed from bondage, they laughed, danced, wept. Some held out fistfuls of wildflowers and offered what little food they could. Others went up to the Germans and spat in their faces.

THERE WERE MORE SKIRMISHES AS THEY HOUNDED THE GERMANS, until their first major encounter at the Dortmund-Ems Canal, about sixty miles from the drop zone. The canal had been bombed the year before by the Americans and had long ceased to be a means by which the Germans could move men and materiel. Nonetheless, it had to be crossed.

The Canadians marched out of Greven in a long column, this time with A Company out front. Their mission was to seize the iron bridge over the canal before the Germans could destroy it. No sooner had the bridge come into view than a fusillade began from the opposite bank. "Incoming!" someone in A Company yelled, and word reverberated down the line. From the back of the column, Josiah watched as the world before him erupted in founts of earth. They were getting stonked by artillery, mortars, whatever the Germans had left. A Company was taking it on the nose.

But they had to get to the bridge. No choice, then, but to make a run for it. Josiah ran as fast as he could through clumps of flying earth and metal, sometimes over the fallen, his gear and vision jostling. He was only a hundred yards from the bridge when it went up with a thunderclap. The air filled with rolling dust, and the bridge fell straight down into the water, and he thought of all the bridges the war had destroyed—on the Divette, the Dives, the Maas. So much of the once-perfect world that had to be set to rights.

He got up and kept running, yelling for Harrison and Somerville to follow, and together they ran for a slit trench on the near side, which the Germans had abandoned. Josiah leapt in first, followed by the others, all of them panting.

The night that followed was quite possibly the longest of the war. The Germans seemed to know exactly where they were and kept pounding them, hard. The worst were the flak cannons, which sent up spectacular fireballs that rained hot shrapnel.

"Where are the Brits?" Somerville asked, shakily. "They're supposed to take out those bloody guns."

"Maybe the engineers haven't set up the bridge," Harrison said.

"We probably don't even know where those guns are," Josiah said. "That's why we had to send out patrols."

Through the long night, as Harrison and Somerville prayed, Josiah thought of his father, maybe because the sky was full of widow-makers. He hadn't seen his father since his first jump at Fort Benning and hoped that meant his father was at peace. He wished his father were alive, but at least he'd been spared the painful worry of a son at war.

At first light, the shelling finally stopped. Their side of the canal was now a hellscape of churned earth, the air thick with black powder and the unmistakable stench of death. Josiah's head throbbed, and his ears let out a single unending note.

And yet, despite the ravages, men crawled out of the ground and breakfasted. Some even managed to boil water and make coffee, to talk and make light. Whenever there wasn't death, there was life.

11

THE WAR WOULD LAST ONLY THIRTY-FIVE MORE DAYS, AND THOSE days would pass both quickly and slowly. Quickly because German resistance began to flag exponentially. Slowly because there was still so much living and dying to do.

They kept slouching toward Wismar, on the Baltic Sea, some three hundred miles from the drop zone. A trek that took them through Minden and Celle and so many other little towns and hamlets that they couldn't keep their names straight. Sometimes they rode in trucks or on the backs of Churchill tanks, ten or fifteen to a deck, blasting through whatever stood in their way. Other times, they took turns on folding bicycles and puttering light motorcycles and anything they could commandeer, including horse-drawn carts. But mostly, they hoofed it, one step after another, until every march they had ever been on, short or long, in good weather or bad, seemed to blur into one long march for which there seemed no end.

ONE AFTERNOON, WHEN THEY TOOK A BREAK FROM MARCHING, MEN did what they always did at such moments: light up. Until now, Josiah had resisted the urge; he'd seen what smoke had done to his father. Poppy had been right the first time they met: his body was a temple. But that day, he finally caved, now that the end was near. He hung a cigarette off dry lips, lit a match, and drew a lungful of smoke, and something spectral entered his body.

"Well, look at you," Walker said. Like Van den Berg and Syd Antoine, Walker had survived the stonking at the Dortmund-Ems Canal, but that night had poured a little more darkness into him, and his voice was cynical, as if Josiah had finally come down off his pedestal. And maybe he had.

Thereafter, Josiah continued to smoke, for all the reasons other men smoked: to kill time, to calm nerves. To have a need for which there was relief. But mostly he smoked to feel close to Poppy. To breathe in the ghost of her.

AS THEY PUSHED ON, THEY FACED NUISANCE ATTACKS FROM THE Hitler Youth and the Volkssturm, the very young and the very old. They were nothing like the SS or the Panzergrenadiers, but they were tenacious in their own way, especially the boys. In youth is fanaticism. Sometimes, after an attack, they found dead boys of only fourteen or fifteen, and it made them angry. Often, when they made boys they had captured dig graves, the boys would cry, thinking the graves their own. Once, Josiah saw a stripling staring at a tattered photograph of what must have been his family and realized they were the same: they just wanted to go home.

WHENEVER THEY STOPPED IN A VILLAGE OR A TOWN, THEY HAD NO compunction about pushing their way into people's homes to spend the night. Some owners were belligerent, others hysterical, fearing the worst. Most were scared but resigned. One night, as Josiah, Harrison, and Somerville entered a town house, a woman and her two children, a boy and a girl, stood with heads bowed, the woman's arms draped around their shoulders. As Josiah passed, the girl, maybe seven or eight, looked up. Her mother tried to push her head down, but she wouldn't relent. Kept staring at this new kind of person she had never seen before. Josiah locked eyes and flicked a smile to say he was no one to fear. That everything would be fine.

MANY OF THE TOWNS THEY ENTERED WERE DESTROYED, AS FLAT and pocked as the moon. Then there were those like Minden that seemed wholly untouched, the streets bustling with life, as if there were no war at all. The brass took over a posh and baronial hotel, and the men took refuge in a fancy department store. When they first walked in, they were stunned. Shopgirls still working on the floor, the shelves well stocked. They weren't supposed to loot, but they couldn't resist helping themselves to the things they needed most: clean socks, clean underwear. In Minden, they also ate like kings. Went rooting through cellars and found every kind of pickled vegetable, every kind of pickled meat. And wine, so much wine. Endless bottles with which to anesthetize themselves.

One night, when Van den Berg caught Josiah writing a letter, he said, "You still moping over that girl?" Then he proposed they go out and anesthetize themselves in that other way.

"Don't you ever want the love of a good woman?" Josiah asked.

"That's exactly what I want!" Van den Berg said, before suddenly turning morose. "Only one woman whose love I ever wanted."

For a moment, Josiah thought he had forgotten about some great unrequited love Van den Berg had had. Then he remembered that Van den Berg's mother had abandoned him before memory.

"Sometimes I think everything I do is to win her back," he said, gravely. "That's why we understand each other, Joe. Neither of us had a mother."

The words came as a shock. For some reason, Josiah had only thought of himself as a fatherless child, not a motherless one.

Van den Berg encouraged him again to go out. When Josiah said no, Van den Berg grimaced, adjusted his beret, and said, "Suit yourself."

ONE MORNING, MOPPING UP AFTER ANOTHER NUISANCE ATTACK, Josiah found another dead boy, this one shot in the neck. He lay in a widening pool of his own blood, staring at the sky in perfect astonishment.

"Got to admire the Jugend," Van den Berg said. "Fighting till the very end."

"It's fucking stupid at this point," Walker spat. "They die and we die. For nothing."

This was Josiah's new fear: that after having come so far, he would step on a booby trap or get picked off by a Hitler Youth. That he would die senselessly. For nothing.

THE BATTALION RECEIVED REINFORCEMENTS. THREE OFFICERS AND one hundred enlisted men, sorely needed after the Dortmund-Ems Canal. But it was strange, seeing new faces so late in the game. Having to work them in and treat them as one. These men had yet to be baptized by fire, and they seemed a little scared and a little sheepish, as they should have been, getting to march on the heart of the Reich after others had paved the way in blood.

IN THE THIRD WEEK OF APRIL, THEY REACHED KOLKHAGEN, OVER two hundred miles from where they had begun, and rested for nine days. Here, they organized a bath parade and received new uniforms and went back to drilling, to daily PT and weapons training, and got their vaccinations updated. It was all a little strange and more than a little maddening, so close to the end.

"They better not let some other fucking unit get to Wismar first," Van den Berg said.

"They can send me back to England right now, for all I care," Walker said.

"Why come all this way and give some other chumps the glory?" Van den Berg asked.

"The glory's in living, brother," Walker replied.

The only good thing about the long delay in Kolkhagen was that mail could finally catch up. Josiah got not one but two letters, both full of quiet confidence. *You're almost there, darling. If anyone can do this, it's you. Send me a postcard from Wismar. Wismar is the new Berlin.*

ALONG THE WAY, THEY FOUND ALL KINDS OF GERMAN MATERIEL, destroyed or abandoned: Panther and Tiger tanks, armored cars and railway guns, Messerschmitts and Stukas and those dreaded 88 mm flak cannons. The greater the fear, the greater the spoils, and the more they wanted photos, like big-game hunters. Some men picked up Mausers or German submachine guns. Others, like Josiah, pocketed a Luger. The tidiest of trophies.

EVERYWHERE THEY WENT, THEY SAW THE SWASTIKA. BLACK ARMS on a white circle in a field of red. Though the Reich was falling, those flags and banners still possessed eerie talismanic power, and men were eager to cut them down, pose for pictures, capture or destroy them. The symbol for the real thing. But the farther they pushed on, the more they saw another kind of flag, made of pillowcases or torn sheets, hanging from the windows of houses, sometimes every house on the main road of whatever village or town they were entering: the white one.

GERMAN RESISTANCE BEGAN TO COLLAPSE. IN THE END, THE BAT-talion was marching or riding past whole German garrisons that simply stood aside, letting them pass. The reason: the Soviets were closing in from the east. Better, then, to fall into Western hands. For the same reason, civilians were streaming west. Many looked glum at the sight of foreign invaders, but a good many cheered, so great was their terror of the Russians. There were so many refugees that nothing could really be done. They were simply sent on down the road, to be handled by some rear unit. The Canadians pressed on.

12

SPRING CAME ON QUICKLY, THE WORLD WARMING, GREENING, blooming. These were the waning days of the war, and everyone knew it.

On the last day of April, after crossing the Elbe River, Josiah was on patrol, walking through a field with half a dozen others. They kept an eye out for any last holdouts, but everything about the day—the azure, the sunshine, the delicate breeze—conspired against a sense of urgency.

A mile in, they approached a copse, with Van den Berg out front. As he tromped toward it, leaves rustled, maybe with wind, but everyone froze. Van den Berg held up his hand, urging the others to stay put, then tiptoed ahead in a crouch, with a rare show of caution. "Easy, Van den Berg," Walker said, but even Josiah, who knew they had to stay vigilant, even he thought, surely not. Surely no one was fighting at this point over such a meaningless piece of land, of no strategic importance whatsoever.

Van den Berg kept inching forward, crossing his legs in a sidestep, until he was almost up to the wood line. He stopped to peer into the trees, craning from side to side. Then he stood up and relaxed, and the men relaxed, too, with a bit of nervous laughter.

At that moment, something resembling a club came flying out of the copse. The way it tumbled end over end, like a juggler's pin, gave it an air of whimsy. Men yelled, dropped to the ground, but Van den Berg just stood there, paralyzed by confusion. Or maybe disbelief. Or resignation. The stick grenade went off with a modest bang, and Van den Berg fell straight back.

The men unleashed on the copse. Josiah shot from the hip, the Bren gun slung around him. He wasn't sure he had ever shot twenty rounds faster, only to load up and shoot some more. For a long minute, the copse thrashed violently. Then the men moved forward, some into the trees, others toward Van den Berg.

Josiah reached Van den Berg first. He was still alive, but barely, his body riddled with wounds, including a sizeable one in his chest that was making a sucking sound. He had lost an eye and most of his babyish teeth and looked ghastly, but Josiah held him in his lap. With his one good eye, Van den Berg raked what was left of the world, trying to make sense of it, but his eye was already glazing. Looking inward, through the deep well of memory and beyond, all the way back to the time his mother had leaned over his crib, touched a hand to his cheek, and disappeared from his life forever. Then the light went out.

In the copse, they discovered more Jugend and Volkssturm, more boys and old men, all dead for nothing.

"What the fuck?" Walker said bitterly. "Just surrender already!"

They dug a shallow grave and buried Van den Berg right then and there, leaving one of his identification discs and marking the grave with his rifle and helmet. Then they made the long walk back to headquarters, in a town east of the Elbe. By the time they got back, Walker was still incensed. In the center of town, a number of German

POWs were penned outside, and Walker strode right up and raised his rifle. The nearest man, dressed in an undershirt, made the mistake of sneering. Walker shot him in the face. The other prisoners shouted, recoiled, scrambled, but Walker was able to shoot another before Josiah launched himself and tackled him to the ground. As they struggled in a cloud of dust, Walker managed to land a punch, flush to Josiah's cheek, before Josiah replied with a heavy blow of his own. Then they were pulled apart.

As other men restrained them, Walker launched a gob of blood. "Whose side are you on anyway, Chang?"

The lieutenant colonel arrived and sized things up, and Walker was taken away. That was the last they saw of him.

THE NEXT DAY, ON THE MARCH TO WISMAR, JOSIAH GOT A TURN ON a motorcycle, a Matchless G3L, and he pulled back on the throttle and went tearing down the road, through rolling green hills, until he was way out front, completely alone in the world for maybe the first time since the war began, and in that solitude cried out. Long, repeated cries that were instantly swallowed by the wind and the roar of the engine. He cried out for the thrill of freedom, and the thrill of crying out, but mostly he cried out for Van den Berg, and for Heikkinen, the lieutenant, his father. But he also cried out for the way the world had driven him from Poppy, and how they had lost so much time, and how they might not have any left.

13

THE FOLLOWING DAY, THEY CLIMBED ONTO TANKS AND RODE WITH the Scots Greys. The plan was to reach Wittenberg by noon, but they met so little resistance they were there by nine thirty. They were now under orders from Churchill himself to take Wismar before the Russians could, so they pressed on, stopping only once to refuel. At sundown, the golden shades of the passing world almost made Josiah wistful, now that the end was nigh. By nightfall, they reached the black waters of the Baltic Sea. There was no sign of the Russians.

C COMPANY WAS SENT TO THE EASTERN EDGE OF TOWN TO SET UP A checkpoint. In the small hours of night, headlights appeared in the distance and grew steadily brighter. When they came to a stop, a shadow emerged from the passenger side and walked into the blinding light. His uniform looked strangely homespun, as if he had sewn on the chevrons himself. Nonetheless, it was clear he was Russian.

Someone from Winnipeg who could speak the language gathered that the officer was the advance party of a Russian armored column headed for Wismar. When the Russian learned the city was already in Canadian hands, he became every bit as surly and pugnacious as he looked, his tirade reeking of alcohol. Then he and his driver turned around and sped off.

The Russians also approached from the north, where they ran into B Company, but there the mood was different. There, the Russians broke out the vodka and gamely plied the Canadians, who caroused with them until morning.

But the mood wouldn't last. When the Russians arrived from the east, they established their own checkpoint. C Company had set up barricades just beyond a large lake; the Russians set up their own a few hundred yards away, on the long stretch of road that led to the next town over. For some reason, the Canadians were not allowed to enter the Russian-held area, but the Russians were free to go wherever they pleased, and everywhere they went, there was trouble. Every night, Josiah heard gunshots, especially on the Russian side, and every day, ever more Germans streamed toward the checkpoint, seeking refuge.

Somewhere between the two checkpoints, a German ambulance lay on its side in a ditch, maybe a hundred yards from the Canadians. One day, a young Russian in jackboots and epaulets crawled into the back and shut the double doors.

"What's that about?" Syd Antoine asked.

Josiah wasn't sure. "Think there's morphine in there?"

The answer came soon enough when a middle-aged woman appeared on the road from the Russian side. As she passed the ambulance, the soldier leapt out and grabbed her and dragged her kicking and scream- ing toward the ambulance.

Josiah started to leave his post, but his new lieutenant told him to stand down. They had their orders not to interfere. "Besides, it's nothing the Germans haven't done to the Russians," the lieutenant sniffed.

"But, sir—"

"Stand down, Chang. That's an order."

The woman was still putting up a fight, so the man punched her viciously in the stomach. Only then was he able to drag her into the back. From behind those double doors came the sound of more screaming. Josiah felt ill.

Eventually, the soldier climbed out, shut the doors, and started back, as if nothing had happened. The ambulance was now silent, and Josiah wondered if the woman was dead. Then the bottom door fell open and the woman crawled out and hobbled toward the checkpoint, quietly sobbing. Josiah and Syd Antoine went out to help her, but she yelled at them accusingly before limping on.

Later that day, Josiah happened upon the lieutenant colonel who had dispatched Walker. When Josiah described what had happened, the lieutenant colonel eyed him from behind his push broom mustache and said his concerns were duly noted, and Josiah thought that was the end of it. But the next day, the lieutenant colonel sought him out to say that he had spoken to his Russian counterpart, and Josiah was surprised to hear what the ranking Russian officer had said.

"I beg your pardon, sir."

"You heard me, Private Chang," the lieutenant colonel said. "If you see more of the same, just shoot him."

THE VERY NEXT DAY, THE SOLDIER WAS BACK, SLINKING INTO THE ambulance. The undercarriage was rotting, which must have given him a clear view of the road.

"We should get him out of there, sir," Josiah said to the lieutenant.

"What did I tell you, Chang? We have our orders."

In time, an older, heavyset woman came trudging down the road, a sack in each hand. Sure enough, as she passed the ambulance, the double doors burst open, and the soldier jumped out and lunged. The woman careened, still clutching her bags, running in a kind of crazed circle before she slipped. Onions spilled across the road.

Josiah began to run, Luger in hand. The lieutenant ordered him to stop, but Josiah ignored him. He would square things away with the lieutenant colonel later. "Hey! Stop! Nyet!" Josiah cried, but the soldier was too far away. He dragged the woman across the road and into the back of the ambulance.

The ambulance was a good sprint away. By the time he reached it, Josiah was already lightheaded, even before he was met by the strange tilt of the box and the sight of the soldier's trousers already down to his knees. At the sound of the door, the soldier craned his neck and started to scream indignantly. Josiah had the urge to shoot him right then and there but didn't want to traumatize the woman any further.

"Get out! Get the fuck out!" Josiah yelled, with no means of being understood except to yell louder and to wave the Luger more insistently. At length, the soldier pulled up his trousers and scrambled out of the ambulance. As Josiah pointed the Luger, the man continued to scream, foaming rabidly at the mouth, but Josiah felt no hatred. He wasn't Walker. He wouldn't give in to darkness. He knew where the line was, that absurdly fine line. He could still tell right from wrong.

He shot the man right between the eyes.

JOSIAH WAS ASSIGNED TO A TOWN HOUSE IN THE GOTHIC QUARTER that hadn't been too badly damaged.

In the morning, he fetched some water from a public hose, heated the water in the kitchen, and poured the water into a basin. After lathering with a brush, he ran a razor over his cheeks in long, raspy strokes. In the cloudy little mirror from his overnight bag, he watched himself transforming. Getting younger and less haggard. A proper shave was a small but important necessity. One of those little things that kept you human.

The other men were upstairs, futzing with a radio, trying to pick up the BBC. As Josiah wiped up the last bits of shaving cream, the house erupted in paroxysms of joy. It sounded as if they were listening to football and some decisive goal had been scored. Then footsteps came bounding down the stairs. It was Syd Antoine, face split from ear to ear. He was hollering wildly and threw himself upon Josiah. Germany had surrendered. The war in Europe was over.

14

THAT DAY AND THE NEXT, V-E DAY, THEY CELEBRATED THE ONLY way they knew how, by drinking indiscriminately. Alcohol overflowed, as if the whole war had been fought to procure it. Not just beer and wine but gin, whisky, rum, and vodka, which the Russians seemed to have no end of. Even Somerville, a teetotaler, partook, to everyone's amusement. Josiah drank as he hadn't since earning his wings in Fort Benning, until the whole world was wheeling.

In his quieter moments, though, he would sit, smoke, and marvel. He had made it. Come through. Walked through the valley of the shadow of death. Now that he had done it, it almost seemed ordained, but he knew it wasn't, not in the slightest, and he savored his every thought, his every sensation of life.

During one of those quieter moments, he went hunting through the half-shuttered shops of the market square for a postcard, until he found one of St. Mary's Church, which towered over the city. He'd pictured how happy Poppy must have been, waking to news of victory in Europe. Now he pictured how happy she would be, knowing he had lived to see it.

Amid the celebrations, Josiah and others went swimming in the inner harbor. As he dove down through the bracing waters of the Baltic Sea, he felt supremely glad to be alive. After rising from the inner harbor, no one could find Oberg, the Frenchman. Many had seen him go into the water, blitzed, but no one had seen him come out. If not for Oberg blabbing away about the luxury of air travel before their very first jump in Fort Benning, Josiah would not have thought to fly back to Vancouver and would not have seen Poppy one last time, so he joined in the search, but the body was never found. No one could understand it. As part of their training, they'd had to swim a hundred yards in swimming kit and fifty yards with clothing on, and Oberg had always done fine—well, in fact. To come through all that and the war, only to drown. Truly, the universe was merciless.

A FEW DAYS LATER, A MEMORIAL AND THANKSGIVING SERVICE WAS held at St. Nicholas Church, which, unlike St. Mary's, had somehow managed to go unscathed. Sitting in the pews, listening to the chaplains, Josiah felt angry and restless. Even if there was a God, it was foolish to think that he took sides in war. That he looked out for anyone. If God spent his time designing the flight paths of millions of pieces of shrapnel, then he was a pedant. The whole thing made Josiah all the more ready to leave. Somehow, days without war were even more unending.

Finally, a week after V-E Day, word came down that they were heading back to England. After trucking a few hours to Lüneburg, where they spent one final night in a bivouac, sleeping in a ditch, they flew to Brussels, then on to bases all over England. Josiah wound up in Newbury, not far from Camp Bulford, and took a lorry back. What a tremendous feeling, walking into Carter Barracks and seeing the old familiar streets. He had lived here for almost two years now, and it positively smacked of home.

Outside his Nissen hut, Josiah saw another ghost, just as he had after Normandy, only this time it wasn't Van den Berg but Heikkinen, or someone who could have been Heikkinen, towheaded and bookish but thinner, much thinner, and Josiah's heart quickened, the way a heart does even when it's wrong. If seeing Van den Berg again after Normandy had been strange and unlikely, then this was something even more uncanny. The two of them walked toward each other, both unsure of what they were seeing. Then came the moment of certainty, and the man fell into Josiah's arms and wept.

THEY WALKED OUT ONTO THE PLAIN, JUST THE TWO OF THEM, THE whole plain yellow with cowslip, the way it had been this time last year, before the whole bloody invasion began. Heikkinen was quiet and pensive, a shell of his former knowing self, but the walk was long and they had time, and the contours of his war emerged. On D-Day, he had landed practically right on top of a German patrol. He and about fifty others, British, American, French, and Canadian, were locked in a barn. Eventually they were taken to Gare du Nord in Paris and loaded into a cattle car, so small they had to sleep on top of each other, a single piss pot breathing its stench in the corner. They were taken to Stalag IV-B northeast of Mühlberg, where they waited out the war. At first, every man got a Red Cross parcel once a week. In time, parcels had to be shared, until there were no more parcels at all, and they got by however they could, making coffee out of acorns, tea out of any leaf. "It got bad, very bad," Heikkinen said, unsteadily.

Then came the bouts of cholera and dysentery, the men immiserated by diarrhea. Scrambling for the outhouse, or just outside, or just out of bed, until even that proved too much. "That's when I thought I was done for, when I couldn't even get out of bed," Heikkinen said. All his life, he'd been desperate to get out of New Finland, little more than a church, community hall, and schoolhouse. Desperate to see and know the world, but in the end, all he wanted was to go back.

Josiah listened, guilty with relief that his war had been different. He would take all the mosquitoes in France, all the cold in Belgium and Holland, and every long and lonely mile of Germany over Stalag IV-B.

As they walked across the plain, Josiah talked of his own war, and he got the funny feeling that Heikkinen, for all his misery, would not have traded Stalag IV-B for all the stonking and the killing. When he got to the part about Van den Berg, Heikkinen's eyes went raw, and neither of them said anything else for a very long time.

HEIKKINEN'S WAR WAS OVER. HE WAS BEING SENT HOME. JOSIAH, ON the other hand, got nine days leave, and he used them to go back to Oxfordshire. Walking from the station to the Fosters' farm, through a world green with spring, he felt time repeating itself yet again.

As he approached the farmhouse, Mrs. Foster stepped outside and clapped her hands together, then raised her arms to embrace him, her face less plain for being familiar. Emily, Beatrice, and Margaret jigged around them, and Josiah handed each of them a tin of boiled sweets. At suppertime, Mr. Foster came in and shook his hand and thanked him heartily for winning the war. For two days and two nights, Josiah sat at that warm and inviting table, dining on Mrs. Foster's still ingenious cooking, and feeling again that this was a life he might like for himself. This time, there was no work to be done, or rather, no work asked of him, so he spent his days out in the garden, sitting in a lawn chair amid the sweet scent of daisies and bluebells, just feeling the warmth of the sun, his eyes closed in a kind of eternal exhaustion.

On the third day, as he sat in the garden, Mrs. Foster came out in a housedress and apron. "This just arrived," she said, holding out a telegram.

Josiah read it, then rose from his chair. "I have to go back to Camp Bulford," he said stoically. There was no explanation why.

"Oh, Mr. Chang," she said, eyes filling. "I'm so sorry."

On the train back, Josiah had a terrible feeling in the pit of his stomach. The war in Europe was over, but the war with Japan was not, and he felt the nightmare beginning again.

"What's this about?" he asked Syd Antoine, once they were back.

"No idea."

The next day, as the whole battalion stood in formation, the lieutenant colonel took to a microphone to address them. The men were short as fuses, and when they heard the news, they exploded. They had passage on a ship. They were going home.

15

THE NEXT FEW DAYS WERE SPENT GETTING READY, CLEANING
huts and returning equipment. They had to surrender any German
weapons they might have picked up, and Josiah had no trouble parting
with his Luger. The feeling was different, though, when he turned in
his Bren. He'd carried the same one throughout the war and had come
to know it and trust it, maybe even love it, the wood of the gunstock
seasoned with his blood, sweat, and tears.

There was one last parade to the post office, where Josiah received
a final letter from Poppy, this one written in response to a postcard
he'd sent from Kolkhagen. *The whole world has been living in a kind of
madness*, she wrote, *but at last it seems that madness is coming to an end.
I almost don't know what the old world was like, or if we can ever go back
to it. But I can almost see it again.* Despite its hopeful air, he sensed
something vaguely threatening, but he had long since stopped trying to parse her every word. He remembered the resolution he had

made on the voyage to England, that so long as she wrote and pro-fessed love, he would keep faith, and here they were, writing to the very end. Though he wasn't sure it would beat him back, he sent one final postcard with the words he'd been longing to write: *I'm coming home.*

1

ON THE LAST DAY OF MAY, THEY LEFT CAMP BULFORD FOR A REPA-triation depot in Farnborough, outside of London. The station in Bulford was draped in bunting, Red Ensigns, and a banner that read LONG LIVE CANADA! Brigadier Hill was there to see them off, and he went down the line, shaking the hand of every last man. When he reached Josiah, he gave him an extra clap on the shoulder, remembering, perhaps, that long-ago battle in Bréville. Eventually, the train began to stir to the strains of "Auld Lang Syne," and Josiah leaned out the window for one last look. He had lived here longer than any other place in his life, and now it was behind him.

From Farnborough, time began to spool in reverse: They took the train back to Greenock, Scotland, where they boarded the *Île de France*. Then they recrossed the Atlantic, only the *Île de France* was nothing compared to the RMS *Queen Elizabeth*. It took three infernal weeks to reach Pier 21 in Halifax, where they were met by a squall of rain and fog and the sound of boat horns blasting in the harbor: dot-dot-dot-dash.

V for Victory.

• • •

JOSIAH WAS DYING TO GO STRAIGHT FROM THE PIER TO HALIFAX Station. Instead, the battalion marched to a homecoming reception with the mayor, then paraded down Terminal Road to Citadel Hill, the streets raining confetti. They were the first complete unit to come home and had to be fêted.

Then more infernal delay: one last night aboard the *Île de France*. "We're never getting off this ship, are we?" Syd Antoine laughed. It wasn't until the next day that they were finally allowed to leave. Josiah shook hands with Harrison at Halifax Station, then boarded a special train, where they were given special treatment. First-class dining and their own cabins. However, at every little town they stopped in, they were obliged to parade. Since Poppy had sent that first newspaper clipping, the battalion's reputation had only grown: the first Canadians into France, the only Canadians in the Ardennes. Apparently, as they had been living and dying in Europe, they had become . . . famous.

In Toronto, after parading on Yonge Street, Josiah found himself back in the great hall at Union Station, which gave him a feeling of eternal return, especially when he entered the very same telephone booth from which he had first called Poppy, lo those many years ago. He still disliked the phone, but he couldn't put off calling any longer.

When the operator called back, she said there was no answer. It was evening in Toronto, not quite suppertime in Vancouver. Maybe Poppy wasn't home yet. The train was about to leave, but he waited five anxious minutes and tried again. This time, the operator put her through.

"Oh my god, Joe! I knew it was you! I was coming home and heard the phone and I ran—" As proof, she paused to catch her breath. "Where are you, darling?"

"Toronto."

She laughed, sparklingly. "I knew you were back. From the papers. But Toronto is better than Halifax."

"Not nearly good enough," he said, "but I'll be at Waterfront Station on Friday."

"I'll be there," she said, "with bells on."

ON THE LAST NIGHT OF THE JOURNEY, JOSIAH LAY IN THE JOSTLING dark, dreaming of reunion, as he had a thousand times before, in every miserable kip and foxhole on both sides of the ocean, never sure the day would come. But now that it was finally here, he felt apprehensive. That things wouldn't be the same. That he was a changed man and Poppy a changed woman. That time had done what it always does: thieve, implacably. All the same, his odyssey was nearing the end. One last night in a strange bed. He had slept in a thousand to get back to the one.

AT THE STATION IN KAMLOOPS, JOSIAH AND SYD ANTOINE STOOD ON the platform, next to the train that would take Syd north, the engine already hissing and blowing, ready to go. When the conductor called all aboard, Syd smiled his exuberant smile and said, "We've got some stories to tell, my friend."

Josiah reached under the pack of cigarettes in his breast pocket and pulled out a piece of paper with an address. "Don't need this anymore."

Syd looked, remembering. "You keep it. She'll know where to find me." And then: "What did I tell you? I knew you'd make it."

They shook hands. And when that seemed wholly inadequate, embraced.

AT EVERY STATION IN EVERY PROVINCE, HE HAD TAKEN LEAVE OF others, until the train seemed his alone, the wretched excitement of seeing Poppy tempered by an ever-growing solitude. His soul swooned slowly, thinking of the men they had left behind. Men who were now shades, lying buried under crooked crosses and headstones in Germany, in Belgium and Holland, and in lonely churchyards all over France, even under the dark mutinous waves of the Baltic Sea. And one man lying in a nameless field so close, so very close to the end.

2

LATER THAT DAY, A FAULTLESS DAY IN LATE JUNE, THE GREAT metropolis finally appeared in the distance, shimmering like a mirage. It brought him back to his very first glimpse of the city three years ago, as a young man, as yet unable to imagine all that was to come. On the outskirts of the city, they snaked along the inlet, with its view of the water and the mountains. All the places he'd been, and none to rival the one he had left. As they passed the inner harbor, he saw where it had all begun, the chain-link fence and the steel, the scaffolds and the five-ton cranes, the yard still going after all this time, and remembered the war wasn't over, not even for him. After thirty days, he would have to report for duty again.

At last the train pulled into Waterfront Station, to the clanging of bells and a final dying sigh, and he walked from the platform to the booking hall, his whole body thrumming. There, under God-streaked light, he and the other men were greeted by a gasp of applause. As the crowd surged forward, he scanned the sudden onrush of faces, but none were hers.

Then, with scuttling lateness, she appeared from the back of the crowd. He only had a moment to register the blue dress, the red headband, the tearful look of regret. Then she was in his arms, and he tasted lipstick and smoke, his head bursting with light. It took a moment to realize that the blinding brightness all around him was not the delirium of his own happiness but so many flashbulbs going off. He touched his forehead to hers, as if to hide. Stave off the world.

"Poppy."

"Oh my god, Joe."

When they finally let go, Poppy laughing wetly, a finger under each eye, all he wanted to do was find the nearest taxi stand and spirit her away. Instead, they were stopped by cameramen who asked for their names. Then someone from the Canadian Army Newsreel asked Josiah for an interview, and reluctantly, he obliged. Toward the end, when the interviewer asked what it meant to be the only Chinese member of the 1st Canadian Parachute Battalion, Josiah stiffened a little. He knew what he was supposed to say. That he was proud. This was supposed to be a feel-good piece, and part of him wanted to give a feel-good answer. But Poppy was watching, and he felt he had to speak in some way to everything they had been through. So he looked into the camera and said, "I just want to be Canadian. Like everyone else."

AT LAST THEY WERE FREE, RACING AWAY FROM WATERFRONT STATION in the back of a cab, Poppy nestled against him, one hand splayed across his chest.

"I'm sorry, Joe. I took too long getting ready, and then the cab was late. I should have been there. As soon as you stepped off the train."

Searching the crowd at the station, he'd felt a dull throb of anger, but now that he was here, with her, the feeling was gone. Yet he felt a little unnatural, like an actor playing a part, maybe because they weren't alone, the driver repeatedly flicking his eyes to the rearview mirror, or maybe because it had been so long. As they crossed the Lions Gate Bridge, to sunlight flickering through cables, he even felt a moment of estrangement. Who was this woman? He didn't know.

The house on Fell Avenue looked the same yet different, the shrubs a little larger, the steps a little worn. As they hurried up the walkway, the curtains next door ruffled, and the woman inside startled with recognition, but rather than disapproval, or mere disapproval, Josiah saw a complicated play of feelings, including what he could only think to call pity, as if she were trying to imagine all he had been through, and the thought of her thinking of him left him strangely moved.

As soon as he stepped inside, he sensed something was off but couldn't put a finger on it. Then he realized the walls were yellow with tar and nicotine, and it hurt him to think that in his absence the place had soured with age. Like last time, they proceeded directly to the bedroom, only this time, Poppy sat down at her dressing table, looked in the mirror, and declared herself hideous. He laughed. Nothing could have been further from the truth. Far from being ugly, those rivulets of mascara lent her a dark and unexpected allure. More to the point, it would have taken an act of God to make her ugly to him after all this time. No doubt, time had passed. She was older, her face a little rounder, softening year by year toward middle life, in ways that might have been imperceptible had he not gone away. But she was still the same alarmingly beautiful woman he had seen from the first, and he felt impatient with desire.

He stood behind her, looking at her in the mirror. Then he brushed aside her hair and kissed her on the neck. She seemed to shrink, to draw back, and he felt that dull throb of anger he'd felt at the station. Surely she knew what he wanted, what he needed, after all this time, and surely she wanted and needed the same. Maybe she was flinching at his caution, when she wanted him to be forceful, unabashed. In many ways, they were strangers again, and it made him unsure. He kissed her neck again, more ardently, and this seemed to relax, then rouse her, until she reached up and ran a hand through his hair.

She turned to face him. In a gesture he had never seen or couldn't remember seeing, she pulled off her headband with a toss of her head. Then they were moving toward the inexorable. At each step, they paused with a kind of worshipful disbelief. They had found each other again in the vast loneliness of the universe, and they were astonished. As they moved together, she buried her face in his neck, as if ashamed. He was already on the cusp when he realized he hadn't put anything on and asked if he should stop, but she said no, don't, don't stop, and he quietly vowed never to leave her again, a moment before his mind went blank.

3

AFTERWARD, THEY LAY SIDE BY SIDE, GAZING AT EACH OTHER. WITH the blinds shut, her blue eyes were almost black, and in them he could see the room in miniature. Already, he wanted to make love again, but he could afford to be patient. The ticking of her clock was no longer the sound of their life together dribbling away but rather stretching into infinity. They had all the time in the world.

Poppy reached for her cigarettes. When he did the same, retrieving the pack in the pocket of his battle blouse, she laughed. "I thought I tasted smoke. When did you start?" When he told her, she said, "I'm surprised it took you that long. The army must be a chimney factory."

As they sat on the bed, an ashtray between them, he suddenly realized why the house seemed off. He'd been so preoccupied he'd forgotten. He went to the window and peeked through the blinds, but the yard was empty.

"Where's Queenie?"

Poppy's eyes brimmed, and he felt a fearful premonition, even before she said, "Joe, there are some things I need to tell you." She rose and put on her pink satin robe. That's when he knew. Still, he wasn't prepared to hear her say, "Queenie's gone. She . . . disappeared."

"What?"

Poppy drew a long breath and gathered herself. "She was out in the yard one day, but when I went to let her in, she wasn't there. A board in the fence had come loose. I did everything I could to find her. You can ask the neighbors. But she vanished into thin air."

He pictured Queenie, her thin face, her thin body, slithering through the breach—just as she had the first time he had come home. "When?"

"You must have been in Germany. I figured you had enough on your mind."

"You should have told me."

"Maybe," she said, patiently, "but I couldn't really explain. She was dying, Joe. We both knew it, and I think she did, too. When she left, I had this overwhelming feeling that she wanted to see you one last time." Poppy's eyes gleamed. "That she went to find you."

Josiah remembered the dog in the trench on his first night in Germany and felt a cold shiver pass through him. "Did you look in the park?"

"I looked, Joe. Believe me, I looked."

Poppy's cigarette had burned out. She sat facing him on the bench of her dressing table and lit another, as if to fortify herself. "There's something else I need to tell you."

He felt a shudder of dread. Realizing he was naked, he got up and put on his trousers and stood across the room, to face whatever had to be faced.

In a sinking yet measured voice, she said, "I'm pregnant."

In his addled state, he thought she meant by him. From last time or just now. But that was impossible.

"What?" he said again, dimly.

"I'm pregnant, Joe."

"Are you sure?"

"I've suspected for a while now—"

"But are you sure?"

"Yes," she said firmly, "I'm sure."

He was struck by a bolt of black lightning. Her changed face, her flinching hesitation, even their novel lovemaking—it all meant something else. The room spun wildly.

"How?"

She drew up, steeling herself. "Remember Jimmy?" she asked, and Josiah recalled the name and the face and the artless way the man had left the storage shed with Poppy, back in his first fledgling days at the yard. Jimmy had left to join the RCAF and had flown as a rear gunner on a Lancaster until he was shot down over the Netherlands. "I told you about that, remember? Missing in action. That was the last I heard. Turns out he was taken prisoner and sent to a POW camp. The camp was liberated by the Americans a few months ago."

Minus fifty degrees, up in those tail turrets. That's what Lieutenant Morrison had said. Then a POW camp, like Heikkinen. Josiah almost felt for the man.

"One day, he just showed up at my door. I was astonished. It was like . . . seeing a ghost. He came in, and we talked. Or rather, he talked, and I listened. That's all we did. For a long time. Then he started to cry, and I held him. He'd been through so much. But then he—"

Josiah saw it all: the sudden closeness, the tender confusion, the famished body, and could almost understand. But it seared him to think his own reunion had already played out once. That his own exploits had helped to bring Jimmy home first.

"Do you love him?"

"No," she said, scoffing a little. "I haven't seen him since."

The tourniquet around him loosened. It almost didn't matter, then. Or rather, might not have mattered if—

"Does he know?"

She shook her head. "And he never will."

The tourniquet loosened again. "What are you going to do?"

"I don't know," she said, touching a hand to her head. "I haven't had time to figure it out. I know what I want to do, but I don't know what I *can* do."

"Didn't you use—"

"Of course, Joe. I don't know what happened."

His thoughts darkened. What were the odds of things going awry the one time—

"How many other men?"

She rolled her lips with forbearance. "There were no other men, Joe."

He felt relieved. But now that the shock was beginning to fade, the nobility of being wronged gave way to other feelings: anger, self-pity. On the mirror behind her, the postcards of Toronto, Orillia, and Fort Benning had given way to ones he had sent from Lembeck, Coesfeld, Ladbergen, Ricklingen, Riestedt, and Bahlendorf, which brought back every interminable mile of the odyssey.

"Do you know what I've been through?"

He thought she would be remorseful. Look at her lap and say, "I know." Instead, she said, "I never wanted you to leave, Joe. I never wanted any of this."

It must have been hard, excruciating even, fearing for him for so long. But hers seemed the better end of the deal. "All you had to do was wait."

He saw the effort to tamp down some froth of emotion. "I was honest, Joe. I was clear from the start. I didn't want to wait, yet that's precisely what I did. For more than two years. It took time, but I learned how to be patient. And except for a day, an hour, less, I was. I want that to count for something."

All that time was not meaningless, not nothing, but he saw they wouldn't agree on the one great exception. If it were simply a matter of forgiveness, he might have found it within him. He had strayed enough himself to understand human failing. But it wasn't simply a matter of forgiving and forgetting.

"What are you going to do?"

She turned away, stricken. "I don't know."

He looked at her, sitting there in all her pain and uncertainty, and tried to rouse some hatred but couldn't. The truth was, she looked beautiful, more beautiful than ever, what with her new body and the strange and dark enchantment of those still bleeding eyes. What he wanted, he realized, was to have her again. Which was why he had to leave.

"I have to go."

Again, she pressed her lips with forbearance. "Okay. If that's what you want."

He finished dressing. Put on his undershirt and his battle blouse and pulled down his maroon beret with strained dignity. Then he picked up his duffel, and she followed him to the door.

"Where are you going?"

"I don't know. I just . . . need some time to myself. But I'll come back when I'm ready."

He could tell she found his answer wholly unsatisfactory, but she didn't argue. Instead, she looked at him expectantly, but he refused to go to her. On that he was resolute. Then he was out the door, his vow never to leave again already broken.

4

JOSIAH STRODE DOWN MARINE DRIVE, PAST ALL THOSE MADDENINGLY identical houses and all the shops and restaurants, until he reached the foot of the Lions Gate Bridge, where he grudgingly paid the toll. As he walked over the water, he looked out onto the great metropolis, including the yard, still nattering away in the distance, and couldn't believe how everything had changed in the short time since he last crossed.

A man came toward him on the sidewalk. One of those old men who always dress warmly, even in the heat. In this case, a sweater-vest and a tweed jacket, plus a plaid fedora. They wound up meeting in the middle, high above the water. For some reason, the man stopped abruptly, and Josiah stopped, too, in case they knew each other. When the man's eyes narrowed, Josiah realized he was expected to step aside, to make way, and this enraged him. The man was walking on the wrong side of the bridge. More to the point, Josiah was in uniform, his goddamn wings on his goddamn chest, having just liberated goddamn Europe.

"Get the fuck out of my way," Josiah said.

The old man's face darkened with loathing, but also satisfaction, as if everything he had ever suspected had been confirmed. Josiah had the urge to throw him off the bridge. Sensing as much, the old man stepped around him and hurried off.

The path Josiah used to take through the park had overgrown, but he would have known the way even in the dark. He recognized the trees, standing sentinel, and felt the mystery of persistence, the way the world changed yet stayed the same without you. When he came to the clearing, he was met by the same feeling. The camp was gone, but there was his chopping block, his stump stool.

"Queenie!" he called.

Her name echoed through the woods, sending creatures scattering. He listened, waited, heart thudding.

"Queenie!" he cried again.

He pictured her alien face, those strangely articulated ribs, and that shock of white on her chest. There was almost no chance she had made it all the way here, and even if she had, it would have been for naught. Worse than naught. There were coyotes in these woods, and he felt her fear as she caught their scent, long before her cloudy eyes could apprehend their vague silhouettes. And he felt her dreaming of him as the first bite came down, to a gargle in her throat.

He kept calling, waiting for the moment of joy. It never came.

5

HE SPENT THE NIGHT AT THE ST. FRANCIS HOTEL, DIRECTLY ACROSS from Waterfront Station. All night, he heard the clanging of the rail yard, his room unpleasantly bright from the sign for the Almer Hotel next door, but he wouldn't have slept anyway. He lay there for hours, just staring at the ceiling. At some point in his endless cogitations, it occurred to him that had she not gotten pregnant, she might not have said anything. Which might have been better, living in happy oblivion. If her condition could have been reversed, safely, she might not have said anything, either. As it was, there wasn't much to be done. He didn't want her to die, doing something reckless. Had he been someone else, they might have been able to live a lie. "Not sure *who* he gets his looks from," they could have joked for the rest of their lives. In this case, though, the truth would always be plain. He tried to imagine it, raising another man's child, possibly with Jimmy himself, somehow returned and ensconced in their lives, but all he could see was the angry child, forever ashamed of the strange man his mother had taken up with, and he knew it wasn't in him.

Maybe his strangeness was the problem. Maybe she would have been true if he had been someone else. They were some of the first to do this, Poppy had said, and it pained him to think they didn't know how. At moments, he felt on the verge of forgiving her, but the feeling seemed to come too quickly, as if innocence were also her birthright, which was why he couldn't do it.

At other moments, he thought, of course. Of course this was bound to happen. What had it ever been but a summer affair. A ninety-day wonder. Too little to build a life on. He remembered his first night with Poppy, when he thought about getting a little house like hers and waiting out the war in comfort. Why hadn't he just done that?

In the morning, as the city began to stir, he left his room in search of food. When he came down the stairs, the matronly woman at the front desk, who had checked him in the night before, lit up at the sight of him. "Congratulations, Mr. Chang! You should have told me!"

On the front desk lay copies of the *Province*, the *Sun*, and the *News-Herald*, and there on the front page of each was a variation of the same photograph, as if they had come from the same contact sheet. The caption in the *News-Herald* read *Private Josiah Chang of the 1st Canadian Parachute Battalion returns to a kiss from his fiancée, Poppy Miller.* The front page of the *News-Herald* was famously pink, which lent the scene an extra dusting of romance.

Josiah was horrified. Everywhere now, others would recognize him as that soldier from the papers, that paragon of love, until they saw the child and the plain truth. Now he understood why Poppy's neighbor had given him that look. She had seen Jimmy come to the house and heard them together through the paper-thin walls. Like a seer, she knew everything, and had looked upon him sadly. This was what he was in for if he stayed with Poppy: a lifetime of pity.

"May I keep these?" he asked, as if he could round up every last copy in the world. "Also, I'll be checking out."

He gathered his things, crossed the street to the station, and bought a ticket to Niagara-on-the-Lake.

6

HE WAS THE FIRST MAN TO RETURN TO CAMP NIAGARA, TO THE quartermaster's surprise, and put up in a field of bell tents, where he spent his days alone. It was now July, the weather sweltering, but he hadn't been issued summer khakis, so he lounged around the tent in his undershirt. In time, men came back, one by one. A few had been discharged, others given farm or industrial leave, but most of the unit returned, including Syd Antoine.

"Here we go again," Syd said.

This time, they were getting ready to join the Americans for the invasion of Japan, but Camp Niagara felt less like the army than summer camp. They spent their days playing football and baseball and cooling off in Lake Ontario. On weekends, they took the bus to Niagara Falls or Hamilton or Buffalo. On Saturday nights, there were dances at Simcoe Park, where they flirted with farmerettes, girls who came from across the province to work on farms around Niagara-on-the-Lake. They were all young and sun-kissed and pleasant to talk to, but never more than that for Josiah.

As summer passed, thoughts of Poppy persisted. He pictured her starting to show, her condition no longer easy to hide, and wondered if there had been a shotgun wedding and the powerful amulet of a ring. At mail call, he still expected letters, a habit he had yet to break. Yes, he had disappeared, but all she had to do was write to the 1st Canadian Parachute Battalion and the letter would have reached him. Any overture, it seemed, should have come from her. But no such letter arrived.

ON A FINE DAY IN MID-AUGUST, SYD ANTOINE PUSHED BACK THE flaps of the bell tent, letting in a blinding burst of light. Josiah looked up from his cot, shading his eyes.

"Have you heard the news?" Syd asked, breathless, and Josiah saw him again on that fateful morning in Wismar. "Japan surrendered. War's over."

7

AFTER HIS WEEKLY TRIP INTO TOWN, JOSIAH RETURNED TO HIS cabin in the woods with a rucksack full of provisions. The last of the snow was gone, and the birch trees shone silver in the clear spring light. Once home, he put things away and fed the dog, then sat down at a long farm table to read the letter he had long been expecting.

When the war was finally over, the 1st Canadian Parachute Battalion was disbanded, and some of the men were shocked. These were the ones who had found their calling, who loved the life and wanted to keep jumping. Some would stay in the army and go on to fight in other wars. Not Josiah. He never wanted to see war again.

After they were honorably discharged, Josiah and Syd Antoine once again took the train across the country to Kamloops, only this time, both of them went on to the Cariboo. As veterans, they each received a one-hundred-dollar allowance for clothing. They also received a war service gratuity, money for each month of service and each day overseas, which for Josiah came out to nearly five hundred dollars. This, plus the not inconsiderable sum he still had in his father's canister of banknotes, was enough to buy a plot of land in the woods near Quesnel.

During the fall, while the weather was still good, he worked on clearing the land and building a cabin with the help of Syd Antoine. Josiah bought logs that were already seasoned, but otherwise, they did everything themselves, from notching the logs to framing the roof to splitting the shakes with a froe, until he had a tidy one-room cabin with a porch and a fireplace. Sometimes as they worked, they would reminisce about the war. On many afternoons, Syd's girl, a handsome woman named Cheryl, would swing by with sandwiches and jars of Saskatoon juice. After the cabin was done, Josiah set about making his own furniture, including a farm table like the one he had seen at the Fosters'.

The cabin proved stout through winter. They had done a good job of chinking and mudding, which kept out the worst of the cold. Some might have found the cabin nippy, but not Josiah. Not with a fire in the fireplace. Not after Belgium and Holland. Plus, he had Prince, who liked to curl up beside him. Mostly, life was good. He liked living in the woods and looking out on his stands of paper birch. But sometimes late at night, he received visitations. From the man he had killed on patrol in Normandy, the one who had flailed so theatrically, or the three in the boat on the river Maas. They would stand at the foot of his bed, silently, their faces obscured by shadow, yet Josiah always knew exactly who they were. Over time, he saw every last German he had killed, sometimes more than once, but never the Russian he had shot in the head.

That winter, Josiah received a letter from a fellow veteran named Arthur Kwan. He had served in the Royal Canadian Navy and was trying to start a dedicated branch of the Royal Canadian Legion. Josiah was not really one for that kind of fraternizing, but he lent his name to the cause. No matter. The application to create the branch was rejected.

So he wasn't optimistic as he sat down to the letter he'd been waiting for from the Province of British Columbia. Earlier that year, he had written to the premier. *I was born in Canada, I own property, and I served in the 1st Canadian Parachute Battalion in Europe. I respectfully request the right to vote in the next provincial election.* He thought the letter more powerful for being brief. Now he had his reply:

> Dear Sir:
> Thank you for your letter of January—. I appreciate very much hearing from you. Be assured that every effort that I can make toward granting full rights of citizenship will be carried on during this year, and hope that the Charter amendments of next year will ask for the necessary changes to give the franchise to your people.
>
> *Sincerely yours,*
> *John Hart*
> *Premier*

This sounded like a polite no. Maybe change was coming, but how long would it take, a year or seventy-four? He had come to realize that some things could not be willed into being. That some things, many things, changed only when others said so, on terms of their own choosing. He folded the letter and tucked it back into the envelope.

Maybe Poppy was right. He should never have taken the bargain. Worse than fighting for nothing was losing her for nothing. He should have just stayed and lived in beautiful ignominy. Every day, he still dreamed of that life, the one in which he never leaves. He also dreamed of that other life, the one in which she never strays. Sometimes he was bitter that she hadn't waited just a little longer, and he would have stupendous arguments with her in his head. Mostly, though, he was sorry that the world had conspired against them. For a long time, he had hoped for a letter, but she must have been a mother by now and busy with her own life. Sometimes, when he pictured a baby clamped to her breast, he dreamed of yet another life, the one in which he is able to love the child, and the child him, such that he can withstand any sling and any arrow. But the dream wasn't to be, at least not yet. He hadn't lied. He'd said he would go back when he was ready. He still wasn't.

8

LATE OF AN AFTERNOON, AS DAYLIGHT BROWNED TO HONEY, PRINCE began to bark, which could only mean one thing: Syd Antoine had come to visit. Syd lived with Cheryl in Quesnel and sometimes liked to drop by—he was the only one who ever did. As Josiah threw more wood in the stove and put on water to boil, Prince continued to bark.

"Easy, boy. It's just Syd."

When the knock came, he told Syd to come in, and the door opened slowly, cautiously. Prince was not only barking but inching back, which was strange. During those nighttime visitations, Prince would always bark at something unseen, and Josiah thought a dead German was about to walk in the door. Instead, it was something else altogether: a woman, peeking through the door at Prince, then squatting to let him sniff her hand, the hem of her day dress riding above her knees. Josiah couldn't be sure of what he was seeing.

He called out her name, or tried to, but she didn't seem to hear. Instead, she scratched the dog behind the ears and nuzzled his speckled face. "My goodness, what a sweetheart," she said, without looking up. "What kind of dog is he?"

Josiah wasn't sure. Probably Labrador and Doberman, with a few other things thrown in. "A true mutt," he said. Like Queenie, Prince had simply wandered out of the woods, hungry and gaunt, back when the cabin was still being built. When he told her the dog's name, she smiled her deep-dimpled smile, eyes glinting. "Of course."

Her day dress was green, and her dark hair fell in waves, and she looked remarkably herself, considering. Motherhood became her, and he felt a thunk of the old desire. But she hadn't come with the child, and part of him wished she had, to see if there was any spark of tenderness in him. Any spark of possibility.

She rose and cast her glance about, and he saw the cabin through her eyes, as if for the first time: the farm table, the posted bed, the wood-burning stove, and the fireplace made of river stone, which he and Syd had built free of the cabin itself so the cabin could settle around it. With a wry smile that made him think of his pup tent, she said, "You're stepping up in the world."

It surprised him how familiar she was being. As if no time had passed and nothing had come between them. In fact, she seemed so blithe that he feared it could only mean one thing: she had come to devastate him in some way. Was Jimmy back in the picture? Had they become happy parents? His heart curdled at the thought, and he wished the man had never come back from the war.

He poured two cups of instant coffee and set them down on the ta-ble. She took a seat and pulled out a pack of Sweet Caporals and offered him one, but he said, "No, I quit."

"Was it hard? I'm thinking of quitting myself."

"Wasn't too bad," he said, though in fact it was very bad. "Just a couple of nights of sweating it out."

He found her an ashtray, and the cabin filled with tendrils of smoke, and he felt a craving he thought he had exorcised. He didn't ask the question he wanted to ask. Instead, he asked, "How did you find me?"

She shifted a little in her seat, then explained. She had found a piece of paper in her room with a woman's name and address. "Must have fallen out of your uniform," she said, and Josiah remembered reaching for cigarettes in the pocket of his battle blouse. "I'll be honest, I was suspicious. Thought you were being a hypocrite." When she needed to find him, she took the train to Quesnel and headed straight for the address. Until the moment she got there, she thought he might be the one to open the door. Instead, she had met Cheryl—"Lovely woman, by the way"—who had directed her here. "I came to bring you this," she said, picking up her handbag and rifling through. "I thought it might be important, but I didn't know how else to—"

She thrust a letter at him. It was addressed to him at Fell Avenue, but he didn't recognize the sender at first, a Mrs. Emma Flanagan from Douro, Ontario. When he did, he had a withering feeling.

"Why don't I give you a moment?" Poppy said, snapping her handbag and rising.

Even after the door shut behind her, Josiah hesitated to open the letter. He knew what it would say and didn't want to hear it said. He pictured his friend and wondered how it had happened. Wondered, too, if he was ultimately to blame. Yes, Bill had gotten a second chance to jump, but he only had two. By pulling him out of the way, Josiah had cut his chances in half.

Dear Mr. Chang,

It saddens me greatly to tell you that my dear Billy was killed in action nearly a year ago on April 14, 1945. He was serving valiantly with the 1st Canadian Infantry Division when he died during the liberation of Arnhem. He always spoke of you fondly and in the highest terms and said you would want to know if the worst ever befell him. I can only hope this letter finds you and there isn't another heartsick mother in the world. I'm sorry this task has so long eluded me, but doubtless you'll forgive a mother in her grief.

Regretfully,
Emma Flanagan

The war. So many fronts, so many battles, so many ways for a man to go down. If Bill had served in the 1st Canadian Infantry Division, then he had probably been in Italy before Josiah had even set foot in England. He remembered RAF Ringway, where their British instructors had been patient. Maybe with a little more patience, Bill might have been a paratrooper yet. The thought made Josiah feel like a bastard.

Then he remembered the Horse Palace and how he would hear not only crying but urgent, syncopated breathing in the night, but somehow it wasn't until he found himself in Piccadilly Circus, where most of the soldiers and sailors seemed more interested in each other than the prostitutes, that he understood what that breathing meant. And it took him a while to understand that that may have been the fear that lay deepest in Bill. If so, he hoped Bill hadn't gone to his death without facing it. Without knowing someone.

In the midst of his thoughts, he was drawn to the window by the sound of clattering. Outside, a silhouette in a day dress was raising a maul. Poppy making herself useful, or maybe just having fun. The image of her in the amber light laid itself atop another, like a palimpsest, and he felt an ache for a lost time.

When she stopped to wipe her brow with her arm, he knocked on the window, and she looked up and smiled and set the maul down.

"I'm sorry," she said ruefully, after he'd explained the letter. "I remember Bill. I remember the drama of whether or not he would jump. In fact, I remember all of them. Walker, Heikkinen, Van den Berg. They were like characters in a long serial novel. If I were you, I would write a book. Write it all down before you forget."

"Millions of people lived through the war. My story is nothing special. Certainly no different than most of the guys in the battalion."

"I disagree," Poppy said. "I think your story is . . . singular."

Josiah explained what he had heard from Arthur Kwan, that five or six hundred Chinese Canadians had served, men and women alike, including a bomber pilot who'd been shot down over France and awarded the Croix de Guerre for helping the French resistance. Josiah might have been the only Chinese Canadian in the battalion, but he was hardly the only one to serve. No, his story wasn't singular. Even if it were, the world would have no interest.

"Well, I still have all your letters and postcards," she said. "One day, they'll be of interest to someone."

This small disagreement seemed a proxy for larger ones, and they sat there brooding until he asked, "How are things at the yard?"

"I wouldn't know," she said, looking away. "I was laid off right before Christmas. Along with the last of the women."

Josiah knew from her letters that production at the yard had begun to slow long before the end of the war. When a contract for fifty ships was canceled, the yard began to drop shifts: first the graveyard shift, then all shifts on Sunday, then the swing shift on Saturday. The labor shortage that had once seemed insoluble was now the opposite problem, and women were usually the first to go. Still, the news caught him off guard.

"The South Yard launched its last ship at the end of January. Now it's closed."

This, too, caught him off guard. The din of the yard had once seemed so unceasing that he couldn't imagine the whole place shuttered.

"I know the war was terrible for so many, but those were the best years of my life," she said. "I doubt I'll ever have it as good."

He knew what she meant. The war was a great upending. For a brief and beautiful season, a woman like her could drive a jitney and a man like him could wield a rivet gun, and they could move through the world differently. Suddenly he was back in the yard, way up on the scaffolds, holding that sleek silver barrel and feeling its power—and his own.

All the guns he had fired for king and country.

But now that the war was over, the old order reasserted itself. Heikkinen had parlayed his service into a job as the manager of an insurance company, while Somerville had become the manager of a bank. Meanwhile, Syd was back to being a high rigger, and Josiah was still living off his war gratuity. And Poppy—

"What are you doing now?"

"Nothing for the moment."

Josiah tried to hide his surprise. "How are you going to take care of—"

"I'm hoping they'll give me my old job back, even though I dread the thought of going back to clerical. If not, I'll have to give up the house. Maybe move back in with my parents." The prospect pained her.

"Can I tell you something?" she asked, looking abashed.

"Of course."

"I'm thinking of becoming a reporter. Maybe even a war reporter." She snuck a look at him. "Think that's something I could do?"

He remembered the war and couldn't imagine going to it if he didn't have to, but the question amused him. He had always thought of Poppy as someone who could do whatever she set her mind to, and he said as much.

She smiled, encouraged. "You're the first person who hasn't told me I'm crazy."

For a moment they were quiet, as if they had both said too much. Then he asked, "How are your parents?"

For some time, she and her parents had been estranged, even though his joining the army had shamed them into a kind of repentance. But now, to his question, she laughed. "They're fine. It's bizarre, but they like to talk about you. Every time the war comes up, they'll say, 'We know someone who jumped in Normandy!'"

He laughed, trying to imagine it. But all of this was just prelude to what he really wanted to know: "And how's the baby?"

Her blue eyes cooled. "Josiah, there is no baby."

His heart started. "What do you mean?"

"I did what I had to do."

"How?"

She smoothed her dress. "It's probably best if you don't know too much. But I went to a . . . professional. Not a doctor, but a specialist. Experienced. Apparently, the war created a lot of demand." She laughed a complicated laugh. "But she wasn't easy to find. I can only imagine many women don't find someone."

No matter what he might have wished for, he hadn't thought it possible. Wasn't even sure he had wanted it to be possible. His vague ideas of how such things happened were lurid, and he didn't wish them on Poppy. Regardless, she had done it, made the difficult decision, but she hadn't felt the need to tell him, not just today but for months, so maybe her decision had nothing to do with him. Still, the picture had changed dramatically.

"Wasn't it . . . dangerous?"

"Of course it was. But so is war."

He thought he understood what she meant, that she had done what she'd had to do, as he had. For them. "Are you still in danger?"

She frowned. "From the law, you mean? I suppose so. But I only care about natural law. By man's law, everything you and I did was illegal. Everything *about* us was illegal. I don't care a whit about man's law."

He should have known she would go to any means necessary. After all, that's what she had wanted *them* to do: live outside the law. He wasn't sorry for what she had done, and clearly, neither was she. Still, he felt a pang for the child he had pictured all these months.

She lit another cigarette, then spied the letter from the office of the premier, still lying on the table. "What's this? A commendation?"

He laughed bitterly and pushed the letter toward her. She read it, eyes fading, then tucked the letter back into the envelope. "I'm sorry, Joe."

"You were right. I should never have left."

"No, look," she said, reaching into her handbag and pulling out a dog-eared copy of the newspaper, which she must have read on the train. "Things might be different soon. We might all be Canadians yet."

He read the article she had squared off for him. Apparently, Parliament was debating a new citizenship act. That must have been what the premier meant by Charter amendments. Under such an act, Poppy couldn't be stripped of citizenship for marrying him, which was progress. But as far as he could tell, there was no promise of citizenship for the likes of him, no matter their record of service.

As sunlight burnished the room, they sat there talking. She asked about the cabin and everything in it, including the table, and he told her about his second visit to the Fosters, which he hadn't had time to write about, and this led in turn to talk of the war, things he would have told her much sooner if he hadn't left so abruptly upon his return.

As she listened, eyes transfixed, he realized how glad he was to be in her presence and how much he had missed her. The Cariboo was a long way to go just for a letter, so maybe she had missed him, too. Now he saw her blitheness in a new light: she had come expecting to find him holed up with another woman, only to discover that he lived alone, seemingly free and unencumbered. Which was true. Since coming home from the army, he had led an ascetic life. No drinking, no smoking, no women. Quit everything, cold turkey. During those terrible nights of tossing and turning and sweating it out, he had imagined every kind of poison leaving his body, including pain, anger, and hatred. When he finally came out the other end, he felt free. At peace. Happy as he was to see her, time had changed him, and he didn't want to go back.

When the shadows grew long, he rose from the table and said, "Are you hungry? Let me get some supper going," but she looked at the fading light and said, "I should get back before dark."

He couldn't tell if she was just being polite. Either way, he felt snubbed. "Do you have a train to catch?"

"In the morning. But I have a room in Quesnel."

So she had time. Didn't have to leave so soon. He could have walked her back, even in the dark, so maybe she *had* come all this way for a letter. "Okay," he said.

She studied him, as if she'd expected him to say something else. Then she brightened, picked up her handbag, and walked to the door. He should have followed, but he held back, as a small reproof. When she turned around, she was surprised to see him on the other side of the room. She tucked some hair behind her ear uncertainly.

"Thanks for coming all this way."

"Of course."

"Do you know your way back?"

"I do."

She stood there primly, waiting to see if he would come closer. At that moment, Prince, sensing a change in the air, stirred from his spot on the floor. Poppy hunkered down again and lavished affection, a little showily, he thought, which was unkind of him, and he realized he wasn't nearly as free as he had supposed. He had cultivated a hard pearl of resentment. That she hadn't waited and had never apologized for not waiting.

At length she stood. Again, she waited for him to come closer, but he refused, and he wondered if the war had done this to him. Made him cold.

"It was nice to see you, Poppy."

Her mouth crimped, and the corners of her eyes shone. "It was nice to see you, too, Joe."

She turned to go, but when her hand touched the door, she paused. "I would have told you sooner," she said, looking over her shoulder at the floor, "if I thought it would have made a difference. But I knew you needed . . . time."

For so long now, her silence had felt like indifference, so it came as a great relief to know it wasn't. Why, then, was he still standing on the other side of the room? Hadn't she already apologized, if not in word, then in deed? What was left to prove? They had both been willing to die for each other. And yet, a smallness, a meanness, stopped him.

The cabin stilled, each of them waiting for the other to speak. Even Prince, lying on the floor, seemed watchful and expectant. Then, in a trembling voice, she said, "Goodbye, Joe."

The door opened to a spray of light. Then her silhouette dissolved, and the fan of light closed, and he found himself alone again, the cabin ringing with emptiness. After a moment, he went to the window. She was already down the path, vanishing into a thicket of shadows, and all at once, he saw everything that had ever happened between them, from the first to the last, the way he sometimes saw the war, in an instant, unbearably, and he knew he was seeing her for the last time. She would not come back, just as he would not go to her, and the tether between them, once so powerfully made, would snap. He hadn't known her in the first flush of youth, and now he would never know her in her middle years, or her late ones, as her beauty faded. They would both grow old, but not together.

Once, when Josiah was a child, a traveling circus had come to whatever town he and his father had happened to be in, and Josiah had begged to see the fortune teller, an old crone with a talking board. As they sat across from each other, the planchette had moved mysteriously around the board, promising a life of great love and great adventure. For a time, his father indulged his brush with the supernatural, but eventually he explained that their own imperceptible movements had steered the planchette, that the fortune teller was a charlatan, and Josiah, humiliated, had promptly shunted the memory away—until now. Now he wondered if the same wasn't happening. If countless small, unthinking choices weren't driving them to a false fate.

He went to the door and opened it. Her form was growing smaller, but he still couldn't bring himself to stop her. What had they ever had but a brief and beautiful season? Better to let it blaze in memory than smolder with recriminations. And the world—the world was still against them. Despite everything, he still had no country to call his own.

So he tried to brick away the last of his feelings. Tried but couldn't.

"Poppy!"

His voice ricocheted through the woods, through darkening filaments of birch, and she stopped in her tracks, almost beyond view. She stood where she was, her back still turned, as if she weren't sure whether she had really heard her name or only just imagined it. He didn't know what he would say until the moment he said it.

"Stay."

She didn't move, and he wondered if his voice had been too croaked for her to hear him. The longer she stood there, the more it seemed she would just carry on, and he scolded himself for being rash and steeled himself again. Then her shoulders began to tremble, and she touched both hands to her face and turned around, and even in the dusky light, he saw those dark rivulets. This wasn't the first time. He had lived this moment before. First, the mincing steps. Then she was running.

ACKNOWLEDGMENTS

Jackie Kaiser at Westwood Creative Artists. Acquiring publisher and editor Sarah MacLachlan and Janie Yoon, formerly at House of Anansi Press. Editors Tara Parsons at HarperVia and Doug Richmond at House of Anansi, who pushed me to be better. Publisher Judith Curr, associate editor Alexa Frank, production editor Lisa Zuniga, and designers Stephen Brayda and Janet Evans-Scanlon at HarperVia. Ithaca College and the Department of Writing. The David T. K. Wong Creative Writing Fellowship at the University of East Anglia and Jean McNeil, my mentor at UEA, for reading the first fledgling pages. Ann-Marie Metten and Historic Joy Kogawa House in Vancouver. The Access Copyright Foundation, the New York Foundation for the Arts, and the Canada Council for the Arts. The City of Vancouver Archives, Museum and Archives of North Vancouver, Chinese Canadian Military Museum, Canadian War Museum, Directorate of History and Heritage, Library and Archives Canada, Wartime Canada, National Infantry Museum (US), and Columbus Museum. *The Dragon and the Maple Leaf: Chinese Canadians in World War II* by Marjorie Wong, *Waterfront to Warfront: Burrard Dry Dock Company During World War II* by George N. Edwards, *Wallace Shipbuilder: Burrard Dry Dock Magazine* (1943–45), *Boys of the Clouds: An Oral History of the 1st Canadian Parachute Battalion 1942–45* by Gary C. Boegel, *Men of Steel: Canadian Paratroopers in Normandy, 1944* by Bernd Horn, and *Paras Versus the Reich: Canada's Paratroopers at War, 1942–45* by Bernd Horn and Michel Wyczynski. Richard Mar, the only Chinese Canadian to serve in the 1st Canadian Parachute Battalion, and the brave men and women of Chinese descent who served Canada during the Second World War. Cory Brown, Eleanor Henderson, Raul Palma, and Jacob White. My parents, David and Judy Wang, and my brother, Holman Wang. My daughters, Zadie and Zoe, and above all, my wife, Angelina.

A NOTE ON THE COVER

Jack Wang had me sold with his debut short story collection, *We Two Alone*, and I've been ready to explore more cover work for Jack since that run in 2020. The writing in *The Riveter* is equally inspiring, and I quickly worked up a folder of potential directions: minimal and abstract all the way to very literal and representational.

The cover we ultimately pursued tells a more expansive story: the paratroopers in the air, dramatic Canadian landscape, snow falling in the sky. The design speaks the same language as *All the Light We Cannot See* but feels very connected to *The Riveter*. The paratrooper imagery is genuine World War II archival photography, and even the typeface used is strategic: simple and elegant but also geometric and authoritative, a combination that echoes the content.

—Stephen Brayda

Here ends Jack Wang's
The Riveter.

The first edition of this book was printed
and bound at Lakeside Book Company
in Harrisonburg, Virginia, in January 2025.

A NOTE ON THE TYPE

The text of this novel was set in Garamond 3, a typeface designed by Morris Fuller Benton in 1936. While Mergenthaler Linotype released two handsome earlier versions of the Garamond font, neither version proved to be as popular in the United States as the Jean Jannon model from American Type Founders. This led Linotype to license Benton's design from ATF, where it was appointed Garamond 3. The third time turned out to be the charm, as Garamond 3 continues to be an appealing and well-liked choice for printed matter.

HARPERVIA

An imprint dedicated to publishing international voices,
offering readers a chance to encounter other lives and other
points of view via the language of the imagination.